In Search Of

— A Small-town Romance —

Mara Dabrishus

— and —

Tudor Robins

In Search Of

A Small-town Romance

Mara Dabrishus

— and —

Tudor Robins

Books by Tudor Robins

Island Series
Six-Month Horse
Appaloosa Summer
Wednesday Riders
Join Up
Faults

Stonegate Series
Objects in Mirror
After Lucas
Throw Your Heart Over

Chris and Tilly Series
Meant to Be
Tilly (coming soon)

Books by Mara Dabrishus

Stay the Distance Series
Stay the Distance
All Heart
Derby Horse
Racing Gods (coming soon)

Other Novels
Finding Daylight

For our readers on Patreon, who helped shape this story.

CAM

THERE WERE SO MANY things that could go wrong.

Coming into something like this you had to tell yourself you were covering them off; all the possible roadblocks, disasters, obstacles. You had to believe that's what all the preparation was for.

But I knew as well as anyone else what a joke that was.

I could seize up. But, for me, that always happens on the bike, right after the swim. When my calf muscles have to transition right-quick from icy water and constant contraction to the flexing extension required for pedaling, while adjusting to the relative warmth of the air.

And here I was in the run with my muscles sliding along just fine.

I could chafe. It seems small but it's nothing to scoff at. A seam, a lace, a thread, a hair in the wrong place, and the burning and bleeding could make me lose – if not the will to live – then definitely the will to finish this race.

So far so good, though. Socks, shorts, shirt staying where they should. A nice breeze wicking the sweat from my exposed skin.

I could crash. But, again, the bike was the most likely place for that where too many riders – nerve-riddled and adrenaline-spiked – converged on narrow, twisting, hilly, potholed roads.

Over halfway through the run the field had straggled out. I ran through dappled shade and flickering sun in my own running space. A trip-up from another runner seemed unlikely.

Of course, for me, with my particular goal of an age-group win, there would always be the possibility of the other guys just being flat-out better.

I figured, coming in, there were half-a-dozen to really worry about. I'd already passed four of them.

At kilometre fourteen I had my eyes fixed on number five, and it was a particular pleasure to put a lock on his lycra-clad buttocks and reel him in.

I did it the way my swim coach taught me to move through the pool – pretending the water is something I can dig my arm into and pull my weight forward – I remembered that, and used this guy's sinewy hind end as my anchor, my reference point; propelling myself past him.

Fifteen strides to go until I passed the guy from Boston. How did I know he was from Boston? Everyone in the bar last night knew where he was from, as we spent what was supposed to be a relaxing evening listening to minute-by-minute details of his training routine, the cost of every single piece of equipment he'd brought with him, and everything he'd eaten for the last seventy-two hours, all in a fortissimo Boston accent.

Ten strides to go and I could picture the shock on the waitress's face as he casually reached out to pinch her ass when she brought him the bill.

Five strides to go and I re-lived the satisfaction of telling him to keep his hands to himself … which led to the even more satisfying memory of how the waitress thanked me, back at her place, our bodies pressed hard against the front door, slamming it open, then again on the kitchen counter while we got side-tracked in our search for a drink, and finally using up all the hot water in her barely big-enough shower.

And still to bed in time for my seven hours of pre-Ironman sleep, leaving me fit and rested to beat the Boston blowhard.

In the final stride before I passed him, my hand hovered right behind his haunches and it took every bit of restraint in me not to pinch.

Hot sweaty man, I reminded myself, and pulled my hand in, hunkered down, and sailed past him.

The rest of the field down, one more to go.

By now I was pretty sure I wasn't going to hit the wall, either. I had six months of training to thank for that. So many, many weekends without beer and without the corresponding morning-after-the-night-before greasy breakfasts to sop up the hangovers.

Brick workouts, using up most of my weekends and leaving my then-girlfriend moaning, "Again? Do you really need to cycle to Kingston today?"

"Yes," I'd said every time.

"This isn't working," she'd said.

Oh, yes it is, I'd thought, while saying, "I'm really sorry, but there's no point in going into an half-Ironman unprepared."

And today's smooth swim, effortless cycle, and limber running legs were the result.

Maybe this training thing could be a permanent way of life after all.

I accelerated, just for fun, and it was easy – my lungs and legs shifted seamlessly to their new gear. In the far distance I spied a speck I hadn't seen before. Could that be guy number one in my age group? The last guy I had to catch?

Only one way to find out – keep running.

Maybe I could meet a woman who also liked to train. Who would be fast, strong, and wouldn't bug me. Who wouldn't make me resort to working out as a creative way to escape her.

The thought seemed so reasonable that I started scoping out the runners around me. All shapes and sizes … nothing illustrated that better than a triathlon. Stocky, stringy, wobbly – all were represented. Sweaty, scruffy, running-catalogue chic – I saw all those, too.

There was a woman off to my right, running with easy strides through the pure, clean Adirondack autumn sunshine. She had a long French braid – not perfect; that would be bizarre this far into a race – but something about its heaviness, the way it swung in a rope down her back, and the suggestion of the thickness of the hair it restrained, was very sexy.

Her legs were long, muscled, and tanned in a training-outdoors rather than a tanning-bed kind of way.

She glanced at me, and I tossed her a smile, and I thought, *It's not that I can't commit. It's not that I'm a womanizer. It's that I haven't met the right woman, and maybe this is her …*

"Stop!"

The girl blocking my way was all wrong.

The hand she held up sported nails so long they scared me, coated in a shade of glossy pink that hurt my eyes.

Her tan … well it was *not* outdoor-natural.

And her hair – not much natural about that either.

Not to say I'd kick her out of bed, but I couldn't imagine ending up there with her in the first place, given the resentment I was feeling at her breaking my amazing running rhythm to allow the organic, athletic, all-natural, newly discovered soulmate and mother-of-my-future-children to pull steadily away from me.

"What is wrong with you?!?" I deked sideways, but her reflexes weren't half-bad; she jumped just as quickly, staying right in front of me, and saying, "There's nothing wrong with me … it's him!" She pointed to a guy sprawled on the ground. While I watched he groaned and pulled himself into the fetal position. His knee was bleeding and so was his elbow.

OK, truth. I was not a very nice person. I wasn't selfless. I wanted what I wanted and I'd already decided I wanted an age-group win. Which, let's face it, was not going to happen if I stayed in this spot any longer.

But … race karma.

No runner left behind.

It's a thing, both spoken, and unspoken. No single race result is more important than another person's well-being.

I knew it … I just couldn't feel it.

But if I kept running, and came first, there would be a dirty film over my win. An asterisk next to my result. He's the guy who left someone in pain / in distress / in trouble just so he could get a trophy. Who does that?

I wanted to do that.

The guy groaned again and rocked his body.

"Do something!" the girl yelled. "Help him!"

I'd like to say that's what changed my mind. I'd like to claim my concern for this guy, and my desire to step in and assist this Good-Samaritan girl, is what made me decide to stop.

In reality, loud-mouthed, obnoxious Boston-Guy pounded by me and I thought, *I don't know if I have it in me to chase him down again*, and there was no way I wanted him to beat me legitimately, so I sighed and met the girl's eyes for the first time, and said, "What, exactly, do you want me to do?"

LYNSEY

EVERYONE SAID THIS WAS a bad idea.

OK, maybe they didn't say that to my face, exactly, but they were thinking it with their quirked eyebrows and their looks of general concern when I said the words "Half-Ironman."

Even my best friend, jockey-extraordinaire Georgie Quinn, gave me that look. That are-you-sure-you-want-to-do-this-to-yourself look, which was a variant of her I-think-this-is-a-bad-idea look. To her credit, that look got me out of bed before the crack of dawn to go running with her every day of the racing meet at Saratoga; my longer stride forced to keep up with her furious shorter one. And also to her credit, Georgie's questioning side-eye at mile four, six, nine, and eleven got me all the way to mile thirteen just as the sun cracked over the horizon.

Then there was the bike for my birthday, and the impromptu lesson on gear shifts after I may have innocently wondered aloud at their purpose like a biking newbie while my older brother, Harris, covered his face with his hands and his shoulders shook from trying to contain his laughter.

I didn't appreciate the laughter then. But now? Now I got it. I didn't belong here. All it took was one look around this sleepy little resort town to see Georgie's morning runs and her infamous eyebrow couldn't exactly compete against the likes of these people, who discussed the merits of various running shoes like my brother might discuss shoeing his racehorses and went over their meals leading up to race day like Georgie, well, *didn't*.

"You know you're not here to win, right?" Georgie said to me in the bar last night as we passed a table of people one-upping each other's best times. I barely heard her because I was too busy realizing I had no best time. None. Nada. What would I do if someone asked? Say something truthful and risk *the look*, or say something to cover it up like "I don't bother with times" and get a totally different, no less horrible look?

"Of course I'm not going to win. This is more of a finishing without embarrassing myself situation," I said to her, comfortable in that reality. The less comfortable reality was coming in dead last, which I did not share with her because of those morning runs and that bike. For as many times as I'd gotten my best friend's look of concern underneath those arched eyebrows, she was also the person – the only person – who actively supported me. And since she bothered to drive up from Saratoga after the racing meet ended, securing my bike to the back of my car herself, there's no way I could tell her my main fear.

Failure. Big, fat failure.

I couldn't have Georgie looking at me like Dad did the day he told me he wouldn't be paying for this semester of college. Not paying for *any* more college.

"And if you're thinking you'll use your mother's inheritance, rethink that," he'd said, right after Tupelo Stud took the Whitney Handicap with a purse of over a million dollars. "You won't be touching it until you can prove to me you can manage it appropriately."

I stood there in the Champagne Room after the race, a glass of bubbly liquid held tightly in my fingers as people toasted to our success, watching my father cruise through the crowd in all his sleek, besuited glory. Like he hadn't upended my life. Like a sociopath.

Not paying. Not anymore.

So I woke up early – not a hard ask, considering the Thoroughbred racing world I lived in – gathered my things, tied a blue ribbon around my ponytail because running gear could use an accent or two, and gathered with the rest of those obsessed people at the shore of Mirror Lake.

Looking up and down the edge of the water, I recognized at least one thing in them that made sense. We were all looking for something. Proof, maybe, that we could do this if nothing else.

I could do this. Couldn't I?

Then the starting gun had us all plunging into the water and thought ceased. The world became breath and the tug of muscles working, bodies brushing by mine, water slapping at my skin. I pulled my way through the water, unhurried through the loop across the lake.

When my feet touched earth again, I felt good. Better than good. I pulled the wetsuit off in a haze of knowing I could do this. Pulled on dry clothes, climbed onto the bike, and spun off into the mountains sure in my belief that this was all going to be OK.

I, Lynsey Armstrong, had this.

The bike's tires shushed over the pavement, the gears clicking smoothly just like the day Georgie taught me what they were. I didn't notice the other bikes aside from avoiding them. My calves burned. My lungs ached. My skin was clammy from the suit and from the sweat, but it felt good, too. Like accomplishment.

When I swept into the second transition area, pulling on my morning-run-battered shoes, my muscles quivered at the shift, but I shrugged at it. Pushed it away. *Look at the road and run, Lynsey,* some part of my brain instructed. *Don't think about anything else.*

Don't think about college. Don't think about Dad. Don't think.

So I didn't. I ran, my ponytail bobbing behind me, little blue ribbon still stubbornly sticking in place. I reached back to touch it every so often, stroking my fingers over the slippery satin, thinking if such a pretty little thing could be that tough then I could, too.

Right up until mile eleven, when the ache in my lungs was more like an angry spike of pain and the burn in my calves was an inferno. The quivering along my muscles was a shaking I couldn't stop, and my body desperately cried at me to stop. Right here. In the middle of the road, if necessary.

Which seemed like such the story of my life. Get so far, but not far enough.

No. Nope. Not today. I poked at my crying body, hardly realizing that I *was* crying. Like my body and my brain had suffered a severe falling out and I didn't even realize it. I swiped at my face, blinked the tears out of my eyes, told myself to keep running. The finish line was so close. I could taste that incoming cup of water already. It would be sweet. It would be the best cup of water I'd ever had in my life.

And then the man in front of me fell down – hard – all road-rash knees and bleeding hands. Runners scattered around him, narrowly avoiding a tangle of legs as he rolled and came to a groaning stop on his back. There was nowhere to go except over or around him, and both of those options sounded exhausting. If it wasn't a straight line to the finish, my body wouldn't do it. No matter what my brain said, this was the end of the line.

Thank god.

I stumbled to a halt at the man's side, listening to him groan underneath my pants for breath as I doubled over and rested my hands on my knees, trying not to throw up. Swallowing the acrid taste in the back of my mouth, I looked the man over and realized quickly that I couldn't tell if he was worse off or I was.

He was – I was pretty sure. I mean, he was the one on the ground. I still had the benefit of standing, but I wasn't sure for how long. My knees were wobbly, and no way was I going to be able to do anything about helping him on my own. The last medical van was a couple miles ago, and with two miles left in the race would there even be another one?

I swallowed again and made myself straighten my spine with a gasp of breath. *Note to self,* my brain cried: *move slowly. Super, super slowly.*

"Hold on," I told the man, who I was increasingly sure wasn't aware I was even there. "I'll find help."

But help where? People swooped past, locked on their increasingly real goal. As I watched them glide by, the man's groans becoming more insistent, the same little voice nagged at me: *no, not today.*

I was Lynsey Armstrong, damn it. If I'd learned anything in my life of never finishing anything, it was that I could always convince someone else to finish things for me.

Which is how I got the irritated attention of Runner 1939. At least, that's what his running bib said, and he certainly didn't seem keen to introduce himself after desperation had me moving quickly enough to stop him, hand out like I belonged in The Supremes.

Stop … in the name of getting me out of this mess.

He tried to skitter around me, but oh, I kept up, even as my knees locked. My feet were pins and needles. My lungs kept working only because they had to keep me alive, and I could feel they were doing it grudgingly. I might have screamed at him, and I really hoped I yelled "Help *him*," rather than the stickier truth: help *me*.

Runner 1939 stumbled to a halt and glared at me full force, then his eyes flickered to a distant point behind me. I glanced over my shoulder to see how close it really was to the finish, only to see that his attention was on the rear end of a woman who was steadily leaving him behind.

OK. Well, now I felt less bad.

"What, exactly, do you want me to do?" he asked, tearing his gaze from the girl's backside, exasperation going full tilt.

I wanted to shout, "Is it not obvious?" But I bit back the urge and gave him a once over – tall, fit, sweat-streaked in a way that made his eyes bright. He would have made beautiful babies with the woman leaving him in her dust, but today just wasn't going to be his day.

My gaze fell to his forearms, which were all defined tendons, making me wonder if I'd even noticed forearms before. Surely I had. 1939 wasn't the only man in possession of forearms.

These will do nicely, I thought, inanely, the tired part of my brain scrambling for words to convince this total stranger to do me a solid.

"I can't move him on my own," I said, watching his eyebrow quirk. It was the *no kidding* look. A cousin to the this-is-a-bad-idea look. "He needs help. Like, *now* help. Not *when-someone-gets-around-to-it* help. Move him with me and maybe your brave sacrifice will get you that girl's number."

Now I got his attention.

"What girl?" he asked, and I mentally patted myself on the back.

"Seriously? I have eyes," I said, and then motioned to the man, who had curled on his side, eyes closed. "I'll take one side, you take the other. We can walk him until we see a van, or a person with a cell phone, or the finish if we have to."

I sounded remarkably assured.

"The finish?" He sounded dubious, no doubt wondering how far I could go myself. I nodded.

"The finish," I confirmed, stepping gingerly to the man and

touching his arm. "Sir," I said, "we're going to try to help you. Can you stand?"

I got a little, halting nod. Not confident by any means, but it would have to do. I motioned 1939 over to me and got a sigh for my efforts before he miraculously stepped toward me, leaning over the man and taking his arm. I stumbled to the man's other side, nearly tripping on my sluggish feet and putting a hand on the man's back to steady myself. I really, really hoped it looked like I was trying to help.

1939 eyed me. "Am I going to be carrying you the rest of the way, too?"

"Not if I can help it." I slid underneath the man's shoulder as 1939 took the brunt of the weight.

"Sir," I said, "I'm Lynsey and this is …" I trailed off, waiting for 1939 to fill in the blank.

"Cam," he said, as though he had to think about it.

"I'm Albert," the man added, wincing as we started moving, one leg totally useless and the other hopping along. "And no one's called me 'sir' since the war, so you can cut that right out."

Cam pressed his lips together, hiding a smile.

"Gotcha," I said, going for bubbly and bright, and coming out squeaking when Cam shifted some of Albert's weight onto me for a step. Just enough for my exhausted body to stumble. I caught myself, hand snagging Cam's wrist behind Albert's back and clinging like a lifeline.

"You OK over there?" Cam asked, sliding those bright eyes of his over to me. There was a shine in them, like some part of him that wasn't thoroughly annoyed with me might also think this was hilarious, deep down. It would make for a good story later at the bar with those half-Ironman die-hards.

I would have finished top of my age group, I could see him saying, *but I had to be a hero instead. Save the damsel in distress.*

And that thought straightened my spine right up.

"Never better," I insisted, letting go of his wrist.

The next step I took toward the finish was sure.

Chapter Two

CAM

WHAT SHE WANTED, AS it turned out, was a way out of the race.

The signs of over-exertion – which I learned in a two-day first aid workshop the university forced all grad students to take – were clear. Her lips were cracked, even as she was trying to help the guy who fell, she stumbled, and as she introduced us all to each other, some of her words stuck in her dry mouth.

We covered about ten feet before I decided while I was willing to not finish this race, I wasn't willing to end up trapped under a pile-up of tumbled-over, worn-out triathletes who had hit the wall.

"Whoa for a second," I said.

The girl's eyebrow lifted at "Whoa." Whatever – she could think I was weird – "whoa" made me think of my horse-crazy sister, Meg. It made me happy. I used it whenever I could.

"Here." I handed her my water bottle. "Drink the rest of this."

She opened her mouth, and before she could protest I said, "A) You're dehydrated, and B) I don't have cooties, so just drink it."

"Cooties!" She snorted but there was a tiny lift to the corners of her mouth. She raised my bottle to her lips and drank it down. While I watched I noticed a vein tracing her temple and the thinness of the skin under her eyes.

I had a compulsion to lay my thumb on that delicate skin – to smooth it out. *Weird*, I warned myself, and successfully quashed the impulse.

"Happy?" She wiped the back of her hand across her mouth and held the empty bottle out to me.

Hmm … let me see … happy? The words formed in my head, "*Yeah, sure. Three minutes ago I was on my way to an age group win. Now I'm about to spend the foreseeable future in extremely close physical contact with an injured old man and a dehydrated girl when all three of us could really use a shower.*"

But *Meg*. She wouldn't say that. Ever since my little sister got her shit together, including sustaining a long-term, meaningful relationship and supporting herself financially doing work she loves, she's kind of become my role model. Hence WWMS (What Would Meg Say?).

I could never be as nice as Meg, but as I took my water bottle back I managed, "I'm satisfied."

"Ha!" the girl said and I had this strange feeling she was looking straight into my not-so-nice brain and seeing the original words I suppressed.

"Let's go," I said. "There's gotta be a medical station some-where up here."

—

ALBERT WAS QUITE AN interesting guy, so at least there was that.

His story was that he'd – not exactly dodged – but *avoided* the Vietnam draft by getting himself a position as an unpaid engineer-ing intern working on the mining Superstack being built in Sud-bury, Ontario – a mining town five hours north along the highway from my hometown.

"Sudbury!" I said. "That's a pretty hardcore place to live in January. You might be more Canadian than I am."

He laughed. "Well, you're right. My first winter made me wonder whether I wouldn't rather ship out. At least it toughened me up for events like this." He frowned and looked down at the leg he still couldn't put any weight on. "At least I *used* to be tough."

"Oh! Sir … I mean, Albert … I think you're amazingly tough," the girl – Lynsey – said. "I'll let you in on a little secret. I wasn't ex-actly enjoying the race up until I stopped to help you."

No shit. I looked away as soon as I thought it – I didn't want her reading my mind again.

Which is when I caught sight of the bright Ironman branded t-shirt announcing MEDICAL VOLUNTEER in block letters. My heart lifted. "Hey! Over here!"

The volunteer slowed from a hurried trot to ask, "What's the situation?"

"Oh, nothing too serious," Albert said. "My old leg just gave out but these kind young 'uns got me up and moving."

Wait … I thought. *Let's not be too hasty with the "not-too-serious."*

"Hmm …" The volunteer hovered. "No other issues? Shortness of breath? Loss of consciousness?"

Lynsey waved the hand not supporting Albert. "Nothing like that. He's in great form!"

OK, could we maybe reserve judgment on how great Albert's form is? I mean, after all, if he was dodging Vietnam, the guy's got to be in his seventies.

"Great!" the medical volunteer said. "I have a call for a potential cardiac issue further up the course. Since this gentleman's in good hands, can I ask you to take him to the medical tent at the transition point?"

"Of course!" Lynsey stuck her thumb in the air. "Glad to!"

WWMS? Meg's nice, but she also loves to run. I think even Meg might mutter, "*Shit!*" at this point.

The medical volunteer resumed his trot, but he paused long enough to call, "Good race karma to you two!"

"Oh, yeah. Of course. Good race karma is exactly what I spent six months training for."

I thought I'd muttered it to myself, but Lynsey must have great hearing. "What was that?" she asked.

"Nothing," I said. Nothing at all – which was exactly what my race had turned into.

—

THE MEDICAL TENT WAS right next to the Finish line.

This was *not* how I'd planned to see it, but through a cruel twist of fate – and the in-and-out nature of the course – the spot where Albert's leg gave out meant the main medical tent was the closest spot to get him medical attention.

When the tent came into view, Albert gave himself a shake and said, "Now, I'm sure it's not that bad. I can walk on my own the rest of the way."

He took one step on his own, away from the lopsided support provided by Lynsey on one side and me on the other, and immediately buckled. We both rushed forward and re-assumed our previous positions.

"I'm so sorry, youngsters," he said and I kept to myself the thought that, actually, I would have been pretty pissed off to have shut down my race only to find the old guy could have walked himself in.

"It's fine," Lynsey said. "Don't you worry."

I didn't know this girl at all and, taken objectively, every single word I'd heard out of her mouth was sweetness and kindness itself, so why did some underlying instinct tell me she was someone not to be messed with? Walk away now and she'd make me sorry.

Come to think of it, she'd managed to put an end to my laser-focused goal with nothing but her lycra-clad body and an iron will, so my instinct was probably well-founded.

Two of the bright-t-shirted volunteers rushed out of the tent. "Oh, sir!"

"His name's Albert," Lynsey broke in.

"Well, Albert, what seems to be the matter? Let's get you in here on a table and have a look …"

As his weight was taken from me, I straightened, rolled my shoulders back, and said, "Well, that's fine. I guess I'll be going."

"You *so* will not." The words weren't even out of Lynsey's mouth before a clipboard-wielding woman I hadn't noticed before stepped forward to back her up, "Actually, if I can just get a bit of information from you both."

"What? Why?"

"In the capacity of next-of-kin."

"We're not his kin." I pointed at Lynsey. "I'm not her kin. No kin here!"

"Well you were kind enough to bring him in, so if you could just provide some basic information, that would be very helpful."

"Of course we will!" Lynsey threaded her arm through mine to yank me closer to clipboard lady.

I spared a thought for those who truly were this girl's next of kin. Kind of like being related to a tornado. Or, maybe, a bulldozer. Either way, something to be avoided.

—

WITH EVERYTHING BUT MY blood type and my inseam measurement provided to the volunteer-but-very-thorough lady, I adjusted my right shoe lace with the aim of finally – *finally* – leaving.

I was missing about 10K of my run – US race or not, the Canadian in me could only ever measure in kilometres – and at some point it had occurred to me I could make the distance up – even if only symbolically – by running back to my buddy's cabin where I was staying.

Back to the cabin, hot shower, beer – consolatory, rather than celebratory – but my drinking companion wouldn't care. And then … *what?*

Back to normal, I guessed. Back to Montreal – to the two-bedroom walk-up apartment I used to share with my friend JP – until he got married last month. I was lucky he paid up his share of the rent to the end of the year and he didn't want any of it back.

I re-tied my left shoe lace. *Lucky.*

Back to my lab assistant job at the university where I could keep preparing slides and replacing microscope light sources. Sure, the assistant professorship that was supposed to materialize didn't come through in this budget, and the funding for the research project I was committed to was delayed by a year, but at least I was still employed. There weren't a ton of academic jobs around – I was fortunate to have one.

I re-settled my running shorts on my hips. *Fortunate.*

Back to getting by. To surviving. To doing fine. Because, honestly, it didn't feel like *living*. I wasn't *progressing*. For the last half-year or so, this race gave me some kind of purpose; a goal, even if a self-imposed one. But with the half-Ironman unfinished, what did I have?

I straightened my sunglasses.

Nothing. No aim. No life.

Shit. This was exactly why I needed to run home. So I could keep from thinking about this. So I could avoid wallowing.

And maybe on the way I'd come across that hot athletic woman – the one that got away, quite literally – and she'd fall for me, and that would be the beginning of life as I wanted to know it.

Yeah. Probably. It was time to go.

"Where are you going?"

Oh my … really?

"Home," I told Lynsey.

She planted a fist on each hip. "No you're not. You say 'eh.'"

"What on earth is that supposed to mean?"

"You say 'eh,' so you're Canadian, so you're not going home right now."

"First of all, maybe I am. The border's only about a hundred kilometres away which, you probably have no idea, but is about sixty miles. I could cycle it in no time. And secondly, do you always take everything completely literally? Like 'home' has to be my permanent home? And thirdly, I do not say 'eh.' And fourthly …" I threw my hands up. "Sorry, my stupid, I don't even know why I'm having this conversation."

"Hi!"

"What now!?!" I whirled around to face an impossibly adorable girl. I mean, she practically had Girl Next Door printed across her t-shirt. She had freckles *and* dimples *and* her hair was in braids.

She stepped back in the face of my roar, but – have no fear, Lynsey to the rescue – Lynsey stepped forward, hand out and said,

"Please excuse him. He's low on electrolytes – 'eh?'" The "eh" was said with a sideways glance and an eyebrow raised in my direction.

That was so not the proper use of "eh."

"What can we do for you?" Lynsey asked the girl before I could correct her use of the most Canadian of interjections.

"I'm Hope …" *Of course her name was Hope.* "… and I'm putting together a story for the *Lake Placid Mirror* on the thrill of victory and the agony of defeat, Ironman-style. The ladies in there told me you guys brought in a fellow racer in distress, and I was wondering if I could interview you?"

I stepped back, then back again, and spread my hands wide – one pointing toward Lynsey, one toward Hope. "I'd hate to get in the way here, with my funny Canadian words, and my electrolyte-depleted attitude, so I'll let you two grab a Gatorade and talk to your hearts' content."

"It's been a slice," I called over my shoulder as I spun on one foot and, with the other, hit the ground running.

LYNSEY

"YOU'RE NEVER GOING TO get that girl's number at this rate!" I yelled at Cam's retreating back. He waved me off and kept going, his towering body getting smaller and smaller as he ran away from me. "Fine! With your attitude any self-respecting woman would give you a fake number anyway!"

He kept going, winding through the craze of finished runners and support staff, disappearing in the melee and making him yet another man who high-tailed it out of my life. Only this one did so quite literally.

It almost made me laugh. Almost. I wasn't here to strike up another doomed relationship, and especially not with a moody Canadian with the patience of a high-strung colt, but something about watching Cam disappear felt familiar. In my experience, men were like this – objectively good for certain things that involved muscle, reaching-out-of-the-way items, and keeping the species going, but otherwise I wasn't too convinced they were good for much else. In my lengthy, unfinished college career I'd run into enough to know they were generally flight risks.

My history was what I liked to call enriching. It was the only positive spin I could put on it, but whenever I thought back on my scattered past with men I would always think at least I learned something.

For instance, I learned about self-delusion with Mason, the pre-law student who was chronically opposed to relationships, which he revealed seven months into ours, ruining college boys for me in the process.

It was a particularly sharp lesson on duplicitousness with Andy, the musician I met the last time the Breeders' Cup rolled through Los Angeles. I should have known better – I know hindsight well now, too – because what chance does a horse girl from Florida with more money than sense, as Dad liked to say, have with a celebrity? Zilch, that's how much. It's one thing to find out your boyfriend is cheating by snooping through a phone or finding lipstick on a collar. It's another thing altogether to find the evidence splashed across the internet.

Then there was Christian. The one. The *Wellington* One. I might have fallen in love with his horses first – in fact, I knew I fell in love with his horses first, because how you could look at a horse like Wordsmith leaping over a four-star course and not fall madly in love is beyond me. The chestnut was all class and neatly tucked knees, conditioned to perfection in the detail-oriented way Christian applied to everything about his life.

I'd taken one look at Christian's properly manicured life, his swept barn, his clipped and groomed horses, and dropped right out of college, to Dad's horror. Took up riding again, a little less to Dad's horror. Rode Wordsmith myself. Felt him soar over jumps with that incredible kick of his and landed softly right into Christian's bed like it was meant to be.

I didn't regret a second of it, until Christian looked me dead in the eye two years later and said three little words: This. Isn't. Working.

Done. Easy peasey. Like it had never happened at all.

And what did I learn from that one?

That good things end. All the time and for no reason at all. Seemed like I should have gotten that lesson a lot earlier, and maybe I had. No. I knew I had. I just hadn't properly absorbed it until I slunk back to Ocala, back to the farm's guesthouse I had once shared with Harris. Hopefully back to school, to find a heading in my life, except Dad wasn't exactly on board with me going back to college on his dime at the ripe old age of twenty-five.

Nope. Turned out he wasn't on board at all.

I rubbed at the tattoo on the inside of my left wrist. The compass on my skin seemed more than a little ironic now. The little inked N shifted under my tendons as I flexed my fingers.

Show me a heading, I thought, and then realized the little arrow was pointing straight in the direction of Cam's path away from me. I sighed. I'd needed a perfect stranger. I happened to get Cam. Sometimes, you can't win every hand you're dealt.

But that wasn't necessarily true. I did get what I wanted: a reason to stop running. I even got a drink of water. I felt a little less like throwing up, and even though my stomach was still sour and my body ached all over I had to admit this turned out well.

For me, anyway. I couldn't say the same thing for Cam. Although I was OK with that. Anyone who bristled at "race karma" probably wasn't too good a person – well-defined forearms or not. I'd just ignore the fact that this not-so-good person helped me out. I had a feeling he was doing a bang-up job forgetting that on his own.

I reached for my blue ribbon, finding it still stubbornly knotted around my hair, and took a big, cleansing breath, ridding myself of Cam forever. Then I turned to the reporter, who was rocking the Pippi Longstocking look.

"Hi Hope," I said. "I'm Lynsey. I'd love to talk."

—

"LET'S START AT THE beginning," Hope said, settling herself in one of the folding camp chairs at the edge of the medical tent, away from Albert, who was busy telling the medical team clustered around him to get a move on, he had animals to tend back at the farm.

My ears pricked at *animals* and *farm*, my mind naturally skipping over the likely cows or chickens and going straight to horses. Although I doubted it was the kind of farm I was inclined toward – Lake Placid didn't exactly seem the place to raise Thoroughbreds or Grand Prix jumpers. Besides, Albert didn't seem the type.

"Sure." I sank down into a chair opposite her, my body doing it slowly as every muscle worked out how to stop standing. Bend knees, sink down, shift balance … there. Parked. I sighed in relief. Hope gave me a small, knowing smile.

"You don't seem the Ironman type," she commented, fiddling with the end of one brown braid.

"I'm not," I admitted. "I think I was mostly lucky to get as far as I did."

"You were going at a good clip," Hope pointed out. "You hobbled in with Albert before some age groups started finishing, so I'm not sure you need to be so modest."

I shrugged. "My best friend trained me like a racehorse the past month, and I was riding horses competitively up until I quit this spring." Rather unexpectedly, I could have added. I didn't, frowning at the memory and shaking my head a little to unstick it from the front of my thoughts. "I guess I retained some form over the summer after all."

"So then why the Ironman?" Hope asked. "If you don't mind me asking?"

"If you didn't ask you wouldn't be a reporter, would you?" I hedged, not exactly knowing how to answer her.

Why the half-Ironman? Why had I thrown myself into this? I didn't have a firm answer other than I definitely didn't want to go home. Not yet. And the triathalon ... well, it let me stretch out my stay a little longer. I had an easy excuse, and I was pretty sure that wasn't what Hope expected to hear.

She laughed. "Good point. I'm not exactly used to talking to anyone who isn't a Lake Placid native. Guess I'm nervous."

"Don't get a lot of outsiders?"

"We do," she said, glancing past the medical tent, at the sleepy community currently overrun with non-natives. "We're a tourist town, of course. But I'm a new hire for the *Mirror*. I'm getting my feet wet."

"Glad to help ... wetten?" I guessed, and she laughed.

"Thanks," she said. "I was told to find a story, and I think I have with you. Albert is a running star – he does the New York Marathon every year and started doing the half-Ironman since they started the Lake Placid event. Always finishes top of his age group. He's the one we all root for around here, so that you helped bring him in ... You're a story, you know?"

I shrank a little into my chair, unused to being the story. That was for my brother and Georgie, with their nationally acclaimed racehorses. It was for Christian and Wordsmith. Hell, it was even for Andy and his band of misfits. It was never for me.

"I don't know," I shrugged. "I just knew he needed help, and I couldn't do it by myself, so I kind of … sort of … dragged Cam out of the race. Which I feel bad about, by the way. Can you print that? That I ruined his race? Because I did."

I didn't feel that bad, but my lack of remorse probably wasn't print-worthy either. Hope nodded eagerly.

"Of course," she said, and looked up at the approaching ambulance, her mouth firming into a pretty, rosy point. "Oh, no."

I craned my neck to see what was happening just as Albert's voice broke through the post-race noise.

"I don't need no ambulance! I'm perfectly fine to walk on my own two …"

Then there was a crash, followed by the scurry of medical volunteers. Hope jumped up from her seat, and I was quick to follow, pushing into the tent just as the EMTs surrounded Albert, who was once again on the ground, only this time he was passed out cold. I got a quick look at his face, which was a bleak gray, before Hope pulled me back and the EMTs could go to work, whisking Albert onto a stretcher and toward the ambulance. Once he was packed inside, the doors closed with a metallic slam; the ambulance giving out a couple of warning wails before pulling away toward the street.

"Does Albert have anyone in town who can help him at the hospital?" I asked Hope, who shook her head.

"He has a son," she said. "He lives in Miami, and I doubt he's here. They don't talk much, from what I understand."

Shame. Although I probably understood better than most the disconnect between parent and child. I certainly wouldn't describe myself as being particularly chatty with my dad. But then there were circumstances. Extenuating ones.

I watched the ambulance rock onto the street, picking up speed as it shook loose from the chaos of the crowd.

"He's the one you all root for, right?" I asked, glancing over at Hope, who looked at me and nodded.

"Right."

I reached to the little blue ribbon, making sure it was still in a presentable bow.

"Then I guess we'd better go root for him."

—

THE HOSPITAL WAITING AREA was dreary and uncomfortable. I sipped at my bottled water, waiting for any news on Albert and wishing I'd had the forethought to stop and grab my bag before jumping into Hope's car. I was phoneless. Walletless. Basically the only form of identification I had on me was my running bib, which wasn't going to get me very far.

I thought about Georgie, who was waiting on me to finish the race. I hadn't crossed the finish line, so she probably thought I was still out there on the road somewhere. At this rate she probably thought I was dead in a ditch. I could see her demanding race officials to comb the area for me, as she conducted a thorough hunt of all the area hospitals.

"There you are!"

I looked up, taking in my pint-sized best friend, who stood just inside the hospital doors with a murderous expression on her elfin face. Her hands were planted on her hips, sharp elbows akimbo.

"Are you OK?" she asked, her concern not registering as much as the frustration. She handed me my bag, and then waved my cell phone in front of my face. Its screen glowed with texts – most of them from her. "I thought you died. And no one at the medical tent could find you on their list, but luckily someone mentioned the ambulance, and then …"

"I'm fine," I assured her, pulling her down onto the seat next to me. She fell into the hospital chair with a little squeak. "Thank you for being the extremely dogged friend that you are, but I'm just waiting on someone."

"Who?"

"Albert," I replied, getting Georgie's narrowed look of confusion. A close sibling of you've-lost-your-mind-haven't-you and run-that-by-me-again. I knew it well, so I filled her in and the look slowly eased away.

"Is he doing OK?" she asked when I'd finished with the story of my daring heroics.

"We haven't heard," Hope said from next to me, her head bowed as she typed aggressively into her phone. It was odd watching such a cute person manhandle anything, but Hope was obviously in a zone. "The good news is this story is almost done, thanks to Lynsey's immensely helpful interview."

I smiled, and Georgie raised an eyebrow. Hope continued stabbing at her phone – writing the story, I realized. She paused, holding it up and reading it through. Then she sighed.

"It could really use a second perspective," she said, lowering the phone into her lap. The screen dimmed. "But Albert is off the table, so to speak. And Cam literally ran away before I could get a question out."

"If it makes you feel better, I'm pretty sure he was running away from me."

"It doesn't," she said, sighing. "This will have to do. No way I can get to Cam in time before deadline."

She picked up the phone again, opening her e-mail, but before she could make me a small-town celebrity the door to triage opened, a doctor striding through with a swish of her white coat.

"You're the two ladies who brought in Mr. Thompson?"

"Albert," Hope said, nodding.

"And he has no next of kin?"

"A son, in Florida," I supplied.

The doctor nodded. "Mr. Thompson is hypoglycemic. In other words, his blood sugar levels are dangerously low. We have him on glucose, and once he's stabilized we'll need to address the fracture in his right ankle. He's been admitted. We'll need to get in touch with his son, if either of you have his number."

Hope shook her head, and I shrugged. Georgie frowned at the situation like she was still trying to parse what I was doing here. The doctor nodded like she hadn't expected us to be able to supply it anyway and assured us Albert was in good hands.

"Will we be able to speak with him?" Hope asked.

"Not yet," the doctor said briskly. "He's still quite groggy. Soon."

Hope deflated.

"I think that's our cue to hit the road," Georgie said, nudging me in the side, which meant it would be time to pack up and head back to Saratoga. Back to real life, with its promise of … what? What was I going to do with myself on the farm in Florida? What *was* I doing with myself?

"There has to be a way to get you a second interview," I blurted out to Hope, who straightened and looked at me quizzically.

"How?" she asked slowly. "Albert is …"

"Not Albert," I said, standing up. "Cam."

"Cam ran away from me, remember?"

I waved off her very solid fact, even though I was still incredibly sure he was running away from me. I seemed to have that effect on guys. Hope? She was too adorable to run away from.

"He couldn't have gotten far," I said. "He did *run* away. It's not like he got in his car and drove back to Canada. I don't care how fit he thinks he is, he's not running home today. He's somewhere close by."

"Well, how do you find him then?" Georgie asked carefully, recognizing the potential of a wild goose hunt. I frowned, detective work clearly not my strong suit. Just like so much else in my life, I could safely consider policing a non-starter in terms of career choices.

"1939," Hope said softly, almost to herself. "His race bib was 1939." Then she brightened. "I can track him through the number on the bib! We'll have an address in no time. At the very least, I can get a phone number."

"Are we seriously doing this?" Georgie asked as I jumped up, ready to go as Hope picked up her bag, already heading for the hospital door and the parking lot beyond.

I knew I was supposed to say no. That this was Hope's story, and she could see it through to the end. I wasn't necessary, but I needed a distraction. A diversion from real life.

A reason to not go home. Not quite yet.

Then Hope paused at the door.

You're coming, right?" she asked, one hand on the door. "I could really use a photo of both of you. Together. And maybe if Albert wakes up, we can get all of you together?"

Oh, Hope, you *genius*.

"Absolutely!" I gave her a thumbs up, and then turned to Georgie.

"We are definitely doing this," I said, grabbing her hand and hauling her out of her seat. "It's time to go find Cam."

Chapter Three

CAM

WRONG, WRONG, WRONG, WRONG. Everything had gone wrong.

I was supposed to finish the triathlon. I was supposed to win my age group. I was supposed to end my race as I began it, with a dip in Mirror Lake, except with the second post-race dip holding no desperate worry about going fast enough while conserving energy, no other swimmers kicking bruises onto my limbs, and accompanied by the sweet knowledge of a medal and the anticipated enjoyment of a well-earned post-race meal of just about anything I wanted.

Instead, I was wedged into Lewis's shower, if you could call it that. It was more like an upright plastic coffin. The rough floor was meant to be anti-slip, but it was more mold-, mildew-, and filth-trapping, and both the pressure and temperature of the water left a lot to be desired.

The icing on the cake (and that was rancid icing on stale cake) was the institutional once-white-but-now-pink-slimed-around-the-edges shower curtain which, because I was a full-sized man, and this was a half-sized shower, clung to me every time I moved.

Y.U.C.K.

I was working hard to get the trickle of water to rinse the lingering shampoo suds out of my hair when I realized I wasn't alone in the bathroom.

To be fair, it didn't have a door, so privacy was a relative state, but a hulking bulk which I sincerely hoped was Lewis was now right on the other side of the very-near-translucent shower curtain.

"Cam!" he hissed.

"Um, yes?" I shrank away from the shower curtain only to have the built-in soap dish dig into my back.

"There's somebody coming to the door."

"OK ... well ... it's your door, Lewis."

"They're women."

While I was motivated to help my socially awkward friend overcome his fear of the opposite sex, I would have been more motivated if I wasn't naked and soaking wet. "Lewis, you were married. Clearly you can talk to a woman."

"I was married for eleven weeks."

Shit. Totally my bad. Bringing up the short-lived marriage was a truly dumb move. Before I could think of anything to say to undo my error, Lewis added, "They're really pretty. And one of them looks scary."

Two pretties, one with scary mixed in. Why did that sound

familiar?

The fact that my even-taller, and much-bigger-than-me friend was still cowering beside the shower stall told me there was no way I was going to convince him to answer the door.

"Oh, for …" I cranked the lukewarm trickle to a stop, grabbed a towel and a t-shirt, and headed for the door.

I had the towel snugged around my waist by the time I rounded the corner into view of the two blurred figures on the other side of the screen door. I lifted my arm to thrust it into the shirt, when I realized it wasn't a shirt.

It was the pair of boxer shorts I'd slept in last night, left where I changed out of them this morning and picked up by mistake.

"Cam? Is that you? It's Lynsey! Hope and I just need to talk to you for a minute."

I shrugged. If the incredibly tacky multi-coloured parrot-adorned beach towel my aunt brought back from Hawaii for my sixteenth birthday wasn't enough to scare them away, I didn't know what would be.

I yanked the door open, spread my legs wide enough to ensure the parrot was on full display, and said, "Well, well, well, long time, no see."

Lynsey took a long, deliberate look at the parrot, then locked her eyes onto mine. "Speaking of seeing … or should I say, *un*seeing … I wish that was possible."

"As you can see, I was previously occupied, and I'm sure you didn't come here to talk about my parrot, so what can I do for you?"

"We … I mean, *I* … I mean *The Mirror* …" Hope's freckles were fading into the general mottled blush of her cheeks. She wouldn't make eye contact with me, or my parrot.

There was a poke at my back and I turned to face Lewis, holding what I recognized as my real and actual t-shirt. Just as I was about to ask what happened, and how he went from hiding in the bathroom to facing not one, but two women, I caught his eyes sliding to Hope.

Oh … It was like that.

Clearly I wasn't going to be sleeping with the cute reporter. Lewis, likely without even being fully aware he was doing it, had invoked the bro code. He liked Hope, so I'd leave her alone. Fair enough. I'd been accused of many not-that-nice things over the years, but I always had my friends' backs.

As I pulled the t-shirt over my head, Lynsey took a step forward, making her surprisingly close to me when my head popped out of the crew neck. Lewis was right – *scary …*

"What Hope means …" Lynsey said, "… is that she has a story to write. She has a deadline to meet. And she needs you to help with that."

No way. I was done with having my plans hijacked. I opened my mouth to say, "Sorry, but …" when a different voice came from behind me.

"He'd be happy to help. Do you need a drive?"

Come on, Lewis … was this really the moment you had to find your courage?

Lynsey snapped her fingers. "Great! Ditch the parrot and let's get going."

—

"I HATE HOSPITALS."

I was with Albert on this one. I was going to need another shower when I left this place – a real shower with hot water and the actual ability to rinse germs away. My skin was itching with all the antibiotic-resistant bugs I just *knew* were all around me.

I have to admit, I was tuned out. There was the bustle and activity that happens when there are too many people in too small a space, and I was mostly busy trying not to touch any possibly contaminated surfaces.

I was hungry, and I was trying not to let my mind race ahead to the gaping space that was My Future, but I was also really trying to avoid being in the moment, because this sick-bed moment wasn't one I had any interest in being in … which is why I was caught totally off-guard when somebody handed me a bouquet of flowers.

"Huh? What?" I cursed my reflexes for taking them, and like a hot potato immediately looked for another set of hands to get them into.

"Lynsey!" I said, and when she turned to face me, I did the bouquet hand-off. Nice work, if I did say so myself.

Click. "So nice!" Hope was saying. "Now, Lynsey, you give them to Albert." *Click,* and that moment, too, was captured for time immemorial … or as long as *The Mirror* stayed solvent.

Hope was on a roll now. I don't know if it was because she

was getting her big story, or because Lewis had stayed outside in the parking lot – possibly it was just because I was wearing proper pants – but her shyness had fallen away and she was saying, "This is going to be a great story!" and herding Lynsey and me around Albert's bed, and *click-click-clicking* away.

She lowered her camera and beamed. "Great! I have exactly what I need!"

"Well, I certainly don't, young lady!" Albert was looking tired, grumpy, and a bit pale, and at his words the sparkle was snuffed out of Hope's face, to leave her looking equally deflated.

Thank god Lewis wasn't here; even I (nearly) wanted to comfort the angelic reporter, and I wasn't the one with a crush on her.

Lynsey stepped forward. Of course she did. I hardly knew her, and I already knew she was going to speak up a good five seconds before she opened her mouth.

"What is it Albert. What do you need?"

"It's not me, young lady, it's my animals."

"Animals?"

"At my farm, of course. They can't feed themselves, you know."

Just as he mentioned food, a trolley appeared at the door. The food arranged on it held no appeal for me, but Albert definitely perked up. "Ah, dinner."

"Albert?" Lynsey asked. "The animals?"

"What? Oh, yes, ask anyone. They'll tell you how to get to the farm." He accepted a tray from the trolley and lifted the plastic cover.

"Albert? Excuse me, what kind of animals? What do you feed them?"

The sight and smell of the liquidy, lumpy dish in front of him, seemed to have taken the edge off Albert's concerns about his animals. "Goodness child. I was under the impression you were a smart young thing. It's not rocket science to feed a few farm animals, is it?"

The staff member who brought the food made a *tsking* noise. "Peace, and quiet, and food. That's what this gentleman needs. Please move on now. You can always visit again tomorrow."

"Of course," Lynsey said. "That's fine." Then she hooked her arm through my elbow and said, "Don't you worry Albert. We'll figure out how to take care of your animals."

The only word I really took in was "we."

We.

"So, you and me?" I asked as Lynsey spun us around and pointed us toward the door.

"Last I checked that's what 'we' means," she said.

"What about Hope?"

"She has a story to write." Lynsey gave my arm a little tug and did something resembling a skip. "Come on. You and I saved Albert. Now we have to save his animals."

"Of course we do."

"I knew you'd understand."

—

"WE'RE GOING TO NEED your friend Lewis's car," Lynsey said as the double glass doors slid open in front of us with a soft whirring sound. She was holding a sheet of paper torn from Hope's notebook with some wobbly lines drawn on it labeled "Hospital" at the bottom of the page, and "Farm" at the top.

"Excuse me? I'm sure Lewis has things to do with his own car. Why should he give it to us … *you?*" Changing pronouns was a pretty weak way to try to extricate myself from this situation, but it was worth a try.

"Because of the animals." There was an underlying *"duh"* in Lynsey's voice.

"They're not Lewis's animals. What about your car?" *Brilliant.* If she was using her own car, she didn't need me.

"What about your car?" she flung back at me.

"They're not my animals either." Her fast-knitting eyebrows told me she didn't like that answer. "Plus, I don't have a car." *Ha! Yahtzee!* There was no arguing with that one.

Except Lynsey seemed willing to try. "What? How can you not have a car?"

"I live in Montreal."

She put both hands on her hips. "I'm sorry, am I missing something? I thought Montreal was a big city – I mean for Canadian cities – I mean, I can see if you told me you lived somewhere everyone got around by dogsled, but that's not Montreal, am I right?"

It was happening again. I was engaging with this girl when I didn't have to. There was no gun to my head. I could just walk away. "Listen, I'm not about to educate you on the use of public transit in major metropolitan areas, or the non-use of dogsleds in most of Canada, I'm just going to …"

"Hey! You guys good? Where's Hope?" If only Lewis knew how vulnerable he was, standing in front of Lynsey, dangling his car keys.

"Oh! Lewis!" I was right. Lynsey was staring at those keys like they were a hypnosis fob watch. "We need to get out to Albert's farm, to feed his poor, starving animals, and Cam here is trying to tell me he doesn't have a car …"

Lewis broke in. "Oh, he doesn't have a car." He shrugged. "I mean, he lives in Montreal …"

I was learning that Lynsey really could raise her eyebrows quite surprisingly high.

"… but it's no big deal," Lewis was continuing. "You can use my car."

Lynsey's eyebrows slammed back into place and the sweetest smile you could imagine spread across her face. "Why thank you, Lewis. It's good to see that somebody around here has some respect for animal welfare."

Since Lynsey was so convinced she and Lewis were kindred spirits, I decided to try my luck. "Why don't you and Lewis go together?"

"No!"

"No!"

They both shook their heads.

Lewis spoke first. "I, uh, was just going to check on Hope. I'm hungry, and I was thinking she might need some food before she starts writing her big story, so ...” He pointed toward the sliding doors where Hope was visible inside, head down, scribbling into a notebook. “So, you two use the car and maybe you can meet us at the diner on Main Street after?”

In one smooth movement Lynsey swooped Lewis's keys out of his hand, threaded her arm through mine, yet again, and smiled. “You're on! I could definitely use some diner food after all my exertion today.”

“You didn't even finish the race!”

She whirled to face me. “Do you know how many calories I burned today? Do you know how many miles I covered?”

“*Kilometres*,” I muttered as she steered us both toward Lewis's vintage hatchback.

She dropped into the driver's seat, and I eased myself more slowly in through the passenger door ... and nothing happened.

In the silence of no engine starting, no radio playing, no nothing, my stomach rumbled long and loud. Lynsey wasn't the only one who liked the sound of a diner visit.

“Come on,” I said. “As you can hear, I'm starving. If we're going to do this, could we please, please, *please* just get going?”

“There's one small problem,” Lynsey said.

“What is it? No leather seats? No satellite radio? Or, maybe, you don't like the cup holders?”

Lynsey tapped the gear stick between us. “I can't drive stick.”

—

I WAS PREPARED TO be bitter. OK, while I backed out of the parking spot, and turned out of the parking lot, and trundled out of town, I *was* bitter.

I mean, Lynsey had coerced me into a car I didn't want to be in, to do a job I didn't want to be doing, and on top of it I was the one doing the driving. Really?

Something happened, though, when we left the final traffic light behind us. When we made a left turn off wide, smooth, well-marked-for-tourists asphalt, onto a narrow road in that kind of in-between state where you can't tell if the pavement is really crumbly, or the gravel's super hard-packed.

My shoulders dropped a couple of centimetres.

There were sometimes trees, and sometimes fields. There were stretches of fencing that was occasionally straight and wooden, but mostly made of sagging wire.

I tilted my head to one side, then the other.

There were mailboxes marking country driveways. Some were painted camo, others had quaint houses tole-painted on them. Many were bare metal with names stenciled on them in crooked block letters.

I exhaled.

A dog ran alongside the car. A pair of ducks erupted from the ditch beside us. We came up behind a tractor. A very slow-moving tractor.

Lynsey straightened in her seat. "I can drive one of those!"

"You what?!?" My shoulders crept up, as did the tone of my

voice. How, oh how, can a person know how to drive a tractor but not a mass-produced Japanese car with a manual transmission?

Before I could ask, Lynsey exclaimed again. "Here, here, here!" She glanced down at Hope's notebook page. "I'm pretty sure this is it. Turn, turn, turn!"

Thank goodness for the stick shift. It was a combination of brake pumping and down-shifting that allowed us to negotiate a very last-minute turn.

Here we were. Maybe. Safely off the road, tires on loose gravel, nose of the car pointing down a long driveway.

"What do you think?" Lynsey asked.

"I think it's not what I expected."

LYNSEY

IN THE MIDDLE OF the gravel driveway, a rust-colored chicken pecked single-mindedly in the dust. It had the attitude of a chicken that ruled the joint – oblivious and assured in a way I felt it shouldn't be. It was a chicken, after all. And it lived … here.

The farm looked like someone had built it several decades ago and promptly forgotten about it. A weathered blue barn, its roof slumping in the middle, was the most noticeable structure. Across the gravel drive, a cabin-type house was ensconced in a wrap-around porch. It looked as weather-beaten as the barn, with peeling white paint flaking up in large chunks all over the siding.

Pastures and fields spread out past the cabin, crisscrossed with broken three-rail fences. Some of the boards were snapped in two, or falling off the posts at angles. In other places, the fence was broken all the way through. It was impossible to gauge the acreage, with the undulating hills receding into evergreen forest beyond the pastures.

It occurred to me I should have asked Albert more about the animals. Namely what they were and where they were, because if they were all at large like this chicken it was going to take a lot longer than expected to feed them.

An empty fruit stand sat askew off the side of the road, the name of the farm painted across the wooden placard hanging from rusted chains under the eaves. I squinted at it, trying to read the sun-faded name.

"Does that say … Little Pipsqueak?" I asked, mostly to myself. Cam glanced up at the sign, head tilting.

"Light Pumpkin," he tried, sounding more sure of himself.

"That's ridiculous," I countered. "No one names a farm Light Pumpkin."

"And Little Pipsqueak is better?" He plucked the directions out of my hand and studied them. "Didn't Hope write the name of the place down?"

"If she had I wouldn't be asking what the name was," I pointed out, snatching the directions back and pocketing them. "It doesn't matter. We'll ask her next time we see her. Let's find the feed and the animals, get everyone settled, and go eat."

"Since you're the one with tractor-driving experience, I'm

assuming you're enlightened in the area of farm animal management as well," Cam said, sweeping a hand out at the farm beyond the decrepit fruit stand. "Go. Feed. I'll supply moral support by staying with the car."

"I know how to feed horses," I argued. "This …" I pointed at the chicken, which stopped its scratching to bob its head at me. "I don't know what to do with this."

Georgie would know what to do, I felt sure of it, but since she'd backed out of my goose hunt to drive back to Saratoga, citing places to be and an actual job to return to, I was on my own. Jobless. Directionless. With a farm crying out for attention in front of me and a chicken eyeing my running shoes like they might be tasty.

I told myself I *wanted* to be here. This was my avenue away from Florida, even for just a little while. I had to stretch this out. Milk it for all it was worth before reality crashed down.

I took a large, fortifying breath. The chicken pecked at my laces curiously.

"Don't you think it," I told the chicken. She ducked her head in her chicken way and erupted into the air – fluffed feathers flapping – alighting on the fruit stand's counter. I jumped, squelching a startled scream before it could turn into a shriek. Cam eyed me like he was dealing with a mental case. "I didn't know they could fly."

"That looked more like a hopeful leap to me," he said, pulling his phone out of his back pocket and tapping at the screen. "I'm shocked it got off the ground."

The bird pecked at the swollen wood, checking out the head

of a nail and tapping at it with rigorous patience. I left the bird to its quarry, turning back to the farm as Cam kept his head down, studying his phone with increasing absorption.

"I'm going to the barn," I announced, hopping onto the road. Cam didn't even glance up, which I figured was expected. He didn't want to be here, and I didn't know what I was doing by dragging him with me. This was my quest, not his.

He can drive a stick shift, I told myself. *You can't.*

Although I could have figured it out, couldn't I? If I'd been determined enough? Did I lack the proper commitment to procrastinate with my life? Or maybe I was simply a masochist, dragging along this man whose personality definitely did not match the promise of his forearms.

Still stewing, I approached the barn and looked up at its weathered boards. Blue was an interesting choice for a barn like this one – a classic Dutch barn with a steep gabled roof. It was more dramatic than the old converted tobacco barns on my family's farm, and a world away from the open shedrows at the track.

I pushed at the door, felt the old wood give under the pressure, and then threw my body behind it. The wood squeaked, the hinges let out a grinding cry, and then the door rolled back in one fell swoop so fast I had to catch myself before I fell straight on my face.

A shaft of light fell down the interior aisle, illuminating a hay-strewn dirt floor. Stalls ran up and down the aisle and my heart lifted automatically, full of the hope of horses. It smelled like them. Earthy and warm, like a summer day.

But the first stall was empty.

The second was, too.

Third, fourth. So on and so on.

"Well, what the hell?" I asked no one, crossing the aisle and peering into another stall, squinting through the dim light to find a horse napping in the center of its pile of bedding.

A *big* horse. The kind you'd hook up to a plow. Its hooves were like dinner plates, ratty feathering curling over them. A manure stain covered the entirety of his hindquarters. The rest of the animal was all bay dapples, so even if he wasn't perfectly turned out at least he was eating well enough.

"Where's your feed, buddy?" I asked him. The horse cocked an ear at me, cracking his eyes open just enough to watch me under long eyelashes. No response.

"Not hungry?" I asked him, and the gelding snorted at that, throwing his massive forelegs out in front of him and shoving his bulk off his bed, looming into the air so suddenly I was taken aback by how much he filled the space. With a flick of his bedding-riddled black tail, the horse turned around and shoved his nose over the stall door, slamming his muzzle into my hip and wiggling his lips, looking for treats.

"Didn't bring any," I told him, picking a piece of straw out of his tangled forelock. "But I promise I'll bring you some if you tell me where the feed room is."

"I don't think he's going to be of any help," Cam said dryly behind me, as the gelding took that opportunity to scratch his head against my side. The force of it knocked me clear to the other side of the aisle, where Cam stood with an amused half-smile on his face.

"What?" I asked, wiping a greenish smear of horse slobber off my arm. He shook his head.

"It must be something about women and horses," he said. "My sister is obsessed, too."

"I'm not obsessed," I said, even though I was. I really, really was. Cam nodded slowly like he didn't believe it either.

"Sure," he said. "And you're up here talking to a horse like that's a normal thing to do."

"Sometimes it is," I defended. "You've never talked to an animal before?"

"With the understanding it wasn't going to be talking back to me," he said. "There's a difference."

"Is there?" I asked, because I really didn't think there was. I talked to animals all the time, and sometimes they did talk back. Just not in the way most people expected. "Horses respond to aids," I found myself saying. "And some of those aids are verbal."

"Training isn't the same thing as a conversation," he pointed out.

"Isn't it?" I asked, and he gave me a weary look.

"OK, fine, you obviously know something I don't," he said, and I smiled my most winning smile.

"I accept your admission of wrongness."

He sighed. "I'm positive there are at least a dozen ways you could have said that better."

"Lucky me I can't seem to bother myself with caring," I said, smiling my way down the aisle. "What are you doing up here, anyway? I thought you had phone stroking to do down by the car."

"I was looking up how to feed chickens," Cam said, surprising me enough to stop me in my tracks.

"You looked up how to feed chickens," I said, meaning for it to be a question only for it to come out like a shocked statement. He shrugged.

"Well, yeah," he said. "I figured neither of us knew what we were doing. You, however, seem to know a little more than I initially gave you credit for, Ms. I Can Drive A Tractor But Not A Car."

"I helped out on the farm in the summers," I said, nosing my way down the aisle.

"Farm?" Cam asked, the word sounding foreign in his mouth. He looked like he was trying to solve a complex calculus problem in his head and it just wasn't coming out right. I couldn't help the laugh that bubbled up my throat.

"I just broke your brain, huh?"

"Nope." He recovered quickly. "I'll just leave all this to you, then. Clearly you don't need the help."

"Don't get too ahead of yourself," I advised, peeking into another stall and finding three small goats blinking up at me. One bleated, its tiny tail whipping back and forth. "The farm in question raises Thoroughbreds. Not …" I motioned to the goats. "These guys are cute, but this isn't exactly my wheelhouse."

"Let's just find the food," Cam said, trying a door at the end of the aisle. The knob creaked in his hand, the swollen wood popping as he pushed his shoulder into the door.

"Doesn't seem promising," I said. "You have to feed animals multiple times a day. Not, you know, once a year."

At that moment, the door gave and Cam let out a triumphant, "Ha!"

I peered over his shoulder, my mouth dropping at the sight of bags emblazoned with plump, white chickens. Next to those, bags with similarly plump white goats. I even spotted the reassuring sign of horse feed, and further back in the room, the ladder up to the hayloft.

I hoped that loft was full.

"This is stupid easy," Cam announced, going to the bags and finding scoops already waiting inside each. He hefted one in each hand, gave me a winning grin, and left me in the feed room. A dry erase board on the wall caught my eye. On one side, the names of the animals, or just the animals in general, written out in a shaky row.

Chickens. Goats. Cats. Horace. Matilda.

The first three were self-explanatory. A silky creature wrapped itself around my foot with a *meow* right as I reached for the Dollar Store bag of cat food on the shelf, uncrimping the bag. I found the bowls on the floor – five in all.

Oh boy.

I filled the bowls and got out of the way as the space was invaded by hungry felines, tails and whiskers twitching as they hunkered down to eat. Putting the food back on the shelf, I found myself staring at the board again. The date on the top was yesterday's, hash marks tallied in shaky black lines under the words *Morning, Afternoon,* and *Evening.*

No wonder the cats were ravenous. I found a cobwebby dry erase marker and wiped away the date with the heel of my hand, then cleared away all the little hash marks.

I wrote the right date, and did the tally, pausing at *Horace.*

"You must be the giant," I said, tapping the name with the end of the marker. Then I looked down at *Matilda.*

Who was Matilda?

"Lynsey!"

Cam didn't seem the type to panic easily, and I definitely heard a thread of desperation in his voice. I dropped the marker, scattering the cats as I leapt for the door. Scrambling to the edge of the aisle, I found Cam running back to the barn – scoops clutched in each hand and a pony galloping up on his heels.

Matilda, I assumed.

Cam dashed into the barn, the pony hot behind him.

"Whoa!" I stepped between them, the pony coming to a stunned halt, her snow-white head yanking up and her eyes a little wild. She stretched her neck past me, lipping at Cam's scoops and letting out an impatient squeal, adding a stamped hoof to punctuate her demand.

"She bum-rushed me," Cam accused, pulling the scoop out of the pony's mouth. "Out of nowhere. I'm certain she nearly killed a chicken on her way up here."

"Poor thing's hungry," I said. "She hasn't had a meal since yesterday."

Cam snorted. "Tell the chicken that."

"She didn't kill a chicken, did she?" I asked, grabbing the pony's ratty nylon halter, yanking her down the aisle. Cam shrugged.

"There were a lot of feathers flapping," he said. "It was hard to tell in the chaos."

Cam dropped the scoops in the feed room and followed me down the aisle.

"Where are you putting the heathen?"

I paused outside of an open stall, catching the nameplate on the door.

MATILDA.

"I think I've got a pretty good idea," I said, leading the pony into her stall and sliding the door shut. She immediately stuck her neck over the partition, nuzzling the latch until it popped open. I jumped forward, latching it again.

"Oh, that's just great," Cam sighed.

"The feed room," I said, pointing down the aisle. "Hurry. And they both need a flake of hay from the loft."

He nodded, hurrying down the aisle and disappearing for a good few minutes until the sound of hay dropping from the Dutch door onto the ground outside the barn made me sigh in relief.

There was hay up there after all.

Cam hefted a flake into each stall, and then dumped the feed into the buckets latched to the walls. Matilda gave him the evil eye and buried her nose in her bucket. Cam stepped back, letting his scoop hand relax at his side.

"Can we go eat yet?"

I eyed the latch on the pony's door. Obviously escaping was something she did regularly. Even though she was eyes-deep in her bucket, there was no telling when the mood would strike her to fly the coop again.

"Help me find something to secure her door," I said.

"She's not our responsibility, you know," he pointed out, correctly. "We're here to feed, and we've fed. There is a diner calling our names."

My stomach groaned at the thought of food.

"Cam, there's a dry erase board in the feed room," I said.

"Yeah, I saw it."

"It's just ..." I shrug. "Albert cares about these animals, enough to make sure they get their three squares a day. The least we can do is make sure his pony doesn't get out again."

"Seems like she does it on the regular."

"Even so."

He sighed, and I looked up at him, knowing I had my pout-face on full force. It was a patented move. Tried and true on everyone I'd ever known. Cam looked at me like he knew exactly what I was doing. He squirmed, shifting his weight, and finally let out a breath.

The breath of surrender.

"Fine, I saw some twine in the feed room. We'll tie the latch down, but then we're going."

I smiled.

Chapter Four

CAM

So, I lied.

I already knew how to feed chickens. My sister lived with a farmer, after all. My parents weren't quite ready to give her the "farmer" title as well – when new acquaintances asked about their daughter they tended to highlight her Bachelor of Education, not the fact that she mostly used her teaching skills on equines and women of all ages who wanted to learn to ride them. Still, I was pretty sure my sister living on a farm, with a farmer, meant I had a very close blood relative who was a farmer.

Meaning feeding chickens was, well, chicken soup. Or, I guess that should have been duck soup, but easy anyway.

What I was actually doing on the phone was having a come-to-Jesus moment sparked by the subject line BIO101.

As in, it was mine to teach.

Which was supposed to be good news.

I went to bat for you, my department chair wrote. We have to cut a TA. I gave you BIO101 because it's got to run. You're safe.

Safe …

While I was staring at the screen, standing at the end of that driveway, in a place which very few people could claim to be the middle of anywhere-at-all, I thought about that. Going back to Montreal. Being safe.

Montreal was a world-class city. Safety was a good thing.

Somehow, though, the two together weren't giving me the feeling of a *life*.

A bird twittered in the evening air. The sun warmed my swim-and-bike-and-run-stiffened muscles. A late-summer / early-autumn breeze chased across my skin, raising a shiver.

This place. It filled me with a peace, a calm, I had only ever felt at our family cottage on an island in the St. Lawrence River.

In the distance Lynsey popped her head out of the barn, then retreated inside again.

That girl. So far she'd filled me with frustration and irritation, true, but also, more than once, she'd made me want to laugh.

The most attractive thing about Lynsey wasn't her curves, or her smooth skin, or the vivid colour of her eyes — although in the short time I'd spent with her, I'd already noticed other guys observing all those things about her.

No; the most interesting thing about her was that I owed her nothing. She owed me nothing.

I might not have known what I wanted from my life but, like me, Lynsey wasn't wearing a wedding ring, didn't have any kids' birthdates or initials tattooed anywhere (that I could see) on her body, and still hadn't made noises about a home she had to get back to.

I knew fewer and fewer people like that. People who didn't look at their watches and say, "Better get going to meet the real estate agent / talk to the wedding planner / take the baby to Tiny Tots swimming."

My spectacularly empty life made it increasingly unenjoyable for me to spend time with spectacularly fulfilled people.

Lynsey, so far, if you discounted the annoyance factor, was easy to spend time with.

Plus, I was getting hungry and I figured feeding these animals was the quickest way I was going to get myself fed too, so I headed to the barn to meet her.

—

"I DON'T FEEL RIGHT about leaving." The barn was filled with the sounds of munching – which was only making me hungrier – so I wasn't sure what Lynsey's issue was.

My stomach growled – louder than the rustling of the horses pulling at their hay, or the goats' occasional contented bleat, and I shrugged. "Suit yourself. Lewis and Hope already have a huge head-start on eating, and I intend to catch up."

Because my earlier analysis about Lynsey held true. I'd hang out with her as long as it was easier than the alternative. Right now, spending any more time at this dilapidated farm was *not* easier than sliding into a booth at a diner serving hot food.

The evening, which had been undeniably charming in its golden-pinkish-sunsetty-magic, was shifting. Clouds had moved in. The light had faded. A current of air, stronger and cooler than a mere breeze, whistled down the aisle of the barn.

I tossed my keys in the air, caught them again, and said, "Someone can probably come back to pick you up after dinner. When we're done. Sometime."

An owl hooted, deep and haunting, and Lynsey clamped her hand across her midriff. "I guess I'm hungry too."

I didn't hear anything from her stomach, but who cared? The deal wasn't to only stick with her if she told the truth. As long as she didn't stand in the way of my dinner, she was welcome to tag along. I had a hankering for nachos anyway, and if I pretended they were to share with Lynsey, that would still make it totally reasonable for me to also order a burger.

In that way, having her along could be useful.

"OK," I said. "Let's go."

With a double-check of each animal's water bucket, and the latches on their doors – especially Matilda's – and with about three – or maybe four – backward glances, we did just that.

———

WHILE IT WAS TRUE that the combination of huge booths, an extensive comfort-food menu, and walls hung with local art gave the diner a friendly, down-home feel, that's not what mattered.

What mattered was that the nachos came heaped high with cheese on each one, the burger was juicy without the bread being even slightly soggy, and the taste of the cherry pie made me declare, "Heavenly …"

With one bite left – a bite oozing with not-too-sweet-not-too-tart cherry filling and nested in rich, flaky crust – I finally lifted my eyes from my plate just in time to see Hope's cheeks flame like the red-sky-at-night-sunset Lynsey and I had driven through to get here.

"What?" I asked.

"I just found out she baked it." Lewis shook his head and spread his hands wide. "Can you believe it?"

"You made this?" I pointed at my final, sacred mouthful.

Hope nodded.

"This very, actual, particular piece of pie?"

She nodded again.

"This is the best pie I've ever tasted. Bar none." The part of me that wanted to finish the pie immediately did silent battle with the part that wanted to wait a minute or two to make sure I really, truly appreciated that last portion. "It might be the best *food* I've ever tasted."

"It's my mom's recipe," Hope said.

"But I don't understand. You're a reporter. How could you have baked pie that's being sold at a diner?"

Hope laughed. "While I appreciate the clout you attribute to my journalistic duties, believe it or not, *The Mirror* isn't exactly a full-time gig."

Lewis leaned in. "She's a baker."

"A baker?" No wonder Lewis's eyes were wide with awe. I was suddenly seeing Hope in a whole new light. An I'm-sorry-my-best-friend-fell-for-her-first light.

She was adorable in that big-eyed puppy way that never really got tired. She was smart enough to write publishable words. I'd already seen that she was kind. And then, to learn she could bake like this …

I mean, this was a girl offering a ready-made life. Step right up, have a beautiful wedding with a beautiful bride, have our first child nine-and-a-half months later, wake up happy every day, and always, always eat well.

Returning from a trip to the washroom, Lynsey slid into the booth, speared my pie, forked it in and, with crust spraying from the corners of her mouth mumbled, "How can you leave any of this on your plate? I inhaled my slice."

Flabbergasted.

An English Major I'd slept with had once used that word and I'd mocked her so mercilessly she got out of my bed at 3:30 a.m., pulled on her clothes – including my all-time favourite vintage Montreal Expos hoodie which I never saw again – and swept out into the minus thirty degrees of a mid-January night.

I'm sorry, I thought. *You were right*. It was a great word. It was a punch to the kidneys, followed by a knee in the gut. It was all the air sucked out of my body at once. It was my brain reeling because there was no way to express the true egregiousness of Lynsey's transgression.

Lynsey elbowed me. "I had a horse that used to let his mouth hang open like that. It didn't look good on him, either." Then she made a move that I assume was meant to pinch my hanging-open-in-astonishment lower lip, and that was the final straw.

I stood up on the bench, stepped over Lynsey, and walked straight to the counter ignoring the calls of, "Hey!" and "What are you doing?" and "Cam!" coming from behind me.

The woman wiping the surface looked up and asked, "What can I get you, hon?"

"Another slice of that cherry pie, please."

She smiled. "It is great, isn't it? Unfortunately, though, that lady got the last piece. She's sitting at your table – maybe she'll share with you?"

I followed her finger to Lynsey, eyebrows raised, giving me a theatrical shrug.

"Fat chance."

"Pardon me, sweetie?"

"Nothing. Thank you."

"We'll have more pie tomorrow. Maybe I'll see you then."

Fat chance. This time I kept it to myself.

I WAS OUTSIDE, USING one of those concrete parking barricades to stretch my legs, when the rest of them came out.

"What happened to you?" Lynsey asked.

I used Hope and Lewis as my excuse not to talk to her. They were walking oh-so-slowly across the parking lot, gazing into each other's eyes, in danger of falling flat on their faces if they encountered even the slightest dip, or bump in the pavement. I pointed at them, waggled my eyebrows, and moved around to the passenger side of Lewis's car.

Polite version of my silent message: *We shouldn't talk in case we disturb the adorable lovebirds.*

True message: *I can't talk to you now because I won't say anything civil.*

Lynsey didn't get either meaning. "What are you doing with your eyebrows?" She swished a late-season mosquito away from her head. "Did something bite you?"

And with that, the tiny amount of patience I possessed was gone. "Bite?" I asked. "Did you say bite?"

Now she was the one with the mobile eyebrows – they knitted together – "What are you talking about?"

"I had one bite left of cherry pie. One. Bite. Of the best cherry pie I've ever tasted, and you swooped in and *stole* it. Who does that?"

"Are you serious?"

"Never more."

"All this about a couple of ounces of cherry pie?"

"*Grams*," I muttered.

She was still talking. "Gawd … if it's that important to you, I'll go in there and buy you another slice."

"No …" I was shaking my head. "No, you won't be able to, because …"

But she was no longer listening to me. She was staring at her phone and it was her turn to mutter, "Shit …"

"What?" I asked.

She lowered her phone and looked at me. "Have you ever heard of a hotel forcibly checking you out?"

"What do you mean?"

She passed me her phone, displaying an email from front-desk@hotellakeplacid, reading Dear Ms. Armstrong. We were unable to reach you using the phone number we had on file. As the hotel is full, we cannot extend your stay and have cleared your belongings from your room. You may pick them up from our luggage storage area at your earliest convenience. Please feel free to contact us at the phone number below.

I waited for her to make a wise-cracking joke about the adventure of being homeless, about how the Hotel Lake Placid was a dump anyway, and she'd rather stay at the Ritz-Carlton, about not bothering to pick up her stuff because she'd just buy everything new.

She didn't do any of those things. Instead she sniffed, and bit at her lip, and her face drained of colour, contrasting with the bright red of her ear lobes.

In one of those completely weird moves destined to make me cringe every time it would flit through my mind for ages afterwards, I reached for Lynsey's ear thinking how mine always went red and hot when I was tired, and Meg's did too – knowing exactly how the skin would feel between my fingers – before remembering, just in time, the ear I was reaching for was neither mine nor my sister's.

Whoops. I recoiled as fast as if Lynsey's ear was a red-hot ring on an electric stove, and thankfully Hope and Lewis reached us just in time to notice the frown wrinkling Lynsey's tanned forehead.

"What's wrong?" Hope asked, and Hope being Hope, everything was sorted out in a very few minutes after that, with Lynsey bundled into the passenger seat of Hope's pick-up while Hope chattered away. "We'll swing by the hotel – and tell them what we think of forced check-outs – and it will be a pleasure to have you stay at the house tonight …"

"You'll be OK?" Lewis asked, three times.

Three times Hope blushed and said, "I've lived here my whole life, silly. Of course I'll be fine."

Even though I knew it was genuine, and even though I should be happy for my friend for finding love after his short-lived and ill-advised marriage (calling his ex-wife a selfish, narcissistic, diva was paying her a compliment she didn't deserve), something about the dreamy look on Lewis's face as the pick-up trundled away, wore my patience right through.

"Oh, snap out of it." And I actually snapped my fingers when I said it.

He jumped. "Sorry, sorry. Of course, you must be tired. Let's get back to the cabin."

We drove a couple of blocks in silence before I gathered the courage and decency to say, "You're right, I am tired. That must be why I was such a dick. I'm sorry. I think it's nice that you like Hope."

"Like her?!? Oh, I don't know if I'd go that far." Lewis's ears were burning as bright as Lynsey's had been, but fortunately I made no attempt to touch his.

The memory of Lynsey, and her red ears, made me confront the uncomfortable reality that my meanness to Lewis had nothing to do with me being tired, and everything to do with the guilt I'd felt for seeing Lynsey at a vulnerable moment – clearly upset – and doing nothing to try to make things better for her, or to change the fact that the last thing I'd done was complain to her about my cherry pie.

I shrugged. *Whatever.* That was par for the course. I often did things that would make normal people feel guilty, and my well-established super power was in not feeling that guilt.

And, truly, Lynsey had stolen my last bite of pie. I was the wronged party and I had every right to point that out to her. And, as to being evicted from her hotel, well that was her fault too. How did she think hotels worked?

Hmm … maybe I was tired after all … there was no other explanation for me going soft in the face of an incompetent girl with problems of her own making who, after all, was right now in the safe care of the very fetching – and culinarily gifted – Hope.

As Lewis turned into the rutted driveway leading to his man cave of a cabin, I decided Lynsey had landed on her feet – to be honest, she struck me as the kind of girl who always would – that she'd have a better sleep at Hope's than I would on Lewis's slow-leaking camp mattress from his Scouting days. She and her Louis Vuitton luggage would be long-gone from this not-quite-big-enough-to-be-called-a-town by the next time Lewis sought out Hope.

Of course, I should also be pretty far outta Dodge by this time tomorrow.

Montreal, and my slow-ascending academic career – propped up by BIO101 – awaited. There was a girl, too; a rising star in municipal politics who'd been resisting my advances but had recently sent me a couple of flirtatious texts.

Life, as I've known it, was waiting for my return.

"Ready to hit the hay?" Lewis asked as he shut off the engine.

Ready to zone out? Yup. *Ready to stop thinking?* Absolutely. "I was ready hours ago."

LYNSEY

IN THE MORNING, I woke up halfway expecting to find myself in my room at Saratoga. The old Queen Anne Victorian – nearly as old as the race track itself and painstakingly remodeled by my step-mother to wipe away all remnants of what she called our "less than happy times" – would be filling with summer light by now. Horses would be stepping neatly across Union Avenue, their breaths misty on their way from their flower-adorned shedrows to the fog-cloaked main track to train. I would have been awake by now, coffee in hand, watching Tupelo Stud's horses by the rail with my brother. It was our tradition in the summer. Wake up before dawn, procure coffee, watch the works from first horse to last.

But summer was over – at least it was for Saratoga. And I was …

The smell of cinnamon and freshly baked bread pulled me to sitting on the sofa, which Hope had fastidiously fashioned into a bed the night before, apologizing for the lack of a guest room after I'd refused to take her bed. I was the one who didn't have a plan. I was the one who should have been apologizing. After all, it's not like I didn't know how hotels worked.

OK, maybe I didn't know how hotels worked. This was the first one I'd paid for outright … not that I was admitting that to anyone.

My stomach grumbled, reminding me that food wasn't going to come on a tray either. I had to procure it myself.

I rolled out of bed and pulled the sheets off the sofa with me, rolling them into a ball like a sloppy but somehow also elegant throw pillow. Picking through my suitcase, I pulled out a pair of leggings and shimmied into them before following the delicious smell down a squeaking set of stairs, stumbling into a flour-dusted industrial kitchen.

I came to a quick stop at the sight of Hope working at a huge lump of dough, flour streaked over one cheek and dotted down an apron emblazoned with the name Irene's Bakery in cute, hand-drawn letters. She looked up, blowing loose strands of hair out of her face.

"You're up early!"

"Habit," I shrugged.

"Me too." She smiled, going back to work on the dough, separating it into smaller loaves and manhandling them like she had a vendetta against bread. "Baking is an early morning thing."

"So are horses," I said. "Screaming for breakfast before dawn."

She laughed. "I'll bet." Then she motioned to the huge oven behind her. "Hey, can you pull the cinnamon rolls out of the oven? Mom is out front opening the store, and my hands are full."

I took the mitts she pointed at and pulled the door down, cinnamon-tinted heat blasting into my face.

"This smells divine," I sighed, maneuvering the giant tray to the counter Hope pointed at with one doughy finger.

"Makes me feel a little bad about stealing Cam's last bite of that pie," I said, mostly to myself. Hope blushed – obviously unable to take any kind of compliment. I should have flushed a little myself, out of shame for thinking I might be comfortable enough with Cam to go eating off his plate.

"I don't think he was upset about the pie," she told me.

"What do you mean?" I asked. "I stole it. Like a lunatic."

"And it really wasn't about the pie." Hope held firm.

I looked at her like she was speaking Latin, and she kept kneading and working, a small smile on her face. Finally, I had to ask. "If not the pie, then what?"

She shrugged. "I don't know. He just seemed … interested in watching you. And watching other guys watching you. It was kind of cute, how he just blew up."

"That was *cute?*" I laughed – the obnoxious barking kind – out of total disbelief.

"Yes," Hope insisted, flicking a bit of flour in my direction. "Because it was so ridiculous. It was pie, Lynsey. No one gets that upset over pie. Not even *my* pie, and as has been stated, mine is the best."

"Well, there has to be a first time," I countered.

"I wouldn't bet on it."

"Even if he was somehow all flustered by my womanly appeal, which he was not, it doesn't matter," I said. "Cam is a closed chapter in my life. He'll be back in Montreal before the end of the day, safe from my pie-stealing ways, and we'll never have to cross paths again. End of story."

Hope sighed. "If you say so."

"Oh, I know so," I told her. "You can call up your boyfriend now. I'm sure he'll tell you Cam is long gone."

Hope sputtered. "Lewis is not … I mean, he can hardly be my boyfriend. We just met! Yesterday!"

"Uh-huh," I snorted. "If anyone was flustered by womanly appeal it was Lewis, and the woman in question was you."

Hope opened and shut her mouth, while I leaned over the cinnamon rolls, taking a deep, appreciative breath.

"It's a family recipe." A woman – Hope's mom, going by the

subtle streak of gray in her hair that was the exact same shade as Hope's – paused in the doorway to the kitchen. "You're our sofa surfer, I take it?"

I ducked my head, suddenly feeling the urge to flush at that particular shame – the being incompetent at life thing.

"I am," I nodded. "And thank you, Mrs. …"

"You can call me Irene," she said. "No need to be formal."

"Irene," I said. "Thank you for the sofa. Can I repay you? Help out …" I cast a look around the kitchen, full of shiny things I'd never used in my life. I could probably do great accidental damage in this room.

Irene eyed me like she knew it. Hope grinned and put a bowl in my hands.

"Glaze the rolls," she said gently. "You can't go wrong."

A tinkling bell announced the shop's first customer, and Irene excused herself with a small smile. I began to carefully drizzle sugar all over the rolls, watching the white stuff pool over the cooling bread and wanting to delve into it with both hands. My stomach grumbled again.

"We should feed you, too," Hope said, separating the dough one more time and beginning to fashion what I suspected were scones.

"Would you accept work in exchange for food?" I asked, thinking about my credit cards and my bank account. There were limits on trust fund distributions, weren't there? I should probably figure out how much money I had, because Dad wasn't going to pick up the check anymore. He'd been quite clear. *Tough love,* he'd said, after taking a sip of his champagne and swanning off to celebrate our massive win, disappearing in a crowd of suits and feathered sun hats.

"You can have one of those rolls after they cool down enough to eat," Hope said, arranging her scones on a baking sheet and pulling me over to her, sprinkling my hands with flour and putting a lump of dough in them.

"And one of these, too," she said, showing me how to turn the dough lump into Irene's Famous Scones. "We work on an if-you-baked-it-you-can-eat-it-free policy here." Then she squinted at me. "Doesn't look like you need free food, though."

"I don't!" I said, coming out squeakier and more forceful than intended. Hope ducked her head, working on the dough.

"Of course," she said quickly. "I didn't mean …"

"I just," I started at the same time, and then we both laughed awkwardly, the tension blowing out. "I'm kind of on my own up here," I said, working on shaping my scone. "If you hadn't noticed."

"I kind of had," Hope said, taking my lopsided scone and evening it out before placing it tidily on the sheet. "You never mentioned having somewhere to be, and when you didn't go back with your friend … I guess I just figured you were either carefree or avoiding something. But it's not my business, so just know you're free to stay as long as you like."

I let out a breath. "Thanks," I said. "That means a lot."

Hope pushed a wayward strand of hair out of her face, smearing another streak of flour on her cheek. "No problem," she said. "Besides, anyone who helps out Albert is a good person in my book."

I paused. "Oh, god, the farm."

Hope looked up. "I'm sure Albert's son has things managed by now."

"But what if he doesn't?" I asked. In my mind's eye, I couldn't help thinking about Horace patiently waiting for his next flake of hay, his big body still wedged in his stall. And Matilda, fruitlessly trying to get out of hers after we'd tied the latch down.

Hope frowned, pushing the baking sheet into the oven.

"Give me one second and we can go check on things," she said, dusting off her hands and pulling her apron over her head, flour drifting around her like a cloud.

"You don't have to," I said, heading for the stairs. "My car's still parked at the hotel. I'll walk over and get it. You have a whole bakery to help run."

Hope paused, looking at the oven. "OK, but report back. If the farm's not getting taken care of, I want to know about it."

Speaking of, since you care about the farm, and you're Lake Placid's number one investigative journalist, do you know what the 'LP' stands for in the farm's name?"

"Huh," Hope blew a stray lock of hair off her oven-flushed forehead. "Excellent question. I would say 'Lake Placid' but I think I'd know if that was it. To be honest, as long as I can remember it's just always been called that."

—

IT TOOK ONLY A few minutes to get out of Lake Placid, the small town falling away to the gradual climb of evergreen-packed mountains. Only a few minutes more, and I was steering my Audi down the county road to the farm, passing ramshackle tracts of land and tilting, rusted mailboxes. I rolled down the windows, letting the early morning air whip around the car and taking a deep breath of it. It smelled different than home – more pine and less palm – but still full of country, and that made my heart settle in my chest as I drove.

I slowed at an intersection, coming to a full stop to let a horse trailer turn in front of me and trundle down the road. I followed, eyes sticking to the dark brown rump of the horse, its tail dangling over the tailgate and trailing in the current like a black banner. Every so often, the horse turned its head, its eye large and wary, as though it didn't quite trust where it was going.

"I feel you, buddy," I whispered to myself, watching the trailer slow and turn off the road, bumping onto an old driveway not far from the farm. I slowed down, getting a look at the rundown property – tiny three-stall barn, a paddock full of abandoned scrap. It wasn't ideal, but people did worse with horses.

I wished the horse well and kept going, turning onto Albert's property and driving past the old fruit stand, all the way up to the barn, which looked just as abandoned as it had yesterday. One foot placed in the barn confirmed for me no one had been there since: Matilda and Horace both came to the front of their stalls, letting out insistent, painfully loud whinnies.

"OK, OK!" I called over the cries, which soon included the plaintive bleats of the goats. I climbed up into the loft, kicking down a few flakes of hay, and distributed it across the animals. Once the barn was full of the shifting, repetitive sound of chewing, I checked the dry-erase board to confirm. No one had been here, and if they had, they didn't subscribe to Albert's rigorous tally mark system.

Stepping over the cats, I texted farm abandoned, animals ravenous to Hope and immediately got a frown emoji in response.

I'll investigate, she assured me in a follow-up. Keep you posted.

I stood in the aisle, shifting my weight and wondering at what to do next. Leave? Stay? It felt wrong to go, but this wasn't my land, wasn't my farm. These weren't my animals. I didn't belong here … but I didn't want to go, either.

Besides, all I had so far was a sofa above Irene's bakery. Hope and her mother were adorable, and I had a hunch they'd let me stay until it became uncomfortable – and still insist I sleep in their living room. But I couldn't do that, because sleeping on a sofa isn't my idea of a long-term commitment, and I couldn't trespass on the kindness of recently acquired friends. My mother raised me right, even if my father didn't.

At the very least, I could get the animals out of the barn. Surely everyone needed paddock time. I trooped out of the barn to assess the grazing situation, finding two paddocks behind the barn with intact fences. And a riding arena.

I stopped dead to stare at it. The dirt had weeds growing in it, the grass encroaching from under the broken fence, but it was an honest-to-god ring with – I squinted at the far corner – standards and poles piled in faded disuse.

"Are you kidding me?" I muttered to myself, turning on my heel to head back into the barn and standing, looking around for another door. There had to be a tack room somewhere. Where there was a riding arena and horses, there was a tack room.

I counted down the empty stalls. No tack room. I checked the feed room again, searching for a hidden door. Nothing. Weird.

Standing in the aisle again, I put my hands on my hips and thought about this, still drawing a complete blank. Matilda shoved her head over her stall door and snorted at me, banging her hoof against the wood and nipping at the latch.

"OK," I told her, opening the door and grabbing her halter. "Because I can't have you destroying your stall while Albert's gone."

Once I had all the animals – goats and horses – enjoying the sunshine, I stepped back to admire my handiwork. Matilda was busy turning circles around Horace, and the goats were kicking up their heels. Everything seemed very quaint and pastoral. Quiet. Peaceful.

I eyed the arena again, and then lifted my gaze up to the house.

I shouldn't do it, but I already had the thought. So I set off, climbing the slight rise and stepping up onto the wraparound porch. The boards creaked threateningly as I crossed to the door, almost telling me *this is a bad idea. Don't do it. Stop right there.*

I ignored those warnings and put my hand on the knob, giving it an experimental twist. The door popped right open, swinging inward with a squeak and revealing Albert's life the way he left it yesterday, when he was sure he was coming home to feed his animals. The worn hardwood groaned under my feet as I walked into the living room, with its burnt orange sofa and dark brown recliner set before a tiny tube television with bunny ear antennas perched hopefully above the set. The corner of the room was taken up by a cast iron object I couldn't identify as I passed into the kitchen, which was all 1970s goldenrod – even the refrigerator – and scattered with the remains of breakfast.

My stomach rumbled, and I steadfastly ignored it, passing into the back of the house, where there were two bedrooms, one bathroom with a lone toothbrush sitting in a cup by the faucet, and two closets. One, full of carefully folded towels and linens. The other …

Bingo.

A saddle, gleaming like it was still new, was perched on a stand. A bridle was draped over it, also clean and shiny. On the walls of the closet – ribbons. Blues, reds, whites, yellows, pinks … they papered the wall almost completely except for one spot that was dedicated to a photo of a little girl, her dark hair in pigtail braids, sitting on a pony that looked suspiciously like Matilda. Albert stood to one side – younger, grinning, but Albert sure enough, one arm thrown over Matilda's haunches and the other resting on the girl's knee. On the other side, a younger man, in his early thirties, obviously

Albert's son.

I looked up at the shelves above the saddle, at photo albums, the years marked on their spines. 1991-1994, 1995-1998, 1999-2005. Three in all, and then nothing. My stomach clenched – a familiar feeling rushing up my throat. I closed the door quickly and leaned against it, resting my forehead against the wood and taking a deep breath. I felt a warm lick of shame.

I shouldn't have opened this door, barging into Albert's life, like I shouldn't have barged into Cam's, dragging him into my quest to procrastinate. What was I thinking? Who did things like that? I took a shuddering breath and left the hallway, crossing the house, halfway to the door when my phone rang, Hope's name flashing across the screen.

"Hey," I answered.

"So, there's a small issue," Hope said, sounding breathless.

"That doesn't sound great," I say, standing in the middle of Albert's living room, noticing the framed photo on the wall – Albert and a woman in a wedding dress, both of them grinning at the camera. Then, next to it, an infant dressed in a pale green romper, arms up mid-wave. I squeezed my eyes shut, eager all of a sudden to leave.

"Albert's been discharged from the hospital," Hope said.

"Good," I said, feeling supremely awkward now as I was still standing in the man's living room, uninvited and unsupervised. "I'm sure he'll be glad to be home."

"Well," Hope said, holding on to the word longer than necessary. "That's just it. He's not going home."

I pause in my reach for the front door.

"What do you mean?"

"I mean," Hope sighed, "Albert's son, Wes, flew up from Florida last night, and he's taking Albert back with him. I only just caught them on the way to the airport. Their flight is … well, it's boarded by now."

I gaped into the phone. "But what about the animals?"

"That's the other thing," Hope said. "Albert said you were taking care of them. That you had it covered."

My knees felt weak. Jittery. I sank down onto the burnt orange sofa and clung to it with my free hand, the sagging cushions scratchy against my newly sweaty palm.

"But, I …" I started, getting ready to say *I can't*. I couldn't look after these animals. I couldn't stay in Lake Placid indefinitely. My life was upheaved, on pause, and lacking in direction, but this little farmhouse with its hints of quiet family tragedy was not exactly where I thought I'd be living it out.

But then, where else did I have to go? Any house owned by my father was a no-go, and Hope's sofa wasn't logical. I didn't have anywhere *to* go … except maybe here.

Stay here.

My mind was still having a hard time wrapping itself around such a concept, even though a few hours ago I was yearning to stay in Lake Placid to drag out the inevitable. But that was when the inevitable was tucking my tail between my legs and going home to grovel, beg, and capitulate upon demand. All of a sudden, if that was my future, it got kicked down the road.

Indefinitely.

"It's so unexpected," Hope was saying, my attention coming back to her. "Wes hasn't been in town for years, not since his daughter passed. And Albert needs his family right now, so I understand. The animals, though …"

"I'll take care of them," I said, my voice wavering, even though I was sure.

"Huh?" Hope's voice squeaked.

"I said I'll take care of them," I said. "The farm. All of it. I can do it."

"Oh!" Hope's surprise did not fail to register. I winced, wondering if I came off as that incapable all the time. It couldn't be a good look. "That's great!" Hope continued. "I have Wes's number in Florida. I'll text it to you. You'll want to talk to him, I imagine."

"I imagine," I echoed, looking around me at my new home away from … Well, this *was* home now. For however long.

After I disconnected the call from Hope, a phone number popped up in a text. I hovered the tip of my finger against it, and then remembered they were on a plane home. To Florida. Where I should be.

I stood up, tapping my fingers against the phone's case, looking around the tiny house wonderingly. Here was the solution to all of my problems, at least for a little while. I took a deep breath, and let it out slowly, feeling lighter than I had in days, since Dad told me he wasn't paying my way anymore. I was floundering ten minutes ago, and now I had a foothold. I could feel it. This little place might be a rundown, goldenrod crime against interior design, but it was saving me right now.

And I intended to save it right back.

Chapter Five

CAM

T HE TREE CAME DOWN at 2:37 a.m.

Of course, I only found that out later, when I also found it had smashed the watch I'd left lying on the floor next to me, leaving the hands marking out 2:37.

All I was aware of at the moment it tore through the roof, was nothing. Blackness. The deep sleep of a person with most of a triathalon under their belt, and then of being heart-racingly, far-too-suddenly awake.

Awake, but far from lucid. Because it was a fretful night, with clouds covering the stars and moon, and nasty licks of wind randomly hurtling down rotten pieces of tree, it was pitch dark outside. And, because the falling tree carcass also snagged the cabin's power supply on its way down, it was molasses-black inside.

With the inside and outside merged, and not a hint of light

anywhere, and what I later found out to be tree branches pinning me to the floor with Lewis's finally-and-forever deflated camping mattress underneath me, I had not a clue where I was, or what was happening to me.

"You're crushing me," I mumbled. "Lynsey …" Then enough of my brain woke up to remember I hadn't slept with Lynsey. "Never will, either," I muttered before cluing in that must mean I was in bed with Amber, my back-up booty-call buddy. Which actually made more sense because Amber did keep a set of ropes under her bed for special occasions.

Except … there was a wedding … oh, yeah. Amber's. I went to it the weekend before the Ironman. She was honeymooning on Turks & Caicos right now.

So, not Amber.

I felt a few things all at once – rough bark under my probing hands, a cool autumn night breeze licking across my exposed skin, and drops on my face. Rain?

I was really tired, and completely confused, and the muscle stiffness from the day's efforts had well and truly set in, making me uninclined to acrobat my way out of whatever was snaring me in, and a big part of me thought it could be a nightmare – I'd had worse ones – and maybe I should just roll over and go back to sleep.

Two things stopped that:

A) I couldn't roll over.

B) Lewis's voice. Yelling. Frantic. "Cam! Cam! Where are you Cam?" Then a stream of light bobbed across me and he told someone, "Oh my god. A tree's fallen on him."

—

LEWIS AND I SAT in a set of folding lawn chairs with webbing of clashing 70's-era colours, and questionable strength, and sipped our coffee, and stared at the cabin propping up the tree, or the tree nailing down the cabin – however you preferred to look at it.

As so often happens, there was no sign of the unsettled weather of the night before. The morning was as sunny and blue-skied as any I'd ever seen, and people living in intact, built-to-code houses likely slept right through without an inkling of last night's passing weather system and its whirling winds, fatal to rotted-out spruce trees.

The members of the volunteer fire department were the first ones there, and the ones to lever me out from under the tree.

A paramedic strongly suggested I go to hospital, but when I resisted reluctantly admitted he couldn't find any injury likely to cause imminent death. I persuaded him to put four stitches in the cut on my brow and when he was done he'd assured me it would add character to my looks.

The police showed up, but didn't seem to know what to do, so mostly drank a lot of coffee, and pointed their headlights on the downed power lines so the utility guys could work their magic to make sure nobody would be electrocuted.

By the time that was all done, it was light(ish) and somebody brought Lewis and me a Thermos of coffee, and we'd been sitting there ever since.

"What are you going to do?" I asked Lewis, and as sorry as I felt for him, it was actually a relief to be able to query his future, instead of dwelling on the question of my own.

He shook his head. Sighed. Rubbed his forehead. Up-ended the Thermos and emptied the final three drops into his cup. "I'm going to need more coffee before I can answer that."

"And some food." I said it partly because I was hungry, and partly because I knew food would make him think of Hope, and Hope would cheer him up.

He straightened in his chair. "Yes. Food." Then he lifted his arm and sniffed underneath it. "But before that a shower."

Which is how I knew my friend was well-and-truly in love. What other guy, after having a tree fall on the only real estate he possessed, would insist on a shower before bacon-and-eggs?

Whatever. I might as well throw him a bone. "OK. Let's figure out a way to get clean."

—

IT WAS A DIP in the river that served as our shower. Which, to be honest, was a step up from Lewis's indoor plumbing anyway.

When we ventured inside to grab towels, and some shampoo, and clean boxers, it was actually astonishing how little the rest of the cabin had been impacted by the tree fall. I mean, the rest of it was substandard in every way, but it had been that way before the evergreen had taken its tumble.

The main damage was centred on what had been the second bedroom. My bedroom. The duffel bag I'd been living out of was pinned to the floor by a branch through the handle. I used the knife blade of the multi-purpose tool I always kept in the pocket of the duffel bag to slice the nylon webbing and dragged the bag out, allowing myself one good gape at the maze of branches and rafters scattered over my former resting spot like a tumbled game of Jenga.

No, wait, not my resting spot. Probably better not to think of it that way.

The place where I slept last night.

And would never sleep again – not even if Lewis restored it to Hyatt Regency standards.

So, a good scrub, a cool rinse, and a scratchy towel-dry later and we were on our way into town to look for food and coffee.

———

We ended up at Irene's. Of course we did. The diner called my name but the trauma from last night's events was over for me – I could have died, but I didn't – whereas Lewis would be dealing with the logistical and financial fall-out for much longer than me, so I let him choose, and the comfort of Hope won out over the comfort of the $5.99 Breakfast Platter.

As it turned out, Hope invited us in, right past the bakery storefront – which did smell amazing – into an industrial-type kitchen, where she fried us bacon and scrambled us eggs, all while exclaiming over my four stitches and Lewis's crushed cabin.

I let the two of them talk, while I sampled Hope's non-dessert wares and found them just as good as her pie.

While Lewis paced up and down in Hope's narrow hallway,

cell phone to his ear, talking to his insurance broker, Hope turned to me. "Have you had enough to eat?"

"Mmm …" I said. "These cinnamon rolls are something else."

"Oh, Lynsey glazed those," Hope said. "I actually like how she did it better than my usual way. I'll probably switch."

Lynsey. Of course. She slept here last night. Hope caught me looking left and right, and under the table, and laughed. "Oh, she's not here. She headed out to the farm pretty early to feed the animals."

Zing. There it was again – that unfamiliar pang of guilt. Why did feeding the animals already feel like a chore that was half mine? I almost died last night – I shouldn't have to feel like a shirker this morning.

But I did.

"How about you?" she asked. "What are your plans now?"

Lewis returned to the room saying, "OK, thanks then. I'll wait to hear from you," then pocketing his phone to turn to Hope. "I'm so sorry."

I didn't even have to dodge Hope's question – I was forgotten – she didn't care anymore. Lewis was back in the room. "What did they say?" Hope asked.

He ran his hand through his hair and pushed his coffee cup forward. "Do you think I could get a refill?"

"Long story?" she asked.

His eyes locked on hers and in front of my eyes his shoulders lowered, worry lines smoothed from his forehead. "Oh, just details."

She poured each of them a coffee and sat down across from Lewis. "I'm listening."

I cleared my throat. "Um."

They both turned to me. Their looks were polite, but slightly surprised. *Oh yeah. You're still here.*

"Maybe … I was wondering … do you think Lynsey could use some help out at the farm?"

The smile that flooded Hope's face was genuine. "Oh! That would make me feel so much better. It's … she's … Albert's … well, I'll let her tell you, but there have been some developments this morning, and I think she might have bitten off a little more than she can chew. She might appreciate a friendly face. Here …" She jumped up and fished a set of keys out of a basket on the windowsill. "Take my truck. I shouldn't need it the rest of the morning."

"If you need anything I can drive you," Lewis said, so it appeared things were settled. I was driving Hope's truck to Albert's farm, and Hope and Lewis were more than happy to see me going.

The question was whether Lynsey would be equally happy to see me.

—

"WHAT ARE YOU DOING HERE?"

I'd just cut the engine of Hope's truck when Lynsey stalked out of the barn and walked right past me, pausing only long enough to hurl her greeting my way. She disappeared around the side of the building and I considered starting the engine again and backing out.

But Hope. She would *not* be happy to see me come straight back without even speaking to Lynsey. And if Hope wasn't happy, Lewis wouldn't be happy. And I'd already concluded he deserved good things today.

I took the keys out of the ignition, dropped them into the cupholder – I'm pretty sure around here that counted as an anti-theft system – and swung out of the truck cab.

OK. Here I went. Getting myself into I'm-not-sure-what. Already rehearsing my explanation to Hope and Lewis. "*I tried …*"

The side of the barn was not a well-frequented area. The mowed area, such as it was – I noted that it was in need of a good chop – ended level with the front wall. I stepped into waist deep grass, still wet with a combination of dew and last night's rain.

As the seedheads tickled my outstretched palms all I could think was "*tick-check, tick-check, tick-check*" over and over again. You could take the boy out of Scouting, but you couldn't take Scouting out of the boy.

Lynsey was more than halfway along, squinting at the barn, frowning, then taking a couple of steps and squinting and frowning again.

"What are you doing?" I used her own words minus the "here." I thought my greeting was friendlier.

She turned to me with flushed cheeks and hair full of twigs and leaves.

"Looking!" She tightened her hands into fists and stamped her foot. "Looking for something, anything, to block a great big hole in the fence which I only spotted *after* I turned the horses out."

She stepped forward and pulled at the grasses and, sure enough, there were rails, poles, posts, whatever you wanted to call them – lengths of wood – lying along the base of the barn, but the main thing you could definitely call all of them was rotten.

"Nothing's right!" She yelled. "Nothing! And I can't move any of it, anyway. And I don't know how you attach fence rails. And, Matilda won't let me catch her, so she's probably already long gone, and for all I know there's a bull in the neighbour's field, so that will be a huge problem when he comes charging through the hole in Albert's useless fence …"

"Lynsey." I said it in my calmest, quietest voice. I dated a girl once who was an Early Childhood Educator. When the kids screamed, she whispered. It always worked.

It worked now. Lynsey stopped, stared at me, and took a deep, shaking breath.

"Have you tried bringing Matilda in with oats?"

She exhaled noisily, blowing loose hairs off her face. Slowly shook her head. "I was too flustered …"

I held up my hand. "Go in the barn. Get some oats. Try to catch Matilda that way. I'll take care of the fence."

"But … but … how …?"

"Go," I said. "I'll sort it."

I pointed to the path we'd broken through the long grass and she went ahead of me, glancing back every couple of steps. I just kept pointing. She, fortunately, kept moving.

When she turned into the barn, I did the most obvious thing I could think of to block the hole in the fence. I drove Hope's truck to the gate, got out, opened the gate, drove through, closed it behind me again, and started driving, very slowly, along the fenceline until I came to the spot in question which, yes, would pose no problem at all to either a sneaky Matilda, or a muscular bull.

Then I used my best parallel parking skills to manoeuvre the truck so that it completely covered the gap and got out to inspect the length of broken fencing.

It did occur to me, on my walk back, that from what I knew of Matilda she very well could already be gone. A classic case of shutting the barn door – or blocking off the gaping hole – after the horse was already gone.

But there was a shake-shake and a "c'mo-o-o-on!" from the direction of the barn, and hoofbeats drummed behind me and, for the third time in less than 24 hours I was nearly killed; this being the second time by Matilda.

So she was still in the field.

I cupped my hands around my mouth and yelled to Lynsey. "It's fine! You don't have to catch her. I blocked the hole!"

By the time I reached Lynsey, she'd done the sensible thing and scattered oats over a wide area, while side-stepping well out of Matilda's way.

"Really?" she asked as soon as I was in earshot.

"Yup. For now. I'll get some tools and fix it properly later, but for now it's a no entry / no exit zone."

She shaded her eyes. "How did you do that so quickly?"

I turned sideways, swung my arm wide and waved to the truck which was an olivey-green colour that kind of blended in with the overgrown nature around it. "I like to call it the half-ton solution."

I waited for her to tell me what a stupid idea that was. To say "Any idiot can drive a truck through a field – I wanted the fence fixed." To shake her head and ask, "Seriously?"

Instead, her chin puckered up, and her eyebrows pulled down, and she gave one very loud sniff, and then another, and before I knew it she was bawling and oh-my-god-give-me-a-hole-in-a-fence-to-fix-any-day-because-I-had-no-idea-how-to-handle-this.

"Um?" I said. "Cup of tea?" Because somebody, somewhere in our ancestry was British.

Maybe someone in Lynsey's was, too, because she wiped her hand across her nose and nodded, and when I put my hand under her elbow she followed me to the porch steps and on the way over there, I used my other hand to text Lewis: Come to farm, STAT. Bring Hope, and tea, and a hammer. Or two. And some of those cinnamon rolls.

—

By the time the tea arrived Lynsey's cheeks were dry, but there was a splotch of pinkness at the tip of her nose, and her eyes were just a little too shiny.

Hope whisked out a Thermos, and mugs, and a small carton of milk, and cinnamon rolls and there was a moment when I took my first sip of hot tea and looked at the other three sitting on the weather-greyed rustic steps, with wildflowers nodding around the porch on either side, and the sun beaming out of a searing blue almost-autumn sky, glossing across Horace and Matilda's coats as they grazed in their temporarily secure field, when I thought, *This is it*, and *What else could you ask for?* And *Where else would I want to be than this?*

Then Lewis shifted and the end of the rotten step he was sitting on gave way, spilling him into the wildflowers which were technically just pretty weeds, and Matilda reached over for no apparent reason and sunk her teeth into Horace, and the sun shifted just enough to hit the windshield of Hope's truck, reminding me of the fallen-down fence it was hiding, and I think Lynsey must have had the same rude awakening because I swear she winced.

Lewis stood up and brushed at his backside and said, "Well, now, thinking of things that need repairing, I have something to ask you, Cam." He looked at Hope, who blushed and nodded, before continuing. "After talking to Hope this morning I've decided the tree was just a small setback. The cabin's my home, I'm going to keep rebuilding it, and I could really use your help. If you'll stick around a while, and work with me on the cabin, I'll pay you as fairly as I can."

"Oh no you don't!" Lynsey jumped to her feet so quickly I had grave concerns for the not-so-solid step supporting her. "I was going to ask Cam to work for me! I need more help than you. I have this huge farm." She spun around and I thought maybe it wasn't going to take the stairs collapsing under her for her to end up on the ground. "Look what an absolute shithole it is … everything's falling apart. How am I supposed to handle this alone? Cam needs to work for *me*."

Her chest was heaving and I was worried the tears were on their way back. She took a deep breath and wrinkled her nose, and said, "And what tree are you talking about, anyway?"

With everyone staring at me, I did the only thing possible under the circumstances. I snagged the last cinnamon roll from the tray and shoved it in my mouth.

LYNSEY

I WATCHED CAM CHEW on his cinnamon roll with narrowed eyes.

He swallowed carefully and wiped his hands together. I glanced down at them, noticing how large they were. Long, tapered fingers. Roughened from outdoor work. Clearly my request wasn't exactly out of left field for him, especially if I was competing with Lewis over his handyman skills.

"You must be a heavy sleeper," he said, squinting up at me. I could feel the frown of confusion building on my lips, and studiously refused to let it bloom across my face.

"What are you talking about?"

"Lewis's cabin got demolished by a downed tree in the storm last night," Hope explained to me, reporter to the core.

I swung a look between Lewis and Cam, who looked no worse

for wear except for the string of stitches knitted along Cam's eyebrow. I'd noticed them earlier, but I'd learned a long time ago not to ask questions if you didn't want to know the real answers. I had a sneaking suspicion I didn't really want to know what Cam got up to in his spare time.

"So that's where the stitches are from?" I asked, feeling more secure in the answer I was going to get. "A tree?"

"A tree that *fell on me*," Cam emphasized. "Where did you think I got them?"

"I don't know," I said, throwing up my hands as threads of my earlier exasperation wove back into my blood. Cam had that effect. I didn't like it. "Maybe you get into bar fights for fun."

"Do I look like a person who gets into bar fights?" Cam asked, face screwed up in confusion as he looked from me to Lewis, who shrugged. "Who does that?"

"Plenty of people," I said. "And since you get all pissy over pie I figured it wasn't too much of a leap, don't you think?"

Cam sighed, rubbing at the bridge of his nose.

"As I was saying," Hope broke in, "Cam has nowhere to sleep. And, I think it should be said, neither does Lewis."

Lewis's mouth twisted into dismay.

"Well, now, I can set up a tent," he insisted.

"And cook where?" Hope challenged him. "You have to eat. You have to shower. Brush your teeth. Where did you do all of that this morning?"

"Your place and the river, mostly," Cam admitted.

I stared at him, trying not to imagine Cam standing naked as the day he was born in the river, but my brain wasn't allowing me to *stop* seeing it. The image was there, and it stuck, parading around in my head in all its tantalizing glory. I wrinkled my nose, irritated. Cam was the last person I needed to imagine with his shirt off, glistening and sleek with river water.

Damn it. I squeezed my eyes shut, banishing the images. *It's just been a while,* I told myself. *You're hormonal. And frustrated. And maybe freaking out a little bit.*

And maybe I couldn't get Hope's commentary out of my head about Cam watching me. About reacting to me, even in his weird, surly way. It wasn't something I was interested in, because obviously his personality was never going to match up with his forearms, but that didn't mean I couldn't appreciate the scenery.

Right?

"So you're just going to continue eating out and bathing in the river?" I asked, opening my eyes. "Indefinitely?"

He opened his mouth and then shut it again, which I took as conceding my point. Then it dawned on me. "Weren't you supposed to be halfway to Montreal by now?"

Cam shot a look up at me. "Weren't you supposed to be in Florida or Saratoga or wherever your family has a sixth vacation home?"

"Hey," I pointed at him. "We only have four vacation homes, OK? And one is more like an apartment."

Cam rolled his eyes, and I huffed, sitting back down on my

rotten step and looking down at my phone. I stroked my thumb over the black screen, wondering if I should call Wes and leave a message. The sooner I got that done, the more real this would seem, even if it was temporary.

"For the time being, Lewis can stay with me," Hope said, getting back to solving the boy problems floating around us. Lewis's eyes rounded, his body stiffening.

"You don't even know me," he protested. "I could be a serial killer or a peeping Tom."

Hope looked up at him patiently. "Even if I weren't an excellent judge of character who has access to public records databases, I have Cam to vouch for you."

Cam raised his right hand. "I vouch for him."

Lewis sighed. "I've camped for longer than it will take to fix the cabin's roof."

"And then you have the matter of the exterior wall having a hole in it," Cam reminded him.

"We'll board it up," Lewis insisted.

"And then winter will be here in three months," Cam added. "You've got a day job, meaning the work will be mostly on me. So take however long you think it will take to make repairs and double it. Triple it to be on the safe side."

"So you're looking at camping into winter?" Hope asked, perky as ever.

Lewis groaned.

"I'm glad you see things my way," Hope announced, taking

Lewis's noise as surrender. "You can stay on my sofa, and Lynsey and Cam can stay here."

"I can do what now?" Cam asked, just as my stomach bottomed out.

"I need someone who can make repairs, not a roommate," I insisted.

"And who better to make repairs than someone who lives here?" Hope pointed out, smiling beatifically as she began to pack the cinnamon roll tray and pick up the empty tea cups.

"If Cam's doing repairs in two places, that's longer I'm staying on your sofa," Lewis argued. "And why is he even doing repairs on a place Lynsey doesn't own?"

"I don't want Lynsey falling through these rotted steps," Hope argued right back. "Or getting hurt on the farm without anyone around to *know* she's hurt. And when Albert comes back – *if* he comes back …" she paused, and shook her head, pushing the tray and cups into her tote bag. "I think this is better for everyone, Lewis. Besides, I don't care how long you stay on the sofa, and it's not like Cam looks like he's eager to leave."

I tilted my head at Cam, who studied his fingernails. Clipped short, clean, drawing my eyes up to those strong hands again. I imagined what they'd look like holding a hammer. Then my brain did a swift veering turn up the forearms I had found so promising, ending in more images of Cam half naked, sweaty from working on the farm during Lake Placid's humid late summer, still holding that hammer.

"There's room for two in the house," I found myself saying, the words out of my mouth like some Pavlovian response. Cam looked at me out of the corner of his eye.

Damn it, damn it, damn it.

I cleared my throat. "What I mean to say is there are two rooms in the house. Two beds."

"Yeah, I think I got that part," Cam said, a hint of a chuckle on his words. The urge to melt into the rotted wood dripped off me, the awkwardness palpable. Cam didn't look concerned. I had the sense that sleeping in beds he wasn't well acquainted with was his normal. Women's beds. And apparently Lewis's floor.

Cam looked out at the paddock, where Matilda was busy gnawing on Horace's withers. Horace whipped his head around, using it like a sledgehammer to send Matilda scrambling. Cam pulled a face, and then wiped his hands over his mouth and down his throat, shaking his head like he couldn't believe the situation he was in.

Yeah, you and me both, Buddy.

"I'll do it," Cam said, startling me. He stood up and stepped to the ground, turning to look up at my perch on the steps. "Now, to the issue of payment."

"Um." It had not occurred to me that he would want to be paid. I went back over my original statement. I had said "work for," hadn't I? Why had I said that? "I would offer you room and board, but honestly I think I can only afford the room part."

He stared at me blankly and then took a deep breath. "You

mean to tell me Lynsey Armstrong of four vacation houses and a horse farm is strapped for cash? How is that possible?"

"One of them is an apartment," I corrected. "And I'm not the one who owns those things, Cam. I can offer you a room, which is actually a lot if you think about it."

"A room *here*," he said, waving a hand at the decrepit house at my back. I felt offended for it, ramshackle goldenrod travesty that it was. "A tree fell on me this morning, Lynsey. A *tree*. I feel like staying here would be pushing my luck, don't you?"

"No," I said, also standing. "No, I don't. This place is solid." I stamped on the step to prove my point, the board creaking ominously. "You'll be fine. Better than fine." I stomped on it again. The board shifted. I ignored it. "And the whole point of you staying here is to make it liveable for the foreseeable ..."

And then the board snapped, sending me teetering. I heard Hope's squeak, her hands clutching at my knees, but it was too late. I was falling, my heart flipping up my throat along with the quick rush of dread that comes with sharp falls to the ground.

But then Cam appeared underneath me, his lean body blocking my fall and his arms wrapping around me, plucking me out of the air. I sucked in a breath, fingers scrabbling at something to grab and coming away with fistfuls of his shirt, my fingers brushing accidentally over warm skin. I got a whiff of soap and something earthy. Like river water.

Damn it.

Cam looked down at me like I was certifiable.

"If that was a demonstration of exactly what we're going to be doing for the next six months, I'm not sure it was particularly selling," he said wryly.

I extricated myself, pushing to arm's length and then remembering to let go of his shirt. I hastily crossed my arms and found my voice again.

"I'm only offering the bed," I reiterated, frazzled, and then found the need to add, "Your own bed."

"Yup," he nodded. "Got it. Again."

"So we're clear."

"Transparent."

A moment of silence passed, both of us staring each other down like we were in a Western waiting for the clock to strike noon. Then Lewis cleared his throat.

"You know, Albert had a solid little business," he said, pointing at the weather-beaten farm stand. "Between the produce and the festivals, he got by. If you kept those things going, you'd probably make a little money."

I tore my gaze from Cam.

"A little money?" I asked, just as Cam said, "Festivals?"

"Sure," Hope added. "This is a working farm. I don't know much about it, but I'd call Wes soon as you can. Get the details. If you're taking care of the place, you might as well make it profitable, you know?"

Oh, I knew. The prospect of staying here just looked a little greener. I shot a look at Cam.

"What do you think? Partners?"

Cam eyed me, looking me up and down like he was tallying up exactly what I was capable of. I wanted to squirm underneath the appraisal, because I knew what he was thinking. I was biting off more than I could chew. Rushing in, panicking later. All those were true. After all, I needed him to be the one to fix the fence. I needed him to remind me how to catch a horse, because I'd panicked. I'd caught horses since I was old enough to walk, and there I was panicked into not remembering. I was the last person who should be running a farm by myself, and I knew Cam saw it clear as day.

But then Cam shrugged. "Partners," he said, and then grinned. "But if there's a tractor on this property, you're the one who's going to drive it."

—

THAT AFTERNOON, I STOOD next to Hope's truck and watched Cam hammer the fenceline back into proper working order. Lewis held each plank while Cam rammed the nails home, giving my traitorous brain enough fodder to expand its folder of fantasy images as I watched Cam's t-shirt stretch across his back, sweat gathering on his forehead, forearms at peak manliness.

I shook myself out of it and looked over at Hope, whose eyes had glazed over. I nudged her and she jumped, shooting me a guilty smile.

"I think that's it," Lewis announced, giving the last plank a good yank as Cam straightened, rubbing one of those damned forearms against his forehead and tossing the hammer in the direction of the satchel of ancient tools they found in the barn. "Shouldn't have to worry about escapee ponies now."

Cam snorted. "You haven't seen her in action. This is nothing."

"Then you might want to invest in better tools," Lewis said. "Kell Hardware in town is my go-to. We'll need to make a stop there on the way back to the cabin, speaking of. Need plywood to board up that wall before a family of racoons moves in."

"And I'll be taking my truck back to the bakery," Hope said, swinging a look at me. "You'll probably want to come get your things?"

"I can get them," Cam said before I could open my mouth. "Since I'm going into town anyway."

I thought about Cam packing up my suitcases, which I had left splayed open on the floor. Cam touching my toiletries, my clothes. Seeing things he was not ever going to be allowed to see and then having to live with that knowledge for who knows how long as we cohabited under the same roof.

I turned a bright shade of scarlet, if the warmth rushing to my face was any indication.

"Nope," I shook my head. "I'll pack myself up and meet you at the hardware store. I managed to compile a list of things this place needs this morning, so I need to go anyway."

"Or you could just give me the list?" Cam asked, furrowing his eyebrows at me.

"I'm going," I insisted. More like snapped. Cam raised his

hands in surrender and then bent to pick up the satchel, the tools clanking.

"Have it your way," he said, putting the tools in the bed of Hope's truck and peering across the sweeping pasture to the barn, where my car was parked next to Lewis's. "Need a lift to your car?"

"There really isn't enough room for four…" I started to say, trailing off as Cam patted the truck's bed. I raised an eyebrow, and Cam pointed across the pasture to the cars. If I stood on my toes, I would just be able to see the hoods.

"It would take you a solid fifteen minutes to walk back," he said. "This place is bigger than it lets on."

"But it would be a short drive," Hope said, opening the driver's door. "I'm OK with a little joyriding if we go slow."

Cam lowered the tailgate with a creaking thunk and leapt onto the bed, turning around and holding out a hand to me.

I eyed the situation from my vantage point on the ground, studying this infuriating man holding one of his equally infuriating forearms toward me, hand outstretched and waiting for mine. When did this become my life? When had I let this happen?

Or did I force it by accident?

No, I'm pretty sure I didn't make Cam say yes to helping out on the farm. He didn't strike me as someone who would care either way if I fell through the rotted farmhouse steps or took a dive from the hayloft. Being here with me wasn't being done out of the goodness of his heart, since I wasn't sure how much goodness he was stashing away in there.

Nope, he had his own reasons. And that was fine, because I had mine, too.

"You coming up or are you walking?" Cam asked, crooking his fingers at me in impatience.

"I'm coming," I grumbled, stepping up to the tailgate. "Keep your pants on."

I put my hand in his as he grinned at me.

"So you keep reminding me," he said, and with that he hauled me into the bed.

Of the truck. Where I immediately pushed away from him and sat down, resting my back against the opposite side of the truck. Cam, still smiling, pulled the tailgate back into place and settled himself across from me. Then he leaned forward, slapping the back window to indicate we were ready to go.

Hope flashed him a thumbs up and started the ignition, rolling away from the fence. The truck shifted underneath me, and I braced myself as Hope turned around, the wheels bumping over uneven ground.

I tried to look at anything other than Cam, who was doing an excellent job of staring behind us, eyes glued to the tire marks pressed through the tall grass.

Of course, I failed. My attention stuck to him like it was hard wired to only focus on one thing. And that thing was Cam. We were really going to do this. Stay here. Together. I couldn't even begin to imagine what that would look like in theory much less in practice. I didn't even know this man. If my mother was still alive, she'd be beet red, screaming at me to at least check his references if this was an actual job. And if it wasn't, what the hell was I doing?

"You don't need to do this," I found myself saying across the truck bed. Cam pulled his gaze from the grass, looking at me for a long moment before he finally nodded.

"You're right," he admitted. "I don't need to."

I frowned at him. "Then why?"

We trundled from grass to gravel, the truck rumbling and my butt vibrating over the metal grooves in the bed. I put my hands on either side of me, watching Cam, who shrugged.

"Maybe I want to," he said, because men are nothing if not cryptic and in need of intense lessons on opening up and actually talking about their feelings.

"Well," I said as the truck squeaked to a halt by our cars. "This is going to be *fun*."

"A riot," Cam agreed, and stood up. "I'll see you in town?"

"I imagine so, unless you intend to walk back here after."

He paused, as though just realizing he didn't have a car of his very own. Then he sighed. "One more thing to add to the list, then."

He jumped down and I climbed out of the bed on my own, brushing at my dirty leggings even as gravel dust billowed up around me from Lewis and Hope pulling out of the lot, leaving me to follow on my own.

Once I was safely sitting on one butter-soft leather seat, finger on the ignition, I looked through the windshield at the farm and paused. My phone sat in the cup holder, dark and waiting for me. Swiping it up, I woke up the screen and tapped at my messages. The link to Wes's number glowed up at me, and I wondered if they were still in the air.

Logically, I didn't matter if they were or weren't. I had to talk to them, especially now that I'd not only roped myself into taking care of this place, but also Cam. I needed assurances. Maybe a bank account. Yes, a bank account would be *amazing*.

I tapped the link and lifted the phone to my ear, listening to the grinding rings. One, two, three, four. It kept going and clicked to voicemail, a gruff-sounding man ordering me to leave a brief message at the beep.

Beep.

I paused, and cleared my throat.

"Hi, this is Lynsey Armstrong. I'm the person taking care of your father's farm while he's, um, away. I wanted to check in with you to discuss the running of the farm. If there's anything that needs any special attention. If there's, um, a fund or something – I realize you won't want me meddling in the financial affairs of the farm, but I know it's a working farm and since your father's asked me to take care of the …"

Beep.

"Damn it." I dropped my forehead to the steering wheel. Brief was not my forte, either.

Shaking my head, I hit the number again and when the call moved over to voicemail a second time I was ready.

"Wes," I said. "This is Lynsey again. Please call me back as soon as you land. I think we have a lot to discuss."

I put the phone back in the cup holder, feeling marginally more in control of my life until I looked back up at the farm. It sat in front of me, spreading so far beyond what I could see from my Audi's front seat that I felt the creeping sense that I was going to need a lot more help that I originally thought.

I thought of the list I made for the hardware store. Not to mention the list for the grocery store. The lists for everything else, like maintenance and animal feed and, hell, *clothes*. I didn't think I was going to get very far wearing what I'd brought to Lake Placid. Running shoes aren't exactly farm appropriate.

"Please call me back, Wes," I murmured, hitting the ignition button. "Please, please, please."

The Audi purred to life, ready to take me into town so I could spend a ton of money I didn't have on a farm that wasn't mine. I glanced down at the gauges on the dashboard and groaned, reaching over to my phone and pulling up the first list I'd made, titled NECESSITIES.

Underneath, I typed *gas*.

Chapter Six

CAM

AFTER NEARLY BEING KILLED, and rearranging my entire life in the span of a few short hours, my head would have been spinning if I'd let it, and I didn't feel like having a reeling head, so I focused on the drive along roads that were either gravel, or so crumbling they might as well have been gravel. I took note of the sky, and the fields filled with golden round hay bales, and I breathed a deep and true sigh of relief when Gord Downie's voice twanged out from Lewis's surprisingly decent radio.

Still being able to get The Tragically Hip on the radio was a small mitigating factor in the traitorous move of me relocating south of the border.

Relocating? Is that what I'd agreed to do?

Uh-oh, the brain spins were threatening. Quick, think of something else.

My phone rang, and decent radio notwithstanding, Lewis's car was not Bluetooth enabled, so I put my foot on the brake, pulled over to the shoulder and fished the phone out of the fold of the passenger seat. "Hello?"

"I'm ba-a-ack!"

Oh god. Talk about spinning heads …

I dropped the phone straight down the side of the seat and pulled back onto the road.

—

HANNAH WASN'T A STALKER, but she had been mistaken for one in the past.

When I first met her at the courthouse cafeteria where I'd been testifying on behalf of a friend in small claims court, and Hannah had been consenting to a peace bond application brought by her last boyfriend, she'd explained, "I wouldn't have hurt him – or the performance tires on his sports car, which is what he seemed most worried about – I just come on strong sometimes." She'd popped a fry into her mouth and said, "I can admit it – I like drama. If he'd waited, I would have lost interest and moved on, but I accept that I freaked him out, so the least I can do is agree to the peace bond."

True, she'd seemed intense, and wild, and over-the-top – and, yes, I could hear my mom's voice in my head saying *"You do* not *want to touch this one with a ten-foot pole,"* but a) I admired her honesty and b) I couldn't help but wonder how all that intensity, and wildness would play out in bed.

So I had touched her. No comment on the ten-foot pole.

Everything Hannah had told me was true. She came on *very* strong for a little while, then it could be months before I'd hear from her again. So far it had never been a problem.

In my current state, with my life flooded with people and responsibilities I hadn't even imagined less than forty-eight hours ago, I did not need Hannah showing up.

Which I well knew she could and would do.

Shit.

By the time I pulled up behind Hope's truck at the bakery and fished my phone, along with half a pack of gum, and a dollar bill, out from the crevasse beside Lewis's driver's seat, there were several texts from Hannah:

- What just happened? Did you drop your phone?

- Your neighbour says you went away for the weekend but you should be back by now. What gives?

- One of your windows is unlocked. I can climb through and wait for you if you're going to be back soon.

A newfound sympathy blossomed for Peace Bond Guy.

The phone rang again. While it was tempting to just turn it off, at the moment it was my only means of communication. I took a deep breath. Hannah was straightforward. She knew she was overpowering sometimes – I would just explain to her that this was one of those times. And right now, while Hope and Lewis were inside, and Lynsey hadn't arrived yet, I had a precious few moments of privacy to do that.

"Hi Hannah." Even as I answered I was mentally rehearsing

what I would say next. How calm and reasonable I'd be. How I'd dispense with this problem.

"Oh god!" she said. "I was starting to think you'd been in a car accident right in the middle of our call. It made me realize I've left it too long; we really need to see each other."

Hannah was going off-script, and Lynsey was rolling her car to a stop, and I started sweating.

"This isn't a good time." As soon as I said it I remembered a very level-headed and calm ex-girlfriend telling me every time I said that to her the red mist descended – her description – "It's the most condescending thing you could say, and it makes me want to punch you," she said.

It seems the less-stable Hannah agreed. "Oh no you don't!" she was yelling while I wondered if Lynsey, now facing me with both eyebrows raised, could hear her. "On second thought," Hannah continued. "You're right. This isn't the time, or the way, to discuss anything. You can tell me where you are and I'll come to you so we can talk in person."

"Shit!" *Double shit.* That wasn't supposed to actually come out of my mouth.

"What!?!"

"Sorry, no, I stubbed my toe …" Lynsey blinked under her sky-high brows, then looked down at my safely-shod, perfectly un-harmed feet.

"Cam, what the hell is going on?" Hannah asked.

Lynsey's facial expression, combined with Hannah's voice, had me flooded so full of adrenaline I had no idea whether to fight or flee.

I copped out. "Listen, we'll talk. Later. Right now I have to do something really important."

I ended the call and held my phone out to Lynsey. "Do you know how to turn off the GPS locator?"

She took the phone, then said, "Hey, wait …" and tried to hand it back, but I threw up my hands, turned on my heel, and began walking toward the bakery.

"What's the important thing you have to do?" she asked.

I pointed at her. "Number one is definitely turn off the GPS." Then I indicated the area below my belt. "Number two is find the bathroom." Then I grinned. "Except not for number two." I was jogging away from her by now. "I'll be back in two shakes of a … oh forget it … you'll have just enough time to fix that phone."

LYNSEY

"Hey, wait just a minute," I yelled after Cam, only for him to disappear from view, too preoccupied with running away to stand and listen to me berate him about how I was not his personal assistant. He could turn his own GPS off, thank you very much. I already had enough problems; it wasn't like I needed to add one of Cam's to my steadily growing list.

I sighed, looking down at Cam's beaten-up iPhone cupped

in my hand. Cracks in the screen spiderwebbed from one corner, promising a future of pulling glass splinters from my fingertips. I tapped the home button gingerly. The phone beamed to life, orderly lines of apps ready and willing to divulge all of Cam's secrets. I blinked at it. Who left an iPhone unprotected?

Canadians, I thought, and smiled to myself at the look of disgust I envisioned gracing Cam's face.

Shoving the phone into my back pocket, I made the trek up to the apartment above the bakery to collect my bag. Once I'd corralled every scrap of non-farm-appropriate clothing and zipped up the Louis Vuitton, I sat back on my heels to contemplate dragging it down the stairs and back out to the car when Cam's phone started buzzing against my butt.

"Oh, for …" I pulled the offending object out of my pocket.

On the phone's screen, the image of a girl winked up at me. The photo was close cropped, full of the girl's face – pursed lips, glimmering nose stud, playful tilt of her head, and messy bangs that brushed over that wink. I was suitably impressed with the girl's eye pencil technique. Her makeup game was on point.

HANNAH, the phone proclaimed in giant capital letters across her face, as if deliberately yelling. It made me pause just enough to wonder if answering it was a good idea. Deliberate yelling couldn't be good, but then deliberately sending someone to voicemail when they didn't need to suffer that horror for no reason wasn't good either.

I tapped the answer button, lifting the phone to my ear.

"Where are you, *exactly?*" The voice was perturbed, to put it mildly. I suddenly felt a deep kinship with Hannah, in an all caps sort of way.

"In an apartment over a bakery, holding a phone that isn't mine," I said to a gasp. "Although that's probably not the answer you're looking for."

"Who is this?" she demanded.

"I'm Lynsey," I replied. "Holder of Cam's phone for the next few minutes."

"That …" The venom in her voice seeped out of the phone and exploded into a guttural grunt of exasperation. "He's avoiding me!"

"Looks like it," I agreed. "He tasked me with turning off the GPS. Can you believe that?"

"*What?*" she asked, befuddled.

"I know," I rolled my eyes. "As if he couldn't do it himself."

"I can't believe the gall," she huffed. "Here I am, just trying to surprise him, and he's giving me the run around."

"Somehow I do not find that remotely surprising," I said, standing and dragging the suitcase toward the stairs.

"Can't you?" Hannah asked. My kinship with her dimmed a few degrees. Clearly, she was in love with Cam or in love with the idea of Cam or she didn't know him at all, because anyone who couldn't see he was a flight risk was being deliberately obtuse.

"No," I said. "I've known Cam for about a day and I can definitely say I am not surprised."

"You've known him for a day?" Hannah asked. "And you're answering his phone?"

"Mitigating circumstances," I grunted, pulling the suitcase down the steps and yanking it around the first landing, trying not to run over my own heels on the way down. "Listen, I can take a message for you or not? It's your call. I just figured someone should answer the phone."

"And you've known him for a day in what capacity?" Hannah asked, ignoring me. I rushed to cover a barking laugh – because laughing was my first impulse at what Hannah was suggesting – and stumbled, catching myself before I took a nosedive down the stairs. The suitcase wasn't so lucky. It lurched, skidded past me, tumbled once, and crashed onto the tile below.

"Damn it," I burst out.

"I cannot believe this," Hannah growled, and then seemed to catch herself. "I mean, I guess I can. It's not like we're, I don't know, *exclusive*. But this is really bad timing for me right now, you know?"

"I don't," I admitted. "Not really. And we aren't actually …"

"I mean, he knows the arrangement," Hannah insisted, cutting me off.

"Does he though?" I asked, retrieving my suitcase and hauling it out the backdoor, dragging it toward the Audi. "Because he seems like a free bird to me."

"Well, that's where he's wrong," Hannah declared. "He doesn't get to ignore me when it's convenient. I'm worth more than that."

"Definitely," I agreed, popping the trunk. "You really are."

"And I'm going to say it to his face," she declared.

"Right on," I said as I hauled the suitcase into the trunk and slammed it shut, feeling Hannah's girl power rubbing off on me.

"As soon as I can get down there," she continued. "He doesn't get to hide away when I …"

"Down there?" I blurted, Cam's harried request for me to turn off the GPS suddenly and painfully shouldering into the forefront of my thoughts. I pulled the phone away from my ear, scrolling through the apps until I found Find My Friends.

Shit.

"I'll have to take the train," Hannah's voice yammered as I put the phone back to my ear. "I lost my license because, well, he knows why. But I'm not going to be ignored anymore. Thank you … what was your name again?"

Oh, dear god. I squeezed my eyes shut, wishing I had never answered the phone.

"Lynsey," I said through a sigh, because I was already so screwed. There wasn't a point in trying to double back now.

"Lynsey," Hannah said. "That's a pretty name."

"Thanks."

"You've helped me out so much, Lynsey," Hannah said, sounding sunshiny and bright, full of happiness at the thought of telling Cam off. To his face. Because the man used GPS for booty calls with people like Hannah. If I cared enough, I would have an impassioned talk with him about privacy.

But I don't care, I reminded myself. This was Cam's problem, not mine, so I wasn't going to do that. Cam was on his own.

"Glad to help," I replied.

"Thanks!" she chirped, and ended the call, no doubt already looking at Find My Friends. I tapped the app's icon and found her dot glowing in the Montreal area. Then I found Cam's, pulsing right in Lake Placid.

Then I turned off the GPS.

Not that it was going to do Cam much good.

Chapter Seven

CAM

As I left the bathroom, I ran into Lewis. "Perfect," he said. "I want to go over the list with you before we head to the hardware store. It's in the truck."

It also seemed perfect to me to have Lewis to protect me when I headed back out to face Lynsey.

She looked at me through narrowed eyes while she held my phone out. I was familiar with the expression on her face. It meant she had questions I didn't want to answer.

"Who, exactly, did I just turn the locator off for?" Lynsey asked.

My inclination was to lie, but thinking of a good lie seemed like more effort than telling the truth. My personally edited version of the truth anyway. I shrugged (first step in injecting a "no big deal" tone into my answer), "Just this girl. She gets a bit fixated at times. On me. On *parts* of me …" As I continued – as I *remembered* – my nonchalance ebbed and the real truth slipped out. "She has this thing about my forearms."

Why did I tell her that? Talk about handing Lynsey the ammo she needed to mock me – and my poor, quite-unremarkable fore- arms – forevermore.

Lynsey's face froze, and she remained unexpectedly, mercifully silent on the topic of my lower arms, then she mumbled something and struck out for the bakery.

Even though I should have just been grateful to avoid being the butt of her jokes, I couldn't resist throwing one of my own after her rapidly retreating figure. "Number two?" I yelled, and got a fierce upward thrust of her middle finger in return. So, whatever sent her into poste-haste flight couldn't be that serious – maybe it truly was just a case of a sudden need for the bathroom facilities.

"You ready to look this over?" Lewis called from where he had a piece of paper spread on the hood of the truck.

"Yup. Of course." With all my women problems solved, I was completely free to focus on plywood, deck screws, and two-by- fours.

Lynsey

Kell Hardware looked like an earthquake hit it approximately two decades ago and no one had ever bothered to clean it up. The place was a motley assortment of dusty tools for rent cluttering the already cluttered aisles. Bins – some open, some not, some labeled, some not – towered over me, full of what I assumed were nuts and bolts. Somewhere in the back of the store, a paint mixer thudded. Overhead, the fluorescents flickered with abandon, making it hard to read my list as I peered between it and a wall of display hardware, all of it labeled with numbers that didn't seem to coordinate with any of the sometimes-labeled, sometimes-not bins.

It was chaos.

Why? Why was it always chaos?

"Can I help you, miss?"

I turned to a man who looked like Santa in paint-dotted overalls. He smiled at me and rocked onto his toes, which were strapped into red Birkenstocks.

"I…" I didn't even know where to start. "Do you work here?"

"Yup!" His smile widened as he showed me his nametag, which proudly proclaimed him to be *ROY, Owner*. Then he tilted his head at me, assessing me from my running shoes and leggings to the oversized sleep shirt I was still wearing. "Now, you must be the girl taking care of Albert's place."

"News travels fast," I said, because I was absolutely sure I did not look like I would be taking care of a farm at first glance. Unless I had hay sticking out of my hair, which was admittedly likely.

The bell tinkled, announcing new customers.

"Roy?" Lewis called out.

"Be with you in a minute!" Roy hollered, turning his attention back to me. "As you can see it's a small town. Everyone knows each other. Sometimes a little too well if you get my meaning."

I stared at him. "Not really."

He pushed his hands into the pockets of his overalls and bellowed a laugh up at the flickering lights. "Oh, boy," he sighed, his laughter ebbing as he wiped at his eyes. "It's mighty nice to have a fresh face in here. Not that I don't miss Albert at all, mind. The two of us go all the way back in the old curling league. Our kids were friends, wives were friends. That's how it is around here. It's a tight-knit community."

I nod, catching his meaning. "I guess I made the phone tree, huh?"

Roy laughed again. "You betcha. Something about a white Lexus parked at the old farm."

"An Audi," I corrected, and he beamed cheerfully at me.

"My mistake," he said, and then peered at my list. "What is it you're looking for?"

Chapter Eight

CAM

AT THE HARDWARE STORE, Lewis made his purchase first and while I left Lynsey to fill her list for the farm I helped him load up Hope's pick-up truck.

Truck loaded, I came back into the store to find both Lynsey and Roy bent over the list with furrowed brows.

When I asked, "What's up?" Roy looked at me with relief while Lynsey did that squint-frown thing from earlier at the farm. *Why did I ask?*

Lynsey pointed at the list. "They don't seem to have anything we need. Like here – that doohickey thingy for Matilda's door. And another one for the gate. Do they not sell those here? Do we have to go to a tack shop? But I've never seen those things at a tack shop …"

"A latch?" I asked.

Roy straightened. "Oh, now, a *latch* we can do."

Lynsey gave me a dirty look. "Thanks for making me look stupid. I could have said a 'latch' …" she paused to put air quotes around the offending word. "… but I figured it had a special name since it was for a horse."

What I said was, "Sure. Let's call it a horse latch. Or a Matilda latch." What I thought was, *I'll call it anything in the world as long as we can buy it and get out of here.*

The order moved forward after that until it was time to pay. The way Lynsey shuffled through credit cards reminded me of a blackjack dealer. When it finally dawned on me that she wasn't purposely trying to annoy me, I shook my head. "Seriously? Four vacation homes …"

She shot me a sideways glance. "And, like I said, none of them are mine."

She took a deep breath, plunked a card on the counter, and said, "This one." Her hand was shaking. I had to restrain myself from reaching out to steady it by mentally reciting *Her problems are not my problems*, and I then had to restrain myself from realizing how untrue that was by making fun of her when the transaction went through.

"First try. Very good."

She stuck her tongue out. "It's just a temporary cash flow uncertainty situation. As soon as we start earning some money everything will be fine."

"About that," Roy said and we both whirled to face him with I, for one, being certain he was going to say the credit card had been declined after all. "Do you want me to put the sign up again? It's about that time of year."

The sign he placed on the counter was sun-yellowed, curled at the edges, and sported multiple smears which might have been squished insects.

Still, the fact that it had only taken him thirty seconds to find, showed he considered it important enough to be filed in some fashion, and the information on it was definitely clear and easy to read.

In bold, black Sharpied hand-lettering, the sign declared:

LP Farms

The pumpkin patch is open again.

Come get your pumpkins.

Same price as last year.

Discount for picking your own (wear rubber boots).

Cash only.

"Really?" Lynsey said. "*This* worked?"

Roy leaned back, crossed his arms and said, "Well, Albert never had trouble paying his hardware bill."

I tried to turn my sharp burst of laughter into anything else – a sputter, a choke – finally I shook my head. "Sorry, swallowed my gum."

Lynsey glared at me. "You're having all kinds of trouble today aren't you? Stubbed toes, swallowed gum …"

I ignored her and tapped the paper. "About the sign – this is probably a stupid question – but can you tell us what 'LP' stands for?"

Roy scratched his head. "Now that you mention it, this is probably a stupid answer, but I have no idea. It's just always been called that."

I shrugged. "Alright, I tried. Please go ahead and put it up."

Lynsey shook her head. "No, no, no. We cannot put that up."

"Why not?" I asked.

"OK, besides the obvious fact that we need a new sign, we need to know if there are even pumpkins first."

"Oh, there are pumpkins," Roy said. "Albert dried the seeds in my garage last year. Couldn't park the car in there for three weeks. Wife nearly killed us both."

I looked at the hardware man. "Put up the sign for now, please, and we might come back and update it." Then I turned to Lynsey. "And you and I are going to go to the farm right now to track down these pumpkins."

I waited for her to snap at me. I waited for a great explanation of why it was a stupid idea. Instead she giggled. "Are we going to sit out and wait for The Great Pumpkin?"

It was so unexpected it made me laugh out loud. "There Will be Pumpkins!" I declared.

"Oh, so is Daniel Day-Lewis joining us in our hunt for pumpkins?" Something about Lynsey actually getting my way-too-obscure movie reference made the whole conversation much funnier.

"No," I said. "I think I'll call Sean Connery to help in The Hunt for Pumpkins for October."

Lynsey and I might have thought we were the two funniest

people in Lake Placid, but Roy clearly had another opinion. He cleared his throat. "Um, yeah, so if that's everything, my delivery guy will swing by with your stuff tomorrow morning."

"Except the horse latch," I said, grabbing it up from the counter. "We can fit that in the car."

LIKE EVERY GOOD CANADIAN, I was equal parts amazed, overwhelmed, and delighted by the Price Chopper.

"Have you seen the price of this cheese?" I asked Lynsey, as I held up a package of Pepper Jack. "And what even is Pepper Jack?"

Lynsey was gone, though, browsing the magazine section. On second thought, the price of cheese – or of any grocery item at all – probably meant nothing to her.

By the time we met up again at the check-out, I had the items we needed for tonight's dinner, as well as five different flavours of cheese which, combined, still cost less than a single package in Canada.

"Are you sure about this?" Lynsey asked. Earlier, as we drove away from the hardware store, she'd lobbied hard for dinner at the diner, at the bakery, anywhere in town. I'd said, no, I was on a mission to find those pumpkins before nightfall.

"But how will we eat?"

"I can cook."

"You haven't seen the kitchen in the house."

"I'll make a fire. I'll cook outside. It will be great. Trust me."

She made a strangled noise, and I thought back to her credit card roulette.

"If we do it my way, I pay," I said.

She mimed putting a gun to her head, while smiling sweetly. "Well, then I can think of nothing nicer."

Now, as we slowly walked forward, following our meal-to-be along the conveyor, Lynsey elbowed me. "You know what?" Once again, I waited for a critique – this time on my choice of ingredients.

Once again she surprised me. "I think we actually got kicked out of the hardware store."

I grinned. "I think you're right. But you started it. 'The Great Pumpkin,' – come on."

"I *did* start it. I started strong. You were really grasping by the end."

I opened my mouth to defend The Hunt for Pumpkins for October, noted the cashier looking at me, and shut my mouth again. We were new in town. Maybe we should only get kicked out of one establishment per evening.

LYNSEY

WITH THE GROCERIES PILED high in the Audi's trunk, I drove us out of town and back into the Adirondack wilds. At least, that's how it felt when I bumped off the maintained-well-enough city road and onto the cracked blacktop headed to the farm. The sunset painted the forest on either side of the road a reddish-gold over the steady, unrelenting dark green. It should have been soothing, and with the insanity of the day receding into the background I should have been letting myself sink into it.

Only I wasn't. Not at all.

Cam jiggled his knee next to me, tapping his phone against the other. He was fidgeting, most likely because who knew what the dynamic would be when we got to the farm. We were going to … what? Settle in and make dinner? Like roommates? And then quietly take over Albert's house, slide into the two beds (I shuddered at the thought of the sheets), and … fall asleep?

What. Were. We. Doing.

I kept glancing at the phone Cam tapped against his knee, Hannah's conversation fresh in my mind. It wasn't like she could follow us out to the farm, could she? If the app pinpointed Cam in Lake Placid, it didn't let her see exactly where he was – especially since I'd turned off the GPS. And it wasn't like the farm was directly adjacent to Irene's – even if she'd had time to trace him all the way to the parking lot I'd been standing in.

But Hannah seemed like the kind of girl who wouldn't let a little blip like GPS stand in her way. She could always ask around, and if the Lake Placid phone tree taught me anything today it's that everyone knew everything already. She'd be standing on Albert's crumbling steps before I knew it.

I was starting to sweat.

Damn it. Damn it all.

We passed the scrapheap farm I'd noticed earlier in the day, when my life had been radically different. I glanced at the sagging barn half hidden in the trees, the mobile home that sat across from it. A patchy dirt lot separated them, marked with scratching chickens and one loose dog that turned to bark at the car as we passed.

Then, along the fenceline, stood the horse I'd seen trailered onto the property on my first drive to the farm. It had to be – it was the only one in the field. It had its head plunged into the grass, ripping at it greedily. Its ruddy bay coat shined in the sunset, light splashing across the horse like a lick of fire. A splatter of clean white birdcatcher spots, like constellation points, trailed up its hindquarters and over its tucked flank and deep ribcage.

I did a double take. Those were the lean lines of a racing Thoroughbred.

Odd.

No one I knew would throw a horse in training into a yard full of scrap, even if they were taking a break from the track for a few months. Besides, it was too early to send horses off to farms for the winter unless this one was injured.

Maybe it was.

I took a deep breath, reminding myself I couldn't control everything. Not Albert going to Florida, not the horse living across the street, and definitely not whether or not Hannah was going to show up as soon as the train could get her here.

It wasn't going to be a problem. Worst came to worst, Hannah would break up with Cam or end whatever they were doing in person and that would be that. I'd probably saved them from dragging on a clearly unhealthy relationship. They'd get some closure.

Yes, things would be fine. I was sure of it.

I glanced over at Cam, watching him stare at the trees as we sped closer and closer to the farm. His fidgeting slowed, and soon he was simply resting his phone against his knee, relaxed in an all-male sprawl across my passenger seat. I envied the sprawl, but the all-maleness of it was going to be a problem.

For him, for me, and probably for poor Hannah. Eventually.

I supposed it was time for me to nip this problem in the bud.

Chapter Nine

CAM

FROM WHAT I KNEW of Lynsey so far, I wouldn't have pegged her as a throat-clearer, but she'd cleared her throat at least three times and we weren't even halfway to the farm.

"What is it?" I asked.

"Huh? It's …"

"Don't say nothing."

She sighed. "OK. Fine. It's just that I was wondering if we need some house rules."

"House rules? Like what? Like leave the toilet seat down, and the toilet paper should roll over, not under?"

"More like …" She cleared her throat again. "In light of me having to turn the GPS off on your phone, is some random stranger going to show up at the farm?"

"Not unless you messed up turning off the GPS."

"Seriously, Cam. I mean, should we have a policy on guests? By which I mean, sleepover guests."

"Why? Are you liable to bring home a parade of men? Because my only ground rule for that would be don't wake me up and I'm fine with it."

"Cam … I mean it."

I sighed. "Fine. *Mom.*" Her eyebrows flew up. "OK, OK, sorry. You're nobody's mom. By all means, let's have house rules. From my perspective, it's pretty simple. Obviously we're not going to sleep together …"

"What!?!" The car swerved slightly and she righted it before continuing, "I mean, why would you even say that, and why would we *obviously* not sleep together?"

I waited until the car had been traveling in a straight line for a couple of seconds before answering. "Well a) I think we're both heterosexual, and you are what some would classify as pretty hot, and I consider sex to be an excellent form of physical exercise, and I was here doing a triathlon, indicating I have a try-anything attitude toward physical exercise so, in a small house … let's just say it's not unreasonable to think we might jump each other at some point."

If I was worried about her interrupting, I shouldn't have been. Her mouth opened and closed a couple of times and it was easy for me to continue. "And b) if we slept together, I'd still want to sleep with other women, and I've been down that road enough times to know it's a bad idea."

At this point Lynsey's hands tightened on the steering wheel

– I could tell by the white knuckles – and her words came quick and sharp. "You know what? You're right. Sleeping with you would make me want to sleep with other women too."

OK, I wasn't stupid. I knew all about sarcasm. But I also firmly believed in seizing the moment, which is why I said, "Really? Because if you mean it, we can have a radical re-think of the house rules. In fact, come to think of it, I could just turn that GPS right back on and we could have a willing participant down here in no time."

"Cam?"

"Yes?" I waited for her to say, 'You wish,' or 'In your dreams,' or 'Don't be stupid.'

Instead what she said is, "I promise you that should the time come that I want to sleep with another woman, I will find her myself."

Zing.

"Also, you should not, in any way, assume you'd be invited to participate."

Zap.

Lots of girls had slept with me, and a decent percentage had slept with me with other girls, but almost none had put me in my place like that.

It was a bigger turn-on than the thought of a threesome.

Although, long-term an actual threesome would probably be more fun than being told off.

Still … *respect.*

I performed the best bow I could in the confines of the passenger's seat, and said, "Young Padawan, you have earned my admiration, and with it the right to make one house rule of your choice." I straightened and looked at her. "So, go for it."

She slowed, flicked on her indicator to turn into the driveway, and said, "You know what? I'm done with house rules for now. Let's find some pumpkins."

—

WE FOUND THE PUMPKINS as the sun set.

If Lynsey had kept walking during her earlier quest for fence rails, she would have stumbled right onto them.

But if she'd done that we wouldn't have first laid eyes on them bathed in the golden glow of a last-days-of-summer sunset, looking like rows and rows of orange suns. Looking like, if you picked one up, you'd own your own celestial body.

And that would have been a pity.

"Oh my …" Lynsey breathed beside me.

"What?" I asked. "You never knew where your pumpkins came from before you carved them?"

She looked at me. "I never carved my own pumpkin. I think the maid got paid to do it."

Of course there's starvation, and war, and all kinds of inequity and unkindness in the world, but in that moment it was the saddest thing I'd ever heard and I wanted to hug her.

I wasn't sure how she'd react though, so I did something else. I made her a promise. "This year, you are carving a pumpkin."

Lynsey

"I'll tell you what," Cam said, reaching into his pocket and pulling out a Swiss Army Knife, unfolding the blade. "Pick one. We'll take it back to the house."

My heart did a little leap at the thought, which was ridiculous because they were pumpkins. It wasn't like I was staring at a field of horses and had a free coupon to pick whichever one I wanted. And wouldn't that be the best fantasy in the world? A coupon for one free horse?

I glanced over at the paddocks, where Matilda and Horace were waiting by the fence to be brought back in for dinner. The goats had their necks pushed between the fence boards, stretching for the blades of grass that were just out of reach. There was work to do, but I looked back at the pumpkins with a lump forming in my throat.

"We need to save them for customers," I said, shaking my head.

"One isn't going to break the bank, Lyn," he said, shortening my name like everyone else in my life. The familiarity reminded me that I had a lot of phone calls to make on top of getting Wes on the line. There was the call to Georgie, and Harris, and – I gulped down the rising panic – Dad, who I knew would find a way to cancel every single last one of my lines of credit if I told him what I was doing. If I was skittish about my finances now, I wouldn't have to be once Dad found out where I was because I wouldn't have finances to worry about.

Which made the pumpkins all the more important, and here I was, already pointing at one large, perfectly round one.

"Good choice," Cam said, bending over the pumpkin in question and sawing it off the vine. He slid the knife back in his pocket and hefted the pumpkin into his arms, cradling it against his chest with the sun diving behind the forested mountains at his back. He looked like he'd stepped right into a photoshoot for a sexy millennial farmers calendar – if such a thing actually existed.

"You know, my kid sister and I have a kind of a tradition every Halloween," he said, stepping over the unchosen pumpkins on his way back to me. "Carve pumpkins to scary movies and get sick on chocolate."

"Sounds like you're a bad influence," I said, watching him grin at me.

"Me?" He shook his head. "Meg is the ring leader. I'm often the innocent bystander."

"Sure," I laughed, feeling a pang of homesickness. Not for home or family, really, but for what I hadn't ever had. Carving pumpkins with Harris, having traditions that weren't easily wiped away. I'd missed that. I'd always missed it. "I'm sure, Cam."

He nodded toward the barn and I fell into step with him on the way. It felt almost companionable.

Almost.

Cam's speech – if one could call it a speech – about our inevitable not-screwing, despite the inevitability of it, hung over us like a looming thought bubble. I imagined an ellipsis in the middle of that bubble, followed by a definite and very bold question mark.

No, I thought. Nope. Don't touch it.

You're only annoyed you didn't get to say it first.

Because screwing? I laughed. Out loud.

Cam gave me a look as he put the pumpkin down by the barn door, and I slapped a hand over my mouth.

"What?" he asked. "Is there something on my butt?"

I stared at him. "Why would there be something on your butt?"

"I live on a farm now, Lynsey," he pointed out. "Why wouldn't there be something on my butt, is the better, more likely question."

I glanced at his butt, which for all intents and purposes I should never do again.

"It's fine," I informed him. "Your butt is fine."

"I bet you say that to all the guys."

I rolled my eyes and turned back to the horses. We led them inside, the goats trotting ahead of us in what was clearly a well-worn routine. After we'd gotten everyone fed and bedded down for the night in silence, I felt better.

As though this wasn't a giant misstep.

On the way up to the house, we stopped by the car and unloaded the trunk, hauling a pumpkin and six overstuffed bags of groceries up the crumbling stairs. At the sight of the kitchen, Cam stopped.

"This is exactly like my grandmother's," he announced, and tilted his head at the ancient, rounded Frigidaire. "Is that a padlock on the fridge?"

"It's the handle," I said, pulling on it. The door popped open and a weak chill crept into the room. "At least it seems to work."

"It does the job," he nodded. "And it's kind of cool. No pun intended."

"Uh-huh." I didn't believe him. Cam was exactly the sort of person to have a whole stable of puns ready for use. "There has to be a pantry around here somewhere."

I picked up the remains of Albert's breakfast and started opening cabinets, finding another cache of cat food that worried me and another bag of chicken feed that *seriously* worried me.

"Do you think there are more cats we should be worrying about?" I asked. Cam peered at me over the fridge door. "Um, possibly a house chicken?"

"Did you just say *house* chicken?"

He slowly straightened, looking at me like I had said something that shouldn't exist in the English language. I lifted the bag, shaking it.

A few seconds later, the pet flap on the back door flipped up. I jumped, whirling, chicken feed spraying around my feet and scattering across the linoleum. "What the …"

"Um, Lyn …" Cam shut the fridge and took the bag from me before I could drop it, where it would have accidentally hit the two cats that had planted themselves there.

And the house chicken.

Chapter Ten

CAM

IT WAS A MIRACLE I stayed awake long enough to cook dinner. Then again, I was as hungry as I was tired, so not eating wasn't an option.

Lynsey was yawning too, but as we carried firewood to the site of Albert's weed-filled yet sturdily rock-lined firepit, I heard her stomach growl as well.

It didn't take me long to get flames licking at Albert's well-dried firewood then, while they caught, I settled on the other end of the log Lynsey had already claimed.

Another one of those moments washed over me.

The ones that had been coming every now and then ever since I got here. This one had to do with light and dark. With silhouettes of trees, and swooping bats, the haunting hoot of an owl, and a tired girl, outlined by the fire, which was already filling the air with the smell of childhood camping trips.

It had to do with a long, jam-packed day, and new possibilities, and tired muscles, and the anticipation of a hot meal.

These moments didn't last forever, but I couldn't remember the last time I experienced them. Not during my last year in the city – that's for sure. Not in my life taken over by work, and traffic, and an endless series of non-committal relationships.

It was these moments that had given me the courage to take a quick moment earlier today, when Lewis was talking to a volunteer firefighter, and text back to my boss: I appreciate all you've done for me. I won't be able to teach 101. Please give it to somebody else. I'll explain later.

Or, come to think of it, maybe not courage. Maybe the fear of what would happen to me if I returned to my old way of life as if nothing had happened.

Not that I really knew what was happening, but I did know it was something different.

"Oh my goodness, I am starving," Lynsey said, and I snapped back to the dinner we wouldn't be having if I didn't move.

"OK," I said. "Here we go. Campfire cooking is all about tin foil. You can make pretty much anything you want to eat if you have the right ingredients and a heap of tin foil."

"Why are you telling me?" she asked.

"Because I'm going to show you how to do this in case I get hit by a bus … or a tractor … or another tree."

"But …" in the rapidly falling night, I could just catch a glint of firelight, and the final rays of the sun in Lynsey's eyes. "… you're not planning to get hit by a tree or a tractor, are you?"

I've certainly been accused of being dense, of not taking a hint, of not picking up on small details, but even I knew she wasn't really asking about a tree or a tractor.

I smiled wide enough that I figured she could see the white of my teeth in the dark. "No, not for the next little while I'm not."

Then I held out the newly purchased roll of tin foil. "Start by tearing off a length about as long as your arm …"

LYNSEY

MY CELL PHONE BEGAN a vibrating dance across Albert's bed stand (fashioned out of two milk crates and a piece of plywood) somewhere before sunrise. It was still dark in the room when I jerked out of sleep to slap at it.

There were only, oh, a good majority of the people in my life who would be calling me before dawn. Georgie, Harris, and Dad were easy bets. Right about now they'd be at Tupelo Stud's dark stretch of training track, standing underneath the old moss-strung Live Oaks as the Thoroughbreds galloped through milky mist. My heart clenched a little at the thought of home, and then jackhammered into a race because I wasn't ready for the conversation any of them would want to have.

Namely, I wasn't ready to discuss anything having to do with wondering what I was doing. Because not knowing? Nope. Dad would have the Gulfstream in the air in thirty minutes when he heard that answer, because cutting the purse strings for Dad didn't mean you're on your own. It meant, *I get to decide what you do from now on.*

I sat up, peering at the glowing phone.

Wes.

I stabbed at the answer button. "Hello?"

"Lynsey," a booming voice answered me. "I sincerely hope you're still not on that farm."

Albert's tiny room felt even more impossibly small. "What do you mean?" I croaked.

"I mean I don't want you taking time out of your life babysitting a rundown piece of property," Wes said. "I realize my father feels comfortable with having you there, but the fact of the matter is I'm not."

"It's really not an issue," I said, scrambling to explain myself. How did one explain irrational thinking? I scurried to try. "Someone has to take care of it and I don't have anywhere pressing to be."

"Like a job?" Wes prompted. I was tellingly silent. "School? Family?"

Silent. Even more silent. Wes sighed.

"You mean to tell me that my father found a squatter?"

"I would not go that far," I said. "I'm between opportunities at the moment. Albert came along at the right time."

"Uh-huh," Wes said, clearly not convinced. "Look, the fact of the matter here is my father has no business running a piece of land that large by himself anymore. This has been coming for some time, and I've finally gotten him to agree to move out. Sell the place."

My voice stuck in my throat, coming out like a little, high-pitched whine.

"Ms. Armstrong? Did you hear me?"

"You're selling," I managed to get out. "I understand. I would too, honestly."

I had to think fast. Going back home wasn't an option, and I'd only just landed here. Sure, it was basically a pumpkin-filled isolated shack in the middle of nowhere occupied by a possible moral degenerate, but it had felt like mine for enough time to get attached.

But who was I kidding? I just didn't want to go home.

"We're having an appraiser out there in a few weeks," Wes continued. "Once Dad gets more used to the idea. I think it's best if you head on home, Lynsey."

"What about the animals?"

"I can have them rehomed."

"Or they could just stay here," I offered, leaping into my most professional tone of voice. Mom always called it the Armstrong in me – the ability to talk my way into and out of things. "Just like your father," she'd said once, offering me one of her barely there smiles. I hadn't taken that comment well. I still didn't.

Everything fell away as I focused on the silence on the other side of the line.

"Look at it this way. I'm already here. I can keep this place running, make sure the pumpkins get sold and the festivals go off without a hitch, and I can take the profits in return for making this place presentable while you get it ready for sale."

"And how are you going to do that?" Wes asked, seeing right through my charm.

Then I thought of Cam.

"I know a handyman who can fix some of the more glaring issues," I continue. "This cabin has real potential as a fixer-upper, and I'm sure Albert wouldn't want to see it bulldozed to make way for a McMansion."

"A McMansion isn't my business," Wes said gruffly. "Once it's sold …"

"Of course," I jumped, agreeing readily. "The new owners can do what they want, but shouldn't we think of what makes Albert comfortable right now? Make it easier for him to sell?"

Wes sighed. "The farm has a small savings account."

I pumped a fist in the air.

"*Small*, Lynsey," Wes reiterated, as though he'd seen my silent celebration. I put my fist down. "For feed and hay and farm maintenance, although god knows Dad should've sold those horses long ago. The house is a lost cause, as far as I'm concerned. Focus your guy on the farm and we've got a deal."

I nodded, shifting my expectations.

"Good, then we're agreed," I said. "I'll stay on and keep the place running."

"In the short term," Wes reminded me.

I nodded. "In the short term."

"I'll be in touch with the account numbers," Wes said. "Dad has most of them locked up in his head, so sit tight over there. Those animals need anything, call up Essex Feed & Grain. They'll take care of you."

"Great," I said, and then paused, an overwhelming wave of relief rushing over me. I didn't have to go home. Not yet. "Thanks, Wes."

"What for?" Then he laughed. "You're the one doing all the work."

Once I hung up, I sat in the middle of Albert's double bed and let my success sink in. A feeling started to rise in my chest. Hope, maybe, that this wasn't as ridiculous as I'd thought. I had what might almost be considered a job, which was more than I'd had a few minutes ago. That was more to arm myself with when the battle with Dad started.

Invigorated, I climbed out of bed and pulled on jeans and a t-shirt, ready to start the day. The house was silent – I assumed Cam wasn't a rise-with-the-sun sort of guy – and slunk down the hallway, pausing at the closet containing Matilda's tack.

A hard pang hit my heart when I opened it, eyes falling to the glossy leather saddle and then down to the pair of riding boots I hadn't noticed the first time. They were tucked in the back on the floor, sitting there for who knew how long.

Then another, more instinctual urge hit me. The horse kind.

Without thinking, I pulled the boots out and slipped my feet into them. They were a bit tight, but they'd do in a pinch.

I smiled at my silent pun. Cam would be proud.

Then I pulled the saddle out of the closet and threw the bridle over my shoulder. Matilda and I were about to have a little chat.

To my surprise, Matilda took one look at the bridle and fairly shoved her face into it, chewing the bit like she relished a challenge. I led her into the cool morning air, the sun barely a hint in the sky. Everything looked silver and inky blue-green. Matilda was ghost-like, her chaotic mane in fits and tangles down her neck.

"We're going to have to give you and Horace a real grooming," I told her, tightening the girth and patting her neck. "It's been a while."

Matilda flicked an ear back at me and then swivelled it forward again, watching the chickens ruffle out of their hen house and start exploratory pecks at the ground.

I gathered the reins and mounted up. Matilda surprised me by standing still. My body relaxed when it hit the saddle. I wasn't too far off the ground, but I was far enough that it scratched the right itch. The horse itch.

From Matilda's back, I couldn't see much more than I would have had I been standing next to her, but it might as well have looked like a different world. The farm looked better. Like it wasn't in shambles. I was seeing it through rosier glasses, and when I put my heels to her sides I surprised myself by sending her down the drive to the road.

Away from the farm.

Matilda huffed at my decision, jigging underneath me. The road was silent, the mare's hooves clacking on the pavement as I sent her to the other side and bounding up the rise. We turned, settling into a brisk walk, shuffling through the long grass down the side of the road, putting the farm in our rear-view.

I asked her to trot. Matilda shook her head and let out a little buck before settling into a quick, unholy bounce of a gait. I pushed her into a canter and started to rock, a grin spreading over me that lasted until I saw it.

The bay with the birdcatcher spots.

I reined Matilda in, bringing her to a walk as we approached. The bay lifted its head, watching us from its position among the rusted-out cars and farm equipment. I winced at the thought of a horse running up against the scrap and found myself wondering all over again what it was doing here.

Sinking my weight down, Matilda halted like the kid's pony she had to have been – well-trained at some point and good at her job of taking care of someone. She pushed her head over the top rail, blowing out a few breaths. The bay twitched its tail, studied us for a long moment, and then let out a big sigh before dropping its head and moseying over for a meeting.

The two horses bumped noses carefully, sussing each other out as I sat silently, ignored. Up close, I got a better look at the bay – a gelding, the birdcatcher spots little dime-sized circles glowing off his side. He looked good – well-fed, glossy, his mane falling neatly along his neck. This was a horse that had seen first-class care and attention. Someone loved him, that was clear.

And he was … *here.*

The mobile home on the far side of the paddock was dark. The sinking barn just as dark. The dog from yesterday was nowhere to be seen, but the chickens were starting to scratch.

I tried to tell myself not to be a classist asshole. Maybe whoever lived here owned the horse. Trained it. Maybe it was just taking a break from track life for a minute before shipping to Belmont or Florida. I didn't know, and that was what ate at me, because it still didn't seem right.

Of course, there was at least one way to figure out who he was. All Thoroughbreds on the track had a tattoo. I just had to flip his upper lip and get him to stand still while I committed it to memory.

Easy.

I snorted at my own little joke, and the bay startled, wheeling away from the fence and taking off like a leaping stag. Matilda tensed at the sudden cold shoulder and let out a plaintive whinny.

A dog barked, and a light snapped on at the mobile home.

"Shit."

I spun Matilda around, hustling her out of there as though I was guilty of something. Or maybe suspicious of something. Suspicious that something was going on and I didn't want to get caught snooping for the truth.

—

AFTER I GOT MATILDA cooled off, I led everyone out into the paddock and turned them loose. By the time stalls were clean and the aisle swept, morning was a stronger yellow streaking the sky and my feet were killing me. I'd need to have Harris send me my riding boots, but that would involve talking to him, which meant talking to Dad, which meant … well, no talking to my brother.

I picked my phone up from the feed room on my way out of the barn, noticing ten texts from Wes about accounts, a mystified text from my horse trainer friend Nick asking me where I was, and six calls from Georgie, all with accompanying voicemails.

My old, stronger instinct was to call her back, although my new, developing instinct was to let it go. She was in Florida, surrounded by questions about where I was, and maybe it was better to let my best friend field them for me than to do it myself.

Then my phone started vibrating in my hand, Georgie's face appearing on the screen. The best kick in the shins she could have given me.

"Hey," I said, answering the call, appropriately shamed.

"Lyn," Harris returned, my stomach sinking. "What the hell?"

"What are you doing on Georgie's phone?"

"We *live together*," Harris emphasized. "She's been calling you unsuccessfully every time she gets off a horse, so I figured I'd give it a go. Lo and behold, you answer."

"I had horses to take care of," I sniffed, as though that explained everything.

"Oh, did you?" Harris replied, unimpressed. "Up in Essex County, bastion of previously unknown equestrian excellence? Or did you leave Lake Placid?"

"That would be revealing more than I'm comfortable with at the moment."

"If you can't tell me where you are, who can you tell?"

"Georgie," I said.

"Whom I live with," Harris reminded me. "So that's probably not the best answer."

"Nick," I tried, carding through all my oldest friends.

"Also my best friend," Harris continued. "Should we run through the Venn Diagram that is our lives, because this is getting old."

"Oh my god, do you have to be this impossible?" I stalked out of the barn and up to the house, wincing the whole way as my toes pinched in the boots.

"I'm your brother," Harris said, an infuriating smile in his voice. "We're just built this way, I guess." Then he sobered up. "Tell me where you are so we can at least send someone to get you. Dad's freaking out down here."

"No, nope," I said, climbing the stairs carefully, avoiding the known weak spots. "I'm not coming home."

"Why?" Harris asked, making me pause at the door, my hand on the doorknob.

"Why do you think?"

"Can we not have a weird circular conversation right now?"

"You know why I don't want to come home, Harris."

"Dad was an asshole to you over the Saratoga meet," Harris

said plainly, "but that's not a reason to traipse off on your own without telling anyone where you are."

"It is if I had a deep-seated reason to believe Dad would find a way to pull strings and get me right back where he wants me to be," I answered.

"Lynsey, you've been doing exactly everything he doesn't want you to do since you dropped out of college," he said. "You're a pro at this point. Dad can't do anything to you."

I laughed, opening the door and storming into the house, yanking the infernal riding boots off and kicking them into the corner. "Says the man who holds the farm and all the horses and basically the entire inheritance in the palm of his hand."

"I really don't want to have that conversation again."

"Neither do I," I agreed. "I don't want the farm or Dad's money, so more power to you. I just want him to leave me alone while I try to figure out what I'm doing."

"Which is where?" Harris pried.

"Is it not enough to know I'm safe?"

"That is a resounding no."

The tea kettle began a high-pitched wail from the kitchen, announcing that I wasn't the only person awake in the house.

"Lyn, you want a cup?" Cam called. "Or do you want to finish your argument first?"

"Oh my god," I squeaked as Harris let out a dramatic sigh.

"Please tell me you aren't shacking up with the guy in Lake Placid," Harris groaned.

"How do you even know about the guy in Lake Placid?"

"I. Live. With. Your. Best. Friend."

"Speaking of," I said. "Tell Georgie I am going to kill her the next time I see her. Since you live with her and all I am sure that won't be a problem."

"Ten-four," Harris replied, treating my threat about as seriously as I meant it, which was not at all. "Have a great day, little sister."

I hung up on him, just as Cam came around the corner wearing – what else? – boxers. Only boxers. I flushed at the sight of him, mentally adding *revise house rules to include wearing clothes at all times* to my to-do list. I could include a subsection about allowing shirtlessness for outdoor work, since I was only human.

Then I flushed harder.

Cam gave me a long look, like he knew exactly what was going through my head.

"Looks like maybe a glass of cold water instead," he said, nodding like that was the perfect assessment of the situation. "Gotcha. Coming right up."

Chapter Eleven

CAM

Cue Lynsey going crazy.

OK, not Hannah's bunny-boiling, restraining order, peace-bond kind of crazy – I suppressed a shiver, *thank god my phone's GPS was turned off.* Lynsey's brand of crazy was a genteel lifestyle blog / Martha Stewart strain, involving mood boards adorned with autumn colours and textures – at least that's what Lynsey told me they were when I tripped over one on my way to the cereal cupboard – and lists made on paper bordered with leaves and scarecrows, and pumpkins.

Pumpkins were taking over my life.

Every day when I came home from working at Lewis's there was a new carved pumpkin on the front steps. "I'm experimenting with different styles," Lynsey told me when she caught me staring at a pumpkin with a leaf pattern scratched out of the skin. "This one's etched. Tomorrow I'm going to try shaving."

Are those actually different techniques? I knew better than to ask out loud. I didn't really want to know.

Pumpkin recipes scattered the countertops. The corner of one of my dirty dishes touched a print-out and Lynsey whisked it away, with a muttered, "Hey, that's important!"

"You can't cook!" I protested.

"I'm taking them to Hope's. She's going to work with me."

I sighed. "Fine. Just as long as I never detect even a trace of pumpkin in my tea or coffee." I lifted my first cup of the day only to have it knocked sideways out of my hand and into the sink.

"What?!?"

"Hmm …" Lynsey said. "The thing is, I was experimenting with infusing yesterday …"

"Infusing my coffee?"

She nodded.

"So did you leave any non-infused?"

She shook her head.

"People have been strangled for less," I said. "In fact …"

Whatever I was going to say next was whisked out of my mouth, and my brain, by a sharp little bleat.

Both Lynsey and I whirled to look at the kitchen floor where a very small goat looked up at us.

I opened the corner of my mouth and said, "Don't look now, but there's a kid in the kitchen," which, for some unknown reason, Lynsey found sufficiently hilarious to send her into peals of laughter and send the kid scampering back out the cat- / chicken- / now goat-flap from which it had come.

"So that's one more thing on my to-do list," I said. "Build an escape-free goat shelter."

"Speaking of, where is your list?" Lynsey asked. "I've never seen it. Here …" She held out a sheet of her fall-themed note paper.

"Um, no thanks." I tapped my head. "I've got it all up here." Then I dashed out the door, mentally re-jigging my drive to Lewis's to detour through town so I could get a cup of good-old uninfused, black coffee from Hope.

—

THERE WAS A MASSIVE line-up at Hope's.

OK, there were seven people ahead of me in line, but off-season in a place this small, seven people was a measurable percentage of the total population.

My phone rang and I decided I wasn't getting served anytime soon, so I put it to my ear. "Yup-ello."

"Yup-ello? What is that? Some kind of south of the border expression?"

My sister's voice made me smile, and I was full-on grinning as I said, "Y'all need to back off on the south of the border stuff."

"Hmm, well hopefully you do remember that the real Thanksgiving is rapidly approaching and you also remember your duty to never leave me alone with Mom over any dinner involving turkey."

"How could I forget? If my life was a cornucopia it would be entirely filled with pumpkins. I'm quite literally infused with the spirit of autumn and Thanksgiving."

"Infused is an interesting word." Something clattered in the background. "Sorry. Pitchfork fumble."

"OK, wait, about pitchforks, how are you even supposed to use them? I feel like I'm doing something wrong because all the poop just falls through the tines."

"Aah, let me guess – metal fork?"

"Whoa … wait … there are other options?"

Meg laughed. "Plastic. You can even get them in different colours. Other than this weird manure-fling thing they sometimes do if the tines get caught under something, they're much better for bedding stalls."

"Meg. I think you might have changed my life. Where do I get such a thing?"

"When you come for Thanksgiving there will be one waiting for you as your table gift."

"Well, now I'll definitely be there."

"Cam?"

"Yeah?"

"Did we just have an entire conversation about pitchforks?"

I rubbed my forehead. "I haven't had my coffee yet this morning, so it's all a little fuzzy, but I'd say yes."

"Does this mean you're a farmer now?"

"Is that Mom asking?"

My sister snorted "Who – our mother, who hounds me every single time she talks to me about what you're doing with your multiple degrees, and whether I think you've actually quit the university, or just taken a sabbatical? No, never."

"Sorry, Meg. She knows I'll tell her where to go if she bugs me."

"Oh, don't worry, I have a good answer for her."

"Which is?"

"Which is that you're happy. You are happy, right, Cam?"

I was standing with my back to the counter, gazing through Hope's very clean front windows onto a sidewalk where two women chatted over a baby stroller. An ancient dog ambled across the street, while a pick-up waited for him to reach the far curb. The only reason I couldn't see the lake was because of a wall of maple trees in full blazing fall colours.

Not very far away, across an imaginary line we called a border, someone was standing at the front of a fluorescent-lit classroom lecturing on membrane structure and function to a bunch of first-year students, of which about ten per cent truly cared. That lecturer was filling a role that should have been mine. I didn't want it back.

There was a tap on my shoulder and I turned to find Hope, smiling up at me, holding a steaming mug of beautiful, black, non-infused coffee which she slid onto the nearest table with a wink.

"I'm happy. Yes."

"Then that's all good," Meg said. "I'll see you soon."

—

WHILE LYNSEY WAS DOING the equivalent of earning her PhD in everything pumpkin, I was making steady progress at Lewis's cabin.

Backed by the combined resources of Lewis's bank account, and the temporary loan of Hope's truck, I'd accomplished my first, most urgent aim of preventing further damage by making it water and weather-proof. It wasn't pretty, but it wasn't going to fall down, either. Unless, that is, another tree toppled onto it.

That thought had make me look up into the canopy around the cabin and put in a call to the nearest arborist.

Which meant a typical work morning at Lewis's looked like:

- Text the arborist to see if this was the day he might decide to show up.
- Continue the mind-numbing process of painting the entire board and batten structure single-handedly, while …
- … waiting for Lewis to make up his mind about the interior work.

Words like "muddled" "confused" and "tailspin" came to mind when Lewis and I stood and stared at his bachelor-pad cabin, and he cleared his throat, and scratched his temple, and wrinkled his forehead.

With Lewis's waffling stretching from days into weeks, there came a morning I was denied my morning caffeine by a "Back in Five Minutes" sign hanging on the bakery door, and my patience finally evaporated. "Listen, Lewis, here's the thing. You want to ask Hope to move in here at some point."

Lewis cleared his throat twice in quick succession and I ignored him.

"I know, I know – you didn't come out and say it, but you're thinking it. And to do that, you need to make some major changes inside." I walked him into his very small bedroom, tapped the wall separating it from the even-smaller second bedroom which had so nearly become my coffin, and said, "Obviously this wall should come down so you can have a decent-sized master, with a closet that Hope could actually put some clothes in."

I walked to the corner. "Then, if you use this tiny closet that's already here, and reclaim half the pantry on the other side of the wall, you can have a bathroom with an actual bathtub in it." I shuddered at the memory of the wet, slimy shower curtain clinging to my skin.

"Then some new flooring, a new coat of paint on everything. I mean, I'm guessing she'll want a decent kitchen, but probably best to let her pick that out from an actual kitchen company, and – boom – you're ready to pop the question."

Lewis made a choking noise.

"Well, not The Question, but to ask if she wants to shack up with you."

Lewis blinked. He shifted from foot to foot. He tugged one earlobe, then the other.

"Do it."

"It?"

"What you just said."

"Really?"

He nodded. "I'll open an account for you at Kell's. Enough for everything but the kitchen. Get what you need, when you need it. Do the work. If I help when I can, will you have it done before the snow flies?"

"Sure. Yes." I silently added '*Pumpkin- and goat- and chicken- and falling-down-farmhouse- and Lynsey-willing.*'

That's not what Lewis wanted to hear, though.

I stepped forward to shake his hand. "And we'll get those trees sorted out so they don't kill you guys once you move into your love shack."

Who ever said I wasn't a romantic?

—

LYNSEY'S WORKLOAD, ON THE other hand, I wasn't so sure about it.

I mean, the animals were getting fed, and she was definitely moving forward on the pumpkin front – although I wasn't convinced the things she was accomplishing were the most practical items from the opening-your-own-pumpkin-business instruction manual.

But … I felt like she had hours unaccounted for. Every day I hauled my tools back from Lewis's to tackle the front porch steps, or the latest board / fence / door Matilda had kicked to pieces, or the yet-unstarted task of insulating the walls of our bedrooms which, currently were just studs clad with enough wood to keep large predators – and Matilda – out.

I had new callouses and new aches. Last month my jeans fit just fine – now they were falling down. On my list of things to-do was 1) buy a new belt and 2) eat more. Nothing with pumpkin in it.

I felt like Lynsey would have time to buy a new belt for me.

However, she also displayed this weird evasiveness / irritation whenever I asked her about her day.

It started innocently, me not really caring, saying, "So, what did you do today?" and her answering, "Lots, OK? Plenty." Her defensiveness, coupled with certain moments where I'd catch her in a secret smile, or with eyes sparkling on the greyest of days, would have me calling a private eye if we were married.

We weren't though, and she could, of course, do whatever she wanted, but I kept it up – coming home from Lewis's night-after-night and asking about her day – because it was fun to see her fists clench, and her eyes shift, and to find out if she was going to go on the attack, "Why? What did *you* do?" or be evasive, "Oh, you know, stuff," or try to distract me, "Hope sent these croissants over today."

As the days became steadily chillier, we developed other routines. I never had to set an alarm, partly because of the morning light that filtered through the cracks in my bedroom walls, but mostly because each day started with a volley of exclamation and commotion from Lynsey's bedroom. "Oh! That's cold. Brrr! Cold, cold, cold! Freezing!"

There were bumps, and bangs, and shuffles until she made it into the shower and cranked the taps and I'd finally hear, "Aahh! Thank god for hot water!"

Which is generally when I got up and ran water into the kettle.

One morning Lynsey cycled through her wake-up routine, while I carried out a stretching sequence I'd set to her soundtrack – *Brrr!* Flex my toes. *Cold!* Pull my knees to my chest. *Freezing!*

Stretch out one side of my neck, then the other.

Then there was an almighty bang accompanied by "Ow! Shit! Oh! Damn!" and I tacked leap-out-of-bed-and-run-to-the-bathroom to the end of my exercises.

"What's wrong?!?"

"Don't come in!" Her voice was high and panic-threaded.

"What happened?"

"There's no hot water – oh my god it was cold – so I jumped backward, but the floor is so slippery and my feet were wet, and they just went out from under me and I'm … I'm on the floor … naked."

"OK, so get up."

"I don't know if I can."

"It sounds like I might need to come in there."

"Oh, Cam. I really, really don't want you to. Hang on, let me try to move my leg …"

I waited. "Lynsey?"

"Still trying."

"Lynsey … here's the thing – I've seen a naked woman before. I'm coming in."

"No! Don't look! Don't …!"

She went quiet as soon as I threw the towel over her. It was a technique I'd used when a squirrel got into our apartment in Montreal. He was running, he was chattering, he was bouncing off walls, and then the towel fell over him and he went quiet and I scooped the whole package up and set him free on the front stoop.

Lynsey was bigger than a squirrel. She also still had use of her arms and used them to claw the towel away from her face. "Why did you do that?"

"I thought you didn't want me to see you naked."

"You've seen my face before."

I shrugged and looked down at her. "People in glass houses … no, make that, women wedged between the toilet and the sink … shouldn't look their rescuer in the mouth."

"You just killed several different proverbs at once."

"As if proverbs are our biggest problem here." I kneeled down, reached my arms around her mostly toweled body and tugged. "*You* are definitely our biggest problem here."

Shit. Forgot. Arms free. She smacked me hard. "I'm not big."

"You're too big for this space." I hauled, and tugged, and she rolled free and my hand slipped and I cupped something which I was almost positive was butt cheek. "Whoa!"

"Get out!" she shrieked.

She didn't have to worry. In my current dress of boxer shorts I should have thrown out at least a year ago, there was no way I was sticking around to let her see what effect a handful of pert buttock was having on my too-long-deprived libido.

I didn't quite drop her – I'd like to call it settling her on the floor – then I pulled my hands back, threw them in the air, and said, "House rules say it's time for me to get out of here."

I put my jeans on before I went to the kitchen for breakfast, and by the time Lynsey joined me – wearing a full-length robe snugged very securely around her – the kettle had boiled. I poured each of us a drink then turned to her and said, "So, here's the question; which do we do first? Insulate the freezing cold bedrooms, fix the hot water, or replace the deathtrap of a bathroom floor? Because, there's no way we can afford to do all three."

Not to mention finding me a vehicle and continuing to feed both the animals and ourselves … but those were old problems; it was so much more fun to focus on the new ones.

Lynsey took a sip, raised her eyebrows, and said, "I think we really, really need to sell some pumpkins."

—

THAT WAS THE MORNING I caught her.

I left the tree guy finally, finally securing the upper branches of Lewis's magnificent – and potentially deadly – trees with guy wires and drove into town to order the first lot of materials I needed to transform his man-shack into a love-nest.

Lynsey's morning mishap was firmly in my mind – probably too firmly – I stared down at the suddenly too-tight crotch of my jeans and told myself, "Think of insulation, think of linoleum, think of fuses …"

That was another reason I wanted to go to Kell's. I was pretty sure the hot water heater just needed a new fuse, which I could buy right away, but I wanted to cost out the other things we needed. I knew Lynsey wasn't used to the cold and it was hard not to feel sorry for a Florida girl stuck in an uninsulated hut in New York State as autumn drew in.

Plus, bottom line, there was no way our living arrangement was going to survive another incident like this morning's. Very *bottom* line.

The more I drove these roads, the more I loved them. Unlike back in the city where the more I traveled a particular route, the sicker of it I got – sighing when my bus encountered yet another traffic snag or, on the rare occasions that I drove, inwardly cursing every red light – here the roads were growing on me.

There was the series of potholes that required a right-right-left manoeuvre to avoid damage I couldn't afford to repair to Hope's truck. There was the bend set on a consistent curve so that I just had to move my hands from ten-and-two to eleven-and-three, and I could coast the entire way with no further adjustments. There was the unexpected up-then-down hill that came out of nowhere and dropped the bottom out of my stomach like a roller-coaster.

There was Lynsey.

No.

Yes.

Especially after this morning, I'd recognize that backside anywhere.

Also, her car was parked on the side of the road.

I pulled in behind it, cut the engine and stepped out of the cab.

She turned, shaded her eyes, and asked, "What are you doing here?" with all the defensiveness, and prickliness, and edginess of the previous days balled up together and lobbed at me.

"I could ask you the same thing."

"My back hurts," she said.

We both knew it was a terrible, pathetic, truly desperate attempt to change the subject.

"I'm sure it does. That was a nasty fall. And, unless there's a traveling massage therapist who sets up a table in this particular field every Thursday morning, it has nothing whatsoever to do with why you're here."

She pouted, and at first I thought she was just mad at being called out. Then her bottom lip protruded even further, and it started to tremble, and she blinked several times in a row, and she took such a deep sniff her nostrils pinched in, and I thought, *Oh no, oh shit, here we go. Hot tear alert.*

"It's him," she said, stepping to the side and sweeping her arm wide so that I could see the horse in the field, and like the moment when I found the right angle to free Lynsey from her bathroom trap this morning, I had another moment where everything aligned and I put horse-crazy girl + deep emotions + slightly erratic behaviour together.

I might not know the exact details but I'd been here before – my sister had brought me here before – I was in a world where a girl believed with every fibre in her soul that she needed a horse. Not just any horse mind; *this* girl needed *this* horse.

For a second I let myself wonder if she truly believed she needed him more than hot water, or weather-tight shelter, then I shook my head. I could ask – I *would* ask – but I was pretty sure I already knew what her answer would be.

LYNSEY

I RECOGNIZED THE LOOK on Cam's face. It was the god-help-me-I've-seen-this-before look. I had no doubt his sister was a horse fanatic. Only people close to horse fanatics got this brand of trepidation etched across their face when they watched their special fanatic approach a new horse.

Not that I was his special anything.

I was just … emotional. That's all. After a full week of sneaking down to the neighbor's paddock with a bucket of oats I was still no closer to convincing the horse to approach me, and I wasn't about to go traipsing across private property. It was hard enough to find a nook on the far side of the paddock with enough distance to keep what I was doing out of sight from the mobile home and the dog.

What I needed was a better plan. And maybe a partner in crime.

"He isn't supposed to be here," I said, giving the bucket another shake. The gelding swiveled one ear toward me, then maneuvered himself so I was seeing more butt than I was head.

"OK," Cam said slowly, as though still determining whether I'd gone crazy. "Maybe explain to me why he isn't supposed to be here? Because aside from sharing his space with old farm equipment he looks pretty at home."

"Well he's not at home," I sighed, lowering the bucket.

"How is that, Lyn?" he asked gently.

I spun toward him, holding up one finger. "He's fresh off the track, for one thing."

Then another finger. "Those white spots on his side? Those are familiar, I just can't place them and it's annoying me."

Another finger. "There are no other horses on this property, which is not where you put a horse, much less a potentially track-fried Thoroughbred."

A fourth finger, god help us all. "Spidey sense."

Cam tilted his head at me, remaining silent.

"What?" I asked after the quiet became oppressive.

"I'm just impressed you can throw around Spiderman lingo," he admitted. "You did not strike me as being a closet nerd."

"I am not …" I started, and took a much-needed breath, wiping at my eyes with the heels of my hands. "Whatever. What I need is that horse's tattoo. If I can get his tattoo then I can find out who he is, but he's not exactly Horace. He isn't making this easy."

"You just need to flip his lip, right?" Cam asked, and I gave him a look.

"Horse-obsessed sister," he reminded me. "Meg's first horse was a Thoroughbred. She showed me his tattoo. Seemed like an awkward arrangement even when you know the horse in question. This horse, Lyn …" He motioned at the gelding. "He's all the way over there. What's your game plan?"

"My plan was to carefully gain his trust over several days – perhaps weeks – with food, wearing him down until he lets me mess with his mouth," I said and paused when the gelding turned his butt more fully toward me. Cam snorted. "In retrospect," I added, "I get that might be an exercise in futility."

Cam watched the horse for a moment and said, "Seems to me you need to switch up your tactics."

He turned to the truck.

"How?" I asked his back. "By … playing hard to get?"

Cam laughed, opening the cab and halfway disappearing as he rooted through whatever he was ferrying back from town, giving me an amazing view – yet again – of his backside, clad as it always seemed to be in jeans that would not stop being worn in all the right ways.

I squeezed my eyes shut, telling myself when I opened them I'd find a new, incredible fascination with the grass. Or the sky. Or the junk in the paddock. Anything except Cam's ass.

"You OK?"

I snapped my eyes open and was immediately presented with a bag with a huge Irene's logo stamped across it.

"Great," I grumbled. "Just determining how we're going to fix this situation with baked goods."

"Watch and learn, Padawan." He winked. It filled me with an immense sense of impending … warmth. Not good. So not good.

"What even is a Padawan?" I asked, taking a step back from him to clearer air, which was more cusp-of-fall and less Irene's-famous-scones, which Cam was busily pulling out of the bag.

"I take back that nerd comment," Cam said, one blueberry scone in hand as he ducked through the fence rails, my protest dying on my lips as I watched him troop out toward the horse, which looked up with a suspicious jerk of its head. Its ears swivelled, muscles quivering, ready to take flight if needed.

But … there was a blueberry scone. Cam held out one half in the palm of his hand and the horse … melted.

I stared. "What the …"

Cam looked over at me, the horse licking the palm of his hand eagerly and snuffling for more. "Hey, Lyn, grab the rest in the bag and come here, will you? I can't do this lip thing and serve scones at the same time."

"For the love of …" I snatched up the bag, marching into the field with scones in hand, eyeing the quiet barn and mobile home just beyond. The dog was silent, and I hadn't seen any activity … yet. But the trespassing? I was from Florida. I knew how people dealt with trespassers in Florida, and it tended to involve a lot of yelling and threats.

Considering we were basically neighbors? Not the greatest way to introduce yourself. Although who was I kidding? Judging by the current situation, we were the crazy ones in this hypothetical relationship. We fully deserved to be yelled at.

I slipped up next to the horse. He turned toward me, ears pricked and attention on the bag, already trying to shove his nose into it. Cam grabbed the bag, holding it above my head like he was trying to tempt me into making a leap for it. Instead, the gelding lifted his head, lips wiggling for more blueberry scones.

Then he took a step into me, and there's nothing like realizing you are standing between a half-ton horse and a bag of tantalizing scones to start moving quickly. I hooked a hand over the gelding's nose, running my palm over the velvet-soft skin until … there.

Flipped.

I peeked up at the numbers.

R23045. Or was that a six?

I tried to get a different angle, only the gelding shouldered me out of the way and right over a tire. I was airborne – and then I wasn't.

Landing hard on my back a second time in one day was not exactly in the game plan, but admittedly this seemed like a likely scenario the second I walked into the paddock. Cam looked down at me, bag of scones clutched in both hands like he preferred greatly to keep his hands around it than helping me to my feet.

Which, judging from this morning might not be the worst of ideas.

The gelding wasn't nearly as startled by my sudden sprawl. In one smooth movement, he snaked his head out, snatched the bag out of Cam's hands, and took off for the opposite side of the paddock to enjoy the rest of his scones in peace. Cam blinked after him, then shook his head.

"Well, OK, I guess this leaves me with one option."

"Nope!" I scrambled to stand, brushing my hands on my jeans

and scooting past him. "I'm fine. We need no repeats of this morning."

"I wouldn't exactly call this a repeat," Cam said, following me. "Given our state of more clothing and the general vicinity being far more outdoorsy but no less …" He waved a hand at the detritus.

"Rustic ramshackle?" I asked, ducking through the fence rails.

Cam eyed me. "You say that as though it's a trendy decorating technique."

"I have plans for the school bus shelter by the farm's driveway," I admit. "Drag it up to the pumpkin patch, throw a pop of color on it, and you've got a perfect staging booth, don't you think?"

Cam didn't say anything, but the expression on his face made me entirely sure I would be rustic ramshackling the bus shelter by myself.

"Anyway, I take it back," I said. "This is more *rustic*. Our stained shower would feel right at home in this paddock."

Cam rubbed at the bridge of his nose. I could almost see the addition of the shower to his mental list of things to do.

"Not that I can't live with the shower as it is," I amended. "The shower is fine. The bus shelter is also, basically, fine. I mean, I can paint it myself, I'm sure. How long could it take? A few hours? With the lead up to what I feel we should be calling Pumpkinpocalypse this weekend, maybe I should get on that sooner rather than later."

I had my hand on the Audi's handle when Cam finally seemed to digest everything I was saying.

"Wait," he said. "You said this weekend?"

I made a face as I opened the car door. "I noticed in town that the pumpkins were already out at the store, so I bumped it up a week. This is prime displaying of pumpkins season, and who I am to keep people from this joy? I meant to tell you but figured one week wouldn't matter."

"You realize I have to go home for Thanksgiving, right?" Cam asked, straight-faced. "I think I told you that somewhere between the pumpkin etching and the pumpkin painting, around the infusing incident. I'm pretty sure I said something about Thanksgiving."

"Probably you did, but Thanksgiving is weeks away." I got into the car, finding my sunglasses and perching them on my nose as I looked up at him through the open window, confused. "Why are we talking about it anyway?"

"Because I'm leaving tomorrow. Canadian Thanksgiving is the second weekend in October," Cam said. "Meg's doing dinner Saturday, so I need to … you know … go."

I couldn't help it. I laughed. Loud, braying laughter.

"No, that can't be right," I giggled. "Come on. Why would two generally amicable neighbor countries celebrate the same thing on totally different days. It doesn't make any …"

Cam's increasingly drawn-out stare sent me trailing off as I realized he wasn't joking. He wasn't joking *at all*. And not only was he not joking, he was telling me in no uncertain terms that I was on my own. Just me, a field of pumpkins, and who knows how many people crawling over the farm to find the prettiest, roundest, orangest one.

Canada.

Canada, with its just slightly different than America *differences* was going to screw up Pumpkinpocalypse.

I took a big breath and held it. Out in the field, the gelding tossed the empty paper bag over the fence and tore into a raucous sugar-fueled display of sheer athleticism. I stared at him as he galloped toward the fence, black tail trailing behind him and muscles bunching. Everything about his body seemed to lift in anticipation, and without realizing it I tensed – waiting for him to take off and sail over the fence, go tearing off into the New York wilderness.

But the gelding veered, swooping to the opposite side of the pasture, hoofbeats fading like a receding storm. For one blissful moment, I forgot about Canada. Instead, I could only think about the gelding soaring over anything I put in front of him. It was irrational – I hadn't even seen him jump – but somewhere in the back of my lizard brain, I knew he'd be able to take that fence if he'd wanted to.

"It's not a problem. We'll just change the date," Cam suggested, opening the door for Canada again. Canada, and its metric system, and its Maple syrup, and apparently an off-brand Thanksgiving.

I let out my breath slowly.

"We *can't* change the date," I said. "When I made the new-and-improved posters to replace Albert's graphic-design disasters, I put Saturday as our opening date. Since we're definitely not changing a national holiday that leaves me by myself."

Cam didn't have anything to say to that, which was as much a confirmation as I needed.

By myself. Fitting, I guess. I'd struck out on my own, hadn't I? This was what I'd wanted, after all, wiggling free of my family and trying to find myself sans the Armstrong name. I didn't need Cam to sell pumpkins. I didn't need anyone's help to talk people out of their money.

So why did my chest feel hollow?

Then I did something to make my family proud: I put the Audi in drive and pulled onto the road without looking, the tires fishing for purchase on the pavement and catching hold when I slammed on the gas, high-tailing it out of there fast and not knowing where I was going.

—

I SPED BY LAKE Placid's gentle, Olympics-obsessed welcome sign. The town spread out in front of me, Mirror Lake sitting beyond it flanked by mountains and reflecting blue sky and puffy clouds. Looking at it made me more aware that I was breathing after all. I had been all the way into town. I was just too upset with myself to notice.

There was only one port in my particularly Cam-shaped storm: Irene's. I parked by the curb, bumping my tires against it with a jolt, and pushed through the front door. It jingled, like I imagined all the doors along Main Street did – merrily and old-fashioned.

Hope looked up from the counter she was wiping off with a pristine, white cloth.

"Uh-oh," she said when I made a beeline straight to her.

"Please," I groaned, a little too loudly if the silent looks I got from the laptop-toting café occupier crowd was any indication. "A piece of pie. Surely you still have a piece of pie?"

Hope considered me for two beats and then folded the cloth into a neat rectangle. Then she put her hands on her hips. This couldn't be good.

"OK, I could get you a piece of pie," she said, arching an eyebrow. "Or you could tell me what's the matter."

"I live in a shanty in the middle of nowhere without any actual home to return to," I said. "I'm a squatter with Cam as a roommate, Hope. *Cam.* Please take mercy on me and give me a piece of pie. I'll even pay for it."

Hope snorted, but bent down to dig in the case between us, presenting a piece of cherry pie with a flourish and taking the last couple of crumpled bills I had in my pocket.

"I did send Cam home with scones," she said, handing me a fork, which I immediately put to good use. "I guess I'm going to have to rethink that recipe if they couldn't get you through Cam-related crazy."

"The horse ate them," I grumbled around the pie, which brought both of Hope's eyebrows up.

"What now?"

"It's a long story," I said with my mouth full, proceeding to tell her everything as I devoured the cherry pie, ending with Canadian Thanksgiving. "So, in conclusion, the horse ate all the scones, Cam isn't helping with the pumpkins, and do I know what I'm doing?

No."

"Yes," Hope said above me, crossing her arms. "How hard is selling pumpkins? You point people to a field and then take their money. You can do this in your sleep."

"That's not the point," I said. "Taking money I can do – happily, even. But I wasn't supposed to do it alone. I was operating on the assumption I wouldn't be, because Cam was here. We were going to do this together and he's bailing."

"To be with his family," Hope said.

"Which is why I can't exactly say he can't go," I said, stabbing at the pie crust. "Besides, it's not like we're …"

I nipped that thought before it could blossom, chewing angrily and swallowing. I pushed the empty plate away and put my head on my arms, letting out a cleansing breath.

"This is my fault," I muttered. Hope patted my head.

"Maybe. But maybe you just need a break," she said, which were possibly the wisest words I'd ever heard. "Look, I've got a few friends visiting from the city this week. We're kicking things off at the wine bar that just opened by the lake. Why don't you come with us?"

I peered up at her. "I don't want to crash anything …"

She shook her head. "When was the last time you had a girl's night?"

I thought of the last time I'd worn heels, which was all the way back on the last day of the Saratoga meet, when I'd wanted to throttle my father with my bare hands. OK, not the best of memories, but heels had carried me through nearly all of the major social gatherings I'd successfully planned at home – from the farm functions to our annual Christmas bash. I'd put together those events with Mom and I'd kept doing them after she was gone, taking her whimsical creativity and giving it firm direction with the use of planning apps and calendars and an iron fist.

I could get Pumpkinpocalypse off the ground by myself. I'd been planning for this my entire life.

But I did want to throw on a pair of heels first, just to remind myself.

I shoved my dishevelled hair away from my face and straightened, pushing away from the counter.

"What time?" I asked.

"Sixish," Lewis announced from behind me, patting my shoulder as he bellied his ridiculously tall frame up to the counter, travel mug in hand. "Hope wrangled me into driving. Swinging by your place is no trouble."

"We're literally in the boonies," I pointed out. "The wine bar is down the street."

My protest fell on deaf ears. Hope was already filling up his mug with piping hot coffee, tilting her head and blushing as though nothing could be more scandalous. Lewis rested both forearms on the counter, leaning in so dramatically he could have reached the coffee and refilled the mug himself.

"OK then," I announced, loudly. "Six it is."

No one responded.

"I'll be going now!"

Still nothing.

"Hopeless," I sighed, and headed for the door.

——

WHEN I GOT BACK to the farm, Hope's truck was nowhere to be seen. Of course, it wouldn't be. If I were Cam, I'd probably be halfway to Canada by now. I wouldn't blame him if he *was* halfway to Canada.

And that was fine, I reminded myself. I could do this alone.

Looking down at my phone, I had a couple of hours to get ready. Then I remembered.

R23045. Or maybe six. I was only a few hyperlinks away from finding out the gelding's identity and here I was more upset about pumpkins. Well, that ended now.

I pulled out my phone on my way to the house, navigating both the Jockey Club's website and the treacherous steps with memorized ease. I tapped the tattoo into the database.

No Search Results Found.

OK, not a big deal. It was clearly a six. I typed that in as I pushed into the house, the doorknob sticking. I wedged my shoulder against the wood and shoved, nearly falling inside. By the time I pushed my hair out of my face to look at my phone, I was greeted with Lost Cause.

My heart stuttered in my chest as I scrolled down all the facts I already knew. Year of Birth. Sire. Dam. I knew all these things because the gelding down the road had walked into the Keeneland yearling sale four years ago as a colt, fetching nearly ten million dollars in the process. By the time the gavel had fallen, *The Blood-Horse* had already written its first article on him. By the time he'd walked out of the sales ring, the entire Thoroughbred world knew who he was.

And what did he do after that?

Nothing. So much nothing it was embarrassing enough to erase him from the Thoroughbred industry's collective memory. But those little constellation points along his side were memorable. No wonder I couldn't let this horse go.

Before I could rationally think of all the good reasons not to call Georgie, I was already tapping her number, wondering if I could catch her between races. The phone rang and rang, finally picking up to a breathless, "Hello?"

"Do you know who is in the paddock down the road?" I opened, being met with a groan.

"No 'Hi, Georgie, it's me, your best friend, ready to tell you where I am so you can talk sense into me?'"

I ignored her. "Lost Cause," I said. "*The* Lost Cause."

"What?" Georgie asked. "Did you go back to Saratoga?"

"Nope," I said to her sigh. "I certainly didn't, which makes this very interesting don't you think?"

"It would be more interesting if I knew where you were," Georgie pointed out. "I swear I won't tell Harris, if that makes you feel any better."

"It doesn't," I said. "He was quite firm in telling me you two live together now or whatever, which I think was his not-so-subtle hinting that you have a solid relationship that doesn't involve lying to each other."

"He makes an excellent point about the not lying," Georgie said, the sounds of the jockey's room filtering through the room. Banter in Spanish and English, the slam of a locker door, the crack of pool balls over laughter. Georgie existed it in so perfectly and so strangely at the same time. "And since our relationship is pretty solid …" Georgie trailed off.

"Yeah, I get it," I said, sitting down on the orange sofa. The fuzzy mystery upholstery grated against my jeans. "Far be it from me to jeopardize the only healthy relationship I have to emulate when I eventually get one of my own."

"Well, Harris seemed to think you were in one?"

"I wouldn't call it a relationship," I laughed. "And if I were in a relationship with Cam I don't think it would be healthy. I'm almost sure he's going to dart across the border tomorrow and never return."

"I feel like there's a lot more you need to tell me besides the horse," Georgie said. "This Cam person is first on my detailed list. Questions like 'Who is he?' and 'Why is Lynsey hiding out with him?' are one and two."

"You have a bullet point list, don't you," I said. It wasn't a question.

"Of course I do!" Georgie burst. "I don't even know where you are!"

"Shouldn't that be number one on your list?" I asked, being

difficult. Georgie groaned.

"You know what? Fine. Let's go back to the one thing you want to talk about," she said. "Why is Lost Cause living in the boondocks?"

"I was hoping you could tell me," I said, knowing one of her eyebrows was raising dangerously close to her hairline. I was glad I couldn't see it.

"Why can't you just go over there and make friends with new people?" she asked. "Ask for yourself why he's in their junkyard paddock?"

"Because I don't know what I'm dealing with!" I defended. "I don't want to walk up to someone's door and get a shotgun in my face. This is …" I trailed off, Georgie's silence reaching for me through the phone. "Look, you *know* where I am, OK? I don't want to play games."

"You're in Lake Placid," Georgie said, affirming for me that she'd known all along where I'd been. "Where you are *in* Lake Placid is something I can find out really quickly if you want me to find out more about Lost Cause. I can do that for you, Lyn, but I want to make sure I'm not going to get any Armstrong-level anger from you when I do."

"I'm asking you," I said. "I'm not hiding from you, Georgie. Or Harris. I'm just …"

"Your dad cares about you, you know," she said softly. I sucked in an audible breath, and she rushed to amend herself. "This is coming from someone who really, *really* doesn't like him."

"I know he does," I allowed. "It's just … what he does in the name of caring? That's unacceptable."

"I'll help," Georgie said. "But I'm telling Harris."

I nodded. "I figured you would."

"I'll swear him to secrecy," she added. "We'll keep it between us, like old times."

"Old times weren't the best of times," I reminded her, and she laughed over the call for the next race.

"I've got to go," she said. "I'll call you when I find out something."

"Thanks, Georgie."

"And maybe you can invite me up to your hidey hole as a reward for when I find something?" she hedged.

It was my turn to laugh. "I'm pretty sure you'll regret using the word *reward* when you see this place, but sure. My door is open to you."

"Can't wait," she chirped just before she was gone, leaving me alone in Albert's cabin, with its view of the overgrown brush and time-worn fences that rambled down to the road. The in-need-of-more-gravel drive cut through it, and I thought of the bus shelter. Guess there wasn't any time for that this year.

This year.

Oh. My. God. What was I thinking?

I shook the thought from my head and stood up, turning to go get ready for Hope's shindig, when the rumbling of a truck brought my attention back to the window. The grimy, streaked window, which still gave me an excellent view of a tow truck slowly hauling the bus shelter up the drive.

I stared as it passed the house, then stumbled out onto the porch as it lumbered up into the field past the barn. I leapt off the steps to avoid the soft spots, jogging after the truck, which squeaked to a halt at the edge of the pumpkin field. Cam pushed open the door, getting out of the cab, already pulling on work gloves and eyes on the bus shelter. He wasn't ready when I threw myself at him.

"Oof," was the first thing he said, followed quickly by, "You hug like a wrecking ball, you know that?"

"Thank you," I said against his neck, and put my hands on his solid chest, pushing back just enough to look up at him. His arms were still wrapped around me, hands spanning my back. It felt ridiculously comfortable, being right here, in full contact with Cam. I was pretty sure it wasn't supposed to be. I was also pretty sure I should be stepping away from him right about now.

I didn't.

"I thought I'd have to let this go," I admitted, pulling my attention from him to the bus shelter.

"Yeah, well, figured I could do this last thing before I take off for the week," he said. "You'll need a roof over your head in case it starts raining during Pumpkinpocalypse."

"Where did you get the truck?" I asked, wondering about how much it took to rent a tow truck. We didn't have this kind of money. I was positive.

"Lewis called in a favor," Cam said with a shrug. "That was

fortunate, because I briefly considered using Hope's truck before realizing she probably wouldn't want me damaging a lot of it beyond reasonable repair with a bus shelter."

I nodded, and then had to bite the bullet. "I'm sorry I panicked earlier."

He eyed me. "You ripped out of there pretty fast."

"It's a family quirk," I admitted. "We do things fast and without thinking about it too much."

"In very different circumstances that's a quirk I would appreciate," he said, a smile appearing across half of his mouth. I decided that was the perfect moment to wiggle out of his grasp. We stood there, a sudden layer of awkward between us. He cleared his throat and moved around me. "You may need to abandon the idea of painting this thing," he said, mercifully changing the subject. "Seeing as how the sun's about to go down and all."

"I will take what I can get at this point," I said. "Besides, I don't have time. Hope has a thing. I'm going to it."

"A thing, huh?"

"A girl thing," I added, and mentally kicked myself when he looked at me over his shoulder, already starting to work on getting the bus shelter off the truck. Work and Cam looked good together, so it was really for the best when I started backing away.

"OK, have a good time on your girl thing," he said. "I'll get the animals fed while you're gone."

I took my first step back, even though I still wanted to stand where I was, mainly so I could watch. Like a crazy person with no social skills. "Great," I replied. "Thanks. I'm going to …" I pointed at the house. "Go."

The tow truck started to lower the shed. Cam looked at me like I was an afterthought, his attention on moving several hundred pounds of shelter onto the ground without breaking it to pieces.

"Yeah, OK," he said, and then looked up at me just as I was in the process of turning. "Hey, Lyn?"

"Yes," I said, spinning back toward him.

"Call me if you need a ride home, OK?" he said. "Fast and without thinking is great in certain circumstances, but I don't think it applies to girl's night."

I blushed. There was no way I was calling him for a ride. Nope. Not happening. I would go the whole night without lifting a glass of wine if necessary, because me after a few drinks anywhere near Cam?

I watched him leap onto the flat bed of the tow truck like it was nothing, a whisper of something tingly hitting places I didn't want to think about where it concerned Cam.

Nope. Not happening.

"Thanks for the offer," I said, taking another step back. "I'd keep it under consideration, but Lewis has already offered to chauffer."

He looked up at me, distracted, but aware enough to look confused. "That was weirdly formal?"

"Another quirk!" I laughed, waving my hands. "Quirky, quirky Lynsey. I am going now."

Then I spun. And then I nearly ran. Quickly, and thinking maybe a little too much for my own good.

Chapter Twelve

CAM

Ways I could tell it wasn't summer anymore:

The goosebumps on my forearms.

The sharpness of the air in my nostrils, tinged with autumn scents – drifted leaves, windfallen apples, and a hint of somebody's distant bonfire.

The sudden swoop of the darkness. For a long time it would steal in slowly, mingling darker hues into the bright sky, the sun reaching rays as long and late as it could – but with the onset of October the blackness dropped like a curtain.

It was that sharp fall into darkness that had me out in the barnyard, doing the evening barn chores earlier than I normally would. Probably too early, Lynsey would say.

But she wasn't around, so *ha!*

Childish, I knew, but I had a reasonably happy childhood,

which made me happy to hold onto many of my old habits.

The chickens were fed and latched in securely and I'd done an extra sweep around the perimeter of the coop. The man in front of me at the cash at Kell's earlier in the day was saying he'd lost half-a-dozen hens to the foxes last night. I wouldn't want to be around if anything happened to Chick or Hen or Little or Red. The day Lynsey named them was the day I knew I'd better double-up on the chicken wire defences.

The goats … well, let's face it … they pretty much did what they wanted, but tonight they were content to trot into the barn and eat the food I'd given them. Of course, I could easily wake up with one staring me down in bed tomorrow morning but, you know, I was a big believer in having the wisdom not to try to change things I couldn't control and the behaviour of goats was definitely one of those things.

Matilda. She'd either trot around the field … or sometimes gallop … tail up, ears forward, often farting, and keep that up until I came to shake oats, or she'd dive bomb toward me the minute she saw me and I've have to jump out of the way like a bullfighter.

The emphatic way Matilda lived her life reminded me of Lynsey. Minus the frequent farting, of course.

Today was a dive-bomb day, with the pony beelining for the gate and the barn, and me just following to close doors and shoot bolts in her wake.

Her nose was in her feed bowl before I had the stall door – with its row of Matilda-deterring latches secured – and it was to the munch-grind of her jaw that I said, "Horace."

He was a gentle soul. Took his time. When all others lost their heads, Horace stood his ground. I'd literally seen goats, chickens, the barn cats, and Matilda bounce off his solid sides with him just lifting his head from the grass to chew and watch as they righted themselves and carried on.

When I went back out to find him he was alone in the field, silhouetted against the orange blaze of the sky. "My goodness, old son, you look positively majestic."

He let out a long whiffling exhale I chose to interpret as a thank you.

I walked partway out to meet him and said, "Come on, then. Git-up," and he stretched out his neck and started walking.

Except, instead of heading straight for the gate, he circled around me. "OK, dude, what's up with that?" I asked as he continued on, overshooting the gate and appearing to head back toward the open field.

But he kept turning. I watched as he circled completely around me, and it was on his second circuit that something swam into my brain. Something I'd watched my sister do.

"T-rot!" I said it the way you say 'sit' to a dog you've just met. Not sure if the animal knows the command – not positive you're saying it in a way they'll understand. Horace understood. Horace trotted.

He pulled in his lip, which up until now had been dangling, and he pitched his normally floppy ears forward, and he moved into the two-beat rhythm I'd seen Meg call a trot and, once again, the word that came to mind was majestic.

Or at least earth-moving. I could feel the vibrations of his hoofbeats as he held the circle around me.

Wow. OK. So this was cool. What next?

"Walk?" I tried. He dropped back to his original pace and immediately started to swing in toward me. "No, no, no. Keep walking." Without hesitating he finished the half-turn-in he'd done so that he was back on the circle but going the other direction. "Ah, clever boy. Keep us from getting dizzy, huh?" One big ear swiveled toward me. I took that as a yes.

I watched him walk for a while, and it was the first time I'd really noticed how a horse walked. How his hips moved separately from his shoulders. How his hind legs swung his back hoofs into the prints left by his front ones. It was actually quite biologically interesting.

"Trot!" This time I said it with confidence, and he jumped forward, and again I watched the swing and rhythm of his gait.

The next time I said, "Walk," I followed it immediately with, "And keep walking!" and he did. He was looking at me quite a bit, though. It was like he was wondering where this was going. I wasn't sure, either, so I did this other thing I'd seen my sister do and I turned and faced away from him and waited.

Not for long, though. I didn't hear or feel him coming because his walk hoofbeats were much quieter than his trot ones – quite stealthy, really, for a boy of his size – but in less than a minute there was hot breath gusting onto my neck, followed by a big muzzle pushed into the backward-curving palm of my hand.

I turned around and he pushed his face against me and – what else could I do? – I wrapped my arms around his big head and nestled my chin into the space between his ears and, from that vantage point, watched the sun set behind the barn.

Awesome.

When I walked back to the barn, Horace followed me and imagine having a dog that heels, then imagine that dog being twenty times bigger and still walking just as close to you, well that's how it felt to have Horace at my side. I was proud, and amazed, and touched.

When he swung into his stall right beside me there was a part of me that almost cried. I couldn't remember the last time I cried.

In that weird emotional moment, with the sounds of animals eating all around me, I tripped over an empty feed bag and an idea jumped into my head.

—

WE DIDN'T HAVE A TV. Which was normally fine. To be honest, I hadn't once, yet, had the urge to turn one on. Or, more like, the time to. Usually, I'd get home from Lewis's already tired, do enough more work around here to make me truly exhausted, then spend the last hour or so before I fell into bed cooking something which registered somewhere on both the nutritional and gastronomical charts.

Lynsey didn't seem to care, but I was determined neither of us should get scurvy, and we should eat at least as well as the animals that were running us ragged.

So, work, work, work, discuss the farm's priorities with Lynsey (usually me: repair a structure, make something weatherproof / her: build a trellis, paint a gate), cook, disagree with Lynsey over the farm's priorities (me: let's be practical! / her: it's practical to make it pretty!), eat, come to some sort of mutually agreeable compromise (if I move the school-bus shed, she can paint it to make it pretty), then bed.

Tonight, with the animals done early, and no Lynsey to argue with, dinner was done fast and I was left with something I vaguely remembered – spare time.

Which was where my idea from earlier came in.

It was a mild night – with a breeze, rather than a wind moving around the farm. I arranged a lantern and my crank radio on the front porch and sat down with the sewing kit I always carried in my duffle bag to stitch up the old feed bag.

I'd learned to sew from my first girlfriend's mom. They'd taken me to their cottage, and when my girlfriend's brother tore the only pair of shorts he'd brought, his mom had sat down with a needle and thread and made a near-invisible repair. She caught me watching and said, "Here, Cam, I'll show you how. It's a great skill to have."

It was a great skill to have. I'd used it many times over the years and something about making the stitches as small, and strong, and even as possible appealed to me. As I focused on doing just that, and as I listened to Canadian voices debating Canadian politics on the CBC station I'd discovered I could sometimes tune into, I was happy.

Happy also when I held up the finished item and found it was just about the size I'd imagined, and that it neatly held the two big scoops of oats I'd brought from the barn. A few quick stitches to seal up the opening and there it was – a warm bag for Lynsey. A couple of minutes in the microwave would heat it to a toasty, even warmth, that would last much longer than the time it should take her to fall asleep.

Sure, it was a temporary solution, but it was quicker and cheaper than a complete HVAC system for the cabin.

I'd just done my first test – one minute in the microwave – and was back on the porch with the nicely warm bundle lying across my legs when headlights swept into the yard.

Lewis, delivering Lynsey safely home from her evening with Hope, and four of Hope's long-lost girlfriends – driving so she could enjoy the wine portion of the evening.

Which, it would appear, she had.

"Well, hel-lo." There was a softness to her words – not quite a slur, but not far off. "Fancy meeting you here."

Lewis was right behind her. "Here she is. Safe and sound, although maybe not quite sober."

"Thanks Lewis. I appreciate it. Did they have fun?"

"I'm here, you know. You can ask me if I had fun."

"Did you have fun, Lyn?"

"Very fun. Much fun. Lots of fun."

Lewis was already heading back to the car. I called after him. "Thanks again. For everything. And I will get the truck situation sorted out."

"Yeah, I know you will. Happy Thanksgiving. Have some turkey for me."

"Will do."

When I turned back to Lynsey she was shaking her head. "I can't believe you're leaving tomorrow."

"I can't believe you decided to launch the pumpkin patch on the day I'm leaving."

She shrugged and the motion set her off-balance, into a gentle sway. "Your choice."

"Uh, no. Thanksgiving is Thanksgiving. Not my choice. Opening date was your choice."

She wrinkled her nose and her eyes closed and took a second too long to re-open. "It's not *real* Thanksgiving."

"I'm not having this debate with you again." Although I really, really wanted to because everybody knows, in this part of the world the harvest happens in October.

"Skunk," Lynsey said.

"Oh, we're name-calling now?" I caught a glimpse of movement at the edge of the circle of light thrown by the lantern. Black-and-white movement. "Oh, shit. *Actual* skunk. Come on, inside."

Lynsey just blinked at me a couple of times.

"How come I feel like you're getting less sober?"

"One for the road," she said, holding up two fingers.

I bent over, collecting up all my things. "One, what?"

"Tequila shots. Except it was two." She switched to four fingers.

Meanwhile the skunk was moseying in our general direction. "OK, listen. I don't see any way you're not going to be hungover tomorrow, so let's at least try to make sure you don't smell like skunk. Move it."

When she didn't, I transferred radio, lantern, sewing kit, etc. into one hand, and circled my free arm around her shoulders. "Walk. One foot after the other. Let's go."

She sang as she walked. "Skunk in the barnyard – pee-yew! Somebody ate it – it's you!" With this she twisted and pointed at me.

"Hmm … yeah. Very amusing."

"Not amusing. Classic."

"Yeah, maybe an American classic. Can't say I've heard of it myself."

"Oh, blah-blah-blah," Lynsey said, making open and shut motions with her hands. "You and your 'this-is-American-and-this-is-Canadian' stuff. How can you not know 'Skunk in the Barnyard?'"

"Probably the same way Thanksgiving is in a totally different month …"

"See?" She said. "That's exactly what I'm talking about … Somebody farted! It's you!"

"Excuse me?"

"The song …" She snapped her fingers. "Keep up with me

here, Cam. It's not a difficult song."

We were at her bed. "Lie down, Lynsey."

And she did. I was finding drunk Lynsey quite interesting. Equal parts defiant and obedient.

She rubbed her arms. "I'm cold!"

"Here …" I pulled the covers over her. "… I can help with that. Just wait one sec." Maybe it was Lynsey singing childhood songs, but the opportunity to show off my craftsmanship had me pleased as a five-year-old. I found myself humming "Skunk in the Barnyard," as my hand-sewn warm bag circled the inside of the microwave.

"OK, here we go …" I stopped in the doorway to her bedroom. Lynsey was lying exactly where I left her, except with her sheets around her knees and wearing only a t-shirt that did not adequately cover her underwear. "Um, Lyn, I thought you were cold?"

"Uh, yeah. I am. But I still had to get ready for bed."

"Of course." I took a couple of steps toward her, covering half the distance between the door and the foot of her bed, then reached the warm bag out to her. "Try this." I ended up tossing it the last few feet and it landed square on her stomach.

"Oh! Is this for me? It's so, so warm." She lifted it to her cheek. "This is the nicest thing anyone's ever done for me." Just as the compliment began to go to my head, she added. "This week." Then. "Except for Hope inviting me to her girls' weekend."

Still … "So, I'm not a skunk?"

"Still a skunk. But now I'm hot. Really hot." She left the bag by her cheek and fanned her t-shirt.

"No, Lynsey. You need to leave your shirt down."

"Why? I'm not the first woman you've seen naked. Didn't you say that yourself, Cam?"

Uh, yeah. Back when I was cupping her bare butt cheek in my hand. *Shit.* "Lynsey, if you're hot, give me the bag back."

"No way – you're not taking my skunk."

"Oh, the bag is the skunk now?"

"Yes, my skunk from a skunk." She repositioned herself, showing a ridiculous length of thigh.

"Seriously, Lyn, you'll freeze in the middle of the night."

"Whatever …" She gave her t-shirt the most vigorous flap yet. "My skunk will keep me warm."

"I give up." I turned to leave the room.

"Where you going, Cam?"

"To the shower."

"Right now?" Her voice had a wheedling, whiny, 'I'm-bored' tone to it.

From the safety of the doorway I turned back to say, "Let's just say I feel really dirty and I need a shower."

She made a gun with her finger and thumb, cocked it, and gave a hugely exaggerated wink. "Gotcha – I have a brother, you know."

Uh-huh. Great. This would probably be much easier if Lynsey was my sister, but my body was clearly reminding me she wasn't. In the bathroom, I dropped my jeans, shucked off my t-shirt and was one whisk away from losing my boxers, when her voice floated down the hall. "Wait, Cam … I just thought of something."

Thought of something. I was thinking of something, too, even though I was trying not to.

"Ca-am! Come back here!"

I grabbed a towel and held it in front of my far-too-flimsy boxers before heading back to the bedroom. *Do not sleep with her. You cannot sleep with her. She's drunk. She can't make good decisions. It might be hard, but just say no …*

I made sure to stop on the safe side of her threshold. "Yes?"

She had the covers back up under her neck. "Just don't use my conditioner, OK? It's super-expensive – I have to mail order it. That cheap stuff from Price Chopper is just fine for your purposes."

—

I GOT OFF TO a much-later start than planned.

Lynsey was konked when I got up. From her wide-open bedroom door, her bed was visible as a tangle of limbs, and sheets, and hair spread on pillows. Any thoughts I had of shaking her awake fled in the face of her gentle snoring. If she was that tired, there was no way I could wake her up.

She was going to have a long day ahead of her.

So, I loaded the coffee maker with fresh-ground beans and water and stuck a note on the front that read *Just flick me on for instant coffee.* I chased the chicken out of the kitchen … twice. The third time it – or its twin sister, because I had a theory our house chicken was actually two, look-alike house chicken*s* – popped back in through the everything-but-cats flap, I gave up. Maybe the chicken would wander into Lynsey's room and wake her up in time to open the pumpkin patch.

My trip put me smack-dab in the middle of tourist heaven. Making my way past the various Olympic venues on my way out of Lake Placid. Rolling along the smooth pavement of the always-scenic highway, at its absolute prettiest this time of year with fall colours blooming on the maple trees crowding in close to the shoulders of the road.

"How many people would give anything to be where you are right now?" I asked myself out loud. I *knew* the sentiment was true, but I wasn't feeling it.

It was true that, in leaving behind big city life and the never-ending responsibilities of the Biology lab, the last month of my life had been one of the most stress-free ever. I mean, sure, I was working really, really hard, but it was good, honest, physical work. And, yes, the farm had some cash flow issues, but those didn't feel personal. In fact, since I still had my own little nest-egg of savings, it was kind of fun to figure out how to stick within a challenging day-to-day budget.

But … alone with nothing but my own company for the next few hours, the old thoughts that used to cause stress were creeping back in. My parents, for one. Or two, I guess. Although mostly one, because it was mainly my mom who would be grilling me over Thanksgiving turkey about leaving behind *full-time work*, at a *world-class university* (emphasis her own) to do, what exactly?

Since I had trouble summing up my current job title, I was pretty sure it wouldn't impress my mother.

And that nest egg … I had a niggling fear at least some of it might be in jeopardy. I'd been pretty much counting on my almost-brother-in-law to come up with some kind of solution to my lack of vehicle. Jared owned a lot of land. Jared had owned a lot of pick-up trucks in his past. Surely one of them would be available for me to take off his hands? Right? Surely?

Up until now, I'd been firmly fixed on that as my solution, but now my brain was pecking away at, 'Why would Jared have a perfectly good extra truck lying around?' and, even if he did, how would I get it back to Lake Placid?

"Aarrgghh!" I cranked the radio on, full-tilt. These were the questions I didn't have to think about when I was avoiding being bitten by evil ponies, and safeguarding the chastity of drunken roommates, and chasing barn animals out of our home.

I should have just stayed there.

Which, no. That's not right. Even thinking about the island, even imagining driving onto the ferry, even picturing my sister's happy face, set up a deep tug in me. An ache for my childhood, and my background, and my country.

And that's not even counting the massive allure of a turkey dinner.

Turkey dinner. Maybe that was it. I was probably just hungry. Hangry, more like. Or, not hangry, but I was experiencing hanxiety. My blood sugar levels were probably rock-bottom. I was almost at

Watertown. I'd stop at the outlet mall and get some suitably salty, fatty, food court sustenance.

Good plan.

LYNSEY

MORNING LIGHT BEAMED IN through the window, hitting me square in the face once the sun climbed over the spike-like pine trees that rambled down the mountains and up to the edge of the farm. I groaned and rolled away, trying to escape impending responsibility just a little longer, and ran straight into something scratchy.

"Mmmf, Cam," I grumbled, throwing an arm out at the empty section of bed and hitting the feedbag. It smelled of barn, the faint scent of horse, and oats, and hay, and dirt.

And it was in my bed.

I pushed it until it took a dive to the floor, thumping onto the hardwood. Dragging the covers back over my bare legs, I tried to curl up and close my eyes again, but a throaty whinny from the barn dragged me right back to consciousness.

Consciousness, which included a truly magnificent headache and a stomach that felt like I'd eaten several rocks, was not a place I wanted to be. I closed my eyes again, fighting off the urge to be sick, and willing Matilda to give it a rest for just another hour.

I just needed an hour.

I drifted, only to be jerked awake by my phone's blaring emergency horn alarm I knew I didn't set. I slapped it, bringing it close enough to glare at the alarm, which was entitled Hungover Lynsey Needs To Sell Pumpkins Like A Champ.

Goddamn it, Cam.

I pushed myself to sitting, which was the worst decision I could have made. My tongue was tacky. My hair stuck to the side of my face, some of it clinging to my lips. And my head … well, my head didn't want to be connected to my body, as though it didn't want to deal with the ramifications of bad decisions.

"Ugh," I muttered to myself. "Tequila was a bad choice."

I made a mental note not to try to run with Hope's crowd, while being simultaneously stunned that Hope's crowd could drink me under the table like they had. Of course, I'd made it easy. Maybe I'd helped along the process just a little.

I had a brief flash to the wine bar, to Hope's friend Sylvia asking me what I was doing with myself and raising an eyebrow when I'd tried to explain Cam.

"You're living in a romantic comedy," she'd observed. "You'll be making out in the hayloft in under a week, and yes I would definitely watch this in movie form on Netflix."

Then, like Sylvia was some sort of witch, I could see it happening. Cam. Me. The hayloft. I'd flushed, and Sylvia grinned like a cat licking its lips over cream.

"I need to forget we ever had this conversation," I'd announced, turning toward the bartender and demanding their wine list. Two glasses of wine later and the hayloft was still at the forefront of my thoughts, which meant tequila was the only sure shot I had to banish it completely.

But then I'd come home to Cam standing on the porch, wrapped up in the farm's pine-scented darkness like it suited him just fine. And, oh, god.

Hel-lo.

I winced at my drunken self. I might as well have telegraphed the hayloft images in one word.

I rubbed at my forehead, pressing my fingers against the one troublesome spot and wishing I could go back a few hours. A few days. Hell, maybe a few months. Years?

I tried to think of one moment in time where my life wasn't a total wreck and couldn't come up with anything. Everything so commonly came down to time with Mom and time after Mom, both of which had their pitfalls because Dad was always involved, or Harris was going off the deep end, or Georgie was trying to navigate her own family's quiet implosion. I'd weathered those storms with my lists and my plans, slipping out into the bright light of day only to walk into my own confusion – ended relationships, ended school, ended jumping. Everything in my life was half-started and most definitely done.

Everything except Albert's farm. This was still half-started. A beginning, and a tentative one at that.

Maybe it didn't have to be ...

I stopped myself, put a pin in it. Temporary situations didn't get to be mulled over, especially when I had Matilda working her way into a scream.

"OK!" I shouted, as though she could hear me, and climbed out of bed. The headache exploded into fireworks behind my eyes, blotting out my vision with cascades of sparks. I stumbled into jeans, pulled on my shoes, whipped my bedhead hair into a pony-tail without pausing to brush it, and walked into the cool October air and into a forming parking lot.

"Ooooh, no." I stopped in my tracks, looking past the barn and up to the edge of the pumpkin field, where I could just see the bus shelter past the people making the trek to pick their own bright, cheerful, seasonal pop of happiness.

Pumpkinpocalypse was upon us, and I'd almost slept through it.

More importantly, I was alone, and a line was already starting to form at the bus shelter.

I did one last major rub at the throbbing point in the middle of my forehead. Then I put on my game face.

Then I really did run.

—

THERE WERE PUMPKINS EVERYWHERE. Dotted over the pasture, plucked up into the arms of the elderly and the young alike, sat upon by small children with camera-happy parents, toted down the hill to waiting cars, some smashed into pieces along the way. Truly, I was sick of looking at pumpkins and so hungry I thought I might keel over if I was forced to make change one more time. But a break?

No. There was no break. There were only pumpkins. I was

only just able to sprint to the barn, throw down hay to the animals, and squelch Matilda's incessant screams before another wave of pumpkin-eager townspeople took on the field.

But the till? The till looked *amazing*. Green, worn bills peeked up at me every time I opened it. Shiny coins. Dead presidents. I was so happy I could have kissed each one of them.

But I didn't, mainly because I was too afraid I might be sick all over them if I gazed on their faces too much.

"You look … terrible," a voice announced, drawing me away from my growing love affair with the money I was raking in. Hope stood in front of me, holding an Irene's bag and two travel mugs. She looked like a lumberjack goddess in buffalo check – somehow, even after the night we'd had. Although in the fuzzy haze that was my night, I remembered Hope waving off that third glass of wine. I had no memory at all of her touching any tequila. Panic gripped me – was I the only one pounding tequila at an otherwise serene girl's night? What was wrong with me?

"I thought I'd come by to help. The other girls are pretty, well …" Hope made a face, which drew all my fears to a quick, lurching halt.

"Oh, thank god," I said, catching the scent of coffee, and something greasy. My mouth started to water. "Are those for me?"

She beamed at me, holding up the bag. "Who else?"

"Come over here right now," I said, pulling her into the bus shelter and giving her a crash course on the pumpkins as I shoved my face full of food.

Slowly … slowly … the headache started to dim. I could see without squinting. Life started to look a little less like pumpkin chaos as Hope chattered with customers and we kept catching the money being thrown at us.

Hope nudged me, and pointed out at the road, which was clogged with cars parked on the shoulders. "Would you look at that?"

All I could do was stare, and for one hard moment I wished Cam was here to see it. Our first attempt at this making money thing was a raging success, and I lifted my phone to snap a photo for posterity. If Albert's farm was temporary, this was a permanent fixture in my life – a plan that wasn't perfect, but still came together. Gelled.

I took a deep, fall-tinged breath and let it out, satisfied, and slipped my phone back in my pocket just as I caught a glimpse of pale white go streaking out of the barn. Hope startled.

"Is that?"

"Matilda," I said, tensing. Hope looked from the streak of gray and back to me, then to the people. Then back to me. She waved her hands between us.

"Go!" she cried, pushing me toward the path of our wild mare. "I'll take care of this."

I went, slipping through people and darting down the drive, gravel skidding out from under my feet. Matilda was a flurry of hooves ahead of me, zig-zagging like a child behind the wheel of a bumper car, her tail and head up, ears pricked and forward.

"Matilda!" I shouted at her butt, and caught her ears swivel backward before they zipped right back to forward-ho. She trotted merrily past one paddock, past a stand of corn I was sure we'd need to figure out how to harvest soon, and then ducked behind a stand of trees. I ran after her, diving under a canopy that was just beginning to flush gold. The sun filtered over Matilda, splattering over her coat and illuminating her as she slowed to a walk, her head lowering to check out the patches of grass along the side of the drive. Grass she had most likely not yet sampled, if the way she tucked into it was any indication.

"You are so ridiculously bad," I told her, walking toward her and pausing at the sight of a barn peeking through the trees, worn wood the color of the rest of its surroundings – brown and dingy, easily hidden in the murky camouflage of pine and oak.

Leaving Matilda to her roadside sampler, I walked up the widening drive to the structure, which looked more and more like a garage the closer I got to it. When I turned the corner, a garage door accordioned at the ground, as though it had sunk down on its own weight. Next to it, a rusty door looked positively unwelcoming.

I peered in through the little square window on the door, the late morning light hitting equipment within. An old tractor perched on fat tires and – I squinted through the dim interior before I let out a laugh and tried the doorknob.

It turned. Of course it did.

Pushing the door inward, I looked around for a light switch. Nada. I pulled out my phone and turned on the flashlight, running the beam over the bright blue, if exceptionally dusty, old truck. Everything aggressively squared-off, not a nod to aerodynamics, a grill made of pure steel.

A Ford. The 1970s variety. A truck I was sure Cam would probably kill to own. Here it was, waiting patiently for someone to discover it. Who knew if it ran – if it was stuck in here it more than likely didn't. I imagined if it were less dusty and sad it might fetch some cash.

Not that it was mine to sell, but if Wes didn't want the property maybe he wouldn't want the truck either. Although he'd likely want to sell the truck, not give it away for me to … what? Give it to Cam?

Cam, who wasn't here.

Who maybe wasn't even coming back, some treacherous part of me whispered. I swallowed hard as I kept the flashlight trained on the truck's nose, wondering what good it was finding the exact thing a person wanted if said person might not be in your life again. And even if he did come back, it was all temporary, wasn't it?

I turned off the flashlight and took a step back, my headache surged forward. To hell with Cam. He wasn't here, and if he ever came back he'd have to earn the truck.

I was out of the garage before I could think more about it, trooping up to Matilda and snagging her halter, muscling her into line and hauling her back toward the barn like she was a petulant child and I was her bone-tired mother.

I pushed her into her paddock, and then retrieved Horace,

slipping his mild-mannered self in with her. When I turned back to the farm, Pumpkinpocalypse still raged on. When I got back to the bus shelter, Hope handed me my coffee mug and offered me a smile that dimmed a little as she looked around, as though trying to find something.

"Oh, I meant to keep better tabs on her," Hope said, casting a look out at the people swarming from their cars to the pumpkins and back.

"On who?" I asked.

"Hannah?" Hope asked, as I came to a very complete halt, staring at Hope as if she'd just casually dropped a grenade between us. Hope nodded, sure of herself now. "Yeah, she said her name was Hannah."

"Are you sure?" I asked, narrowing my eyes. Hope looked at me as though I'd just asked her something scandalous.

"Yes?" Hope asked back. "I mean, she said she was looking for Cam. I figured they know each other?"

Looking out at the people, I saw a pint-sized woman talking animatedly with someone who looked quite desperate to get away. She looked like a Bohemian princess – her dress was all crochet and lace, her scarf a delicate explosion of colorful birds, the tips of her hair dyed purple, the nose stud winking in the sun.

Then she turned to the bus shelter and paused. Then she waved, as if she knew me from long ago and couldn't wait to catch up.

"Oh my god," I said softly as Hannah began a floating walk

toward us, all the lace and crochet delicately waving around her legs.

"Oh my god," I said again as she descended on the bus shelter. Hope shifted nervously, concerned.

"Is there something I should know?" she asked. I didn't know how to answer. The words stuck in my throat, wedged there, not even allowing another 'oh my god' out when Hannah finally stopped in front of us and grinned. She smelled like every incense stick scent ever made all at once.

"Hi!" she exclaimed. "I'm Hannah. You must be Lynsey. Is Cam around? I can't *wait* to surprise him."

Chapter Thirteen

CAM

THE THING WAS, EVEN after eating an upstate-New-York-chain-restaurant-food-court version of a Philly cheese steak, I was still thinking of turning around.

So it wasn't an empty stomach, or low blood sugar.

I couldn't really describe it – it was just a feeling I knew where I should be, and that was Lake Placid.

I phoned Meg. The spotty cell coverage on the island meant if I wanted to actually speak to my sister, and not have the line crap out, I used the landline at the farm. Which meant, between horses, and farmwork, and running, and life, the chances of catching Meg at the end of the line were slim-to-none.

"Hello?"

"You're there!"

"Um, yeah, elbow-deep in a turkey."

"You're cooking the turkey? You don't even like turkey."

"Well, Jared's mom's having Thanksgiving with his aunt …"

"… and our mother isn't exactly the type to stand in front of a hot stove all day."

"Bingo. Which leaves me."

"You should totally go get take-out from the turkey supper at the church like we did that one year."

Meg made a soft *hmm* noise and I could picture the smile lifting her eyes. "That was fun."

For a second I felt horribly guilty about what I was about to do, but that was the thing – I'd already decided I was going to do it.

"Um, Meggers …"

"You're not coming, are you?" She made it sound like it was always inevitable that I wouldn't.

I needed to prove the worthiness of my intentions. "I'm in Watertown!"

"What? No phones in Lake Placid?"

"Don't be mad, Meg."

"I am so not mad. I'm actually a bit relieved you've come to your senses."

"And what's that supposed to mean?"

"You're a farmer now, Cam. Farmers don't get holidays off. They don't go away for long weekends. Especially not during harvest time. Do you know what Jared's doing right now? Let's just say it involves mud, and the great outdoors, and his tractor. He'll come in for a couple of hours but then he'll go back out. No hockey or football for him. Aren't you guys running a pumpkin patch? Isn't this prime pumpkin season?"

Prime pumpkin season. When she put it like that, my stomach twisted into knots. *What was I thinking?*

"Meg?"

"Yeah?"

"I've got to get home."

"Cam?"

"Yeah?"

"You called it 'home.'"

So I did.

—

I SCRAPED MY TRAY into the garbage and headed back for the mall doors. On second thought, I decided on a detour via the Walgreens for a caffeine-based drink and some peppermint gum – the long straight highway, three more hours of driving, and the cheesesteak in my gut were all likely contributors to me falling asleep behind the wheel without something to keep me awake.

On the way, I passed the wide-open entrance to a department store with stacks of "sidewalk sale" items out front.

I'm not a big one for marked-down, deep-discount crap, but when that crap has horses on it … I slowed, stopped, re-traced my steps.

In addition to being horsey, the print was actually appealing, even to me; a non-horse-crazy guy. And the kicker was, the print was on long johns.

In my mind horses + long johns instantly equaled Lynsey.

I reached for a pair, then stopped. She was pretty rude about me leaving. She called me a skunk. And despite that I gave her a warm bag, made with my own hands. I wasn't really sure if she deserved another gift.

The price, though. Fourteen-ninety-nine. I mean, really. I was pretty sure this was one of those purchases that would always figure in "the one that got away" section of my brain if I just walked away.

Meg.

Meg would also love these long johns. And Meg and Lynsey would be pretty much the same size. So, I could buy them, stuff them deep in my bag, see if I felt Lynsey was sufficiently deserving of them and, if not, I'd already have a leg up on Christmas shopping for my sister.

There. Decided.

Except … my hand hovered. What size to buy?

I'd been standing around for too long because a sales girl had found me. "Hi!" She had a ponytail that swung as she bounced over to me. "Can I help you out?"

She was chewing gum, which I'm pretty sure wasn't retail-service best practices, but it fit in with her upturned nose, lightly freckled cheeks, and her too-tight t-shirt that proclaimed, Happy :).

"Um, just looking at sizes, here."

"Oh!" She tilted her head, leading to more ponytail swing. "Well, if you like, I could totally try them on for you and you could see how they fit me." Then she winked.

Which was basically not-code-at-all for, "I could sleep with you if you like."

The first thought that flew into my head was, "*I have standards.*" The second was, "*Yup, and normally those standards would very much include a quickie with a cute and bouncy sales girl.*"

When did they change? What was happening to me?

Shit.

Even though I said, "No thanks. I'm good," I did allow myself to watch the sway of her hips as she went off in search of other needy customers.

I mean, after all, I might have standards, but I also had twenty-twenty vision.

In the end, the sizing decision got a lot easier when I realized the options went straight from small to large. I tried to picture Lynsey's face if I offered her size large. I thought my face might get smacked.

And as soon as I'd brought Lynsey to mind I had a sudden, vivid image of her in the horsey long johns. First thing in the morning, with her hair mussed up, and maybe one leg hitched up, and if the small was a little too tight, after all, that wouldn't necessarily be a bad thing … or, of course, Meg would like them, too. So, yeah. They were a good buy.

Very practical. And sensible.

I bought them and I left.

—

I couldn't get the miles behind me fast enough. It was probably the caffeine in my system.

I should be feeling guilty about my sister having to sit down to a turkey dinner she didn't even want, doing the heavy lifting of entertaining my parents all by herself.

I wasn't though. I couldn't retrace my route fast enough.

Getting a speeding ticket will slow you down. The thought helped me ease back on the gas.

Crashing the truck will really slow you down. I slowed another two miles an hour and tried not to think about the truck and how getting my own vehicle so I could return Hope's was something else I didn't fix this weekend.

Whatever. I had bigger things to worry about.

Like what?

Like … like checking to see if Lynsey actually woke up in time to open up today. Like making sure Matilda wasn't terrorizing any of our pumpkin customers. Like calming Lynsey down in the not-impossible case that no customers showed up.

Yeah, those important things.

Finally, finally, I was turning onto narrower, and bumpier, and more familiar roads. Finally, I was turning into our driveway.

It was lined with cars. OK, so no despondent Lynsey. One disaster averted.

There was a row of cars blocking my access to the cabin, so I found a place to leave the truck where it wasn't completely boxing anybody in, and I swung to the ground.

Walk fast … because it would work the cramps out of my legs.

That was why.

There were arrows pointing to the pumpkin patch. They looked pro. I had to admit it, if I didn't live here, I'd believe it was a true business.

People passed me going the opposite direction. Cradling pumpkins. Smiling and chatting.

Wow. Good job.

A group of four went by and when they passed, and I could see behind them, there was Lynsey in the doorway of the school bus hut.

She looked up, caught my eye, flushed, and smiled, and my insides lifted in a smile right back at her except, as quickly as the happiness had flooded her face, her eyes went even wider, and her nostrils flared, and she gave a small, but clear jut of her chin, and my eyes slid right past her to Hannah.

Holy Hannah …

If there was one thing I knew about Hannah it was that subtlety didn't work around her. Blunt, decisive, definite were the way to go.

One decisive stride took me right up to Lynsey, where I said, "I missed you, babe!" and cupped her face in both my hands, staring deep into her eyes. It was a move women loved. It always worked. It was guaranteed to make Hannah believe Lynsey and I were totally in love.

It was such a good move that I forgot about Hannah for a second as I marveled about how amazingly wide and shimmery Lynsey's eyes were. Wow. Then she narrowed them and she pushed forward, and brushed her lips across mine and, holy-oh-my-god, this was ridiculously hot, like I was washed with heat, and since I was already holding her face, I pulled it that much closer, and brought our lips more firmly together, and …

A child's giggle drifted across the pumpkin patch and I remembered, *this is not real, this is just for show*. And, speaking of children, the pressure in the front of my jeans reminded me I was about to put on too much of a show if I didn't pull back.

In a second.

OK, this second.

OK, now.

On "now" I made the tremendous effort required to step back.

Lynsey licked her lips, then with a huskiness I'd never heard in her voice before, said, "I found you a truck."

"Oh." Turned out my voice was kind of husky, too. "I bought you horse-print long johns."

Hannah, never one to stay quiet for long, spoke up. "Well, aren't you two a combination of weird and wonderful, all rolled into one?"

LYNSEY

TEMPORARY INSANITY. THAT'S WHAT Hannah could have very well been saying. We were temporarily insane. It was the only thing that made sense.

Kissing Cam certainly wasn't exactly rational, but I'm a quick study. I knew what he was asking me to do. I'd done it despite the phrase looping through my thoughts: *"This isn't happening, this isn't happening, this isn't happening."* Then, when he'd deepened what I'd started, sending a warm rush down my spine, a current of *"What have you done?"* warred with *"Now what?"*

Because, seriously, now what? At least one enquiring mind wanted to know, and if I went on the small smirk on Hope's face and the bemused, wide-eyed stare emanating from Hannah that was two more to add to the list. Not to even mention the healthy chunk of the Lake Placid area standing in our pumpkin patch. I remembered the phone tree.

Yup, we were so screwed.

Cam's hands dropped from my jaw and settled on my hips like that was a common, everyday occurrence and was not in any way abnormal. The space he'd put between us wasn't enough – *not at all*. My breathing was still a little ragged, my heart rate spiking well past my usual sixty beats per minute. I didn't know where to put my hands. On his arms? No – dear god, *no*. Touching Cam's forearms was absolutely forbidden. His chest?

I wanted to laugh and die at the same time.

"I thought you two weren't a thing," Hannah said, wagging a finger between us. Hope's mouth dropped in realization. Then she slapped a hand over it, as if keeping in the inclination toward truthfulness that wanted to pop out.

Cam squeezed a gentle reminder into my hip bones.

Play along.

He was still looking at me like I was the only person here. Like we were the only people here, which sent another flare across my skin in a full-body shiver. That was just great. Just *great*. I might as well have just lit up like a sparkler. He gave me a half-smile that also did things to me I did not want to linger too much on given the company we were keeping.

"Can't very well let a girl like this get away, can I?" he asked, working a thumb underneath my shirt and grazing against skin. I swayed, inching closer, and licked my lips again. Intentionally, I swear. Cam's eyes dropped to my mouth.

Not real. It isn't real.

Goddamn it, Cam.

"Excuse me!"

We all jumped. I yanked away from Cam and spun toward the growing line, which was headed up by a small woman with round glasses perched on the tip of her nose. Blue-gray hair sat like a poof on top of her head, not a strand out of place. She tapped her wallet against the bus shelter and then pointed at the girl in front of her, a pumpkin held in both hands.

"My granddaughter would like to purchase a pumpkin," she said. "And she's only nine, which I feel is too young to be exposed to this sort of public display of indecency."

My jaw fell open. The girl turned beet red and whispered, *"Grandma."*

"Whoa, wait a second," Cam started, just as Hope leapt in front of us.

"I can take care of you, Ethel."

"Of course you can, dear," Ethel sniffed. "Irene's is such a family-friendly business. I didn't know you partnered with these new owners."

She sniffed again, as if her first sniff was not heavy enough with disdain.

"Oh, for Christ's sake," another woman sighed, elbowing her way around Ethel and plopping a pumpkin down in front of us. She shook her long gray and black braid over her shoulder and gave an exaggerated eye roll. "Everyone knows what you always got up to during Summerfest every August, Ethel. It was a secret to absolutely no one. Let the young people be young. You certainly were once."

Ethel gave the other woman a pointed stare, which was met with a cheeky smile. The girl slipped off with her pumpkin. Hope quietly made change. Ethel snatched the bills from Hope's fingers and sniffed again, turning away from the booth and weaving through people back to the cars.

"Dang," Hannah whispered. "Is it like Puritan times down here?"

"No," the other woman barked, digging in her purse and producing a worn pocketbook. "Ethel is simply an unpleasant person."

"Mimi," Hope said, admonishing.

"It's true, isn't it?" Mimi insisted.

Hope made a face and shrugged helplessly.

"We were being a little, um …" I trailed off, not knowing where to go. Next to me, Cam tried, "Obvious?"

I blushed when Hannah slid a look over at us, most likely wondering why I'd lied to her. Or, even more likely, wondering if we *were* lying. After all, it wasn't like it was that long ago when I'd laughed at her when she'd flat out asked me if Cam was more than a friend. From her standpoint, I'd basically encouraged her to come here.

This had to look suspicious. Like a show. It felt obvious.

Too obvious.

Mimi dug through her pocketbook and produced the exact amount she needed, handing it straight to me. "Then it's nice to see a little obviousness around here. Lord knows this place has needed it. Now, when's Winterfest?"

—

BY THE TIME THE sun dipped under the horizon, and the last of the pumpkin-pickers had trundled off, my headache was gone. That was a win. The till was also stuffed full of shiny coins and velvety money, which was a *huge* win. I should have been fantasizing about dumping it all on my bed and taking a selfie with it. Actually, no, strike that. I knew I would have done exactly that if I'd been alone.

If Cam hadn't come home.

If Hannah hadn't shown up.

If Hannah hadn't *decided to stay*, which she declared right after I was done counting the precious, beautiful money.

"You know," she said, hands on her hips and crochet dancing

around her legs as the breeze kicked up, "I took an Uber from town to get here."

Cam, who had committed himself to being as obvious as humanly possible and was busy tugging playfully at my ponytail, stopped what he was doing and looked up at her with trepidation.

"Hannah …" he started, moving around me as I clutched the money bag to my chest, for the moment unwilling to part with my selfie plans. "I don't think …"

"Oh, I won't get in the way of you two," Hannah said, waving at me like I was a mere afterthought. It struck me as calculated. I narrowed my eyes, and Hannah sent a beaming smile at Cam as he approached her like she was feral kitten – mostly cute and harmless but armed with needle-sharp claws. "But I could really use a place to stay. The next train out isn't until tomorrow, and they kind of cut my credit card in front of me in Montreal. Who does that? I thought it was only done in movies."

"It *is* only done in movies, Hannah," Cam told her, and Hannah pouted. It was the pout of a professional.

"Well, that doesn't change the fact that I really need a place to stay for the night," she said, glancing up at him through her eyelashes. "Please?"

Cam was silent. It was unnerving.

No, I whispered to myself, willing him to say it. *Say no*.

"Why are you even here?" Cam asked.

Hannah cut a quick look over at me, because this would be a perfect time to point a finger at me, say I was the one who basically told her *"Come on down, Hannah! Go you! Girl power!"*

Which is probably why she wasn't totally buying the show, I thought gloomily, which meant I was still buzzing with Cam's little touches and flirty innuendo for absolutely no reason.

That bothered me, even when it shouldn't. Cam's problem wasn't my problem, I repeated to myself. It didn't matter if I'd had a secret phone call with Hannah. I could have blatantly invited her to the farm. I could have left them to figure it out, end their insane thing like rational adults, even though I was starting to wonder if any of us were at all rational.

"Look, I'll be honest," Hannah said, pulling her attention from me and snapping back to Cam. "I was upset earlier. I thought you didn't want to see me, which sucks because you know how I react to people not wanting to see me. I just … I get a little forward sometimes, which isn't fair to you. Just because I know what I want doesn't mean you know what you want. I should respect that, and I do."

Oh, ouch. That would've hurt if I'd been in a normal, loving relationship with Cam, man who didn't know what he wanted.

Then I felt it. The sting.

Damn it. Now I was pissed off.

Cam wasn't saying anything, which meant Hannah knew how to weasel her way in where she wasn't particularly invited.

Well, I could play this game.

"Hey, Hannah," I called. They both turned to me, Hannah startled that I was still there, and Cam startled that I was inserting myself. I wound an arm around Cam's, smiling first at her and then up at him, lingering as I kept talking. "Sure. Stay. You're welcome in our home."

"Wait," Cam started, only to be cut off when I put both hands on his face and tipped onto my toes, kissing him perfunctorily on the mouth, like we did it all the time. A hello kiss. A goodbye kiss. Unsexy but devastatingly secure.

"I'm going to go down and bring the horses in," I said, and fell back to my heels, still smiling and playing the game like a freaking champ. "Want to help? I'm sure Hannah will want to get herself settled."

"I …" Cam started, looking confused. I wanted to shake him, get him back on point. Game face, Cam. Come on. I raised both eyebrows, and he tried, "Yes?"

I kept smiling, serenely, like nothing was weird about any of this, and turned to Hannah.

"The guest room is the first bedroom down the hallway," I told her, taking Cam's hand in mine and making sure to weave our fingers together. Then I tugged, pulling him toward the barn as I kept talking. "It has Cam's things in it – storage is such an issue in small houses, you know? Don't mind it; make yourself at home. We'll be up in a little bit. Just have to feed the animals and pull some *hay* down from the *loft.*"

Hannah tilted her head, confused by my need to accentuate certain words. I didn't care. They still filled me with a kind of joy that should have deeply disturbed me if I took the time to fully consider what I was implying.

I squelched the need to laugh, and spun toward the barn, taking Cam with me.

Chapter Fourteen

CAM

"SO ... WHAT?"

"What, what?" Lynsey asked.

What just happened? What's going on? What's Hannah doing here? What are you doing inviting her to stay?

"What, *everything* ..."

Lynsey furrowed her brow. "I don't even know what that means."

We were nearly at the barn now. "You know what? Neither do I. Maybe by the time I've shoveled some manure and tossed some hay, I'll be able to articulate it."

Lynsey shrugged. "So you're saying barn chores first, talk later? That works for me."

There was something too quick, too compliant, too agreeable in her acceptance of my answer. Lynsey was not one for accepting my suggestions, for making my life easy. Lynsey's middle name could be Backchat. Something was up, but I was hungry again, and tired, and I had enough confusing things spooling through my brain without adding a too-nice Lynsey as one of them.

I picked up a pitchfork and started pitching, and let my mind wander.

By the time the stalls were bedded, and the water buckets were clean and full, and each hay net / manger / feed bin was full of pellets / hay / grain, I had a list of organized and prioritized questions in my head.

Then I simplified them. Because really, they all boiled down to one, main question, which was:

What are you not telling me?

That was it. Bottom line. There was a feeling in the air of concealed information; a sensation that always made me squirm.

I'd experienced it before, when I was nine and the goldfish I'd won at a booth at the Eastern Ontario Fair suddenly looked bigger, and perkier, and a slightly different shade of orange than it had when I'd gone to bed the night before, and a solemn, five-year-old Meg led me to the kitchen garbage and showed me the discarded "Pet Haven" plastic bag.

I'd known it not long after I moved in with a girl I quite liked, and while I was out shoveling the driveway our neighbour had stopped to chat and mentioned all the UPS packages we received. "Every day," she'd nodded. "Sometimes twice." The next day I'd been in the drug store when the UPS guy came in. He was tall, he was wearing shorts in January which showed off some very buff legs, he smiled with huge, white teeth, and the woman behind the counter giggled when he handed over an envelope. I went home, straight to our recycling, where I found not one single cardboard box, but did notice our sheets whirring around in the washing machine. For the third time that week.

"You good?" Lynsey called out, which was code for *"I'm letting the animals in – prepare for the stampede."*

"I'm good."

I opened the stall doors as wide as they'd go and stood in my favourite quiet corner where I could watch Matilda scramble, and the goats scamper, and the chickens bob and weave, on their way through the barn and into their respective stalls.

Horace came last, and instead of plodding straight into his stall he strolled over to me and pushed his face against my chest, and sighed, and Lynsey, walking in behind him, said, "Is there something going on here I don't know about?"

I bit back the right-on-the-tip-of-my-tongue retort of, *"Why don't you tell me?"* because of the peace, and of how badly I didn't want to shatter it.

Instead I said, "Horace and I have come to an understanding," and once I walked him to his stall, I turned to Lynsey and said, "Now, how about you show me this famous truck?"

—

As we set out, those words keep spooling through my head, *"What"* step *"are you"* step *"not telling me?"* But as I followed Lynsey down our drive, and along the shoulder of the quiet road – as my feet crunched on the gravel, and the cold hit my cheeks and filled my lungs, and as my eyes followed the wash of bright-as-day-moonlight bathing the worn-flat road surface and picking out the tallest plants in the tangle of past-its-prime wild undergrowth beside us, I relaxed.

This was where I wanted to be. This was why I came back. This was OK.

After not-that-many steps we came to a second – not quite a driveway – but a sort of graveled inlet. I was surprised I'd never noticed it before, but it was the opposite direction from the way we turned to go to town and before the leaves started to fall it would have been more hidden.

"There it is," Lynsey said, pointing at a slightly lopsided building, and those were the first words she'd said since we left the barn, and that was also weird, but *focus*, I told myself, *truck*, and I walked up and grabbed the handle on the garage door just as Lynsey said, "No! I don't think that's a good idea!" and the entire door came away in my hand.

I made a valiant effort. I really did. The words *I don't know my own strength* spooled through my head, except, actually, the limits of my strength became very clear when I was up against an awkwardly oversized metal door completely detached from any kind of mooring.

In retrospect, the thing to do would have been to let go and run backward. Fast.

Which, of course, is exactly what I didn't do. I took one step back and thought, *Buck up, Cam, hold this thing up.* I took another staggering step – with my knees beginning to buckle, and told myself to count to three and give it one good heave and I'd be fine. *One-two-three* and a deep breath and the final surge of effort I expended did nothing at all, except completely deplete me and that's when I gave up and let myself go down with the big door on top of me.

"Cam!" There were scrabbling noises; they sounded like fingernails on metal, followed up by more, "Cam! Omigod, Cam! Are you dead, Cam? Say something, Cam."

Turns out, when spread across my entire body, the door wasn't that heavy. More like a weighted blanket. It was actually kind of comforting. Sound was muffled in the contained space and I took a few seconds to just slow my breathing and flex and release all my muscles and confirm nothing was broken, or even strained – I was just a stupid guy lying under yet another broken item on this farm.

Lynsey was kind of freaking, though. And the ground was fairly cold, with particularly sharp bits of gravel connecting with bony parts of my body. What finally motivated me to move was the fear that Lynsey might throw herself on the door in some kind of misguided attempt to move it and then it would be dangerously heavy.

Not that I'd tell her that.

"I'm OK," I said.

All the sounds from the other side of the door stopped. "You are?"

"Yes. Fine."

"Are you sure?"

"Uh-huh. How about we both push the door in the direction of my feet and it should just slide off."

"Where are your feet?"

"Oh." I kicked. "Got that?"

There were scurrying sounds and the moonlight that was trickling in from the head end was blocked by an obstruction I assumed was Lynsey's body. "Got it," she said. "Heave?"

I answered, "Ho!"

I gripped the corrugated metal as best I could, and the whole door slid a good several feet down so I could feel a current of fresh air on the top of my head.

"Good," I said. "One more? Except be careful because my head's right here. Maybe lift a bit if you can?"

There were noises very close to my head and Lynsey said, "OK! Heave again!" and I did, and she did, and suddenly my head was out and I was lying on the ground looking up at Lynsey's legs straddling my head and I said, "This is not how I imagined our first date would go."

She dropped the door a little too quickly, given it was still on the bottom half of my body, and kneeled on the ground beside me, and made a noise that could have been a sob, or could have been a laugh, and said, "Thank god you're alive."

Then she contorted herself in some weird, pretzel-like way

that allowed her to lie half-beside, half on top of me and grip me in a hug that – perfectly honestly – felt more likely to smother me than the door had, but she offered body heat, and I was pretty sure I'd glimpsed a tear in her eye so I kept quiet and hugged her back.

She smelled of hay, and horses, and the autumn night. She smelled of home.

"Oh, Cam …" Her voice came from somewhere south of my ear and was filtered through layers of hair and clothing. "It's my fault Hannah's here."

"I figured."

"I didn't turn your GPS off when you asked me to."

"I figured."

"And, also, she phoned and I answered and she might have kind of said she was coming, and I might have kind of said, 'Go for it,' or maybe it was, 'Right on, sister,' or something like that, but, in my defence, I didn't think she actually would."

"Lyn?"

"Yeah?"

"I met Hannah in court."

A muffled snort traveled to my ear. "What was she in court for? Stalking?"

The night was so quiet I was pretty sure I could hear the penny dropping in Lynsey's brain.

"Oh. Shit. Really? *Stalking?*"

"Well, close enough."

"You should have told me."

I tried to nod, but some part of Lynsey's neck, or chin, or jaw limited my movement. "I probably should have, and I didn't, so let's just call it even. But, Lyn?"

"Uh-huh?"

"Maybe let's try telling each other stuff from now on?"

"Hmm …" She lifted away from me, and I was suddenly so, so cold. Against the moonlight I could see the silhouette of her head tilted to one side and she said, "Sure. I can make that deal. So how about we start with you explaining why you're back here?"

Oh. That.

Somehow it hadn't occurred to me that Lynsey might ask. Which, yes, stupid since Lynsey's not the type to just let things go.

The thing is, I hadn't concocted a ready-made explanation, so I was left half-trapped under a door not sure exactly what to say to the girl staring down at me.

"How about we get me on my feet, and I finally get a look at this mystery truck, and we'll talk about it on the way back to the house?"

—

THE TRUCK WAS A thing of beauty. Even I could tell that, and I'd just spent the last ten years vigorously avoiding vehicle ownership by cycling through winters where temperatures frequently hit minus thirty and the average winter snowfall was over two metres.

The engine was also so, so simple that I felt like I could probably fix it myself. "Not that I'm going to try to," I said. "We can ask Lewis and Hope who to call, and I'll pay for them to come out this week and give it an overhaul."

"Do we have the money?" Lynsey asked.

"We'll need to," I said. "If we're going to keep living here, we need a truck."

"*If* we're going to keep living here," Lynsey said.

I was running my hand over the hood, trying to figure out what kind of shape the paint was in under the multi layers of grime. "Yeah. That's what I said."

"*If.*"

There was something in her tone that reminded me of the sob-laugh of earlier. A hint of hysteria.

"What's wrong, Lynsey?"

"Well, we've never talked about it, have we? I mean I've pretty much given up my entire life to feed chickens and sell pumpkins – at this time of year I'd normally be somewhere much warmer than this." She lifted her hands and waved them through the increasingly chilly night air. "Much cleaner, too. Whichever house I was living in, my room would be bigger than the entire shack I'm now shar-ing with you. I wouldn't have to rinse chest hair down the shower drain in the morning …" She shuddered, "… at least I tell myself it's chest hair. I wouldn't have had to learn that orange juice comes from concentrate …" She dropped her hands to her side like that was the final straw, which is when I unwisely interrupted.

"I actually prefer orange juice from concentrate."

"Oh, hell! Of course you do, Cam! And that's also why any day now you're going to decide to go back to the biggest metropolis within spitting distance of the Arctic circle, where everybody's getting their igloos ready for winter, and where I can't even pronounce any of the street names, and you can shack up with some girl called Marie-Josee, or Marie-France, or Marie-frickin'-Pierre – like, seriously, what kind of name is Marie-Pierre? – but you won't care about her name because she'll be all exotic, and French, and cigarette-skinny, and she'll say your name with an accent, *"Oh, Ca-méron,"* and she'll keep you warm at night while I'm out here in the sticks freezing my boring old run-of-the-mill American ass off."

When she finally stopped she was breathing hard.

Again, with the benefit of twenty-twenty hindsight, what I should have said was, *"There's nothing run-of-the-mill about your ass."* What I actually said was, "We totally don't live in igloos."

I should have known better, but it just came out, and that's when Lynsey balled her little hand into an effective-looking fist and let fly, and I ducked out of the way, and tripped on a rut in the dirt floor of the garage and on my way back up caught my nose on the wing mirror and, well, let's just call the result a major blood-letting.

I couldn't see, because of having to lean forward to try to let all the blood bypass the front of me and land straight on the floor, but I could hear Lynsey's hiccupping sobs.

"Don't cry," I said.

"Oh, Jesus, Cam ..." She took a juddering breath. "I'm so sorry, but I'm laughing my ass off."

"In that case, help me." I held my arms behind me. "Pull my jacket off."

"Why?" Fortunately, she was pulling while she was asking.

"So I can do this." I reached for the hem of my shirt and pulled the whole thing up and over my head, and held it there, in a ball under my nose, seeping up the blood.

"Now …" This time it was my voice that was muffled. "Do you want to know why I came back here today?"

"Yes."

"Because …" I was very close to another quip – something that would round out the orange juice concentrate, and igloo comebacks with a perfect three – but I'd made a deal with her earlier.

I tentatively lowered the shirt and the former waterfall seemed to have slowed to a trickle, so I risked talking with no facial obstruction.

"I got to Watertown and I called Meg and … how do I explain this? … have you ever gone outside in the cold with something not tucked in properly, or maybe without socks on, or a scarf?"

Lynsey pointed at my shirtless torso and held up my jacket.

"Yeah, yeah, point taken." I placed the bloody shirt on the hood of the truck, and shrugged into my coat, zipping it all the way up. "Anyway, the point is, when you do that – when I do that – I can always feel that place where the cold's getting in. I can feel the missing piece and it doesn't feel right until I fix it."

Lynsey looked at me the way only a Florida girl could look at a Canadian guy using cold weather as an analogy.

I plowed on, though. I was committed.

"That's how I felt in that mall today. There was a piece missing, and the further I went, the worse it felt, and that piece was here; it was this place …" Lynsey's mouth was open, lips parted, eyes fixed on me the way a kid's eyes fix on you when there's only one present left under the Christmas tree and they're waiting to see if you'll say it's for them. "… and you, Lyn."

She flew at me, full-tilt, arms open, and by the time I said, "You'll get covered in blood," it was too late, because she was already hugging me.

I put my hand on the top of her head, and said, "There's no 'if' and I'm not going anywhere. I'm living here. But I'm not living here with Hannah. So, let's go get rid of her."

Lynsey stepped back and looked up at me. "How?"

"Well, now that you mention it, I just had a thought about that." I pulled the truck door open – because, of course, it wasn't locked – and reached in to find the key carefully stowed in the ignition – which, of course, is where everybody stores their truck keys – and I turned it.

The engine caught. Then it rumbled to life.

It might not be quiet, but it was a beautiful sound. "Hop in!" I yelled over the noise of the motor bouncing around inside the garage.

Once Lynsey was in the passenger seat beside me, and we had closed the doors, it was actually possible to speak. "This is how."

"How, what?"

"You asked how we were going to go back."

"*Communication* …" I'd heard that tone from women before.

Exasperation was the polite description. I was also familiar with the I'm-going-to-say-this-really-slowly-so-you-understand way Lynsey continued. "*No*: I asked how we were going to get rid of Hannah."

I grinned. "Oh, that. I actually have a pretty good idea. You just practice saying that thing you said before – '*Oh, Caméron,*' – that's absolutely perfect."

Then I eased the truck forward, rolling through the puddle of blood on the ground, and taking a wide detour around the garage door strewn across the driveway.

LYNSEY

"Should I maybe know a little more about the plan?" I asked as we left Cam's truck parked in the driveway and approached the house. Light blazed from nearly every window, and I wondered how our house chicken was faring with Hannah. Part of me suspected we'd open the door to a heap of feathers and a pot boiling over in the kitchen. Cam squeezed my hand, and the thoughts thankfully scattered.

"The likelihood is you'll nix it if I tell you," Cam admitted.

"You realize, I hope, that goes against our telling each other things decision," I point out. "You remember that, right? It happened literally a few minutes ago."

"Hey," he said, pulling me to a stop and drawing me around to face him. "You trust me?"

Any words I could have chosen to answer him with got caught in my throat when he put his free hand on my jaw, looking at me like he did when he was trying to be obvious in front of Hannah and everyone with access to Lake Placid's phone tree. Cam stroked his thumb along the edge of my chin, and I wanted to bat his hand away because it was both bloodied and too distracting for me to think properly.

I didn't. Even though by all rights I should have, because who were we pretending for here? What were the chances Hannah was looking out the window? And even if she were, twilight had fallen dramatically. We were standing in near darkness with Cam's confessions swirling around us, making me wonder if any of this had ever been pretend.

The flush on my skin certainly didn't feel like pretend. Neither did the strong urge to inch further into Cam's space and see what he'd do if I kissed him again. I'd never been anyone's missing piece before – that much I knew with complete certainty – but the farm was temporary. Cam was temporary. That meant, even for all the ways this might very well be real, *we* were temporary.

We had an expiration date, and I had no idea when Wes would call up and kick us out.

"Then what?" I whispered to myself, realizing too late that the words had come out of my mouth when Cam's eyebrows drew together.

"Huh?"

I pulled away, throwing a hand over my mouth. "Nothing,"

I said against my palm, and then rolled my eyes, putting my hand down. "It's nothing. Of course, I trust you." I waved at the house behind us. "Walk on."

"OK," he said slowly, taking my hand in his again and walking us toward the treacherous steps. "Just follow my lead. Remember she's already suspicious, and if experience has taught me anything it's all or nothing with Hannah."

"So there's no chance you'll just sit down and have a rational conversation like adults?" I asked, hoping there was still a way out of this even as I tip-toed up the steps after Cam. "Can't we just have a heart-to-heart and call her an Uber? Hell, I'll pay for it. I'm sure I still have at least one functional credit card."

"You're a horse racing person," he said, leading me across the creaking porch. "Surely there's a colorful term for no shot in hell?"

"Personally, I don't think *long odds* really encapsulates …" I squeaked when Cam spun me around like we were dancing, only instead of performing a graceful waltz across a ballroom I tripped over an exposed nail and landed against the front door like I'd been thrown against it. My shoulder blades and the back of my head stung from the impact, and Cam winced.

"Yeah, sorry, one more thing to fix," he said, and put his finger to his lips to quell my rising need to speak loudly and with force. It was when he put his hands on my hips and pressed me gently back into the door that the need to tell him to handle this himself dissipated. And mainly that was out of curiosity to see what he would do next, which I could see coming a mile off but still stood with bated breath, waiting with my heart thumping chaotically like I was still in the middle of the Ironman, gasping and eager to cross the finish line.

Cam closed the miniscule distance between us, squeezing out the cooling autumn air. I tipped my chin up, following his motions and standing right on the edge of pretend and real life as he paused, looking into my eyes like he was standing right there with me, wondering the same exact thing.

"You ready?" he asked, which pretty much destroyed my theory.

"Are you kidding?" I asked, ire rising again.

He grinned and ducked to my level, kissing me. I fisted my hands in his coat, as though trying to strangle some part of him in effigy, only then he pulled me away from the door and hauled me up against him. I made a little, girly gasping noise. It was a noise that made the part of me who was pretending cringe because it sounded entirely too real. Breathy. And then there was Cam, who was a man who could only take that sort of noise as blatant permission to deepen everything.

Which he did. Of course he did. He was Cam, after all. Man with no morals, which seemed like a diminishing problem when his hands climbed up my sides and his mouth slanted over mine.

My back met the door again, the thunk barely registering as I let go of his coat and wound my arms around his neck, keeping him against me like I was afraid he was going to sprint off into the night and leave me alone with Hannah.

Hannah. Right, *Hannah*. Who surely had to be right on the other side of the door by now. Where the hell was she? What was she doing? Taking a nap? It was past six o'clock. No one takes naps past six o'clock.

"Lyn, I …" Cam started to say against my lips, his voice going past husky and verging on something that made me so warm I suddenly didn't care what we called this. Pretend, real, temporary, whatever. I liked it. That was enough for me.

"Stop talking," I ordered against his mouth, kissing him.

"No, really, I just need you to be prepared," he said, curling an arm around my back – a firm bar of pressure that kept me locked between him and the door. "You might …"

"Why are we even talking right now?" I asked between kisses. "We could be doing other things."

He groaned, and I smiled, letting myself melt against him, which was the exact wrong thing to do because the door fell open with a whoosh of air and a surprised squeak that definitely wasn't mine.

Mine was more of a guttural yell. Only Cam's damned forearms kept me from hitting the ground.

"Oh my god!" Hannah gasped. "I heard scratching outside and thought maybe it was a raccoon family nesting under the porch, but …"

"No," I said, stopping her there as I tugged my clothes back to presentableness before remembering I hadn't been presentable from the start. "It's just us being insatiable or whatever the kids are calling it these days."

Hannah tilted her head at me like a collie, which was when I noticed she'd changed into a short, shimmery bathrobe. Pale pink silk, printed all over with flying cranes. She was barefoot, a toe ring winking from her left foot. Her hair was piled high on her head and artful tresses were left to frame her face, like she'd been caught in preparations for a long soak in a bathtub we definitely did not possess.

Well. Not suspicious at all.

I glanced over at Cam, eyes widening at him to silently send all my raging thoughts at once. He only nodded and rubbed a hand over his mouth to hide all reaction to the glowing beam Hannah sent his way.

Oh boy. This was going to be harder than I thought.

"Are you both … OK?" Hannah asked, her eyes falling to the balled up, bloody shirt in Cam's hand. We were still speckled with red droplets, and probably looked rough enough around the edges to presume we'd gotten into a fist fight between the barn and the house.

"Better than fine," Cam said as I blurted, "Accident!"

That earned us another head tilt. Then she shook her head, waving off our weirdness.

"Well, I'm glad you're both finally here," Hannah said, gliding past us and padding into the kitchen, motioning for us to follow. I went tentatively, peeking inside to find her patting the house chicken, which was roosting on the countertop next to the ancient toaster.

"Does the chicken have a name?" she asked, as I began to pick up on clues that Hannah had cooked. The kitchen smelled like rosemary with a hint of jealousy.

"It's a chicken, Hannah," Cam said. "So, no."

Hannah considered the chicken. "It looks like a Caroline."

She nodded her head definitively.

"Strong name," I said, and she grinned at me just enough to show teeth, which meant maybe it was actually genuine. It was hard to tell, especially when she quickly abandoned the chicken – Caroline? – and picked up a wine glass, which was far too sparkling to think she'd pulled it out of wherever she'd found it without cleaning it.

"I brought wine," she announced, picking up the bottle – already open and waiting – and pouring several glugs into the glass. She handed it to me. "Originally I had planned to share it with Cam, but since the situation on the ground has changed, I want to make a toast."

She poured two more glasses, handing one to Cam and lifting hers toward the ceiling. I made a half-hearted effort to join her while Cam watched us with bemusement, refusing to move. I elbowed him in the side, because I was raised to have manners no matter the situation, and he sighed, holding the glass in front of him.

"To Cameron and Lynsey," Hannah said, sugary sweet. "Sometimes you find love in the strangest places and with the least likely of people, surprising everyone along the way."

Cam looked up at the ceiling and pressed his lips together. I forced a smile.

"And who knows?" Hannah asked, bouncing on her bare toes. "If the two of you can make this work then anything is possible!"

"OK …" Cam started, moving to put the wine glass down. I grabbed his hand, keeping my forced smile until it felt strained.

"This is really kind of you, Hannah. Both Cam and I …" Cam kept looking at the ceiling, staring at it with such abject focus I thought for a moment he'd found something he was adding to his mental list of home improvements, like a mysterious water stain or cracks signaling our impending death via cave-in. I considered the ramifications of getting trapped with Cam and Hannah and started talking faster.

"We're grateful, honestly," I said. "Sometimes we get home after all the farm work is done and there's just no time …"

"Especially considering I have an incredibly hard time taking my hands off you," Cam broke in, effectively cutting off my babbling. A flush hit my skin, and if the satisfied smile on his face was any indication I must have looked as pink as I felt. Cam took a swallow of wine and shrugged a shoulder. "It's really too bad Hannah here thought there were raccoons under the porch, considering what I had wanted to …"

My phone mercifully cut Cam off before my skin could go from pink to an atomic red. I pulled it out of my pocket, letting out a breath of relief at Georgie's name.

"Hold that thought," I said, and then paused. "Better yet, let it dissipate."

Cam smirked, and I pointed at him, mouthing *be good* on my way out of the kitchen. The second I knew no one could see me, I ducked back out to the porch, took a gulp of wine, and answered the phone.

"Please tell me there's good news," I whispered into the phone. "I need good news."

"Why are we whispering?" Georgie whispered back. "What's going on?"

"I'm in a bit of a hostage situation," I said, slipping further down the porch and taking another sip of wine as I explained how I had gotten into this mess, from the finer details of GPS to making an entire town believe I was in deep, oblivious lust with Cam. "In short," I concluded, "I'm glad someone cooked dinner, but I'm also fairly sure she's not wearing anything under that robe."

"Can we backtrack just a little to the kissing?" Georgie asked, somehow straight-faced even as I was beginning to wonder how I was making it through this day without breaking into maniacal laughter. "I thought this wasn't …"

"It isn't," I insisted. "Cam and I are very good roommates who …"

"Kiss," Georgie finished for me. "That's called something else, you know."

"I'm aware that logically it is called something else, but these are mitigating circumstances."

"Which you chose to mitigate through kissing," Georgie pointed out. "So whatever this is – good friends, roommates, mutual squatters, *whatever* – you now have to add *with benefits* at the end of it until the situation changes." Then she paused while I tried to grapple with the thought of benefits associated with Cam. If Hannah hadn't been inside the house, what happened on the porch just now would have led to benefits. Of that I was sure. Of course, none of this would have happened had Hannah not been in the house, so my thoughts were a circle. A maddening, rapidly cycling circle.

Georgie said something muffled, like she'd deliberately put the phone down. Then I winced through the sounds of grappling, Georgie's muted "Harris!" all I needed to be prepared when my brother commandeered my best friend's phone.

"So I was right," Harris said, making me roll my eyes and take another sip of wine. "You *are* shacking up with the Lake Placid guy."

"The only thing you're right about is the vicinity and the shack," I grumbled.

"Oh, no, little sister." Harris sounded entirely too amused. "I think I'm right about all of it. Call it brotherly intuition and advanced eavesdropping skills."

I heard a squeak, followed by a sound I could only describe as Harris attempting to avoid Georgie's swipe. More grappling followed, with Georgie reclaiming the phone and announcing she was putting it on speaker.

"So how's the living together thing going?" I asked. "Sounds super solid."

"Are you seriously trying to turn this around on us?" Harris asked, incredulous. "I'm far more interested in finding out how the mutual squatting with benefits with the nameless man you picked up seemingly at random is going. Dying to hear about it, actually."

"Harris, don't take this the wrong way, but you're probably the last person I will be asking advice in regards to Cam."

"Ah, the nameless man has a name," Harris chuckled. "That's a start."

"In fairness," Georgie broke in, "it might not be a bad idea to get Harris's opinion on this. He is, you know, male."

"But is that a good enough qualification?" I asked.

"Wait," Harris said. "I'm not playing armchair psychologist for you, Lyn. You can make all the questionable decisions you want; just make sure you use condoms. That's all I ask."

"Oh my god," Georgie groaned. "You know what? Let's start over with what I was originally calling about. The horse."

"Yes, please, the horse," I agreed.

"The horse is a good story, actually," Georgie said, only to be immediately followed by Harris's, "I'd say it depends on your definition of 'good'."

"It's *good*," Georgie reiterated over him. "Lost Cause may have been a flop as a racehorse, but he could have plenty of talent doing something else."

"Back up," I said. "What's the story?"

"Just a high-priced dud," Harris said. I could picture him shrugging one shoulder, being so unflappable in the way he threw his words around. "But what would you do if you paid through the nose for a dud?"

"Put him to stud," I said immediately.

"And what would you do if he was found infertile?" Georgie asked.

I blanched. "How much bad luck can one horse have?"

"Worse," Harris said. "Owners gelded him and brought him back to the track thinking a change of mindset might fix things, but …"

"Nope!" Georgie broke in cheerfully. "Still horrible."

"Finished up the track the same day we won the Whitney," Harris continued. "Last time he ran."

Huh. I leaned against the house, thinking I must have seen him. He probably walked right past me, those little dots glowing in the sun, and I hadn't even noticed.

"But then he fell off the radar," Georgie admitted. "Last time anyone saw him was Saratoga. I called up his previous trainer and he said the owners wanted to wash their hands of him."

"You know how it is, Lyn," Harris said. "Friend of a friend knows a kid who's interested in a jumping prospect. He put him on a trailer and sent him north."

"He said it was a good home," Georgie added.

"Apparently that equates to a junkyard," Harris countered. "They heard good home and didn't bother sending anyone to check out said home to find out if it was much good."

"We don't know anything about it," Georgie pointed out.

"Not really."

"I know a former record-setting yearling is sitting in the middle of nowhere with a puncture wound waiting to happen," Harris said. "Even if he weren't who he is, and even if the intentions are good, it's still reckless and stupid."

"But what is Lyn going to do about it?" Georgie asked. "He's literally not hers to do anything with. So far, the only thing lacking is less than perfect environmental conditions, which is not a deal breaker as far as I'm concerned."

"How am I living with someone with this much optimism?"

Georgie laughed, the grappling beginning again. "You love it."

"OK," I broke in. "I'm hanging up before this gets awkward."

"Fine by me," Harris replied, over a girly shriek.

"Tell me when I get to come visit!" Georgie called, followed by the sudden clattering of what I suspected was the phone falling to the floor.

"I'm hanging up now!" I yelled into the phone, hoping they heard me and then wondering why when it was clear no one was paying attention. I pushed the phone back into my pocket and stood in the dark, happy for my brother and Georgie while also feeling incredibly … flustered. Flustered with the horse across the road and what I was going to do about it, and with Hannah and how I was going to get her out of the house. And, of course, Cam.

Flustered didn't even come close to describing what I was going to do with Cam. Harris's words about reckless good intentions pinged around in my head, right along with Georgie's. All of this might be reckless and stupid, that was true. The big question was what was I going to do about it.

I looked down at the glass of wine, trying to drum up some courage that wasn't liquid-based. I was going to need it.

I took a sip anyway to steel my singing nerves, and marched back into the house with my game face on. I wasn't sure how well I accomplished it after a day of hungover pumpkin wrangling, but by the way Hannah jumped back from Cam as though I'd shot a gun at the ceiling I figured I managed well enough.

Cam was where I'd left him – perched against the table and wine glass untouched – but he'd changed into a fresh shirt and cleaned the blood off his face. Hannah fluttered through the kitchen, her silk rippling in her wake as she crashed through the effort of looking like she'd never had her thoughts on anything other than dinner. I raised an eyebrow.

"Sorry about that," I said. "Call from home. What did I miss?"

Cam held out a hand to me and I took it easily, watching him as though from outside myself when he reeled me in until I was tucked against his side like I simply fit there – a puzzle piece recently found.

"Absolutely nothing," he said, kissing me lightly and lingering a little too long, going that one moment past a socially acceptable hello kiss and crossing into blush territory. Get a room territory. I half expected Hannah to scream it at us from across the kitchen.

Cam pulled back just enough to break the kiss. I leaned forward instinctively, my forehead brushing against his. He lifted a hand, cupping the back of my head, our eyes locking. The kitchen fell away. The table we were sitting on, Hannah on the other side of the room, every lie we'd told to get here … it all stopped.

It was just us, staring at each other, stuck in an improbable situation that felt heavier with each passing second.

But then the timer on the oven began to buzz, and Cam let me go, and Hannah cried, "Dinner!" The kitchen snapped back into crystal cut clarity and I needed to put my game face back on.

First things first: get rid of Hannah.

Everything else would have to wait.

—

"So this is true exhaustion." I collapsed on my bed, the springs squeaking. "Like, there's mental exhaustion and physical exhaustion – both of which I think I've felt before, but this …"

I rolled a look over at Cam, who was pulling on a t-shirt at the foot of the bed. His hair was still damp from the shower, as was mine, since we'd unified into a front of two – never apart. Dinner? Together. Clean up? Together. Shower? If it wasn't technically together, at least we'd let Hannah think it was, and that was the important thing.

"I'm going to sleep," I announced. "Like the dead. Then I'm sleeping in. Think Hannah brought artisanal coffee, too? Or would it be too much to hope?"

The corner of Cam's mouth lifted. "If you're incredibly lucky Hannah will be gone before you ever find out."

I closed my eyes. "You describe bliss," I groaned. "Imagine, if you will, just the two of us. Why does that sound so impossible after one night of your ex-girlfriend running the place?"

"'Ex-girlfriend' isn't exactly the label I'd use," Cam replied.

"Right," I nodded. "Momentary Lapse in Sanity would be better."

"Come on. You haven't had a lapse in sanity?"

I heard Cam move around the bed and I cracked my eyes open, watching his approach. His hair was in toweled disarray, forearms deliciously bared, and all of him very … close. Especially when he stopped by the bed, nearly brushing against my legs.

"My family doesn't do sanity very well as a general rule," I said, pushing onto my elbows. "It's entirely feasible that I was someone else's lapse, not the other way around."

He shook his head. "Just so you know, I strenuously doubt your entire premise."

"Oh, do you?" I arched an eyebrow.

"I do," he said simply. "First, if you had lapse tendencies we'd be in very different positions right now."

I snorted. "You mean we'd be naked."

"Yes," he nodded. "In the simplest of terms. Clothes wouldn't be involved."

"In this scenario, would Hannah still be in the house?" I asked. "Because these walls are incredibly thin and …"

I trailed off when his eyes bounced to the wall separating the rooms. Then, as if on cue, the floorboards squeaked – the telltale sign of restless pacing. Hannah was on the move. Cam cleared his throat.

"So, here's the thing," he began while I stared at him with wide, unblinking eyes, realizing what he was going to say before he said it. "We've been on point all night and I am very proud of you for keeping this going, Lyn, but we need a clincher. Right now, those thin walls are the best opportunity we're going to have."

"I am not having sex with you," I blurted. He looked down at me, confused.

"What? No. Of course not, at least not with Hannah …"

"If you keep talking the slim likelihood of sex ever happening goes down by the syllable," I threatened.

"I'm simply proposing we fake it," he said, lowering his voice.

"Do I look like an even marginally good actress to you?" I whisper-hissed. "I can't even fake an orgasm; how do you suggest I fake a deliberately fake orgasm?"

"This is a lot of information I would rather not know right now," he said while I waved my hands in the air.

"Then help me out here, Cam!"

"OK," he nodded, and leaned over me, putting a hand on each side of my hips. The crappy mattress sank down, both of us shifting. I tipped my head back, eyeing him suspiciously when he asked, "Are you ticklish?"

"What kind of question is that?" I asked. "Of course …"

"Because my helping is dependent on your being ticklish."

"Oh my god."

"Lyn," he said, stopping when I shook my head.

"Fine." I poked his chest with one finger. "But I swear if this doesn't work you are …"

I bit back a shriek when his hands moved to my sides, already anticipating the inevitable. He worked his way up until his fingers met my ribcage and I fell back on the bed, which let out an impressive, bouncing squeak.

"Cam!" I cried, biting my lip when he raised an eyebrow at me and wiggled the tips of his fingers until I gasped and twisted. "Oh my god!"

He smiled, and I smacked his arm. The pacing in the other room stopped, the floorboards going silent, meaning all attention was on us. Cam climbed onto the bed with me, the mattress sinking and no doubt rusty springs protesting loudly. Then the rickety metal headboard slammed into the wall. I covered my face with my hands, sheer embarrassment warring with an increasing need to scream.

Cam crouched over me, hands moving down my sides and eliciting a breathy gasp out of my throat when he trailed fingers over my abdomen, finding another spot that was way too close to actual intimacy for comfort. I nudged him with my foot, which he captured in his hands.

I glared at him. He mouthed, "Oh, Cam," and dragged a finger down the sole of my foot, making my back arch off the bed involuntarily.

"Oh!" I slapped a hand over my mouth, also involuntarily. Cam squeezed my big toe and I ripped my hand away, digging deep within myself to find the acting skills necessary for this sort of insanity. "Cam! Oh my god."

I hit the wall for added effect, ignoring the chuckling from the foot of the bed, which squeaked merrily underneath us, the frame trembling, sounding like a bolt was coming loose.

When he finally stopped, my hair was in my face, chest heaving, all of me a bright pink blush. The stopping by itself might as well have been orgasmic by the way I sighed.

Cam tapped my ankle, reminding me.

Oh, Cameron.

The words came out of me easily, my eyes locked on his. He grinned crookedly, and let go of my foot, placing it softly back on the bed and crawling up to lay down next to me, letting out his own sigh.

From Cam's room, the door opened and slammed shut. Heavy footsteps trundled past my door to the bathroom. Another door slammed, and the shower began its cacophony of spits and gurgles.

I threw an arm over my flushed face. "She better not use the good conditioner."

Cam laughed. "After that performance, I think I owe you all the good conditioner you want for life."

I rolled a look over at him. He watched me hopefully and I shook my head. "You're still sleeping on the floor."

He sighed, pulling a face.

"I thought as much," he admitted, sitting up and grabbing the blanket off the foot of the bed while I wormed under the covers and reached for the light.

"Hey, Lyn?" he asked, his voice drifting up from somewhere near the foot of the bed. I paused.

"Yes, *Cameron*?"

"Thanks."

I grabbed the extra pillow and tossed it to him, smiled at the answering *oof*, and turned off the light.

Chapter Fifteen

CAM

WHEN I WOKE UP, everything was stiff.

There was, of course, a tried-and-true, old-as-the-world-itself solution to that, but so far the only sex Lynsey and I were having was fake, so I opted for the second-best solution and, trying not to groan too loudly as I rose from my sleeping spot on the floor at the foot of the bed, pulled on loose clothes and running shoes.

I left behind a coffee-maker ready to be switched on, two sleeping women (snoring, I might add – both of them), and a chicken. Hen, I think. I could tell by the three white feathers at the tip of her otherwise-reddish-brown wings. "You're not a Caroline, are you Hen?" My eyes strayed past her to the coffee can I'd just emptied and I experienced a lightbulb moment.

Two minutes later, with the help of a Sharpie and a pair of scissors, I settled our new coffee-scented self-serve money bank on the windowsill of the bus shelter next to a sign reading *All remaining pumpkins $2. Please leave cash in our can (or give it to us next time you see us).* I signed it with a smiley face and *Cam and Lynsey*, and looked at our two names side-by-side for just a second too long before shaking my head and remembering. *Run.* That's what I was here to do.

As I set off down the driveway I was trying to figure out whether it would be a good or bad thing if Hen wandered into Hannah's bedroom and woke her up.

Then I thought about one or two fun ways I could have woken Lynsey up. Then I reminded myself this run was about getting less stiff, not more, and I conjured an image of the dusty truck I'd just left behind. Tires. A muffler. The engine block.

Gorgeous in its own way, but the opposite of titillating. Just what I needed.

Run, Cam, run.

Lake Placid was rewarding me for coming home.

At least that's what it felt like. There was a softness in the air I wouldn't have expected after last night's frosty temperatures, and the unseasonable mildness was raising a mist in the fields I ran by.

My muscles warmed and loosened quickly, and even the rubber soles of my shoes seemed softer than they had for several weeks now. They made a spongy *thwuck-thwuck* sound as I ran, as opposed to the more definitive *slap-slap* of colder mornings.

What to do today? I didn't need a calendar, or an organizer – I just needed my morning run to get my life in order.

Well, all the farm chores, of course. Plus pumpkin clean-up. I'd made a point of keeping my head turned away from the pumpkin patch as I ran down the driveway. Now, in the daylight, I was afraid to face the amount of work to be done following yesterday's onslaught.

I needed to go into town for some food – I had a vague idea of finding a turkey breast at the Price Chopper and cooking a mini-Thanksgiving dinner for Lynsey and me. Which led to something else in town. The bus station. Please, please, please let me be driving Hannah to the bus station today.

There was one more thing, too. Coin rollers. What I'd seen of the cash box yesterday told me many people had paid in quarters. And a surprising number in dimes and nickels. This was odd to me. Ever since Canada adopted dollar and two-dollar coins, and got rid of the penny, Canadians don't tend to think of nickels and dimes as "real" money. Clearly that was not the case in Lake Placid, and since Lynsey and I needed all the any-kind-of-money we could get, we needed to roll those suckers.

Maybe it was because my run started with thoughts of Lynsey. Maybe it was because my dreams had been full of Lynsey. Maybe it was because having heard her giggle with complete abandon in a way that sent little bubbles of joy popping in my chest, I wanted to hear that giggle every single day … or, probably not, maybe it was just because there were only so many running routes around here and this one was particularly pretty …

… whatever it was, I ended up standing at the fence right

where I'd encountered Lynsey the other day, staring across the field at the horse who appeared as a dreamy, soft-edged silhouette in the morning haze.

"Hi, buddy-buddy-buddy." I started quiet, voice low and sing-songy. I was also feeling soft-edged and like a dreamy part of the morning. I had an image of him ambling toward me, head out, giving me a Horace-like greeting.

He totally ignored me.

"Hey. You." Soft edge gone. Clarity. Enunciation my lawyer mother couldn't find fault with.

The ear he flicked toward me was almost worse than no response at all. It essentially said, *"Dude, it's not that I don't know you're there. It's that I don't care."*

Finally I resorted to "Yo!"

Which resulted in a lifted head. *That was more like it …*

He faced me, flared his nostrils, tested the air – I can only presume for bakery scones – and, finding nothing of interest gave a very long, loud, rattling, and – to my ears – insulting, snort, then dropped his head back to the grass.

Why did Lynsey want this horse?

She did, though. Just the same way my sister Meg had wanted the horse she called her "heart horse." The difference was, at that time, our family was in the market for a horse. Meg had to do some convincing to get that particular horse, but an equine was definitely in her future.

Lynsey and I, on the other hand, already had two more horses than we had the time or money to take care of. Not to mention the goats. And chickens. I mean, if the pumpkin field hadn't already been planted, I'm not sure we could have afforded the big orange squash.

Movement. Camouflaged by the mist, but definitely there. Up by a trailer I'd assumed wasn't fit for human habitation.

It might not be – fit, that is – but unless there was an animal around here that walked upright and coughed – because that was definitely the sound of a cough floating through the still morning air – then somebody was living in that trailer.

And I had to assume that same somebody owned this horse. The horse Lynsey wanted.

Then again, Lynsey also wanted a cappuccino maker, an en-suite bathroom (with heated towel racks), central vac, and a perpetual supply of fresh-squeezed orange juice. And those were only the requests she'd mentioned this week.

She found me the truck …

What would it hurt to knock on the trailer door?

The morning might be unusually mild, but it still wasn't warm enough to stand around in sweat-dampened clothes indefinitely. So … walk up to the trailer, talk to the inhabitant, ask about the horse, then resume my run.

A plan. Good.

Turns out there was no trailer-door-knocking required.

Once I got within the range of visibility afforded by the still-dense morning mist, I could make out a woman, sitting in one of those webbing-woven aluminum folding chairs – the kind that are so old that funky new companies have sprung up and started making them again using words like "vintage" and "retro."

I had a feeling this woman's chair was an original because, from her beehive hair-do, to her garment which, with its light quilting and shapeless construction my grandmother would definitely have called a "housecoat," she herself was coming across as pretty vintage.

Her long, thin cigarette holder completed the impression.

As strange as this encounter was, my mother's conditioning was strong. It made me establish eye contact, walk up to the woman, hold my hand out, and say, "Good morning."

She looked me up and down, and said, "Well, look what the cat dragged in."

An important lesson in perspective. If you think someone else looks weird they, looking back at you, will probably also see something strange.

Fair enough – young guys wearing shorts and a t-shirt, arriving on foot and steaming excess body heat into the cool fall air were probably not this woman's everyday kind of visitor.

"Yes, ma'am. I'm sorry for the first impression. I hadn't expected to speak to anyone this morning."

She took a long, slow drag, lifted one carefully penciled-in eyebrow and said, "Yet here you are, speaking to me."

"Yes, well, it's about the horse."

"What about the horse?"

"My friend has become fond of your horse."

"Are we talking about the crazy girl who comes and stands by my fence?"

"With all due respect, ma'am, that girl is not the craziest woman in my life."

She gave a short, sharp cackle, which turned into a gasp, which turned into a long, hacking cough. When she regained the ability to speak she said, "I've thought of setting the dogs on her."

"I really wouldn't recommend that, ma'am."

She drew herself up straight in her lawn chair, and said, "And why not? This is my property."

I shook my head. "Oh, it's not that. It just wouldn't work. Animals love Lynsey."

She narrowed her eyes. A long column of ash fell from the end of her cigarette to sprinkle the ground. "Do *you* love Lynsey?"

Whoa. I did *not* see that coming. I had been starting to feel the morning cold but I was suddenly flushed with heat again. "I've become very fond of her."

She crossed her arms, shook her head. "That's not good enough."

"I'm sorry? What do you mean?"

"You look me in the eye, tell me you love that horse-crazy girl, and we can make a deal on the horse. Otherwise, piss off, don't come back, and tell that chick you're so 'fond' of not to trespass on my property, because if dogs don't work, I own a gun."

—

FORTY-FIVE MINUTES LATER I led the horse up our driveway.

The screen door slammed open, the chicken ran out, and Lynsey followed her. The difference was, where the chicken half-flapped-half-kind-of-sort-of-flew down the stairs, Lynsey mostly tripped. She somehow got one foot down on a lower step, then another one under her on the ground, then took a few stumbling, running paces toward my equine companion and me and said, "What!?!"

The horse threw his head up, ears forward, nostrils flared and I was pretty sure he was also thinking, *"What!?!"*

"I brought him home."

"You what?" She might have been asking me but she was fixed on the horse. Hands out, eyes wide, not blinking, hardly breathing.

"He's ours. Yours. I brought him to you."

"To live?" She was whispering now, focused on the horse reaching his nose out to her.

"Yes. To live. Forever. Yours."

So much for horse whispering. She squealed, the horse took a four-legged sideways leap, he landed on my toe, and that's how Lynsey's dream horse came home to live with us.

—

I WAS INSIDE, FOOT hiked up over my knee, examining the place where my toenail used to be. Lynsey was supposed to be making me toast and coffee. Except she was permanently glued to the window.

"Lyn?"

"Huh? Yeah?" She didn't even look my way.

"The toast popped a while ago."

"Uh-huh … sounds good."

"Lynsey. Normally I'm all for getting up off my ass and taking care of myself but I've kind of lost a toenail here."

She smiled out the window which I assumed meant the horse had done something incredibly adorable like take a step, or eat a blade of grass, then said, "You might not lose it, Cam. It might still be OK."

"Lynsey. It's gone. Ripped off. Strangely enough, my running shoes don't have steel toes."

"Who has a steel toe? Ewww … yuck!" Hannah glanced at my foot on her way past. "You've just gone from a nine-and-a-half to, like, a seven. Or maybe less. I just can't do …" She waved her hand toward my foot. "*That*. Feet things."

She nudged Lynsey. "Hopefully somebody else feels differently about that than I do."

"Mmm … yeah. He does have beautiful feet. Although on horses they're called 'hooves' Hannah."

Hannah snorted. "Boom! Didn't take you long to get thrown over for a horse." Then she popped my two pieces of toast onto a plate, reached for the butter, and said, "These are a little cold. It's going to be hard for me to spread the butter."

HANNAH AND I WERE cruising down the road on what was turning into a truly beautiful morning. I wasn't living up to the aesthetics of the day, though.

I ran my hand through my hair. Dried sweat made it stay

where I pushed it – I needed a shower. My stomach tightened and growled – I needed food. I blinked, rubbed my eyes – I needed coffee.

But that could all wait. Hannah had asked me to drive her to the bus station and, figuring out I wasn't going to get any special treatment for my injury, I'd decided to suck it up and shove my toe into a sock before shoving my foot into a work boot.

It was all worth it to get Hannah back to Montreal, because as soon as I did that I could go home and have a shower, and drink coffee, and get back to normal.

Whatever that might be.

We passed the now-empty field where, up until this morning, Hazard used to live. I hadn't gotten around to mentioning his name to Lynsey. It somehow didn't fit with the bubble of blissful sweetness-and-light she was floating around in.

"Eyes on the road," Hannah said.

"OK, OK, it's just …"

"Just what?"

"That's where the horse was living."

"Oh *the horse*. Yeah. *That*."

"What's that supposed to mean?"

She waved a hand in the air. "We'll get to discussing your love life in a minute. However, first there's just one little wee, tiny thing I have to mention."

Wee. Tiny. These words, coming from Hannah spiked my heart rate. She had once asked if we could take a small detour on our way to dinner, and we'd ended up at a jazz bar in the old city of Quebec. Which was a two-hour drive from Montreal. It had snowed while we were there. I didn't get back home for twenty-four hours.

"The thing is," she continued. "I don't actually have money for the bus."

"Oh!"

"Why do you say it like that?"

"Because *that* I can help you with. In fact …" We were on the edge of town now, and I flicked my indicator on, and turned left into a parking lot. The bank parking lot.

I hopped out of the car, wallet in hand, and found I was whistling. As I reached the bank machine I recognized the tune – Jay-Z's *99 Problems* – once more my subconscious was working away.

How much could a bus ticket to Montreal cost? The balance in my bank account was lower than I'd like it to be but I didn't hesitate to double the amount I was thinking of taking out, just in case. There was no way I was entertaining Hannah for another night because I was too stingy to withdraw a bit of extra money.

Money shoved in wallet, wallet shoved in pocket, I was about to turn back to the car, when I noticed movement in the bank. A teller. It was open.

A sixty-second detour got me what I wanted and I was back to Hannah, dropping into the driver's seat, still humming.

"You look happy," she said.

"That's because we're going to get scones."

"We are?"

"Definitely."

True, the scones hadn't been part of the original plan, but this balancing act with Hannah was a delicate one. If she decided driving her to the bus station was the source of my happiness, I might as well call Lynsey up and tell her to put a mint on the "guest" bed pillow for Hannah's return.

Besides Hope's scones could put anyone in a good mood. Even spiky, suspicious visitors from Montreal.

—

SCORE ANOTHER WIN FOR Hope.

Hannah and I were sitting on the bench in front of the Visitor Centre that also served as the Lake Placid bus terminal, and I had every reason to believe Hannah intended to get on the bus when it arrived.

She had a ticket in her pocket, twenty dollars for the ride, a coffee in one hand, and a goody bag from Hope in the other.

We were cruising. We were trucking. Hannah could go on with her life, and I could go on with mine.

Win-win. Mutually beneficial result. All good.

Hannah turned her face to the late-autumn sun, stretched like a cat and I took a deep breath because a relaxed Hannah was a manageable Hannah, then she turned her face to me, opened her eyes wide, before narrowing them again, and said, "Now, for that talk about your love life."

Sh-i-i-it ...

"Ye-e-es ..?" I was both desperately wondering when the bus

might arrive while knowing, with every fibre of my being, that checking my watch, or my phone, would be a death sentence.

"So, here's the thing. Yesterday's storm-in-and-kiss-the-girl move." She gives a yes-no-yes flip of her hand.

"I mean, Lynsey seems to be a pretty cool, independent, kick-ass kind of girl … why would she be interested in you? Don't get me wrong – the kiss was pretty hot – but, I mean, some of my most smokin' kisses were with people I've never seen before and will never see again – there was actually this one guy I just happened to run into outside the bathroom at a truck stop …"

"Hannah …" I warned.

"Yeah, yeah, OK. This is not the time for my sweet memories. Back to yours. Specifically, the horse thing. Frankly, that was over-kill. On its own I would have pegged it for a big fake – I mean, who randomly picks up a horse for a girl, no matter how serious they might be?" She shook her head. "So, if I say I was fifty-fifty on the homecoming kiss, and you got a failing grade for the horse stunt … that leaves last night."

Last night.

The thing is, thinking about last night sends a genuine flush through my body. There's nothing fake about the increase in my heart rate. Because the way Lynsey giggled made me want to bury my face in her neck and nuzzle her with my day-old stubble.

The way she squirmed made me want to wrap my arms around her and hold her close.

The way she said my name … well that was a whole other

ballgame. That's where the pick-up in my heart rate came in. That's why I suddenly felt uncomfortable manspreading on the bench with Hannah. Because I wanted to make Lynsey say my name that way again, but this time for real.

Preferably without Hannah in the next room.

"Hmm … yeah, that's what I'm talking about." Hannah had her head tilted on the side. "Because that was real, wasn't it? I mean, if anyone should know real, good sex, it's me … am I right, Cam?"

I blink. "Yes, sure."

"No, seriously Cam, remember the time we used my yoga trapeze?"

"I … sure … I remember." I pulled something deep in my groin, and had to climb stairs facing the wrong way for a week while it healed. I was pretty sure that wasn't the memory Hannah was trying to stir, though.

She sighed. "OK, I give up."

"You give up what?"

"If the mention of the yoga trapeze doesn't make you want to buy me a ticket on a later bus so we can spend a couple of hours tackling new adventures here in upstate New York, then you really are well-and-truly gone."

"Gone?"

She made a *pfft* noise that sent stray bits of hair blowing away from her face. "Past hope. A lost cause."

"Lost cause?"

"Oh …" She leaned forward and a genuine grin spread across

her face. "You didn't even realize it, did you, Cam? Maybe you actually thought you were faking it …"

There was a rumble, a roar, and the noise of gears shifting, and a hulking bus lumbered around the corner.

Hannah rose to her feet, snugged her bag firmly over her shoulder, and when I stood as well, she leaned in tight, placed her lips by my ear, and whispered, "You, my former lover, are in love with that girl. A completely lost cause."

—

I DROVE BACK TO the farm wondering if I should be driving at all. I felt … I wasn't sure. Drained? Emptied out? Exhausted? Definitely detached from reality. Not drunk, but as though I was nursing a hangover.

It had been a long, eventful twenty-four hours. I'd been torn between homes, caught between girls. I'd secured us a horse – funny that the very real act of getting the horse was the one Hannah had doubted the most. I'd balanced truth and pretense. I'd kissed Lynsey, and only pretended to kiss her.

I'd been asked if I loved her, and told that I did.

What was true? What wasn't?

I turned off the road, trundled up our driveway, and said out loud, "As if I know."

When I brought the car to a stop, I wasn't at all surprised to see Lynsey, foot up on the bottom rail of the fence, chin propped on her arm resting on the top rail, watching the horse.

I grabbed the bakery bag Hope had packed for her, stepped

out of the car, and walked over.

When I reached her, she half turned to me. Like Hannah, back at the bus stop, her head was tilted, her eyes narrowed against the sun.

Unlike Hannah, I wanted to cup Lynsey's face with my hands and kiss her until we both fell backward into the long grass.

"Lost cause," she said.

My heart stopped. Breathing ceased. The whole world was quiet for one, then two, long seconds. I swallowed, but no words came out, which is when Lynsey – now with eyebrows furrowed – repeated. "Lost Cause. The horse. That's his name. I never thanked you properly for bringing him."

Oh. I let out a long, shaking exhale. "It's, um, fine. My pleasure. All good."

"Are you OK?"

Check. Heart beating again. Lungs pumping. "Yeah, I'm fine. I'm great. Hope sent baked goods."

"Perfect!" Lynsey reached for the bag and I settled in to lean on the fence and eat sugared scones and think if this was what being lost was all about, maybe it was OK.

LYNSEY

"So what's the story with this guy anyway?" Cam asked, fishing in the bag and pulling out a scone. Out in the paddock, the gelding lifted his head, nostrils flaring for the scent of sugar. Ears pricked, a low nicker rumbled up from his throat, and he swung into a walk with gusto. Scones were about to be served.

I nibbled on the corner of my own scone, wondering how best to put my answer to Cam's question into words. Why this one? This horse, in particular? It was as good a question as any, since when it came right down to it when was there ever a concrete answer?

This one. That's all I'd been thinking since I'd caught sight of him, like a fateful loop. A siren song. Over and over.

This one.

I looked at Cam and found him watching me steadily, eyes bright and searching, like he was reading the answer right off my face. Then they dived lower, to my mouth, and I wasn't prepared for the flush that hit my cheeks.

"Oh, I don't know," I said, tearing my gaze away and focusing on the gelding's approach. "I guess there's something intriguing about finding a formerly 9.6-million-dollar yearling in a scrapyard."

Cam gagged on his scone, coughing loud enough to startle the horse, who leapt into the air like a spring and tore into a huffing, overly dramatic retreat to the opposite side of the paddock while Cam hacked into one cupped palm, his eyes watering.

"What?" he managed to sputter. "Nine point *how much?*"

I tentatively smiled, raising my shoulders. "Million. Million*s.* Lost Cause was quite the stir."

"How the …" Cam shook his head, trying to fashion words and failing. "What did he … Why …?"

He smacked a hand against the top rail of the fence and leaned against it, while I eased into his space and rubbed what I hoped was a comforting circle on his back. Finally, he took a large breath and began again. "9.6 million dollars."

"Uh-huh," I said softly, more like a humming than anything else.

"Do you even want to know what I paid for him?" he asked.

"I'm really hoping it wasn't a lot, because he's seriously not worth 9.6 million dollars now," I said, my circles coming to a stop. I let my arm rest on his back, caught up in cocooning within his warmth. The early autumn air was cooling, but here, next to Cam, it didn't seem so chilly.

Cam shifted next to me, and I lifted my hand, intending to give him space only for his arm to come around me, keeping me anchored to his side by the fence. I swallowed; mouth suddenly dry around the prospect of whatever precipice we were standing on together. The will-we, won't-we.

Now, without the need to put on a show, the atmosphere was different. Heavy with an impending series of decisions I didn't know how to make. Instead of facing them head on, I looked out at the paddock, watching the gelding lift into an airy trot – striding down the far fence with enough lift and upward motion to make me think I might get into dressage yet.

Eventing. I could do eventing.

"Bit of a dud, huh?" Cam rumbled against my hair, surprising me that he'd managed to get so close while I was busy fantasizing about all the things I could do with this horse.

Wow, I was a goner.

I pulled back and looked up at Cam, refocusing.

"Oh, big time," I laughed.

"And they named him Lost Cause?" Cam asked, incredulous. "Right off the bat?"

"Big ticket yearlings tend to be embarrassments more than not – really they're pissing contests between the Emirates and the old Irish farms. The guy who paid all those millions had a sense of humor about it. Guess he knew deep down what he was getting into. So if you spent some secret nest egg on him, *please* tell me you didn't do that, and thank you, again, because this is ..."

I ran out of words to describe what this was. No one had done this sort of thing for me before – the big grand gesture that sets hearts aflutter in romance novels. I was half convinced they didn't happen, because who was ever this good to someone else?

But that was old Lynsey talking. Lynsey of the family Armstrong, who would never give away a horse for nothing. Mine was a family of contracts and stipulations, money changing hands as horses walked through auction rings and crossed finish lines. Life was a transaction. There wasn't any room for what Cam had done, and even worse, the very concept would only earn a smirk or a sneer. Contempt. That's what I was used to, so the warm fuzzy feeling in my chest was a high I wanted to curl around, keep close forever.

The corner of his mouth lifted, and he let me go. Cooling air rushed between us, and I visibly shivered, then rushed to cover it by hugging my arms to my chest. If Cam noticed, he didn't say anything.

"I wouldn't worry too much about the secret nest egg," he said, "because I didn't pay for him … as such. Just promised to shovel Agnes's stairs every time it snows this winter. Hope it's not a snowy winter …"

"Agnes?"

"She's a firecracker, that Agnes."

"And she just gave him to you, for free snow shoveling?"

"That was the deal," Cam nodded. "After she threatened to chase you off her property if she ever saw you again – which she did, by the way, see you. All the time, apparently. You were right not to go trespassing, although honestly I can't really envision her aiming a shotgun at anything …"

I blinked at him. "So, his papers?"

Cam shrugged a shoulder. "I don't think Agnes had them. She was calling him Hazard, not Lost Cause."

I let out a short, loud laugh. "That's quite the barn name."

He gave me a look. The you've-got-to-be-kidding look. "She didn't seem to be using it out of what I'd call great affection."

"Well, I like it," I said. "Hazard. Seems appropriate for all the money that was lost on him."

"Speaking of money," Cam said, reaching into his back pocket and pulling out a small stack of papers – all a dull cardboard brown and marked with blue, orange, green, and red stripes. I caught the markings on the one facing me – $2 Nickels. "How about we finish the wine Hannah brought and take care of the ridiculous amount of change Lake Placid emptied on us?"

"By, what, wrapping it in paper?" I asked, taking one of the slips and discovering it was really a tube. "Do people spend time doing this?"

"Here they do," he said. "Back home …"

"No, wait, let me guess," I said, handing back the wrapper. "Canada banished coinage from their lands."

"I detect the sarcasm, but they actually did banish the penny," he said. "That Americans still pay for things like pumpkins with loose change is honestly appalling."

"We're a people of great mystery," I smiled up at him, shifting ever so slightly into his personal space, like an unspoken challenge. "However will you cope?"

Cam paused, looking me over while I waited for him to react in kind. Move closer. Closer still. I wanted to tip onto my toes and see if the scone had left sugar on his lips, and then I wanted …

Oh, hell, where did I even begin?

Cam took my hand, and a surge of adrenaline rushed through me, letting me know without any preamble that I already knew.

"I've got a few ideas," he said, and then tugged me gently toward the house.

—

"You were serious about this," I said after I made my last fold on my second roll of dimes. Ten dollars down and – I eyed the pile of coins on the scuffed coffee table, then picked up my wine glass, taking a sip to fortify myself. Next to me, Cam chuckled to himself and kept sliding nickels into a blue-striped sleeve.

"Deadly serious," he said. "You asked me about coping mechanisms? Here's one: finding just a little control in madness. That's a fine way to cope because in case you hadn't noticed we're surrounded by a lot of madness."

He motioned to the pile of coins, just as the house chicken strutted across the shag carpet, pecking at a few fuzzy tufts. Cam swept his arm toward the hen, giving me a look like all of this was the perfect example. Stray change, a chicken no one could account for, the sagging roof, the rundown farm, Matilda screaming at Horace, and Hazard's inexplicable history. All of it – ours and not ours. Madness.

"Today it's a pile of coins and an ex-girlfriend," he said, while I gave him a sidelong look at the word *ex-girlfriend*. He hustled past it. "Tomorrow the porch steps might finally fall through, and if we're lucky neither one of us will be on them when they go."

"Is this you saying you're finally going to fix the porch steps?" I asked hopefully.

Cam gave me one of his crooked smiles as he finished up his sleeve of nickels. "I was actually just using it as an example in my extended metaphor about life here being wildly satisfying in an insane kind of way."

"Wildly satisfying?" I asked.

"In an insane kind of way," Cam reminded me. "America in general, this place in specific, and you …"

He trailed off, and I stopped sorting through the pile for more dimes, frozen. "Me?"

He shrugged a shoulder, finishing the sleeve of nickels and laying it gently on the table and picking up a new sleeve, fiddling with it.

"What about me, Cam?" I asked, pushing.

He let the sleeve drop to the table, sighing as he leaned back into the sofa.

"I had a job lined up in Montreal," he said. "A good one – a stepping stone to a faculty position. In seven years I would have had tenure, enough successful grants to fund my own lab. I'd have been doing research most people only dream about."

I stared at him, realizing I knew very little about Cam's other life. This man who sat here with me had a whole history, and I'd never asked about any of it.

"What happened?" I asked.

"I didn't take it," he said, simply, like that was the beginning and the end of the story.

"Why not?" I replied. "Montreal, tenure – whatever that is – it all sounds safer than staying here with me."

He laughed and scrubbed a hand through his dishevelled hair, only serving to stir it up more.

"That's the point," he said, "right there. I could have gone back to Montreal, lived the day-to-day by the syllabus I was teaching and planning weeks worth of experiments, knowing exactly what I had to do each day down to the minute. But then a tree fell on me, and everything that's happened to me since that moment hasn't exactly convinced me that safe is necessarily the better way to live."

"All thanks to a tree," I said. "Funny how things work out that way."

"Not just the tree, though," Cam said. He leaned forward, rested his forearms on his knees and looked at his hands for a long minute. Then he looked up at me. "Everything that happened while Hannah was here was a show."

"Um, yes," I agreed, even though my hackles went straight up. I looked away, busying myself with the coins as he kept going.

"Lyn, hey, come on." He snagged the coin roller out of my hand and eased me to face him. "I'm not trying to …"

"You don't have to do this," I said before he could tell me sensible things, like how none of this could work, not really. That he's not my type, and I'm not his, and this is at best an experiment like the kinds he planned in Montreal. Some grand attempt to see if the good life is chaos on a rundown piece of property you don't even own before scurrying back to real life. Well, I had an answer for him.

"I'm used to people coming in and out of my life," I said. "And I'm used to people hardly being there, who are so on the periphery that they don't matter despite having a defining say over how my life is run. If you're here to get a better heading in your life, I'm here just to see if I can live one on my own. Just me. So, you see, I'll be fine if you want to go, if you want to end this before Wes ends it for us. It's how it should have been from the outset anyway."

"OK, whoa," Cam said, raising a hand to stop my verbal implosion. "What happened?"

"Nothing that hasn't always been happening," I said and sucked in a shaking breath, forcing myself to focus on the pile of coins. My coins. Coins I earned and weren't handed to me. I scoop up the dimes I separated and begin sliding them into a sleeve, forcefully, the paper tearing at the edges.

"Tell me," Cam said, his presence solid and sure next to me. A weight that could shoulder a few of my worries for a while. I frowned, trying to right a dime that had spun and gotten stuck crooked in the sleeve. Cam slid closer, pulling the sleeve from my hands. "Lyn," he said quietly, sliding his fingers into my hair and cupping the back of my head, looking at me with worry lines creasing between his eyes, "tell me."

"Poor little rich girl," I said. "It's nothing people haven't rolled their eyes at before."

"Try me."

"OK," I said, pushing my shoulders back and digging down for the ability to tell him a story I didn't tell anyone. No boyfriends and no friends outside of Georgie, who didn't count since she'd been enmeshed since the beginning. There was never any hiding myself from Georgie, not even when I'd actually really tried. She'd known anyway.

"I told you my family doesn't do sanity very well?" I reminded him, looking up at his carefully set face. "That's not an exaggeration. My mother died when I was in high school." I swallowed, my voice sticking when I thought about all the things I didn't see. "My brother found her," I added. "My father was too busy with the farm, and with the neighbor's wife, to really notice how quickly everything had fallen apart, so aside from bailing Harris out of jail and reprimanding me for dropping out of college he's been a non-factor since. Except, of course, this summer, when he told me not to expect my mother's inheritance. He wouldn't be giving it to me. And nothing else. Not ever. Not until I proved to him I deserved it."

Cam didn't say anything for a long moment, and I hastily laughed to cover the silence.

"So, it's a story old as time, right?" I asked. "Have and have not. It's not interesting, and I get that. I do. When you met me, I was just trying to see what good I was on my own, what I can even do by myself, but then you came along and I found myself wondering … maybe being alone is overrated, you know? You've done things for me no one else would have done, and you did them without motive, which I'm not used to in the slightest. You're a good person, Cam. And I'm lucky you're here with me, even temporarily. When this ends …"

I couldn't say the rest, because I couldn't see past the end of living on the farm. The end of Matilda and Horace and the house chicken and maybe even Hazard, because where would I put him? Everything was a mess, and I turned to Cam to say just that – this was a giant, completely impossible, hopeless *mess* – but the second I turned he was there, so close my voice died in my throat.

Then he kissed me, softly, as though testing the waters. It was a simple catch of lips, but it stirred up the more serious problem: us. Me and Cam – once nothing, once fake. Now here we were again, my heart pounding and my thoughts spinning, unable to land on anything other than *more* and *now*.

And this time it was real.

I pushed into him, steadying myself with a hand to his chest, fingers digging into his shirt. Our catch of lips deepened, opening into something more flush-worthy. My whole face felt warm, little zips of need singing across my skin with each drag of fingers and slide of tongue.

I was in his lap before I realized I'd done it – a practiced swing of a leg without any of the settling into a saddle. Cam still had one hand anchored in my hair, and the other found my hip, found skin underneath the hem of my shirt, and then palmed across my back to keep me against him when I wasn't going anywhere.

Cam pulled back from my mouth, hovering just within an easy shift slide to kissing again. I only needed to cross the tiny gulf of space between us.

"You realize," he said through his crooked smile, "with your kind of attitude you'd have been just fine on your own."

"Oh yeah?" I asked, my nose brushing against his. "What's my kind of attitude?"

"Independent, charming, charismatic. When you decide to do something you go all in, and that, Lynsey, is sexy as hell. I'm honestly shocked you don't have a cult following at this rate," he said, tracing his fingertips down the length of my spine. I shivered against him. "What I'm trying to say is you don't need to prove yourself to anyone."

"Even you?" I asked, my eyes locking on his as I let myself finally sink the rest of the way into his lap, brushing against a hardness I knew would get a response.

CAM

Whoa. I'd forgotten about this.

I mean, sure a part of me had forgotten about *this* – about getting a hard-on when touching a real, actual human being, as opposed to having a little help from the $3.99-for-half-a-gallon Price Chopper hair conditioner and my own two hands – but there was more.

I'd forgotten about this *level* of excitement. I hadn't felt this kind of first-time, I-can't-breathe, can't-think, can't-process kind of brain-freezing, crotch-throbbing stimulation since I was sixteen, armed with a pocketful of condoms in packages that said I Will Not Be Your Father in Star Wars font, which I'd scooped out of the basket in the boys' Phys Ed changeroom.

"*Shi-i-it …*"

"What?" Lynsey's eyes on mine. Sending a simultaneous tug

through my heart and my groin. Something very premature could happen just from staring into those eyes.

Condoms. That's what. As in, I wasn't prepared. Hadn't been for some time.

"I ..." *Think about it later.* I gave a thrust, and her eyes opened wider, and she held her position with her hips, and maybe that was a riding-girl thing. Or, no, the riding-girl thing was probably the slow grind-thrust she gave back and, "*Oo-o-oh ...*" I put both hands on the small of her back, then slid them up, along her spine, finding the edge of her bra, springing the clasp, which caused a tumble in her t-shirt right in front of me.

Oh, wow, I wanted to go there next. I also knew where I wanted to go after that, and after that, and all roads ended in needing a condom. Or, preferably, a carton of condoms, but one would do for now.

The temptation to barrel ahead was almost insurmountable. But we weren't going to do what I wanted to do without a condom, and I could face that problem now, when I still had pants on, or have to deal with it later, in a trouserless state.

I pulled her tight to me and, for a blissful second, buried my face in the soft warmth of the t-shirt not doing very much to hide her breasts, then I forced myself to mumble. "One second."

She stiffened against me. Not in a good way. "Excuse me?"

I gave her body a half-lift, and I did a sneaky slide, and somehow I was out from under her and she was kneeling alone on the sofa, and I said, "Really. I'm sorry. You have no idea. Please don't move. I'll come right back."

Then I ran to the bathroom.

Please, please, please.

Even though I knew there were no condoms in here. I hadn't put any here. I'd never seen any here. But if you were looking for a can of tomato soup, you'd go to the kitchen first, so I had to look in the medicine cabinet – floss, toothbrushes, painkillers, eye drops, but not a condom in sight – and pull out the spare rolls of toilet paper – just in case – and rifle through Lynsey's make-up bag – mouthing a silent *"Sorry Lyn!"*

Nothing.

I dashed back and she was slumped against the couch and her face said it all; she didn't even have to ask *How could you possibly run away from me in the middle of that?*

Instead of answering, I dropped to my knees in front of her. She lifted one eyebrow and rolled back her shoulders – which, also, just happened to thrust her chest forward. She gave me a look – direct, challenging, *let's do this* – which, combined with her slightly parted lips and quite-a-bit-more parted knees, replaced any rigidity I'd lost during the futile hunt for latex.

"Oh, Lyn. You are so, so hot." I knelt between her legs and pulled her body tight to me. Lifted her shirt and kissed her soft skin. I was about to ask if what I was doing was OK, when she laced her fingers through my hair and arched toward me, and gave a soft moan.

Oh, Lord. I had to find a goddamn condom.

"Lyn, I … just …" I pushed back and up, and dashed down the hall to my bedroom where I made a mess worthy of a house-breaking burglar, or a rampaging toddler, or every goat in our barn, in two minutes flat. No. Frigging. Condoms. Anywhere.

When I came back into the hall she was there. Hair messed, shirt rucked up, skin flushed. The most beautiful thing I'd ever seen. "Cam, what the hell is going on?"

I reached out and cupped her cheeks, and kissed her, hard. "Lyn …" I dropped my hands to the back pockets of her jeans and tugged her toward me. Another kiss. "I …"

Between kisses she was saying, "What …? You what?"

I finally took a deep breath and said, "Do you know that poem?"

She was breathing hard, too. "What damn poem are you talking about?"

"The one that ends, 'And it was all for the want of a horseshoe nail.'"

Understanding flooded her face, and made her even more adorable. "Oh. We're not talking about a horseshoe nail, are we?"

"No, we're not talking about a nail. And I am dying here, Lyn. I want to find not-a-nail so badly I can't even tell you."

She leaned against me. "I thought you would definitely have not-a-horseshoe-nail."

"Yeah, well, normally …" My brain was lust-scrambled, and sexually frustrated but suddenly it latched onto something. "… wait. A nail. That's it!"

"That's what?"

"Don't leave! Don't go anywhere! I'll be right back."

I knew it was good to do this while I was still wearing pants. I bolted out of the cabin, took the stairs in one leap, and sprinted to the shed where my triathlon bike had lived since we got here. Yanked the door open, grabbed what I wanted, and retraced my steps.

Panting. Head spinning. Lynsey was where I left her.

"Here!" I yelled.

She looked at the small case I was thrusting out, then at me. "It's a tire patch kit. Which would be fine if we were talking about an actual nail."

I shook my head. "No, no, no. No, Lyn. It's an emergency road kit. My friend Thomas packed it for me back in Montreal. He said I needed something to cover anything that might come up …" While I was talking, I fumbled in a zippered pocket. After a couple of slips from shaking hands, I pulled out not one, but two lovely, crinkly, squishy, square packets and held them in front of Lynsey's face.

She looked at them for a second, then fixed her eyes on mine. As I watched, a huge smile spread across her face. "Well, *hel-lo* Thomas …"

"Really? Thomas?"

She grinned. "Why not? Especially because, thanks to Thomas, we can do this now, and have another go after dinner."

"You …" I leaned in, and when my lips found hers I could

feel the shape of the smile still on her face. "… are …" I gave her lower lip a nibble. "… the sexiest girl …" She pulled her lip away and made a grab at mine. "… I've ever known."

"Mmm …" she mumbled. "Thomas …" and placed her hand flat against the front of my jeans which instantly felt far too tight. She gave the slightest of squeezes and I felt the twin packets in my hand and remembered this time I could just enjoy it, so I did. I whispered, "More, please," and when she squeezed harder I said, "I haven't felt this excited since I was sixteen."

She put her mouth by my ear, and just the feeling of her breath was making me lightheaded, and she said. "I remember what sixteen-year-old guys are like, and can I please, please ask that we actually both get undressed before this comes to a premature end?"

I backed her up against the wall, and my fingers found the hem of her t-shirt and as I lifted, I said, "Your wish is my command."

LYNSEY

MY SHIRT CAME OFF in a tangle of fingers and wadded cotton, both of us fumbling and overeager. I threw my bra in the general direction of the shirt, not sure where it landed exactly, and I hardly cared once Cam's hands skimmed up my sides and cupped my breasts. I arched against him, a little hum of approval climbing up my throat. Then he was cradling the back of my head again, pressing against me so entirely I hardly felt the cold of the bare-bones hallway wall against my back.

"This is amazing," I said against his mouth, grazing a hand down to the hem of his shirt. "But the clothes, Cam."

"Right, right." He gave me that lopsided grin again and tore his shirt off, all manly grab-and-pull, his hair in wild tufts I had to spear my fingers through.

"Better," I approved, because shirtless Cam? Well, this was a lot better than watching him glisten from an appreciable distance. "Now we can either do this here or we can move two feet to the right …"

I pointed at the door to my room, with the unmade bed mere strides away.

"Are you seriously suggesting wall sex?" he asked, pulling back just enough to stare at me part in awe and part in what may have been confusion.

"I used to ride horses professionally," I told him. "I know how to use my body in unnatural situations."

He stared at me. Silently.

"That is not to say I would prefer wall sex, but … you know … it's not out of the …"

Cam hauled me up against him and picked me up, a squeak of surprise popping out of me before I could stop it. I clung to his bare shoulders and began to laugh as he took us the two feet to the door and into the room. I kept laughing as he dropped me onto the bed and climbed up after me, the bedsprings protesting with rusty shrieks with each move. He settled above me, hovering easily with bed sheets tangling under each outspread hand. I tipped my chin up and caught him in another kiss, while I deftly went to work on his jeans, pulling at the insanely strong button closure and then yanking on the zipper.

"Why do men's jeans have to be made to withstand the apocalypse?" I grumbled as he grinned against my throat. "Seriously," I kept going. "It's like they're made from Teflon. And that's not even getting into the appropriately-sized pockets … ah-ha!"

The zipper finally gave way, and I started tugging them down his narrow hips.

"I do actual work while wearing these, you know," Cam said, shoving them down his legs and kicking them off. Then he attacked mine. "These things …" He peeled them off easily. "What purpose do they really serve? Besides cause me immense sexual frustration day in and day out?"

I grinned up at him. "Dual purpose. One's more obvious than the other."

He threw the jeans across the room.

"OK, come here," Cam said, pushing off the bed and yanking me to the edge of the mattress. My heart sped up at the thought of where this was going to lead to – where all of this was going to lead to, really – and pushed up until I was sitting on the edge of the bed, Cam standing between my knees. Cam, with his lean runner's body and perfect forearms. I reached out toward him on instinct, running a hand over his flat stomach and trailing my fingers across the edge of his underwear, which was still, somehow, frustratingly present.

"Clothes," I said, hooking a finger underneath the elastic and palming the hardness just south of it. Cam let out a hissing sound and snagged my wrist, holding on to me but not pushing me away. I raised an eyebrow. "Are we having a sixteen-year-old moment again, or …"

He kissed me hard, cutting off all thoughts of the awkward teenage fumbling I assumed other people had done in high school, since I certainly hadn't. Who had the time with horses, horses, family implosion, and more horses? It was a miracle I learned how to do *this* at all. This rolling around with other human being thing.

Then Cam broke the kiss and pushed me back to the bed, trailing his hands down to my hips. I inched closer to him as his fingers caught on the band of my panties, pulling them off on his way to sinking to his knees.

"Oh my god," I groaned, looking down at the top of his head. He raised an eyebrow at me from between my legs.

"I haven't even done anything yet," he said.

"No, but you're going to," I said, a flush sweeping over me when he kissed the inside of my knee.

"Oh, yeah," he said against my skin as he moved closer to his destination, my nerves coiling up in anticipation. "I intend to do a lot of things, but I'm just going to park myself here for a while and enjoy the noises you make."

Then he was there. Right there. His mouth moved over the

center of me – just one sweep to settle in – and my hips came off the bed, a squeak of my own adding to the protesting bedsprings. He lifted his head, eyeing me like I was an unpredictable wildcat, and some part of me felt that wouldn't be an entirely baseless accusation.

"That tickles," I said, propping myself on my elbows.

"So … slower?" he asked, breath warm against my skin. I shivered.

"I'll get over it," I proclaimed, waving it away. "Pick a speed, and I'll adjust."

"OK," he said, maneuvering back to where I desperately wanted him to be. I was quivering – shameless and so totally on edge I thought I might be on the verge of jumping out of my skin.

His mouth found its target, and my hips had a mind of their own – jerking up and right into Cam's hand. He spread his fingers over my belly and I threw my arm over my eyes, wiggling and unable to stop. To stop wiggling under such attention didn't even seem possible. I felt so hot I didn't even register that the room was full of autumn chill. I just kept trying to get closer to Cam, my body completely unable to be either still or quiet, especially when he slid a finger inside me.

I gasped, and he chuckled, obviously enjoying my complete inability to get it together.

This had to stop. Only … not. God, I never wanted it to stop.

"Cam," I blurted at the ceiling.

He leaned back from me. "Lyn?"

"Come up here," I demanded. "Now."

The bed shifted underneath me as he climbed up, working his way up my body until he met my mouth with his. Then I pushed my hands into his chest, kept pushing until he rolled on to his back, and I threw a leg over his hips.

"How are you still wearing boxers?" I asked, noticing the regrettable amount of fabric between us.

"I have an astonishing level of self-restraint?"

I snorted and did a hasty dismount. "Condom. We need the condom. Also," I pulled on the irritating material struggling to contain Cam's erection. "These come off."

"I can comply with that," he said, handing me the condom package. I ripped it open while he shucked off his boxers, throwing them somewhere over my head. Once we got through the mechanics of condom placement, a near-hysterical giggle caught in my throat at the thought, I threw a leg over Cam's hips and shimmied myself into position.

Then … there. *There.* I closed my eyes and sank down.

"Je-sus," Cam sighed, hands going to my hips and then up to my waist, holding onto me hard.

"Yes," I managed, tipping backward just a bit. Cam groaned underneath me. "Very much in agreement."

"The talking is sexy, you know," Cam said, and I smiled.

"Not usually a talker." I leaned down to kiss him. "Just proud of our teamwork right now."

He laughed and flipped us over. The bed did an uneasy shudder, and I briefly worried it might collapse underneath us, but then

Cam got to work again and all thought ceased. There was only this, us, a steady coiling sensation as we rocked with and against each other until …

I buried my face in his neck, coming completely apart. Then him, his body tensing against mine.

We stilled, aftershocks racing through my system and breath still heavy, sated. I rested my calf across the small of Cam's back and brushed my nose against his. He did the same, then pulled back, his glassy eyes focusing on mine.

"We need to make dinner," he announced.

"Why?" I asked. "Work up an appetite?"

"That's one way to put it," he nodded, "but mainly I was thinking we need to get that out of the way so we can get back here for round two."

I paused, the post-sex haze clearing just enough to remember our serious lack of protection and all the ways it wasn't meeting the current demand. I gave him one sharp nod.

"OK, let's go."

Chapter Seventeen

CAM

LYNSEY'S BED WAS SURPRISINGLY comfortable. This time, when I woke up, only one thing was stiff.

And that was fine. Lynsey and I could take care of that together.

What an awesome thought.

I lay still for a while contemplating it. I admit that, eventually, over time, this mattress might prove to be too soft to adequately support my manly frame, but after one night, it was like a fluffy cloud. Also, Lynsey had somehow scored flannel sheets. I'm not sure where the southern girl came up with those – especially while I'd been shivering all these nights in impossibly low-thread-count polyester – but I focused on stretching out my toes and feeling the heavenly warm softness, and I decided these flannel sheets could be mine from now on, so no harm.

A slice of sun fell across our bodies, and that was blissful, too. It also drew my attention to the bulge that was Lynsey's body.

More like a swell, really. High at her shoulders, dipping at her waist, and rising again where her hips pushed the sheet up. Her hips, and her backside. Her round, firm backside.

I let my mind drift back to cupping it. To holding one cheek in each hand. To how well that had worked to pull her closer, tighter, deeper …

Oh … stiff. Stiffer. I was on my way to being as stiff as possible.

I needed to wake her up. Soon.

I was trying to decide whether to use my lips or my fingertips when the decision was taken out of my hands.

Phones ringing. In stereo. One from each bedside table.

What the …?

An amber alert. It must be. What else could make our phones ring at exactly the same time like that?

Must. Shut. Phone. Up.

Must get back to daydreams-that-could-turn-into-hot-sex immediately.

I fumbled for it, got it, and shook my head at the name glowing on screen: Mom.

No, no, no … there was no way my more-than-perfect mother could in any way be present in this shabby, drafty, bedroom with its 1950s marmoleum tiles which even the most optimistic of realtors would struggle to sell as "vintage," and window coverings made from loosely stitched together feed sacks.

This perfect bedroom. This bedroom where my life had changed in a way I couldn't imagine how to explain to her.

I was going to swipe it off, but Lynsey was already grasping her phone, already mumbling, "'lo?" so I jumped out of the bed, scooping yesterday's jeans off the floor and detouring into my bedroom to grab a pair of clean-but-not-yet-put-away boxers, before saying, "Hi Mom."

"You sound chipper."

"I am chipper."

"Well, that makes me very happy for you, Cameron. And I have something to tell you that I think will make you even happier."

I reached our combo living / dining / kitchen which, twenty-four hours ago I would have said looked like nothing much, but now looked just like home, and a surge of something very much like joy tripped my mischief switch. "I'm going to be a big brother!"

"Cam …"

I righted a chair which had somehow been knocked over last night. "You're raising my allowance."

"Cameron. MacIntosh. Traherne."

"I give up. What is it, Mom?"

I headed toward the kitchen counter as she started talking.

"… case …" she said.

Coffee, I was thinking.

"… research …"

Filters … where were they?

"… subject matter expert …" my mom said.

I concentrated on jiggling the carafe into the only position which would prevent a massive java puddle from forming on the floor during the brewing process.

"… a hundred-and-seventy-five dollars an hour," she said.

"What?"

"'Pardon?' Cam, not 'What?' People who say 'what' don't get paid a hundred and seventy-five dollars an hour."

"I don't get paid a hundred-and-seventy-five dollars an hour." My eyes fell on the stack of abandoned coin rollers on the coffee table. The truth is, we hadn't rolled anywhere near a hundred-and-seventy-five dollars last night by the time our activities were interrupted.

Interrupted activities … Now, that was a nice thought.

Unlike me, my mom's concentration hadn't wandered from the topic under discussion. "You could, though, Cam. That's the point."

While she provided further details of the high-paying, sub-ject-matter-expert, contract gig that could be mine if I just came to my senses, and went home, I picked up a pen lying on the table and jotted *$175 / hour* on a napkin. Added an exclamation mark to show how crazy that amount was. Scribbled in stars, and circled the whole thing.

When she paused I said, "Mmm …"

It was a trick I'd learned a long time ago. Don't say no to my mother. Don't try to cut her off. Just let her speak her piece, then don't act on it.

It was why I was pretty much always on speaking terms with her, while she and Meg went through periodic interludes of frosty silence.

My mom was still talking as I shrugged into a hoodie and yanked the ancient, swollen front door open.

Stepped out into something worth far, far more than a hundred-and-seventy-five dollars an hour.

Not a road in sight. Not a vapour trail in the sky.

Golden sunshine touching the tops of autumn-browned grasses.

A picturesque – if falling apart – barn containing a horse worth nine-point-six million dollars, who I brought home for a girl worth … well … she had to be worth more than that horse, but adding up those many millions felt crass, so I just classified her as priceless.

This was what my mom was up against. This was why she was going to have to find another limnological subject matter expert for her big case. Also, a-hundred-and-seventy-five Canadian dollars took a pretty big hit the minute you brought it across the border.

Not that I was going to tell my mom any of that now. I'd let ignored e-mails and unreturned texts deliver my rejection.

There was a squeak behind me, and I turned to see Lynsey in the doorway.

She was a picture of romantic dishevelment – all blurred edges and soft focus – or maybe that was because she was standing behind the screen door, but she still looked pretty cute.

"Listen, Mom. Something's come up here." I winked at Lynsey and gestured toward my crotch in an admittedly childish, but surely endearing move. "So, thanks for calling, and you have a really productive day, and I'll say good-bye."

As I slid my phone into my back pocket, Lynsey stepped out from behind the screen door. Still cute. *Phew.*

Her eyebrows arched. "A productive day?"

I nodded. "The best kind of day my mother could ever possibly have." When Lynsey's eyebrows went even higher, I added. "You, my angel, do not hold a monopoly on family dysfunction."

I didn't think there was still room for the eyebrows to lift, but they did. "Angel? That's not going to become a thing now, is it?"

I shrugged. "Just wanted to try it out."

What I wasn't about to tell her is I had a bizarre desire to call her, "Mrs. Traherne." Just for fun, of course. However, despite knowing Lynsey had a pretty solid sense of humour, I wasn't sure how well that particular joke would go over. "Angel" seemed relatively safe.

"Hmm ..."

"I hope you don't mind me saying that you don't seem quite as transcendentally blissed out as I might expect you to be after a night of traveling to heaven and back multiple times ..." I stopped myself just short of tacking "Angel" onto the end of my sentence.

I stepped forward to put my arm around her shoulder, to pull her to the edge of the porch and point out our surroundings that nobody's hundred-and-seventy-five-dollars-an-hour could buy. To have us both breathe the same air, and gaze at the same view, and say, "Yeah, we've got it good."

She stopped me with a hand on my shoulder, locked her eyes onto mine, and said, "Oh, Cam. Albert's died."

Lynsey

My heart was firmly lodged in my throat, fluttering and choking off most of the air I needed to tell the rest to Cam, who looked at me like a wide-eyed, stone-faced statue. He was completely still, body rigid against mine. I ducked my head, my phone still in my hand, dark and quiet after all the things Wes had to tell me.

"We should sit down," I said, motioning to the weathered steps, which I supposed we didn't need to fix. Not now. "I'll tell you everything."

His arm dropped from my shoulders, the chill in the morning air washing over me. I shivered and dropped down next to him on the creaking porch, sandwiching the phone between my palms. Cam's shoulder brushed against mine, and I forced myself to look up at him, surprised to find him watching me intently.

"He died a few days ago," I said, unsticking my tongue from the roof of my mouth. "Heart attack, Wes said. What happened at the race must have been a precursor, but …" I trailed off, and let out a big enough breath for it to come out as an exhausted sigh. "The realtor's on her way now to put up a sign. Wes didn't want us to be surprised."

"That's generous of him," Cam muttered, stroking both hands through his hair and leaning forward, focused on the driveway as if he expected the real estate agent to come bumping up the potholed gravel any second.

"He didn't have to tell us anything," I point out. "We knew he would be doing this one way or the other."

Cam nodded tightly and stood up. "The agent is coming now?"

I looked up at him, squinting as the morning sun broke over the pine-covered mountains and washed the entire farm in yellow, glinting light. I swallowed, hard, and nodded.

"Bright and early," I said. "The sellers are motivated, so …"

"Right." Cam said, already starting down the steps. "Motivated. That's understandable, since – hey, look at that sun – I should probably get a run in now before I head over to finish that drywall on Lewis's cabin. Hope will never want to move in if there aren't paintable, photo-ready walls, you know?"

"Wait, what?" I asked his quickly retreating back, trying to wrap my head around what Hope would be doing in Lewis's cabin while grappling with watching Cam run away from me. Literally. Again. "Cam! You're wearing jeans!"

He waved me off. "It'll be fine!"

I stared at him, silently, from the top perch of the stairs as he took off into a sprint – sans warm up, in jeans, with question-ably old running shoes, without any semblance of a plan. He disappeared from my line of vision without a glance back, head down and plowing ahead like none of that mattered, leaving me in a cocoon of farm silence – the kind of peace I usually sleep through before the roosters remind Matilda that there is a feeding schedule, and I will be held to it.

But the roosters were silent, still sleeping in their coops, so Matilda was equally silent, probably still snoozing in her stall, leaving me with nothing to do except deal with the fissure that had opened up – again – in my life. Although, if I wanted to face facts, I'd have to admit the fissure hadn't ever really closed. It had just gotten wider, becoming a gulf I didn't know how to cross, much less close.

I wrapped my arms around my legs and let my forehead fall onto my knees, curling up into the fetal position as if I could block out every problem while still being perched on top of one of the more dangerous problems in my life – the stairs.

But I didn't care. What was the point in caring? The stairs could crumble underneath me and that would be fine. We'd be out of here before it would matter, Cam back to Canada and me back to Florida, where I would have to face my family, face my father, and meekly do as I was told. No more running, no more playing at having a life of my own, no more independence.

I'd failed. Spectacularly.

A thick chunk of emotion lurched up my throat, threatening to pour out of my mouth in sob-like form, and I pushed backward onto the porch before it could. Standing with enough force to stumble, I swiped hard at my misting eyes and determined to put myself to use before I could become an emotional pile of useless jelly.

If Cam had drywall and running to do, I had horses. Three of them now, one of them at least definitely mine. I'm sure Dad would love that, coming home with not just my frosty attitude but a failed racehorse not worth the sticker price.

A throaty rooster call crackled through the early morning quiet, like a warm up for the greater chorus. Then again, clearer. Again. From the barn, the first thud of hoof meeting stall door echoed up to the house, just as the realtor's shiny, sensible sedan trundled up the drive and pointed its nose at the house.

"Perfect," I grumbled to myself, pushing my hair out of my face and pulling it into a messy ponytail. My hair was still a post-sex rat's nest, impervious to smoothing. My fingers caught in the tangles, and I winced, which was the first face the real estate agent saw upon climbing out of her car.

"Are you …?" she asked, peering at me from over her bifocals, clearly searching for a name.

"Lynsey," I supplied, tip-toeing down the steps and presenting myself.

"Of course." The agent afforded me a cheerful smile, offering me her hand in a warm, practiced handshake. "Wes did say there was a caretaker on the property, but I confess everything has been such a whirlwind …" She shook her head, waving her free hand in a sign that life was chaotic and we could only cling to what we could.

I nodded sagely, like this was all expected. "I'm Cheryl Johnson. I'm here to get things started."

That seemed like the simplest way of saying "I'm here to ruin your life," but I let it go.

"Sure," I said, gulping down the need to scream. "Do you need to take photos …?"

I waved a hand at the house, and Cheryl gave it the big, hairy eyeball.

"No," she said after a long pause. "It won't be necessary to take photos of the interiors. We'll be listing the property as is with the understanding interested buyers will be developing the land."

"Oh," I squeaked.

Cheryl beamed at me. "There's such a demand for gated communities, and the Lake Placid area is woefully behind the times. A property like this, with the trees and the proximity to nature, well. A few exterior shots to showcase the acreage should do it. We'll have nibbles and bites before the day is out, I just know it."

"Um," is all I could muster, which didn't faze Cheryl at all. She turned to her car, rummaging through the front seat and pulling out a camera bag, giving the farm a good scan in efforts, I assumed, of finding the best vantage point.

I could have told her to start with the pumpkin field, with its very pretty views of trees and mountains, now picked nearly clean. The pumpkins had been a nice little earner. We'd have to plant more next year … *next year* … at this rate I'd be lucky to be living here next week.

The sound of an indignant Matilda beating down the barn walls had never been more welcome.

"I'll be feeding the horses," I offered, taking another step. "If you need any help."

Cheryl only nodded, pulling her camera out and fiddling with the settings. It whizzed and chirped, prepared to take equally knock-you-down photos of the scenery. I took that to mean she didn't need me to point out what was obvious, so I turned and beat a quick retreat.

—

"OK!" I shouted down the aisle, hardly coming close to out-decibeling Matilda. "I'm here, give me thirty seconds!"

Matilda's head popped over her stall guard, ears pricked toward me and lips waggling. Her give-me-food-before-I-starve face. I sped by her, taking care to arc away from her stall when her ears swept backward and those waggling lips lifted to reveal teeth.

"So bad," I told her on my way back from the loft, throwing a flake of hay into her stall before Horace and finally Hazard, whom I found sprawled in his bedding like he was jetlagged from his arduous journey across the street.

"Hey, buddy," I crooned, making a tsking cluck of tongue behind teeth. Hazard simply flicked an ear and cracked one eye open, watching me enter his new stall. One he'd be leaving soon. I swallowed down the tightness in my throat, and crouched down next to his shoulder, putting the flake of hay down by his head. He stretched out his neck and nuzzled it, ripping a few strands free and beginning a leisurely munch.

"I think I'm starting to see what made you a pretty terrible racehorse," I said. "Sleeping in and eating in bed isn't your normal track routine, buddy."

Hazard snorted and craned his neck off the bedding, rolling to upright and throwing his legs out in front of him. I scrambled out of the way as he lurched to a splay-legged standing, lowered his head, and did a full-body shake. Without giving me so much as a second glance, he dug into breakfast with the calm swish of his tail, completely relaxed, like he'd lived here since day one.

That *also* made my throat close up, which was the last straw. I couldn't keep thinking like this in terms of what I did and didn't have, what I thought I had and what I wouldn't. Life didn't work like that. I needed to start making plans, and I needed to start now.

Sniffling, I marched out of Hazard's stall and returned with the only grooming supplies I could find – a hoofpick, a stiff curry comb, and a worn body brush – and went to work. Hazard grunted under the attention but kept eating as I turned his coat from dusty-brown to glistening mahogany, the white birdcatcher spots glowing off his sides. Then I lifted his feet each in turn, which he picked up dutifully and held aloft while I pried loose all the packed dirt and every stone he'd picked up in Crazy Lady's scrapyard.

Once I'd worked my way around him, I stepped back and stared, round-eyed at the gelding I knew I'd seen at Saratoga – Lost Cause, who'd floated down the walkway to the paddock like he'd owned the place, when he definitely did not. Strutting around, turning heads, his white spots catching in the unrelenting sun.

That was the horse I was looking at now, and he was something else standing here in my falling down barn.

My.

I winced and had to scrub at my eyes again, just as Hazard gave my hip an inquisitive nudge, as though testing out my balance and treat-packing potential.

"I'm in a pretty sorry state right now," I admitted to him. "I promise I'm usually more put together."

The gelding sighed in my face and lifted his head, resting it casually on my shoulder. I leaned into him, taking the opening for what it was – a horsey hug. I needed it, desperately, and pressed my face into his warm neck, breathing in the smell of horse and barn and hay.

And I felt myself calm down, as though I'd floated out of my body and could see how at home I was, curled up against a horse I barely knew in a barn that wasn't mine. Maybe it didn't matter where I was; if I could take Hazard with me everything would work out.

If. I didn't like that iffy part.

My phone began a distinctive ring from my back pocket, and I pulled it out, swiping over my brother's face.

"I have him," I said into the receiver, to Harris's unimpressed snort.

"And now what are you going to do with him?"

"Jury's still out," I admitted. "Especially since I don't have a place to live anymore."

"The squatting thing didn't work out?" Harris asked. "I confess I'm not entirely shocked."

"Shut up," I told him, and he laughed.

"Seriously, Lyn, I'm sorry upstate New York isn't panning out, but at least you can escape before winter hits."

I thought about that for a moment and realized he wasn't entirely wrong. A Florida girl in winter? That had madness written all over it. "Still," I sighed, looking up at the rafters, "I was really hoping I could make something of this, you know?"

There was silence on the other end of the line.

"Harris?"

"What happened?" he demanded, transitioning from my goofing-off older brother to Tupelo Stud heir so quickly my head spun and I told him before I could think better of it, my sob story rising out of me with an increasingly hysterical edge to my voice.

"So now I'm back where I started," I concluded. "Or worse. Now I have a horse with me, and I don't know what to do anymore, Harris. I really don't."

He sighed. "You want to know why I called?"

"Not really," I grumbled, resting my forehead against Hazard's shoulder as he went back to eating.

"I'm moving to Red Gate," Harris said over my gasp.

Red Gate was across the street from Tupelo Stud, owned by Georgie's family until Dad bought it a few years back, saving it from financial ruin in what may have been his one charitable act. Georgie hadn't thought so at the time, no matter if the deal had also gotten her a share in our most famous race mare, Sweet Bells. The farm was a sprawl of Spanish Moss and dilapidation until Tupelo bought it, sinking enough money into it to refurbish the barns, resurface the track, and reopen as a yearling division and secondary broodmare site, where all our girls vacationed as their weanlings started learning the ropes at Tupelo without them.

"What are you going to do over there?" I asked. "Let down race mares and train babies?"

"It's not like the track can't train a few racehorses with the babies," Harris pointed out, "but that's not what I'm doing over here. The point of this phone call that I feel is flying right over your head is I asked Georgie to marry me and she said yes."

My shriek was not advisable. Hazard tore his head up, eyeing me like I was not the calm, level-headed human I'd led him to believe. I put a hand on his neck, shushing and apologising.

"But," Harris went on, "there were stipulations ..."

"Let me guess."

"I already told you," Harris pointed out.

"You're moving to Red Gate because you're marrying my best friend," I whisper-hissed excitedly. "And you're going to renovate that crumbling farm house and have, like, a bazillion small children and I will be their doting spinster aunt."

"This got out of hand so quickly," Harris groaned. "There will not be a bazillion small children. Maybe, like, two. Two seems doable."

"I'm going to be a doting spinster aunt," I reiterated. "You'll never get rid of me once those babies are on the ground."

"They're children, Lyn," Harris said. "Not foals. And they don't exist yet."

"Point still stands," I said.

"No kidding, especially since I'm offering you a stall at Red Gate for your horse if you want to come home."

That put a stop to the smile stretching across my face.

"But, Dad …"

"Dad will deal," Harris said. "You want a road block between you and Dad, I can help you with that. You know I can. The stall is yours if you want it."

I swallowed, curling my hand on Hazard's neck into a tight fist. I thought about how quickly Cam hightailed it out of here this morning, about how I couldn't possibly know what our next move would be because there wasn't an *our* in the first place. There was only me, and Harris was offering me a chance to do something only for me. A path across the gulf and back to safety.

But then there was the chance that Cam was more than just the guy who was helping me out, with the farm and the horses and the occasional romp in bedsheets. Maybe he was more than that.

"I appreciate that, Harris, I really do."

"But you need to think about it?"

"That's what you'd advise, isn't it?"

Harris laughed. "Hey, if you have a better deal somewhere else, I remind you that I've got hypothetical kids you can spoil."

"Not fair," I pouted. "Using your nonexistent children as leverage is low, Harris."

"Not if it means I get you back home," Harris said quietly. I bit my lower lip and looked down at my feet, not knowing what to say. After Mom, genuine emotion out of Harris had been so hard to wrench free that even years later it startled me when he let me see it.

Harris cleared his throat, laughing at himself. "Georgie misses you. Hell, I miss you and that's saying something."

"Again, shut up," I told him.

"Fine by me," Harris said. "Keep your phone handy. Once Georgie's off these horses she'll be calling."

"I'm sure," I said softly. "Congratulations, Harris. I'm super thrilled for you."

"I know," Harris said and disconnected, the phone going dark in my hand.

—

I HID IN THE barn for the better part of the morning, only emerging to let out the horses and start chores I didn't need to do – like reorganize the feed room – on top of the ones I did need to do – like clean all the water buckets, muck the stalls, and sweep the dirt aisle until it was perfect and I was a dusty, sweat-streaked mess.

When I walked back up to the house, Cheryl's car was gone. Happiness should have been the first emotion that hit me, but Hope's truck – Cam's for a few more days while his "found" truck was being overhauled at the town garage – was still parked in its spot, which reminded me that Cam was still gone, and I was still alone with this empty feeling lodged in my chest.

It sucked, that feeling. Like having a hollow where your heart should be. It felt like I couldn't get in a solid breath, and I was left sipping on air, never getting enough to feel fully alive.

I needed a shower. And coffee. And a plan. That's what I needed. Things wouldn't be right after, but at least I'd be doing something.

I pushed into the house and stumbled into the bathroom, taking the hottest shower the old pipes could manage. Then I checked the cold carafe in the kitchen. With microwaved coffee in hand, I sat down at the table and took my first sip, instantly feeling better when the hot liquid zipped into my stomach and delivered its payload of caffeine.

Next, a plan. I looked around for something to write with, finding a pen conveniently sitting in the middle of the table, right next to a napkin. I plucked it up, ready to write down all of the ideas I didn't yet have, when I noticed there was already writing on it.

$175 / hour.

And stars. And exclamation points. Like a teenage girl had broken into the house while I was gone to doodle her dream wage on one napkin and disappeared immediately after.

I thought about Cheryl, then dismissed it. Then I thought of Hannah, only there was no way anyone would pay Hannah $175 an hour for anything. Which left Cam.

The old, hollow hole in my chest grew, expanding until a shiver ran down my spine. I dropped the napkin just as my phone rang.

Georgie. I mustered up enough enthusiasm to scream with her about wedding plans while my life had veered sideways and completely fallen apart.

I was an idiot. An idiot with a horse and not much else.

"Hey, Georgie?" I asked as we took a breath from squealing over how much of a romantic my wonderful older brother was, deep down. "Think I can take Harris up on his offer of a stall at Red Gate?"

"Of course!" Georgie laughed, because of course she knew. Couples who were actually couples did that – talked to each other, were on the same page about everything. That's why they got married eventually, and had kids, and raced horses, and ran farms together.

They were in love, and I most certainly was not.

Chapter Eighteen

CAM

Did I feel badly for running away from Lynsey?

Only after I straightened up from the spot at the end of the driveway I'd reached just in time to bend over and throw up behind a bush.

Poor bush … it was kind of scrubby. I wondered if my contribution would help it flourish, or kill it off altogether.

Focus, Cam – you're not a landscape gardener.

No, that was true. I was just a messed-up dude who'd been completely overwhelmed – positive I'd either haul off and punch any realtor who got in my way, or that I'd burst into tears in front of Lynsey.

Or both.

With neither seeming like a good option, I'd run, and discovered I still didn't really know my body, because it turned out what it really needed was a good hurl.

I saliva-swished my mouth as best I could, and tried to figure out if I felt better. Decided on yes and no. I didn't feel like I was going to puke again, so that was better from three minutes ago, but I'd woken up satisfied, in a relationship (because, yes, sleeping with Lynsey definitely made her my girlfriend), with land that felt like mine in front of me, and now I was … bereft.

The word came from deep in my brain – from an English class long, long ago – and it was perfect. I remembered it meant "deprived" or "robbed" and that was exactly right. Of all the things I was stripped of, the biggest one was optimism.

I didn't know what to do, or who to talk to. No, that's not true. I wanted to talk to Lynsey. But … the running away, and the rawness of this news that we'd both received – I wasn't sure that she'd want to talk to me. Maybe Meg would be better. I'd love to talk to Meg right now, but this was an in-person kind of discussion and she was so far away.

My brain did this funny thing where it combined Meg and Lynsey and produced a third person.

Hope.

I needed Hope right now. Both Hope and hope.

And, as though signaling the return of optimism, I remembered there was a lone stick of peppermint gum left in the back pocket of my jeans. If I was going to talk to anyone, I needed some peppermint gum first.

So, plan made, breath freshening with every chew, I patted the shrub – "Hope you make it buddy," – and turned my worn running shoes toward town.

—

THE RUNNING WAS SETTLING me. It was impossible to panic and run at the same time without literally running out of breath and passing out. I'd learned that the hard way in high school when, partway through a track practice, our school's star high jumper had whispered in my ear, "I'm two weeks late." This was after a condom failure incident we'd experienced together.

I'd hit the track hard, and our school didn't even have one of those posh rubberized surfaces.

Ever since, *breathe-in, breathe-out* had been my running mantra. No matter what.

So, I was doing OK in the breathing department. My muscles were sliding just fine. Even my Hazard-mangled toe wasn't giving me grief.

But the chafing. I could feel it starting. Double-seamed jeans were never designed for running.

I couldn't give up now, though. The thought, picture, idea of sitting in the bakery, talking to Hope was the only thing keeping me going. If I slunk back to the farm with my tail between my rapidly chafing legs, well, let's just say I feared for my brand-new relationship status with Lynsey.

I needed to have a plan. I needed to feel positive for myself before I could be there for her.

The answer was obvious.

I stopped under a tree branch hanging low by the edge of the road and hopped out of my jeans.

That was better. I mean, the breeze alone was awesome, and the freedom of leaving the heavy denim behind – amazing.

I congratulated myself for taking the time to spread them carefully over the branch. I could pick them up on my way back and they'd be dry, and smell like autumn breezes.

As I set out again I thought how fantastic it was that the boxers I'd grabbed happened to be the long, form-fitting brief-style ones. To anyone else they'd look like compression shorts.

Perfect. This was going to work out just fine.

———

"Cam, are you wearing your underwear?"

Hope was out front, sweeping the sidewalk in front of the bakery.

"What? No. They're running shorts."

"Cam. I may look sweet, but I have enough experience to recognize men's boxer-briefs when I see them." She waved in the general direction of my crotch. "The Y-front is a dead giveaway."

"Oh, that's just to make them look hardcore. It's not even real. See?" I slid my hand down my front, and it slipped right into the very real Y.

"Cam! Get in the bakery. This is exactly how rumours get started in small towns."

She shooed me in with the broom and pointed to a tall stool at the counter. "Sit. I'll be right back."

It took her less than two minutes to disappear through the door at the back and return holding a pair of turquoise pyjama pants adorned with flaming pink flamingos.

"Uh, no," I said.

"Uh, yes. Non-negotiable if you're going to stay here."

A shaft of sunlight warmed the counter. A fan hummed gently in the background. The air smelled of yeast, and sugar, and comfort. I couldn't leave this. I blinked hard. It was OK. That's why I was here. Gathering resolve so I wouldn't have to leave this.

I took the pants, and wriggled into them, and Hope nodded. "Well, that's settled, then. What can I do for you?"

—

BY THE TIME WE were halfway through our coffees, we'd each shed a few tears. "Oh, Albert ..." Hope sighed. "He was a character." She blew across the surface of her hot drink and said, "Although, I'm a bit surprised you're taking it so hard – you didn't have a chance to get to know him that well."

When I hesitated, she said, "Oh, wait. You're not upset about Albert, are you?"

I took a sip of my coffee. "I mean, I'm sorry. As much as I knew of him, I liked him, and I know a lot of people will miss him ..."

"... but," Hope interrupted. "Him dying lets the fox into the henhouse."

What? I tilted my head and looked at her with lifted eyebrows.

She elbowed me. "Oh, come on Cam – you must know that

expression. It means 'causes trouble.'"

"I think you're talking about the cat amongst the pigeons."

"Am I? I'm sure there was something about a fox and a hen-house."

"You're not supposed to let the fox guard the henhouse."

"*Duh* … who would ever do that? The fox would eat the hens."

No wonder I liked this girl. She mixed up her expressions more than I did. God, she was sweet. Wow, she was perfect for Lewis.

Just like Lynsey and I were perfect for each other … or, wait, no … maybe not *perfect* in the way Hope and Lewis were – like two nicely fitting pieces of a jigsaw puzzle – but Lynsey and I were … fun together, dynamic together, Lynsey and I at least deserved a *chance* together.

"Oh …" Hope was cupping her mug in two hands and study-ing my face. "I'm sorry for not getting it at first. You're afraid of losing …"

"Everything."

"Yeah," she said. "Well I don't think we should let that hap-pen, do you?"

—

HOPE POURED OUT TWO extra coffees, loaded a bag with baked goods, then, gesturing to me to bring my coffee with me, led me to the sidewalk, hanging a Back in five minutes sign on the bakery door – "Because nobody will ever know when the five minutes started, right?"

I followed her three storefronts down the road, where she

pushed open a doorway that led onto a flight of stairs and mounted, calling out, "Uncle Forrest! Get your legal pad out!"

She turned to me and stage-whispered, "My uncle's been the town lawyer forever. He knows all the land around here, and he's also just a wee bit *slippery*." She winked.

A large man was at the top of the staircase. "Now, dear Hope, we like to call it 'canny' rather than 'slippery.'"

As I drew level with him I held out my hand. "I recognize you, sir. You were at the pumpkin patch."

"Yes, indeed. That is true. Although I'm surprised you noticed me, as you seemed to be quite preoccupied with an attractive young lady."

I wasn't sure whether the observation was positive or negative, and perhaps it was simply that – an observation – because he kept talking. "Eleanor and I have never once missed a trip to Albert's pumpkin patch, and we were pleased to see how busy you young folks were this year."

"It's the pumpkin patch we're here about," Hope said. "If we don't do something it might not be there for you to go to next year."

"Sit down, sit down. I'll get Eleanor to join us and we'll talk."

Hope started with the news of Albert's demise. Eleanor reached out, took a tight hold of my hand, and next thing I knew we were all holding hands around the table, heads bowed, while Eleanor said, "Dear, dear Albert. You brought riches to our community and our lives. You will be missed." She lifted her head and said, "I will organize a memorial. Now, please continue."

I explained about the phone call, and the realtor, and Forrest was shaking his head before I even finished. "I'd bet my last dollar it's Cheryl Johnson." He pushed his glasses up on the bridge of his nose. "She'll be calling up her developer friends, whispering sweet nothings about plans of subdivision and lakefront estate lots."

"Developers? Subdivisions?" I crossed my arms over my gut. Maybe I wasn't done with the puking after all.

"Now, now ..." Eleanor patted my arm. "Don't you worry, son. You've come to the right place. Forrest and I have been preparing for this day ever since Albert had his first stroke, haven't we, Forrest?"

"Indeed we have, my dear. You brought the file?" He held his hand out, and Eleanor placed a blue file folder in it. Forrest tapped it. "Everything we need to save that land, is right in this sweet little folder."

It was a list.

- Short-Eared Owl
- Tiger Salamander
- Bog Turtle
- Indiana Bat
- Queen Snake
- Well-Marked Cutworm
- Allegheny Woodrat

Oh, wow. And here you could argue I was the crazy one. Running into town in my underwear. Visiting prospective lawyers while sporting retina-searing flamingo PJ bottoms.

But this …

"The young man doubts us, Forrest," Eleanor said.

"He does, indeed, Eleanor."

"He wonders how a salamander can save his home and his new way of life."

Forrest nodded. "And I can see why. It's not an unreasonable reaction."

If I were to slam my coffee cup on the table, jump up, and storm off in my flamingo attire, I wondered if that would be a reasonable reaction.

Hope leaned over the list, forehead furrowed, nodding. "Are you sure about the woodrat?"

He paused from fishing through her bakery bag. "Oh yes. Most definitely. I've seen the latrines."

I wanted to take heart from Hope's interest. I still believed in Hope's sanity. But we all had our weaknesses – maybe familial delusion was one of hers.

"Latrines?" I asked.

Having settled on a cruller, Forrest took a bite, leaned back and crossed his hands over his ample belly, and said, "Oh yes. Very telling. Woodrats make latrines from their feces and the latrines are accepted as confirmation of their presence. There is a remarkable network on a portion of Albert's property."

I turned to Hope. "Help me. Please."

She laughed. "What Uncle Forrest and Aunt Eleanor are telling you is that Albert's land is crawling with endangered species.

Developers cringe at the mention of even one species, but this list …" She lifted both hands in a worshipful motion. "… well, to me this looks like a developer's worst nightmare."

"Really?" I asked. I took a better look myself. "The Indiana bat?"

Eleanor smiled. "If you've done chores at dusk, you've probably seen one."

"This could save our land?"

Forrest picked up a pen, and scribbled a couple of figures on his legal pad, then turned the whole thing toward me. He circled the first figure. "This is what I expect Cheryl has told Albert's nephew he can list the land for." He underlined the second one. "This is what a typical fifty-acre farm of middling quality, with no prospects of development could reasonably be sold for in this area."

There was a two-zero difference in the two numbers.

There was every difference in the world between those two numbers. There was promise, there was hope, there was possibility.

Like, actual possibility. As in, I had a good chunk of the second number in my nest egg bank account.

—

I WAS SITTING IN Hope's passenger seat trying to gather my thoughts. Trying, more practically, to gather the notes and business cards Forrest had doled out to me.

First: "Call Winston – he's forestry, fisheries, and wildlife – and explain the situation."

Second: "Oh, and get in touch with Harriet Serpent – she's a reptile specialist at the local college." My eyebrows had lifted, and he'd chuckled. "Oh, I know, 'Serpent' – isn't the world a wonderful place?"

I was starting to think it just might be.

Finally: "Cheryl Johnson isn't the only real estate agent in the area – even if she declares she is on social media – give Brian Morris a call. He'll come over from Saranac and give you an accurate appraisal based on that land staying zoned Rural Countryside."

"Thanks," I said to Hope. She was so wholesomely adorable, and she'd come to my rescue, and there was something about a girl driving a truck … and I didn't care. Wasn't tempted. Wouldn't go there, even if my best friend wasn't head-over-heels for her. Because, *Lynsey*. Now, Lynsey and I could have a future.

"That was exactly what I needed to hear this morning," I added.

Hope nodded. "Not just you. Me too. And Uncle Forrest and Aunt Eleanor. And the whole town. This place would be worse off without Albert's land."

"Do you think your uncle meant it about his fee?"

"That he'll take payment in the form of he and Eleanor being able to come out to the farm to get their Christmas trees as long as they're spry enough to put them up?" She nods. "Yes. I do. I also have to advise you to seriously consider just paying him – there's longevity in our family, and Forrest is a stubborn man. He'll make sure to get his full value out of that arrangement."

I rubbed my hands together. "If this works out, he can have

two Christmas trees every year." Even I could hear the relief in my voice.

That's when I saw the jeans.

"Whoa. Hope. Can you pull over here please?"

She gave me a sideways look, but she pulled over, right alongside the low-hanging branch.

I stepped out of the truck, lifted the jeans off the branch, and stood for a couple of seconds, holding them, before meeting Hope's eyebrow-lifted look. "I think I might, perhaps, have had a bit of an irrational moment earlier this morning."

The eyebrows arched higher. "You think?"

I grinned. "Yeah, I guess you were the one who caught me running into town in my underwear."

"Oh, Cam. It wasn't the underwear. It was the denial of the underwear. I was seriously worried about you."

I gave my flamingo pants a little tug. "Well, as you can see, I am now dressed in a completely normal fashion, so all that's behind us."

"Thank goodness for that," she said.

—

"Just drop me off this side of the mailbox, please. I don't want Lynsey to know about any of this yet. I want to get some things moving before I get her hopes up."

Hope obligingly pulled over on the side of the highway for the second time. As I reached for the door handle, she said. "Um, Cam?"

"Yeah?"

"I mean, I didn't go there, because of everything else to talk about, but does this mean what I think it does about you and Lynsey?"

Instead of answering, I leaned over and hugged her. When I straightened up, she was blinking really fast in the way my sister did when she first saw the horse of her dreams, or the way my mom did when I got the letter offering me a scholarship at her alma mater.

"Oh, wow," she said.

I reached for the handle again, and again she said, "Cam?"

"Yes?"

"The pants."

"Oh, yeah. You think she might notice?"

"I sincerely hope so if you two are actually some sort of couple."

And, so, three minutes later Hope was backtracking into town with a gaudy pair of pyjama pants on the seat beside her, and I was walking up the driveway in my jeans, and I didn't even spare a glance for the For Sale sign swinging in the breeze because, really, it just didn't matter.

LYNSEY

THE NAPKIN WAS STILL pinched between my fingers when I spotted movement coming up the driveway. Cam, long legs still in jeans, walking like he didn't even regret that particular decision, appeared with a spring to his step.

Rage, sudden and Armstrong-level swift, hit me full on. I almost couldn't see straight as I pushed back from the table, the napkin drifting to the floor. I wanted to do everything at once – scream at Cam, slam a door, break something satisfying, tear off into town and brood moodily at Irene's while shoveling Hope's pie into my face. All seemed like such good options that I couldn't decide what to do first, so I stood, trembling, watching with increasing panic as Cam trotted up the steps.

Was he … was he *whistling*?

My hands curled into fists, halfway through my first step toward the door when my phone began to ring, vibrating into a rattle on the table. I stopped midstride, sucked in a big breath, and made myself look at the phone.

Hope. Literally and figuratively. I snatched the phone off the table.

"I'm assuming you heard the news?" I asked by way of answering.

"About Albert?" she asked, her voice barely carrying over a hum in the background. She was driving. "It's so sad."

"It is," I confirmed, eyes on Cam as he walked up to the house. I could definitely hear the whistling now. I was going to kill him.

"But," Hope continued, "more immediately, I just saw Cheryl Johnson's car drive past on my way from dropping off Cam."

"You dropped off Cam?" I asked, momentarily confused. "So

… how far did he get this morning?"

"Oh, he made it to the store," Hope laughed. "And he's going to have to reveal the rest, because I don't think I'm qualified to both tell that story and drive at the same time."

That sounded about right on course for this day, even though Cam looked positively normal as he approached the house stairs. There were worlds of difference between the Cam who went sprinting out of here this morning and this Cam. This … *whistling* Cam.

"Interesting, huh?" I asked, instead of cursing, like I wanted to.

Hope barked out a laugh. "Understatement of the year. Maybe the decade? But that's not important right now. What is important is the part about Cheryl. Did you hear that?"

"She was already here," I started, only for Hope to make a little fluttery noise, cutting me off.

"Yes, I know, she's *going back*," Hope said, enunciating slowly and loudly enough to break through my Cam-induced haze of unparalleled rage. "There was also one of those really fancy Teslas following her."

That got my attention. "A Tesla."

"A white one," Hope confirmed. "Suspiciously quiet."

"They tend to be," I muttered, Cam's whistling piercing through the door before he opened it, appearing in the doorway with a little jaunt. I glared at him. "Unlike some people."

"Huh?" Hope asked, while Cam's eyes snapped up to mine, a question appearing in them. Before that question could fall to his lips, Cheryl's sensible sedan appeared on the gravel drive, the Tesla carefully crawling behind her.

"I've got to go," I said hastily over Hope saying something about a lawyer. We didn't need a lawyer. We needed a horse trailer, stat. "The Tesla has arrived."

"Tesla?" Cam asked, and wisely scooted out of the way for me to barrel past him, thundering down the stairs and breaking straight through the final step, my foot hitting the dirt beneath the rotten board.

"Oh, for …" I pulled my foot free, scrapes beading red around my ankle. I took a deep breath that did not make me feel any more relaxed, and immediately tensed when Cam carefully made his way down the steps after me.

"Lyn, let me look at it," he said carefully, obviously having come back to reality and read the situation, which was not so much light-and-airy-tra-la-la and more spooked-horse-panic.

I stood stock-still on one leg, looking between him and the cars with their people climbing out of them, surveying the land with oohs and aahs on their lips, and felt a curling in my chest. Like a little bit of me was slowly turning into iron.

"I'm fine," I said through gritted teeth, taking a limping step back. "It's no big deal. Let's just …" I glanced at Cheryl and her developers – a man and a woman, both wearing sunglasses and business-casual, completely out of place as one of the chickens strutted up to them and pecked an impeccable leather heel. The woman let out a little eek of surprise and laughed, fluttering a hand to her throat.

"It's ..." she said, her voice floating up to me. "It's certainly rustic, isn't it?"

"That's one word for it," the man replied, perching both hands on his hips and sweeping his gaze around the farm, skipping right over us like we weren't there.

Cheryl let out a little laugh, waving a hand dismissively. "Look past the structures," she advised.

"Oh, I am," he said.

"There's a pond on the property," Cheryl said, spinning to begin the tour and pointing toward the trees. "Right where the fields hit the forest, of which a good chunk rests on this parcel. The previous tenant sells trees for Christmas, so much of the land is forested."

"Nothing the land movers can't take care of," the woman said offhandedly, shading her eyes and standing on tiptoes as if she could see the water from the driveway. "The pond should be an excellent feature, Adam. Maybe a central point to the community?"

"We'll see what the surveyors come back with," Adam said, then paused in his sweep to focus on us. "You must be the current owners?"

Cheryl laughed, high and fluttery. I froze, unhelpfully, screaming at myself to do or say something smart and cutting only for Cam to shake his head calmly and thrust his hand out for introductions.

"The caretakers," he clarified. "For the past little while."

Adam brightened. "Ah, then you're the perfect tour guide. Care to show us around?"

I sucked in another breath, only for it to come out in an extended hiss when Cam grinned.

"Sure." He winked at me, then nodded toward the pastures. "Follow along."

My jaw dropped, right along with my stomach. What the ever loving …

I snapped my mouth closed and scurried to catch up with the group, drifting at the edges as Cam began the tour. The scratches on my ankle burned during the hike through the pumpkin patch, and my sanity was beginning to fray as we approached the rise to view the pond I hadn't noticed existed, then I was nearly on the tip of despair when the woman – Kim Something-or-another from a city I immediately forgot the second I heard it – stopped dead.

"Horses!" she exclaimed, childlike glee stretching across her mouth and lighting up her eyes, which had only a split-second ago been giving the barn a dirty glare. She quickened her step to the paddock fence, where Matilda was grazing with a single-minded, bordering-on-angry focus. Near the middle of the paddock, the boys stood shoulder to shoulder, Hazard almost hidden by Horace's bulk.

"Oh, this is such a treat! I haven't been to the barn since Jacqueline was born. Adam …" Kim shoved her phone into Adam's hand, "take a photo, will you?"

She skipped over to the fence and draped herself across the weathered boards in front of Matilda, who lifted her head to look at what was going on, her ears swiveling.

"You know …" Cam started forward tentatively, while I watched Matilda's muscles quiver along her shoulders, nostrils blowing as she assessed the situation. "You might want to take a step …"

Matilda finished Cam's sentence, throwing her neck over the fence and using her head like a battering ram against Kim's side, rubbing hard against what I felt sure was a previously quite expensive skirt, and finishing up with a hearty bite to the hem, pulling until I heard cloth tearing.

"Oh my god!"

Gone was the childlike glee. It had been replaced with an exasperated dismay I had a sinking feeling would be paid for in rolled coins, but before I could insert myself in the drama unfolding along the fence my phone started ringing, giving me a perfect opportunity to slip away from the crowd.

OK, maybe it was more like slithered. I slunk into the barn, hopefully unnoticed while Cam attempted to unlatch Matilda from Kim's clothing, and found my brother on the other end of the line.

"Please tell me there's a trailer on its way," I whispered, ducking into Hazard's stall and leaning against the battered wall. "Tell me it's ten minutes away. Please, please, please."

"Lyn," Harris sighed, "it's been like thirty minutes since I last talked to you. The trailer hasn't moved from its spot in Saratoga and you know it."

"Ruin my fantasy," I grumbled. "That's just like you."

"Yeah, also the guy who gave you a stall," he reminded me.

"But sure, fantasy-ruiner. That's fine."

"I'm sorry." I rubbed at my forehead. "It's been … well, it's been a day."

"Well, brace yourself," Harris said. "It's going to get worse."

I tensed, staring at a spot in the stall bedding with intense focus as I asked, "How can it possibly get worse?"

"Dad is in Saratoga," Harris replied.

I sank down to my butt in the stall, collapsing into the straw. "But …"

"And he's not letting the trailer go anywhere until you've talked to him," Harris continued.

"I can't just call …"

"In person," he finished.

"What?" I nearly shouted it. "I can't! You know I can't! Harris, you said …"

"Hey," Harris cut into my rising tirade. "I know just fine what I said. The facts, however, remain as they are. I can't get the trailer to you without Dad letting the trailer get to you, because he's right there with it at this current moment, and I happen to be in Florida."

"Why isn't he in Florida? He's supposed to be in Florida!"

"We left the girl at Saratoga," Harris replied, forever referring to Sweet Bell's stakes-winning juvenile filly as "the girl," simply because he knew it drove Georgie crazy. She was probably in earshot, glaring at him. "She's shipping out to California this weekend."

"The Breeders' Cup," I groaned, closing my eyes and resting my head back, my hair getting caught in the splintered wood. "Of course."

"Of course," Harris echoed. "You've got shitty timing."

"My life is basically comprised of shitty timing," I corrected. "So what does he want me to do, kiss the ring?"

"He wants you to talk to him, Lyn," Harris said, sensibly, as if he'd never had a problem talking to Dad.

I narrowed my eyes. "Easier said."

A beat passed, pregnant with silence.

"I guess I need to remind you that you're the talker in this family," Harris finally said. "If anyone can rise to this challenge and come out on top, it's you."

"Against Dad?" I asked, because the last time I went up against our father my throat had been too tight to let any words out, which didn't matter because there hadn't been any. I'd only had panic, sheer and silent, coating me like the sweat on a hot Saratoga day. Now Harris wanted me to go back to where this all started, to somehow convince a man who wasn't interested in helping me … to help me?

It wasn't possible.

"You can do this, little sister," Harris said with a calm confidence I didn't feel. My heart was a trapped thing, vibrating in the cage of my ribs. I let out a shaky breath and stood up, moving to the barn door and peeking outside, where the woman was staring at Hazard, her hem frayed along one side.

My skin washed cold. I recognized the look on Kim's face, the eager strain in which she leaned into the fence now that Matilda was a safe several yards away, Hazard at the end of her pointing finger. That was the look of a girl who wanted a horse. *That* horse. Right now.

Hazard, who kicked into a riotous canter from a stand-still, Horace trotting to keep up with him.

Hazard, *my horse.*

And even though I didn't have any confidence whatsoever, I nodded.

"Guess a road trip's in order, then."

Harris laughed. "Guess so."

—

"Now that gelding," Kim said as I stalked past the group on the way back to the house, Cam's eyes itchy on the back of my neck, "I would offer five figures for him right now."

I stalled so fast I almost pitched forward onto my face. With a scuttle of kicked gravel, I caught myself and spun at the same time, ready to fight. Everything was up – my blood, my temper, the little hairs along my arms. I must have looked rabid, a gleam in my eye, because Cam pulled himself to his full height.

"No," he said, simple and to the point.

I stopped and blinked, like someone had thwacked me on the nose with a rolled newspaper, too stunned to keep up my attack. Kim jerked her head back, looking up at Cam like she wasn't quite sure what he was telling her.

"Did you hear me? I said …"

"I heard you," Cam said, and then locked eyes with me, a shiver building on my spine. "The answer's no."

"Are you sure?" Kim asked. "With motion like that, I'd love to see him over fences. The scope on him could be …"

"The gelding isn't for sale," I bit out, all I could trust myself to say.

Kim snorted, waving a hand around her, the all-encompassing look-at-this-place-are-you-mad? smirk on her lips. "If you feel you can turn down that sort of money," she said, shrugging a shoulder. "It's too bad."

"For you," I pointed out, uncaring if everyone stopped to look at me, which they did, Kim's nose wrinkling like she smelled something gross. "It is for you," I pressed, "because he's staying with me. The farm my not be mine to save from you vultures, but that horse is off limits."

Kim's mouth dropped, Adam's hands went to his hips, and Cheryl laughed nervously, clutching her clipboard to her chest like a shield against my spitting words.

"Lyn," Cam started, eyebrows furrowed as he eased toward me. I lifted my chin and kept my jaw tight, because if I didn't, I was sure it would start wobbling, teeth clacking, tears only moments away. Cam's fingers brushed mine, a warm rush spooling into my stomach to war with the acid churning there. "Hey," Cam said softly, only for me to hear, "want to take a break for a minute?"

No, no I didn't. I had too much to do and not enough daylight to do it in. I shook my head and turned around, walking fast all the way back to the house. I leapt up the rotted steps, my ankle twinging a little at the memory, and barreled through the front door thinking only one thing: underwear.

I needed underwear if I was driving all the way down to Saratoga at this hour. I threw my phone on my unmade bed, the twisted sheets making my face flame. Quickly, I turned away from the memories and snatched up the satchel that came with my Louis Vuitton set, throwing a clean pair of panties and a pair of leggings in for extra measure. I didn't know what I had left in the drawers at the Saratoga house, but it was best to be prepared.

Pausing in the bathroom, I snatched my stick of deodorant and the good conditioner. Because like hell my father was seeing me at anything less than shiny and smelling of faint, fresh cotton.

"Lyn?"

I winced at Cam's voice and turned for the front door, pushing past him and back down the steps, leaping over the last one and taking off for the car. The keys sat in the cupholder, because who on earth was around to steal it? I yanked open the door, and it met Cam's hand, his fingers curling around the edge.

"Lyn," he said again, ducking his head just a bit to meet my eyes. "I'm reasonably sure I would love to play chase with you in different circumstances, but this is concerning me."

I wedged myself between the door and the car, refusing to meet his eyes. He reached around and caught my hips in his hands, keeping me stationary before I could sink into the car and do what I'd done before – speed off, leaving him eating dust.

"Hey, look at me," Cam said, and when I wouldn't he kept going. "Is this because of this morning? When I went running? Because I'm sorry about that. I just couldn't be here when the realtor came, not with everything on my mind. I probably would have punched her, and if that had happened I'd definitely be in jail by now, so ..."

"Stop," I said, raising both hands and then letting them fall with a gust of air. "This isn't about you running off because of a realtor, Cam, this is about you running *off* because that is exactly what you're doing, isn't it?"

He tilted his head at me, confusion twisting his lips. "I think you need to maybe give me a little more to work with here, Lyn, because I'm ..."

"The note." I pointed to the house, my voice rising to the point I was sure our tour guests could hear. I didn't care, because my throat was open and the words ... oh, they were tumbling out faster than I could think them. "The $175-an-hour-stars-and-ex-clamation-points note that you left on the table like I wouldn't see it? Who does that? You have an opportunity, and that's amazing for you, it is, and I wish you all the luck in the world."

Cam made a face, letting go of me to rub at a particular spot his forehead. "OK," he said through a grimace, "I think we have some wires crossed here ..."

"Do we?" I asked. "Because you're obviously eager to show this place off. Speaking of, tour guide Cam has a tour he needs to get back to."

I waved in the direction of Cheryl, who waved back with a cheerful smile. I gave Cam a pressed-lip smile and turned back to the car, falling into the seat and hitting the ignition. The Audi roared to life.

"Lyn, I need to stress to you that we're really not on the same page," Cam said, lifting his voice over the engine. "I'm only doing this because I have some really excellent news I didn't get a chance to tell you about earlier."

"The $175 an hour," I muttered, finding my sunglasses and shoving them on. "I got the news, Cam. No need to keep repeating it. I get that we can't stay here together, and I get that you have an opportunity that sounds *really excellent*, but I have my own thing that just popped up and I need to go."

Cam stopped, brows furrowing. "What kind of thing."

It wasn't a question. I sucked in a breath and held it, then made myself smile up at him. "I need to see a man about a horse."

———

SARATOGA IN THE OFF season was just as beautiful as Saratoga in the racing season, the green canopies tinged amber and the Victorians licked with sunset light. Pumpkins sat on their stoops, some carved into grinning, fanged faces. It even smelled good. I rolled down the windows and got a lungful, fortifying myself for the fight ahead.

Our particular Victorian sat off the main thoroughfare, a quick jaunt away from the old Oklahoma Training Track. One glance at the white columns on the wraparound porch set my heart racing – and not from homesickness.

From dread.

I pulled into the driveway and sat for a good five minutes,

still trying to formulate a plan that hadn't gelled in the two hours it had taken me to drive south. The silence in the car was oppressive, which made me wonder what was up with my phone. Surely someone would be interested in my whereabouts – Cam and Harris the two most interested parties, even if I'd told at least one of them to go eat rocks in the last few hours.

I grabbed the bag I'd hastily thrown together, digging through the underwear and spare leggings, shoving my wallet to the side and finding … nothing.

Damn it.

Now I didn't even have my phone to distract me. It was just me and my cycling thoughts, which whispered *you can't do this* and *turn the car around and go home.* Then I laughed, out loud, because if Lake Placid was home I might as well keep driving until I hit Florida, where I could beg Harris to fight my battles in person.

Asking what I needed to ask would go down so much better in person.

Then I groaned, picturing Harris doing that irritating wink and gun-finger-point thing that he did when I proved his point for him.

"Fine," I grumbled to my absent brother. "I get it. I'm sure you're looking extremely smug right now."

I slammed the car door. The Victorian loomed over me as I walked up the steps and stood in front of the ornate stained-glass door. I briefly considered ringing the doorbell, because all of this felt foreign to me, and yet intensely familiar. Like I'd lived here decades ago and was coming back to see the house after another family had made it home.

It was familiar and unfamiliar – both things at once.

I shoved my shoulders back, and put my hand on the doorknob, pushing the door open. It swung inward soundlessly, presenting me with glowing hardwood and opulence, every inch dusted and maintained to designer magazine perfection. A giant vase of hydrangeas exploded off of the foyer table, as though announcing, "Yes, the owners are in town."

Melanie, our housekeeper, must have put them there. I could picture her sprinting to the florist and rushing back to the house only moments before Dad arrived and swept through the door, barely noticing the flowers were even there in his well-trodden path to the office.

The dark, wood-paneled office, with its leather furniture and gold-edged books, famed portraits of horses on the walls. It smelled like cigars and single-malt scotch, and I could still smell it as I drifted toward the open door, where I could just spot Dad behind his desk.

He was reclining, his feet up on the desk, playing on his phone. I stopped in the middle of the doorway and stared at him, and jumped when he finally spoke.

"Your brother said you were on your way."

I cleared my throat. "Yes."

"You couldn't have given me any forewarning?"

"I left my phone in Lake Placid."

Dad didn't look up at me. "Melanie didn't know what you wanted, so she did her best. Dinner's in the kitchen, being kept warm. Also thanks to Melanie."

"I didn't really come here to eat."

Then he did look up at me, a sweep of his eyes right up my body before pinning me down with a look I knew meant it didn't really matter at all what I'd come to do. I was on his time now.

"Amuse me," he said, one corner of his lips pulling up in a half-smile. He pulled his feet off the desk and stood to his full height, towering well above me. He was still in dress shirt and slacks, his handmade Italian leather shoes spotless, as though he hadn't been to the track at all that day. He looked like a Wall Street banker, fresh from trading other people's money and loving every harried second of it.

He put an arm around my stiff shoulders and steered me into the kitchen, which smelled like Melanie had either gone all out or had made another panicked dash for take-out from a restaurant not used to such orders. I watched as Dad pulled plates out of the oven, sliding one across the marble countertop toward me.

"It's hot," he said, while I rolled my eyes and got the utensils.

We ate silently, standing, the kitchen island between us. Dad said nothing. I said nothing. Eventually, midway through slicing through a chicken breast that had somehow maintained its juiciness, he paused.

I held my breath.

"Wine," he said, smacking his hand against the counter, and

disappeared to the basement. My body deflated in relief, giving me a moment to regroup while Dad tried to figure out what vintage went best with warmed take-out chicken.

I didn't get far – Dad popped back out of the cellar with a bottle in hand, already cranking the cork out of the neck. It released with a startled pop.

"So," he said, setting two glasses between us and beginning to pour. I watched the red liquid gurgle into the glass, trying desperately to think of something – anything – worth saying when it was eventually my turn to speak again. "Your brother says you're coming home."

"To Red Gate," I clarified, and Dad smirked against the rim of his glass.

"Yes, I heard about your horse. I'll get to that in a minute. Where are *you* going to stay?"

"Red Gate has workers' quarters," I said slowly, the words formulating on my tongue and tumbling into the air before I'd had a chance to really look at them. "I don't see why I can't say there."

Dad took a swallow of his wine. "I've been brought up to speed on your living situation," he told me, licking his lips. "It must be rather dire if you think the workers' quarters at Red Gate is acceptable housing."

"It is for the people who work there," I pointed out.

He looked at me steadily. "And you're not those people."

I stared straight back, something in me twisting until …

"How do you know?" I blurted out, Dad's eyebrow twitching

up. "Do you even know who I am, or have you gone my entire life presuming to know without ever once attempting to find out?"

Dad patted his lips with one immaculate napkin and tossed it on the counter.

"I know you have a closet dedicated entirely to handbags and drive a luxury car you definitely were not the one to pay for – your third white Audi, I believe?"

I glared at him. "Those are things, Dad. Things do not a person make."

"Regardless," he waved a hand. "Let's entertain for the moment that you will stay in the workers' quarters. What will you be doing with yourself while you make your cinderblock compartment a home?"

"You can cut the sarcasm at any moment," I crossed my arms over my chest and forced myself to uncross them. It was a sign of weakness, a defense mechanism. Dad laughed.

"Fine," he said, picking up his wine glass. "I'll cut the sarcasm. My question still stands. What are you going to do with yourself, Lynsey? It's all I've wanted to know, and you've acted like sharing such information is a violation of your privacy. Educate me."

He took a sip from his glass, and I couldn't shake the sudden image of him, weeks before at Saratoga, a champagne glass in his hand after the Whitney Handicap.

"No more college," he'd said. "You're not getting anything out of my pocket anymore, Lyn. Not until you've proven yourself."

College, Mom's inheritance, a future padded with safety nets and feather-soft landings – gone. Ripped out from under me at the same time I was shoved out the door. And I'd let him do it – push me out, take everything that had been willed to me away, and hadn't bothered to come looking for me when I'd done the Armstrong thing; storm off with a squeal of Audi tires.

Well. Not anymore.

I tipped my chin up. "I have Hazard."

"Who?" Dad asked, swallowing his wine.

"Lost Cause."

"And what's a failed racehorse going to get you?"

I spoke without thinking about it – instinct taking over like it usually did when I didn't know what I needed to say.

"I'll retrain him," I said. "He's eligible for the Retired Race-horse Project. People know this horse, and they'll want to see him land in a good post-race career. He practically comes with his own PR, and since I just got an offer of five figures for him all he needs to do is show potential at the Makeover to sell well."

I couldn't imagine parting with Hazard, but Dad didn't need to know that. He just needed to know I intended to sell him, even if I never did.

Dad lowered his wine glass, the clink against marble making me cringe.

"And you'll do this out of Red Gate?" he asked, eyes steadily on mine. It was unnerving, but I knew what he was doing. The full-court press was something I'd experienced since I'd learned to toddle.

I nodded. "Why not? It has plenty of space to train one horse, and if I need a cross-country course I have plenty of friends."

Dad was silent, hand on the stem of his glass. "And the future?" he pressed. "After Lost Cause?"

"Take the sale money," I said, "and buy more Thoroughbreds. Retired racehorses are trending up, Dad. It's not all about imported warmbloods anymore. We can make our horses into more than stressed out speedballs. They deserve the opportunity."

"Good causes are not often the financially sound ones," he pointed out.

"Maybe you'll be willing to donate a few horses to this one," I said, leaning into the counter. "Look at it as good PR for Tupelo. After all the sport's been through in the past few years, an olive branch will make you look like a saint. Think of the glowing praise in *The Blood-Horse* or *The Chronicle* and tell me that doesn't look spectacular for you."

"Assuming you can retrain this one horse," Dad said slowly. I raised an eyebrow.

"You think of all things I can't retrain one horse?"

Dad laughed. "No, Lyn," he shook his head. "Of everything I know about you, retraining horses is well within your capability."

"And no college education required," I said, smiling smugly. "You can keep your money."

Dad was quiet for a beat, finally looking down at the counter. The lack of eye contact made me catch myself, drawing in a breath I hoped he couldn't hear. Finally he nodded.

"Concerning the money, it's not mine to keep from you."

My breath squelched in my throat.

"What do you mean?" I managed.

"Your mother's money," he said, looking up at me. "I spoke with Harris and he's right, in the end, that it's not mine to keep from you. I admit, I thought I had good intentions by keeping the trust out of your hands, but if you're serious about this idea of yours I can see where some seed money could come in helpful."

"Seed money," I repeated, like a parrot.

"Indeed," he nodded. "What do you think?"

"What do I *think*?" I nearly shouted. "Of course. Of course, Dad. Thank you."

If a counter hadn't been between us, if we had been anyone other than Lynsey and Oliver Armstrong with a messy history and probably a contentious future, I would have hugged him. Instead I felt full of vibrations, my whole body buzzing with all the potential that had suddenly opened up like a door at the end of a dimly lit hall.

I took a big breath and let myself grin. Even Dad managed a small smile.

"I'll want to see your expenditures," he said, pointing at me. "Reports on everything. The money is yours, but I'm involved now, Lyn. If I give you horses, I'm a client. I want cuts – we can talk about the percentages later."

I considered him. "A silent partner?"

"Not quite," he shook his head. "An investor."

I swallowed hard but nodded. "Understood."

Then Dad really smiled and lifted his glass. "What will you call this endeavor of yours?"

I looked at the wine sloshing in his hand and a name hit me hard, ran up my throat and was out of my mouth. The old instinct taking hold.

"No Turning Back," I said, and lifted my glass to his.

Chapter Nineteen

CAM

HOW MANY TIMES TODAY was I going to have to – literally, and figuratively – put on my big boy pants?

I'd already plunged into the pit of despair once, and clawed my way back out. Mustered optimism. Made a plan. Put my pants on. Following the fake-it-till-you-make-it school of thought, I'd even whistled.

Then, before I could properly enjoy the fizzing hope of The Plan, Lynsey had told me off and accelerated out of sight at a rate far too speedy for the rutted condition of our driveway. Meanwhile, too-smiley Cheryl was still here with too-rich Kim and Adam.

I rubbed my forehead, massaged my temples, then grabbed my waistband, hitched up my jeans, and whistling a fresh, new tune, sauntered out to information-gather from the enemy.

—

I LOOKED AROUND THE kitchen. What did I feel like having for lunch? It would be much easier if Lynsey was here. She'd pick something and I'd realize that was exactly what I wanted, too … but there was no sign of her.

It occurred to me I could text her. It wasn't the way we normally communicated, but there was nothing normal about today. I found my phone in the basket on the coffee table where I left it most of the time these days, and found her in my contacts. Thinking of lunch. You coming back? Anything you want? Then I stared at it for a while, during which time it didn't vibrate or make any sound.

Was she really that bent out of shape? Over … what? A note? A misunderstanding? I didn't even really fully know what she was thinking … she hadn't stuck around long enough to tell me.

I ran through the list of rationalizations I'd accumulated over the years:

1. If she couldn't give me the benefit of the doubt, did I really want to be with her?

2. If she couldn't work out this tiny misunderstanding, what would happen when we had bigger ones?

3. If she wasn't prepared to let spontaneous and uninhibited make-up sex get us past little bumps in the road like this one, was she the right person for me?

These questions were tried-and-true. I'd applied them many, many times before.

Of course, when I met Lynsey, I was single, so the number of women who'd successfully navigated all my questions to date, was

… zero.

Whatever. The questions weren't unreasonable. I wasn't unreasonable. Gunning it down the driveway when we were in the middle of a crisis, with some mumbled explanation about a man and a horse was unreasonable.

Lynsey was unreasonable.

Fine then. Peanut butter and jam. I'd eat it alone and I'd enjoy it. Then I'd go to Lewis's. If I could follow Forrest's instructions and make this plan work, I wanted to be done working for Hope and Lewis. I wanted to be free to work with Lynsey, on our farm.

—

WHITE PAINT. IT COULD drive you crazy. Literally. The endlessly repetitive motion of rolling it on. The difficulty in judging which parts of the wall were already painted. The cloying scent that seemed to stick to the inside of my nostrils.

There was this condition I heard about from one of my fellow students who studied in the North. *Pibloktoq*. I'd seen it defined as a little-understood hysteria seen in people living in the long Arctic winters. It would be oversimplifying to say it was from too much white, but the endless snow certainly wouldn't help.

I was pushing through with the painting, though, because I wanted to be finished. Wanted this behind me. Wanted to hand the keys to the neat, tidy, freshly-white-painted, *completed* cabin to Lewis.

To maintain some level of sanity, I took occasional breaks to make phone calls and left messages with Forrest's experts.

I was standing sideways to the wall, peering across the surface to try to determine the wet and dry areas so I'd know where to put an extra coat, when my phone rang.

Winston would meet me at the farm at 9:00 a.m. tomorrow.

Before I could even pick up the roller again, Harriet had returned my call. Would 11:00 tomorrow morning work for me?

OK, this was good. Two down, one to go, and the two I'd already secured had to be the tough ones, right? I mean a real estate agent was pretty much guaranteed to show up.

I hoisted the roller, not even wincing at the particular spot on my thumb where it had first rubbed, then popped, a blister.

I was on the right track. I had to believe I was. Suddenly, keeping this from Lynsey seemed silly. I took a mini-break to text her *Things coming together – can't wait to talk about it.* After all, we were in this together. Lynsey could spend the day meeting experts with me tomorrow. We could have a drink together after. Then we could …

… the thought of what we could do after allowed me to blur out the tedious repetition of the final bit of white painting.

—

LYNSEY STILL WASN'T HOME.

I'd never thought of "seeing a man about a horse" as a time-consuming activity.

Yet, even though I'd worked so long (and rolled on so much white paint) that it was dark when I coasted up the driveway, there was no Lynsey. No Lynsey's car. No sign that either Lynsey or her car had been home.

One of those signs would be barn chores being done, and since the horses were still out, as shadowy figures grazing through the dark, and the chickens might as well have been an advertisement for fox food, exposed as they were in their daytime run, it appeared I had work to do before I could enjoy the frozen pizza I'd picked up at Price Chopper.

The super-deluxe, expensive, rising-crust kind of pizza that I'd only splurged on because I thought it would be nice to open a bottle of wine and share both wine and pizza with Lynsey, and I could bring her up to speed on all my appointments for tomorrow, and united nobody could beat us … and she wasn't here.

My stomach rumbled long and loud and I thought, *Yeah, well screw you Lynsey.* I was getting hungrier by the minute and I'd have no problem eating the entire pizza by myself.

As soon as I fed these animals, that was.

I pushed the double doors open and called out into the night and was answered by rustlings, and hoofbeats, and a low whicker.

Somebody in this world was happy to see me.

—

BY THE TIME I'D taken care of the animals, alone, and eaten my pizza, alone, and written out a list of bullet points and questions for each of the people I was meeting tomorrow … and, let's face it, I was pretty sure by now that would be alone, I was good and mad.

I hadn't felt this way for a while. Hadn't cared about anyone enough to let them make me angry for a very long time.

My normal modus operandi was to shrug and walk away. Which, believe me, tended to inspire fury in other people, but my blood pressure always stayed low and even.

Tonight, a headache was creeping in, and I realized it was from the clench of my jaw and the tightness in my temples.

First thing this morning, waking up beside Lynsey, it felt great to have somebody to care about.

Now ... I was starting to wonder why I bothered.

One thing was for sure – I wasn't sleeping in her bed. If she showed up in the middle of the night, she could stumble into a cold empty bed without disturbing my sleep.

Right before I went ahead and climbed into my own bed, I texted her. OK. I'm officially angry now. I was feeling too petty to even stick a good-night on the end of my message.

—

I WOKE UP FREEZING cold and terrified.

What if Lynsey was – as my mother would say – dead in a ditch? What if her car had broken down? What if she'd stayed away because she got some devastating news?

What if something was very wrong with Lynsey, and the very last thing I'd ever texted to her was that I was angry?

My breathing was short and sharp. My heart was hammering. I scrambled for my phone. I take it back. Just tell me where you are.

There. I'd unjinxed myself. She'd be OK now. In fact, maybe I'd walk out to the barn to find her feeding the animals.

Phew. Alright. Today would be a better day.

—

I FED THE ANIMALS alone.

Winston and I followed Forrest's directions to the woodrat latrines without Lynsey. When he swept his arm around in a wide circle and said, "I believe this area could be a seasonal wetland of some environmental significance," it was left to me to take note of the twin spruce trees marking the outer edge of the possible wetland.

Likewise, Lynsey missed it when Harriet Serpent turned over a rock to reveal what she assured me was a Queen snake (although, to me, it just looked like something to be avoided at all costs).

Winston promised me a report. Harriet promised me a report. I didn't even have to wait for a report from Brian Morris, the alternative real estate agent. Nor did he even want a tour of the place.

"I know this farm well," he said. "If you can even call it a farm. It's too rocky for crops, too swampy for much in the way of livestock, and too far out of town for a subdivision — no matter what dollar signs Cheryl Johnson may have dancing through her head." He scribbled a figure on a business card, said "If I was listing it, I'd start twenty-thousand higher than this, but I'd accept this offer in a heartbeat," and handed me the card.

"No offense meant," he added.

I looked at the figure he'd scrawled out. "None taken." I shook his hand. "None at all."

I sat on the top step, holding the card, watching the real estate agent drive away, and took out my phone. Lynsey. We can do this. Really, we can, if you'll just come back.

Then to keep myself from being completely pathetic and staring at my phone, I drove to Lewis's for what I hoped would be the last time as a labourer.

Once there I took a few minutes to distance myself from the stress of my own current anxiety, uncertainty, and loneliness to look around the light, open, airy – and, yes, *white* – space and think, *This place looks great.*

Lewis and Hope would be happy here.

At least someone would be happy.

I shook my head. *Don't be stupid.* If anyone deserved it, it was those two. In fact, maybe this was just the final reckoning up. The good-people-getting-good-things, and those with a less stellar track record suffering.

By which I meant me. Because Lynsey – well, she might be many things, but in my books she was a pretty good person. She deserved happiness.

Maybe that's what she was out seeking right now. Far away from me.

Not answering my texts.

I snapped a picture of sun slashing across Hope and Lewis's floorboards. Of their brand-new-to-them, big, bright space and sent it to Lynsey. My work here is done. If you like this, I'm pretty sure I could do it again. Come home and we'll talk about it.

Then I locked the door, and pushed my temporary set of keys

back through the mailslot.

—

THERE WERE REPORTS IN my inbox when I got back home.

I sat on the porch and sipped a lemonade and read through them, and thought.

The gist of my thinking was that it was time to talk to Forrest again.

Which meant going into town.

My stomach rumbled. There was food in town, which was more than I could say for the kitchen here.

So.

Time to make a plan.

I didn't want to make these plans alone. I took my phone out again. Please. Lynsey. Please just text me. Just call me. Please.

I can't believe I sent that text and I wasn't even drunk.

There was a squeal from the field where Hazard had invaded Matilda's personal space, and she'd reminded him just how close goofy young geldings were allowed to come to sophisticated mature mares like her.

Answer: Not very.

I had responsibilities here.

My stomach growled again.

Feed horses. Feed myself. Hope for divine inspiration.

Or, track Hope down for divine inspiration.

—

BACK IN THE CABIN, horses fed, I paced while I brushed my teeth. If

I did this place up like Lewis's would I miss the charm of the hallway so narrow only one person could fit through at a time? Of the uneven floors that would send me sprawling if I dragged my feet across the threshold into the bathroom? Of the chicken sitting in the middle of the kitchen floor?

I'd definitely miss the chicken, and I think Lynsey would too. But a new, improved, cabin could incorporate a new, modernized chicken flap – right?

Thinking of Lynsey, I could hear her voice in my head. "*Why do you always have to wander when you brush your teeth? In no way should you ever be in the living room with a toothbrush in your mouth.*"

I picked up my phone. Brushing my teeth in the living room while texting you. It's called multi-tasking. Deal with it.

Animals snug, teeth brushed, my string of I-have-no-pride texts growing, I had a few minutes before I had to leave to meet Hope.

I knew what to do. I was going to steal Lynsey's sheets.

Lynsey's warm, soft, flannel sheets that, since she'd sailed off without a word, or explanation, I felt completely entitled to.

I flung her quilt to the side, so I could get at the corners to pull them loose. With those liberated, I went to the head of the bed and yanked her pillows out of the way.

And stopped. And stared.

No. *No, no, no, no, no …*

Lying there, sharp and bold against the crumpled, brushed fabric of the sheets, was the high-contrast graphic horseshoe that adorned Lynsey's phone case.

If I felt stupid texting a girl who was completely ignoring me, I couldn't even fix on the word for how I felt once I knew she didn't even care enough to take her phone with her.

"Fine!" I dropped the pillow I was holding.

I spun on my heel, and grabbed my own phone and my keys on my way out, pausing only long enough to tell the chicken. "I give up."

"On Lynsey," I added. I could be sad, or I could be angry. I could give up the farm or I could fight for it.

I decided while I was still angry I might as well fight and see how far that got me.

I was pretty sure the sadness would come later.

—

SO MUCH FOR DIVINE inspiration. So much for Hope.

There was a sign on the bakery door saying Closed early. Gone to Granite. Join us for some good news!

I stood, and stared, and a dog licked my leg, and the woman walking him said, "You look lost dear."

I turned to her. "I've lost Hope." Then, realizing how it might sound, added. "That is, not hope: *Hope.*"

Even though that made no sense either, she nodded, peered at the sign, and said, "You haven't lost her. She's at the Granite."

My face must have looked as blank as my mind, because she snapped her fingers and said, "Rufus and I will take you there."

The walk wasn't far, but turns out Rufus was arthritic and

it was nearly ten minutes before we stopped walking / shuffling. "Well, here you are." As though he understood his owner's words, Rufus flopped to the sidewalk with a huge sigh.

"Here?" I asked. The door we were standing in front of was just that – a door – there wasn't a window in sight. "Am I allowed to go in there?"

"Of course, dear. Everybody's allowed in. Well, except Rufus, I'm afraid, which is why we'll leave you here."

I squinted at the faded sign over the door. Granite Club. Est. 1953. *OK, then.*

I turned to ask a follow-up question, only to find Rufus had hauled himself to his feet and they were shuffling off. "Good-bye, dear," the woman called. "Once Rufus is moving, I have to go with him."

I put my hand on the well-dinged steel door. A steel door … it made me think of protection, of security. It made me think of places I'd learned to avoid while living in Montreal. Biker clubs, unofficial casinos, and so-called pubs that were maybe one or two steps up from the first two.

I'd been kicked out of one of the latter as an undergrad student when I'd gotten caught going from table to table emptying the remnants of pitchers into my pint glass. "You're lucky 'broke' just describes your financial situation," the bouncer had told me. "I catch you in here again, and something else will be broke."

I pushed the door open with trepidation, uncertainty, and much more effort than I'd expected – it was *heavy* – and stepped into the unexpected.

Enough shoes to open a shoe store lined the narrow hallway in front of me, under signs that said Please remove outdoor shoes, as debris is easily transferred to the ice.

At the end of the hall the space opened up. On the left was a seating area created of overstuffed leather sofas and a fireplace. Next to that were nearly a dozen round tables, and at the end of the space, a bar.

On the right, lines of cushioned chairs faced a huge sheet of glass behind which people were scattered around a wide sheet of ice.

It was a curling club.

The smells, sounds, look, and feel rushed back to me. As a kid, I'd spent several years in a Little Rocks program. I'd even curled for my high school team … as a spare … when they were desperate. I'd never known friendlier people than curlers, or a friendlier place than a curling club.

I walked in with the feeling of coming home.

"Ho! Young Cameron!" It appeared the club was also some sort of office-by-proxy for Forrest, since he was hailing me from one of the large round tables, where he was sitting with a couple of other people, surrounded by a spread of papers, pens, and – no surprise – pint glasses.

Hope's uncle gestured to an empty seat. "I'm not going to even pretend I'm getting up to greet you. Sit yourself down, and say hello to Stu Connelly, our esteemed mayor, and Ann Bradshaw, our town planner. We've just been running over some final details of the town's involvement in Albert's memorial for tomorrow …"

"God rest his soul," Mayor Connelly and Planner Bradshaw chorused together, before Forrest nodded, "Yes, of course," and continued, "But we're just about done, and since we're talking about Albert, this would seem to be a good time to hear your latest update."

—

A ROUND OF PINTS later, Mayor Connelly and Planner Bradshaw had been fully briefed on the farm situation. Despite telling me to speak, Forrest had jumped in to cover the first part, only letting me take over to summarize my meetings and the reports I'd had from Forrest's recommended experts. I'd finished by sliding Brian Morris's business card, bearing his scribbled appraisal, into the middle of the table.

Mayor Connelly pocketed the card, nodded at me, "Nice to meet you, son," said, "I have to see a man about a horse," and strolled off.

It was a struggle not to ask him to say hi to Lynsey while he was seeing said man about said horse.

I followed Forrest to the glass where we watched a beautiful take-out win a hotly contested end on Sheet Four, and I said, "He didn't seem that interested."

Forrest never lifted his eyes from the ice. "He's interested enough."

And that was when my blood pressure spiked, and my fists clenched, and I started telling myself "*No four-letter words, Cam,*" and "*You cannot punch a man forty-years older than you.*"

"Forrest ..." I was fighting to keep my voice even. I was battling to keep my fists low.

"Yes?"

"With all due respect, Forrest ..."

"Yes?"

"What, exactly ..." The pitch of my voice was creeping up. My fists were inching higher.

"Aah ... here we are." Forrest stepped sideways to reveal the Mayor, holding out a phone.

"Call for you." Mayor Connelly held the handset toward me, and not having any clue what else to do I took it.

"Are you my tenant?" asked the voice on the other end of the line.

"Uh ..."

"At my father's farm. Well, my farm now. Living with that eccentric girl. Is that who I'm speaking to?"

"Wes?"

"Yes, I'm Wes, but that's not what I asked."

"Um. Yes. This is Cam."

"Well, Cam, Stu tells me you have an offer for me."

"He does? I do?" I whirled around to look first at the Mayor, then at Forrest. Both were nodding and smiling.

"Yes, well, here's what he told me ..." I nodded as he recapped the information I'd passed on to the Mayor – the information I'd thought he'd completely ignored. I listened as he said, "... Stu tells me there won't be a development meeting to address any of this for quite some time, and I have no reason to disbelieve him, since he's coming here to meet me for a fishing getaway."

"Oh, I …"

"At any rate, Stu told me the price Brian recommended for the old place, and he says you'd like to put that in as an offer."

I would? An offer? "I …"

"Well, not so fast. The wife's still out on the golf course and even with Stu's recommendation, I'll need to discuss it with her – more than my life's worth not to – so don't go thinking your offer's accepted."

I swallowed. "OK. Of course. I definitely won't think that."

"I'll call you back at the club." The dial tone hummed in my ear.

The mayor held out his hand for the receiver. "What did he say?"

"He said he'll call me back here."

He nodded. "Well, then. Guess you'd better settle down with a pint and watch some curling."

As Forrest and I watched him walk away, Forrest said. "They were all in school together, you know. Wes, and Stu, and Brian. Albert gave them all driving lessons in his old truck."

My hands fell open. My jaw relaxed. "So, you pretty much knew what you were doing all along."

Forrest shrugged. "Just giving advice. Doing what I can. Trying to honour the memory of Lester Albert Parkman, God rest his soul."

"Wait, did you say 'Lester?'"

"Yup, his father was also named Lester, so he went by Albert, except for really important things, like the naming of his farm. He said land should bear the name of the person who loves it."

"Is there anything you don't know, Forrest?" I shook my head. "Cancel that question – I already know the answer. Why don't I buy you a pint?"

"I won't argue with that."

—

MY HEAD WAS SPINNING. Or floating. It made it hard to finish the text I'd been composing to Lynsey. The one that started, Even though you buggered off and left your phone behind, I'm sending you an update …

I'd been trying to finish it all night but was distracted by Hope and Lewis coming off the ice, holding hands, looking particularly sparkly, and smiley, and in love and I thought, *"No, that's not right, Cam. You don't describe a person as sparkly."* Except, of course you do when they're flashing a ring as big and bright as the one Hope was wearing.

Forrest had it figured out well before me. It was while he was hugging his niece and reaching out a hand to Lewis that I clued in. "You're getting married?"

After I did my share of hugging and back-slapping, and even sniffed back a rogue tear – oh, and bought a celebratory round – I added that tidbit to my ongoing text to Lynsey. Oh, and by the way,

Hope and Lewis are engaged. WHICH YOU WOULD KNOW IF YOU HADN'T ABANDONED US.

I couldn't finish it then, though, because a girl came in. A girl I could hardly believe. She was all smiles, and pink skin, with freckles brushed across her cheekbones, and shiny hair bouncing in a pony-tail, and curves … Oh my god … the curves on the girl.

And she was Hope's cousin.

"Is she single?" I asked Lewis while we were both at the bar for the I-don't-know-how-many-times-it was.

He looked at me. "Um … but aren't you … I mean, Hope kind of mentioned …"

"Who am I standing here with?" I asked. My voice was slurred, yes it was, but the facts were crystal-clear. I was standing at the bar with me, myself, and I, alongside my best friend who was now de-serting me for married life.

Lewis sighed. "She's single."

"Yup," I said. "OK." I picked up my fresh pint. "Not that I care."

And that was the terrible, horrible, most-disappointing thing about falling in love. It was why I'd resisted it at every turn. I'd known, deep down, that falling in love would ruin everything and, sure enough, it had.

There was a little gap between the buttons on the shirt stretch-ing over Hope's cousin's breasts. It let me peek inside. It showed me lace.

I didn't want to take her shirt off.

On her way to the bathroom – which I'd already seen was downstairs, next to a quiet, and private, lounge – she brushed by me closer than she needed to, and wobbled just a little bit, and placed her hand on my thigh, and said, "Oh, I'm sorry, maybe I need to get away from the crowds for a little while," and I knew, for a fact, I was supposed to follow her.

And I didn't.

Loving Lynsey had probably wrecked my life completely and forever – or at least for the length of the future I could foresee – so I told her that. I hate you. Everyone here is happy, and I'm just drunk and sad. And alone. And it's your fault.

I blinked. The top of the text was long-since out of sight. This was really more of an essay than a text. Yeah. I know this is too long. Deal with it.

I caught sight of Forrest's wife, Eleanor, studying notes with Planner Bradshaw. Not that you care, but Albert's memorial is to-morrow. I guess I'll go alone.

My finger hovered over my screen. Drinking and texting. Somewhere in the recesses of my brain I knew it was a bad idea. Even if the person I was texting wasn't in possession of her phone. I should delete my long and rambling message.

Someone tapped my shoulder, my finger slipped, and the message was sent, just like that.

I didn't have time to worry about it though, because the bartender immediately handed me the now-familiar curling club phone. "It's for you. It's Wes."

I took a deep breath, placed the receiver at my ear, and said, "Hi Wes. Let me just get somewhere a little quieter."

—

"WE'LL ACCEPT YOUR OFFER."

Oh wow, oh whoa, oh my.

"Could you run the details by me … just so we're both clear?" I knew the exact details didn't matter. I knew it was a big "yes-or-no" decision. But I needed a few seconds to think.

While Wes rustled papers in the background I pushed the back door of the curling club open and breathed in the crisp, autumn air. Gazed up at the star-sprayed black sky. Thought of leaving here. Thought of not leaving here.

Wes read me the number I knew so well it was seared on the inside of my eyelids when I closed them. He went on to say, "And that's for everything. You take it as-is. I don't have to come back, or dispose of anything, or find homes for any animals. Nothing. If anything collapses the day after you take possession, it's on you. Those are the terms. Take it or leave it."

A roar sounded in the club behind me. Either a curler had pulled off a wicked steal, or a drinker had put down their credit card for a fresh round.

"I'll take it." I didn't really know how I was going to pay for it, but I'd figure it out, right? People figured these things out. If I waited until I had the money, the farm would be gone, and that thought sent a shiver running right through me, making me blurt. "Done. Deal."

Wes made a grunting noise. "If I was there, I'd shake your hand, sir. But since I'm not, I'll fax these details to Forrest and he can draw up a proper agreement for us."

I walked back into the club, skirted around the packed tables, and handed the bartender the phone. Then, before Lewis could buy me another beer, or Forrest or the mayor could quiz me about Albert's land, or Hope's luscious cousin could come back to tease me, I jogged to the front door, pushed through it and started the long walk home.

I left the village behind, passed Hazard's former pasture, knocked my knuckles on the jeans-hanging tree as I went by it. I'd run these roads, driven these roads, and walked these roads with Lynsey.

These were my roads now.

One more text. Just one. I just bought us the farm. Or, if that means nothing to you, I guess I just bought me the farm. Thought you should know.

I stopped in front of the For Sale sign at the end of the driveway and, for the first time, noticed the panel that said "For Sale" was on rails. I tugged at it and it slid into my hand. When I flipped it over, it read "Sold."

Which is how I slid it back in.

———

THE WALK HOME HAD converted any remaining insobriety to sheer, deep-seated bone tiredness.

I wanted to sleep, needed to sleep, craved sleep in the worst way.

I stood in the hall between my bedroom and Lynsey's and stared at each of our beds and had no desire to climb into either one of them.

This was *my* house now. I would knock the rooms together and make one big room which would be mine. I'd turf out both these old beds and buy a brand new one just for me.

I could invite Hope's cousin back to share it with me.

Oh, god. The thought still wasn't exciting. *Shit.*

I yawned so long and wide it popped my jaw. I'd check on the horses. Make sure Matilda hadn't broken into anyone else's stall. Or the feed room. I hadn't swept earlier, so I'd do that now, and when I came back in I'd be so tired, I'd have no qualms about which bed I slept in.

The barn was its own ecosystem. Several degrees warmer than the rapidly falling outdoor temperatures. It held its own smells. Its particular brand of quiet was made up of all the small, comforting noises of animals shifting, and chewing, and breathing.

For once, everything was peaceful. Everybody was behaving. Matilda's ear tracked me as I walked by her stall, but she didn't even pull in her drooping lip.

I yawned again.

Horace was down, legs tucked under him. He fixed his eyes on me but showed no sign of getting up.

"That's right," I said. "You stay down there."

I let myself into his stall and padded through the deep straw to his side. He reached his nose to my outstretched hand and gave a long exhale. "Hey you. It's funny to be taller than you."

So funny, that I crouched so I wouldn't be anymore.

There was a spot, a kind of circular inlet formed by his front and back legs, and his big body. The thought came to me that I'd fit in there.

"Is this OK?" I was already settling myself in, leaning against the drum-like tautness of his side.

Oh, it was warm. Smooth, too.

I was so, so tired.

I slumped, and my ear rested against him. There were sounds inside him. Whooshes and gurgles. Interesting and soothing. Better than any white noise machine I'd ever heard.

White noise, warmth, companionship, exhaustion … it took less than a minute for me to conk out completely.

LYNSEY

WHEN I PULLED OFF the highway, the engine of Tupelo's truck kicking into a rumbling whine as I brought it slowly down to a stop, the sun hadn't yet cracked over the horizon. I hit the blinker at the stop light, intending to follow the sign for Lake Placid pointing west, into the mountains. While I waited, I took a sip from the travel mug that had made the journey mostly between my thighs.

I didn't need the coffee. With the adrenaline running in my

system I hadn't been able to sleep, not after a day full of signing paperwork and visiting banks, transferring funds into my name and watching my bank account go from enough to hope it could cover my next phone bill to visions of Hermes saddles flashing through my thoughts. I could already feel the leather under my hands – smooth, warm, and buttery.

Hazard deserved a saddle like that, and I wanted to see it on his back. But first I had to get him to Florida, and there were 1,300 miles between here and Ocala. That meant I'd be spending the better part of a week driving down the eastern seaboard, and I'd wanted to start early. Crack of dawn early.

As in, today.

Lake Placid was still a sleepy sort of dead as I drove down Main Street. The only signs of life beamed out of Irene's – warm light washing out the front windows, even though the doors had to still be locked. I ducked a look through the windows as I passed, finding an empty storefront. Hope was probably working on the cinnamon rolls in the kitchen, her mother finishing up the scones, both preparing just like I was.

I didn't want to interrupt them, but there was something about goodbyes. If you didn't do them in person, were you ever really friends? I didn't want to run the risk of Hope thinking I didn't care enough about her to stop and see her before I ran out of town, and there was a snowball's chance in hell I'd be able to do it once I was trundling out of here with Hazard in tow.

So I pulled over, taking up all the parking spots along the

front of the shop in one fell swoop, and killed the engine, leaving it ticking as it cooled to rap my knuckles against the shop's glass front door.

No response. I kept knocking, wishing I'd not been a complete idiot and left my phone behind. I'd managed to get in contact with Harris over the landline at the house to let him know I was on my way, but I'd never memorized Cam's number, so I'd have to be a surprise. Same with Hope, who stuck her head out of the back kitchen, a worry crease between her eyes and flour streaked over her forehead.

When she saw me, her shoulders visibly lowered and she hurried over to throw the latch on the door, ushering me inside.

"Where have you been?" She pulled me into a hug, flour transferring from her apron to my shirt. She tried brushing it off, then shook her head as she gave up.

"Saratoga," I explained. "One thing led to another, so I was late getting back."

"I've been so worried," she said, pulling me into the store and moving to latch the door behind me, her hand pausing midair at the sight of the trailer attached to the truck.

"Tupelo Stud?" she asked, reading the farm's logo. "That sounds like a strip club."

I nearly choked on the sip of coffee I'd been tipping into my mouth. "It's my family's farm."

"In Florida?" she asked, turning round eyes toward me.

"The one and only." I shifted uneasily in my spot. "I wanted to say …"

A little bit of sparkle on Hope's finger caught my attention, completely derailing what I wanted to say. I snatched her hand into mine, pulling the diamond so close to my face I could have kissed it. "Where did this come from?"

Hope gave a little shrug and smiled, like she knew but didn't want to tell. I gave her hand a shake and she laughed.

"Lewis," she said, her smile finally showing teeth.

I stared at her like she was speaking in tongues, then dragged her over to the nearest table. "Sit," I commanded, hauling out two chairs and falling into one. "I leave for a day and miss everything. How did this happen?"

"Well," Hope said slowly, pushing a tendril of hair out of her face and back into the messy bun on the top of her head. "He's been staying here while the cabin's fixed up, you know, and I guess one thing led to another."

I shifted impatiently. "You are being entirely too vague right now," I said. "Details, Hope. I was asking about details."

She grinned. "He wanted to show me how things were going with the cabin, you know? And, it's beautiful. Honestly, he's done amazing things with it thanks to Cam. The two of them have worked so hard …"

I motioned for her to get to the good bit, not intentionally trying to hustle her past mentions of Cam but figuring it couldn't hurt. "And?"

"And," she laughed, "he showed me the walk-in closet that

they built off the master bedroom. It's cedar-lined and huge for that house, and I mentioned, you know, he didn't need all of this space just for himself, which was when …"

I scooted to the edge of my seat. "He confessed his undying love for you?"

"He happened to mention something like that when he said he hadn't designed it for himself," she said, blushing. "He'd had me in mind all the while."

"And that was when …" I prompted, and she blushed all the harder.

"Well, you know."

"Yes." I sat back in my chair, realizing I wasn't going to get much more out of her concerning the passion that more than likely occurred somewhere in Lewis's reconstructed cabin. I decided to give Hope a break, since it probably wasn't possible for her to pinken any more than she already was. "I do think I know."

"He asked me afterward," she said, twisting the ring on her finger. "And I know six weeks isn't a long time, but I look at him and I just feel … home, you know?"

A pang hit my heart. Home sounded perfect. Like somewhere I wanted to be, with the person who wanted to be there with me.

"It's cute," I said. "How this all went down without anyone realizing a thing."

"Cam knew," Hope said, making my grin falter. "All the while, I think. Lewis told me that Cam was the one who pushed him into upgrades to the cabin that he wouldn't have done otherwise."

"Cam the Matchmaker." I tried for a laugh, but it died before it could really soar from my throat. "Who'd have thought?"

"I thought you might," Hope said, considering me steadily. "I mean, Cam kind of told me a little about you two. He seemed really …" She paused, twisting her lips to one side as I wondered about all the things Cam was. All the good – generous, hilarious, incomparably hot – with everything else I knew – that he was most likely already gone. Why wouldn't he be? He'd already had a foot out the door when I'd left myself.

"… happy," Hope finished, sending a flare of warmth sweeping through my stomach. "Just over the moon."

I leaned back, narrowing my eyes at her. "When was this?"

"Oh, when he ran in here with no pants on," she said, laughing. "I'm pretty sure he was a little loopy at that point, but the happiness – that wasn't loopy. He was really eager to get back to you when I drove him back to where he'd dumped his pants."

"He …" I didn't know where to begin with this. Nothing was jibing with what I knew and what Hope was saying, leaving me with only one image that I couldn't quite shake. "Pants?"

"Pants," Hope nodded, her eyes darting to the trailer and back.

"But you're leaving?" she asked, shifting the conversation so suddenly I felt myself deflate like a popped balloon, all the air whooshing out of my lungs.

I hesitated, and then nodded. "As soon as I can load up Hazard and find my phone."

She tilted her head at me.

"So, you haven't heard the news?"

Now it was my turn to tilt my head. "There's more news?"

Her eyes went wide, and she waved her hands in classic *no, nope, nuh-uh* fashion. "Oh my gosh, you've got to go back to the farm and talk to Cam. Now."

"It's not even six yet," I pointed out, and Hope waved her hands again.

"Wake him up," she demanded. "He's probably still a little drunk, but you need to talk to him before you load that horse and leave."

"Wait, still drunk?"

I wasn't sure I wanted to know more, but Hope was still talking. "We were at the Granite Club last night to celebrate – the curling club, you know? – and a lot went down that you need to know about. Like, right now."

"What kind of things went down?" I asked, surprised when she stood up and grabbed my hand, hauling me out of my seat. My chair scraped on the hardwood as I scrambled to keep my feet underneath me. I pulled back on her hand. "Hope, seriously, what kind of things?"

She shook her head, still plowing toward the door. "He's got to tell you, not me."

I dug in my heels.

"Look, if this is about what he did when he was drunk, it's fine," I said, which sounded false even to me. "We aren't really together. He's free to do what he likes with …" I swallowed, hard. "…

with whomever he wants."

Hope lifted the door's latch, pulling it open. Fresh morning air swept into the shop, dissipating the smell of baked bread.

"This is really not about that," she said, pushing me onto the sidewalk, "but even if it were, considering I haven't seen Autumn so bummed after a night out in a long while I'd say you have nothing to worry about."

I didn't have time to ask who Autumn was, or what happened, because Hope had shut the door in my face.

"Talk to Cam!" she called through the glass, and then latched the door tight.

—

I HAD NO CHOICE other than to get back into the trailer and keep driving, now with my heart lodged somewhere in the vicinity of my throat. It kept fluttering away, obnoxiously worried about what I'd find at the farm, even though the rational part of me kept insisting it didn't matter. It never mattered. Cam was going back to Canada, and I was going back to Florida. Red Gate was home now, and Hazard was my future. I kept that thought close. Clung to it with all my might.

Because when I made the final turn toward the farm, I saw it.

The For Sale sign on the side of the road, the little placard underneath it reading SOLD in big bold letters.

It was interesting, to feel all the breath leave my body. Even after everything I'd told myself, it still hurt. Four little letters, one big word. It made a difference. Slammed a chapter of my life shut, no matter how short it had been.

I tightened my grip on the steering wheel and turned onto the driveway, taking care not to take out the sign on my way. The property was someone else's now, and I wasn't much for revenge. Kim and Adam and Cheryl had their future gated community and I had my horse. I just had to load him up and get out of here.

I drove up toward the house and its empty lot. Hope's truck was gone, which meant Cam was gone, which meant …

I didn't need to do the meaningless math, because I knew exactly what it meant. Hope might know Lewis in and out, but she didn't know Cam. Whoever Autumn was, I'm sure her bed was a bit crowded.

The house was quiet. I moved through it feeling like a ghost – in possession and not at the same time, and maybe a little malevolent about it. Cam's door was wide open, the bed still made. Mine was a mess, sheets still askew. I gave it a wide berth and set to work packing, throwing everything I owned into the suitcases without bothering to fold and tidy like I normally would.

I just needed to get out. Slam the chapter closed for good.

Once my suitcases were zipped up and ready to go, I turned toward the bed, shoving the sheets aside until I found my phone. It woke up with a chiding message about low power, which I swiped away in favor of the texts that littered my notifications. Dozens of texts. From Harris, from Georgie, from Hope, and finally from Cam.

Most of them were Cam. The most recent greeted me like a

slap to the face.

I just bought us the farm. Or, if that means nothing to you, I guess I just bought me the farm. Thought you should know.

All I could hear was a strange ringing in my ears. I sank down onto the bed, nearly missing its edge and almost toppling onto the floor. I grabbed the edge of the mattress to keep myself upright, heart pounding.

What? The hell?

My eyes had gone misty, and I scrubbed at them quickly, beginning to scroll through the texts.

I hate you.

I'm officially angry now.

Just tell me where you are.

We can do this. Really, we can.

Things coming together – can't wait to talk about it.

As I scrolled, I didn't know whether I should start laughing or crying. I wanted to do both, like a mad person, which I guess I kind of was. We both were, clearly. I was an unreasonable wreck of a human, and Cam had blown what had to be all his money on *this*.

This place.

I wiped the wetness from my eyes when I stumbled across a photo Cam had sent of a room. Spare, clean walls, sun filtering across gleaming hardwood. It was the cabin Lewis and Cam had built for Hope, and if I'd had my phone on me when I'd gotten this text I'm sure I wouldn't have been surprised at all by the marriage proposal.

If you like this, Cam had written, *I'm pretty sure I can do it again.*

I stood up quickly, and then sank back down again when I realized there was nowhere to go.

Cam wasn't here.

I couldn't rush up to him and explain myself, make things right, because I held in my hands all the evidence I needed to know that ship had sailed.

I hate you.

I hovered my fingers over the phone, wondering how to reply. What was there to say that could ever be appropriate over text? Hope was right after all. I needed to find him and talk, but if he was with Autumn what was the point of talking?

I powered down the phone, standing and feeling as wobbly as a newborn foal. Like I was stepping into a new, alien world and my balance was all off.

Wait, I thought. I'll wait him out. He owned the farm now, so he wasn't the flight risk. He was never the flight risk. That was all me.

I sucked in a breath and counted to ten, then stepped out into the brisk, rising dawn.

—

THE HORSES WERE STILL mostly asleep when I walked into the barn. Matilda's pale head stuck into the aisle the second I pushed the barn door open, her eye gleaming in the reddish light that cast toward her stall.

"I'm not in the mood," I warned her, walking past and climbing into the loft for the hay. I threw down enough for the horses and the goats, then lugged it to each stall, throwing flakes into each opening as the barn started to rustle awake. Matilda squealed and circled her stall, tossing her head in her best impression of a war horse before battle, her pint-sized stature of no significance to her as I threw her enough hay to keep her from knocking down her stall door. Then the goats, who bleated cheerfully. Then Hazard, who sniffed at his hay from his sprawl in the middle of his bedding, still half asleep.

Then I moved on to Horace, throwing the flake in without paying much attention, so when I heard a startled shout followed by a "Jesus Christ!" I stopped.

In my tracks.

Then doubled back, peeking into the stall, my mouth dropping at the sight of Cam stumbling up from Horace's side with hay sticking from his hair.

"You're supposed to be with Autumn," I blurted.

He shook the hay out of his hair, then stumbled out of the way of Horace, who was on the rise.

"Who's Autumn?" he asked, and then held up one finger, as though rethinking everything about this exchange and deciding it wasn't worth it to continue down this path. "You know what? No. That's not how we're starting this conversation."

"But," I started, only for him to shake his head again, walking up to the stall door unsteadily. I eyed him as he got close enough to smell the bar on him and wondered exactly what happened at curling clubs. I had always envisioned nice people playing ice shuffleboard, but I supposed I was sorely mistaken. "Are you still drunk?"

He waved a hand in the air. "Maybe a smidge."

I stared at him, a deep and increasing worry wedging into my thoughts. "You didn't buy the farm when you were drunk, did you?"

He laughed. "Ah, so you decided you needed your phone, *did you?*"

"I always need my phone," I said. "I didn't leave it on purpose. Why would I do that?"

"I don't know," he replied, "why would someone just take off without said phone and not bother getting back in contact for *forty-eight hours?*"

Because I was a terribly unreasonable person. And I was running. And the only reason I came back was to get my things and my horse and run again. Because I was, ultimately, terribly unreasonable.

I wanted to say that. But I didn't.

"Why would someone buy a farm they can't afford?" I shot back instead. "Because this?" I waved my hand at the barn's rafters. "You can't afford this, Cam."

"Do you even know my finances?"

I frowned.

"I didn't think so," Cam pointed out, looking smug. "And I can do what I like with my money, which is purchasing this place for us, but if I'm being honest it's mainly for me. I like it. I wanted it. I bought it."

He paused, looking me up and down. "I suppose you can stay here. If you want."

"That's big of you," I said, pausing, telling myself I had to get it out there. I had to smooth the waters. He was right here. He wasn't with Autumn. He wasn't with anyone other than me, curled up with one of *his* horses, being undeniably amazing to the point that I felt incredibly small in comparison. "Considering …"

"You left," he said for me, rubbing his hands through his dusty hair before dropping them on my shoulders and pulling me as close as I could get despite the stall door between us. He sighed against my hair, smelling overwhelmingly like cigarette smoke and craft beer. "We slept together," he rumbled against my skin, "and I fell in love with you and you left."

I tensed.

He paused. "I probably shouldn't have said one of those things."

"The loving me part?" I asked, the word tacking on my tongue. Four letters, one word, so big it could shake apart everything I knew.

"Yeah," he said. "The loving you part."

"I don't know," I said, daring a look up at him. He was watching me, waiting. "It sounds pretty good to me."

He moved a hand into my hair, twisting a good chunk of it into his fist.

"Where did you go?" he asked quietly, coming close enough

to lower his voice until it was a soft thing, intimate.

"I had to see my dad," I said. "I needed a trailer to move Hazard, and he wanted to talk to me before he'd let me have it. It worked out in the end. I got my mother's inheritance back. I have a plan now."

He considered me for a solid silent beat, then said, "You were running."

A wash of shamed heat flooded over me.

"Why were you running?" he asked, and I closed my eyes, telling myself it would be OK to say it out loud. That of all the times such honesty was required, this was it. Right here. With a man who proclaimed to love me.

"Because I thought you were," I admitted.

He shook his head. "I was never going to run. The napkin you saw was an offer I was never going to take."

"The evidence is mounting in your favor, I have to admit."

He gave my hair a gentle tug, sending a flurry of sparks down my spine. I inched closer to the stall door, wishing he'd push it open, remove the barrier. He didn't.

"Think you can modify your plan and stay put with me?" he asked.

I licked my lips, and his attention dropped to my mouth. "Think you can live with me?"

"I did just admit to loving you," he said. "Cat's out of the bag on that one, I think."

"Good point," I nodded, then I took my opening, lifting

onto my toes and sliding my hands to his jaw, brushing my mouth against his. "If you're staying, I'm staying with you."

Then, with his mouth moving over mine, Cam opened the door.

Chapter Twenty

CAM

MAYBE I WAS STILL drunk.

Strike the maybe. I was still drunk.

I had to be. It explained why I couldn't really feel my feet. Or my knees. Why, actually, not much below my waist had any strength. Except … with the stall door out of the way, I pushed my hips against Lynsey's and her, "Oh …!" mumbled against my mouth, confirmed that, yes, there was a fair amount of power left there.

The drunkenness, though … My turn to mumble, "I must have the worst morning-after-the-night-before breath."

She murmured back, "I've had a gallon of coffee this morning, we're even," and the way she kissed me pretty quickly blurred the lines between her mouth and mine.

I was happy to just kiss her for a while. Considering I thought

I'd never see her again, it was amazing to run one hand up the back of her neck, spreading my fingers wide through the warmth of her hair, pulling her closer to me.

Meanwhile the other hand was, well, kind of checking she was really there. Smooth back with just a ripple of ribs: check. Inward-dipping waist: check. Firm, curved butt: check. Wait … better double-check that. Yup. Still there. Still firm.

"How are your breasts?" I asked between kisses.

"What?"

I slid my hand between us, cupped her breast – a perfect, round, handful – and she pushed against me. All good.

Except the just-checking, just-kissing wasn't enough anymore. I brushed my lips across her cheek, and over to her ear. Gave a teasing tug and nibble on her earlobe and whispered, "Are we all good for make-up sex?"

There was a pause in her response. A stiffening of her body against mine. I pulled back and tried to meet her eyes, but they skittered under my gaze. She lifted them to me just long enough to say, "Make-up sex isn't really in my playbook."

Of course not. As I'd learned the hard way, Lynsey was a runner, and running away kind of nixes opportunities for making up.

I could have called her on it. Could have pulled a completely legit "I told you so" out of my back pocket.

Or I could move forward. Make sure we both knew exactly how to handle any future disagreements.

I slid both my hands into the back pockets of her jeans and

on my way in for another kiss said, "Well, we have to fix that, don't we?"

I walked her backward toward the pile of hay she'd thrown down. With every step, I pushed my thigh between her legs. With every push, she moaned. With every moan, the pressure in my crotch got more insistent.

When her calves hit the first bale, I kept pushing. "Wait!" She threw her arms around my neck and wrapped her legs around my waist. "Too prickly!"

I wanted to be lying on top of her, but I also quite liked her clinging to the front of me. I put my hands under her backside, and lifted her against me. "This …" *Kiss.* "… is quite hot …" *Kiss.* "But I don't know how long I can hold you." Another kiss.

She laughed. "Just grab that rug and throw it over the hay."

A half-step sideways, a one-handed grab, an awkward throw, and the hay was covered by a horse blanket. Lynsey locked her eyes onto mine. "Now you can teach me how to have make-up sex."

Butterflies rushed my stomach. Despite my past, everything with Lynsey felt new. "First step," I said, "is to keep looking at me like that."

Don't look away, I told myself as I lowered her to the hay. *Don't look away*, as I held my body over hers.

Her eyes were pretty, no doubt about it – wide, framed with feathery lashes, flecked with gold – but it was the look in them that had my breath coming so short my head was spinning. There was trust, yes, but also equal parts eagerness and lust. "What now?" she whispered.

"Now," I said, "Get angry."

"Excuse me?"

I sat back on my heels. "Tell me why you're angry …" She opened her mouth – probably to protest – until I added "… take your shirt off while you're doing it."

"Oh …" Everything about her was sexy. The perfect circle her mouth formed when she said "oh" made me want to kiss her – made me want her mouth on me. She sat up. She rose to her knees. She fixed me with those sexy, shimmer-flecked eyes and said, "You always put the toilet paper roll on the wrong way."

Wait a minute … but before I could say anything she crossed her hands in front of her, grabbed either side of the hem of her shirt, and yanked the whole thing off over her head, leaving her breasts tumbled in her bra, and her hair tousled around her face.

I nodded. "Yes," I said. "I do that."

She lifted one eyebrow, and I peeled my shirt off the same way she had. She blinked, just a bit too fast, then said, "You twitch in your sleep. You kick me."

Which I totally would have denied, except she was undoing her jeans, and easing the zipper down, and her panties were pink and lace-edged with a repeating horse print all over them, and I wanted to laugh and tell her she was adorable, and rip them off her with my teeth at the exact same time.

I swallowed, hard. "My bad."

She gave me the same "your-turn" look as before, and I fumbled the button on my jeans. I was thinking my boxers were nowhere near as cute as her panties, but once my jeans were down she made a gulping noise and inched forward.

"I thought you were leaving me forever." There it was. This one wasn't a joke.

Her eyes were shiny, and there was a catch in her voice, and I said, "Oh, Lyn. No, never."

I reached out and pulled her close and this time it was so much better, because her skin was warm, and soft. I kissed her and said, "I wouldn't … I won't."

The thin fabric of my boxers was no longer really doing anything, so I pulled them down and reached for her cute-sweet-sexy horsey panties. "I don't have a condom," I whispered.

She took my hand and slid it between her legs and said, "Given the circumstances, I think we're committed enough to do without. I'm on the pill."

She was warm, and wet, and it would have been torture to go on another hunt for latex, so I fluttered my fingers against her gusset and breathed, "Oh, thank god for that."

"Lie down," I said, and when she did, I took the cotton of her panties between my teeth, just the way I'd wanted to, and tugged them off, and she lifted her hips to let me, and while her hips were still raised, I eased right back into place, and with nothing between us at all, hesitated for just a second – just to savour it, just to mark it – and she lifted her hips higher and I was in, sinking into her, and pressing our bodies together, moving in rhythm.

"Cam …?"

With her legs wrapped around my back like that, the most coherent response I could manage was, "Mmm …?"

"I have to tell you something."

"Now?" I gasped. *Really?* Then she did this shift, shimmy, squeeze thing like I'd never quite felt before. She could tell me anything as long as she kept doing that. "Sure …" I panted. "Shoot."

"I love you."

Whoa. Head spinning. Not breathing. I'm not sure how there was still blood left to rush anywhere else in my body, but my heart was definitely swelling.

I wrapped my arms under her shoulders, gathered her to me as tightly as I could, and said, "Oh wow … that's going to make this even better …"

The simplest things became intensely arousing: the grip of Lynsey's fingers across my back, the warm, familiar smell of her skin, the tiny moans punctuating her breathing.

We found a rhythm, then she stilled her hips, and skipped a beat, which made the next thrust even more exciting, and when our movements synced up again I knew I couldn't last much longer.

"I can't …" she gasped.

"So don't …" I urged.

"Now?"

"Now …"

Then nothing mattered except for the explosive relief of my body releasing into hers, and her deep shudders in return. Just when

I thought it would stop, she gave another elaborate shiver, and with a response like that it was impossible not to rush ahead and think about our next time, and the time after that, and all the times in the future.

With this girl. This one. She was all I needed, and she was everything I needed.

I collapsed beside her, trying to avoid crushing her while still keeping her close enough to hug and hold. She wriggled around so we were forehead-to-forehead, face-to-face, and she said, "Did it?"

"Did it, what?"

"Did it make it better?"

"It made it incomparable."

She wrinkled her nose, hummed a little tune, and said, "I'm *incomparable*."

I kissed her nose. "Yes, you are. Absolutely." Then I rose up on one elbow and said, "And now, we have a memorial to get to."

"We, what …?" Lynsey ran her eyes up and down our naked, hay-sprawled selves. "We're still going to go?"

"Here's the thing, Lyn. All those people in town – all our new neighbours …" I winked at her. "… think Albert's story is ending. Don't you think we should show them we're going to keep it going?"

She took a deep breath, reached out and took my hand, threaded her fingers through it, and said, "And going …"

I laughed. "And going …"

"And going …" She smiled. "OK, then let's go."

—

I SAT IN THE passenger seat of the huge, gleaming pick-up with my arm hanging out the window, and my hand brushing the sun-warmed Tupelo Stud logo on the door. The late-autumn breeze smelled of fallen leaves, with the tiniest promise of snow to come not too far in the future, and life was good.

The girl beside me was more beautiful every time I looked at her. Because she was part of my life, now. Not going anywhere.

The day I met her I'd noticed the lines of her body, the smooth-ness of her skin, and the sway of her hips that told me, *Yeah, she could be fun.*

Which she definitely was.

Through the fall we'd become friends. In the deep full-on-been-through-everything-you-could-imagine – not to mention a whole bunch of things you couldn't – way. The kind of friend who bugged you, you could tell them they bugged you, then you could sit down and eat pizza together. There weren't that many of those in the world.

I didn't know the exact moment I realized I wanted more – everything – her body, her friendship, and also her dedication, her commitment, her *love.*

I did know there'd been a few agonizing days there where I waited for her to catch up to me, but now that she had, everything she did was special.

The way she bit her tongue when she had to lift a really heavy bale of hay.

How every time she sneezed it was three times in a row, and that she was the only person I knew who sneezed when she sipped her first cup of coffee each morning.

I'd even come to love the way she put the toilet paper roll on the holder. Even though it was wrong …

"What?" She'd caught me looking at her.

"Oh, nothing."

"I love the way your voice lifts an octave when you're lying."

I grinned and she asked again, "What?"

"Just, I think you really do love me."

"I really do love you."

We were at the end of the driveway now, indicator on, waiting to turn onto the road. She started to ease the truck forward. "Wait!" I yelled. "Stop!"

"Why?" But she'd already re-applied the brakes and tapped the truck to a halt.

I jumped out and ran to the ancient farm sign, doing a spread of my arms reminiscent of Vanna White, except the letters I was showcasing were faded and ancient.

Lynsey scooted over and perched on the edge of my abandoned seat. "What are you doing?"

"Believe it or not, there's actually something I failed to text you while you were away."

She laughed. "Given the state of my inbox, I do find that hard to believe."

"I found out the name of the farm."

"You did?" With her heels hooked on the bottom of the door frame, elbows propped on her knees, and chin resting in her hands, she looked as adorable as I'd ever seen her. "So? Come on – tell me!"

I pointed to the L – "Lester" – then the P – "Parkman" – then said it all together "LP Farm – Lester Parkman Farm."

"I don't understand." This was accompanied by a brow furrow that made it really hard not to dash back to the truck and kiss her.

"Forrest told me Albert's name was 'Lester Albert Parkman,' and he named the farm after himself because he believed land should bear the name of the person who loves it."

Lynsey straightened and clapped her hand to her breastbone. "That is unbelievably sweet."

"I believe it, too."

"What do you mean?"

"What I mean is when we repaint this sign – which I suggest we do as soon as we get back from Lester Albert's memorial – I think the farm should become LC Farm."

Lynsey repeated it back, "LC …? What? … LC …?" until I heard the sound of the penny dropping in the changing tone of her voice. "Oh! Lynsey Cam!"

I only had the chance to start asking, "What do you think?" before she leapt out of the truck and into my arms in one smooth move.

With her mouth at my ear, she whispered, "Because we love the farm."

"Yes, we do," I said.

"And, also, we love each other."

I squeezed her as tightly to me as I possibly could.

"Yes, we do."

Acknowledgments

So, we wrote a book together.

Did we know what we were getting into?

No. Absolutely not.

Did we do lots and lots of research, and try to figure out the best way to go about it, and discuss pros and cons, and get expert input?

No. We wrote. The outline flowed like crazy. The ideas whizzed around. Were we smart?

Did we think, OK, this is really a big step — this co-writing thing — maybe we should just do one out-there thing at a time?

No. We created a Patreon page, because if one experiment is good, two must be better — bonus points for conducting an experiment in public view!

It was great.

It was great because of all our Patreon patrons. Some provided fantastic support in the background (thank you – we felt you there) and others had lots of thoughts/comments/ideas … and helped us find mistakes and inconsistencies (our proofreader thanks you!).

If you were a Patreon patron, we love you and thank you. If you were Linda Shantz, Bailey Brogan, or Kristen Patching, thanks for showing up in the comments section. Again and again. Every time.

We also need to send a shout out to Natalie Keller Reinert, who supported us when she has her own Patreon page to run (if you want to read more horse books, check out Natalie's!). Heather Voltz was an early and generous supporter, and Donna Huang lives very far away but is always there, supporting me (Tudor speaking!) as a loyal reader.

We have to thank each other. We'd be lying if we said it was always easy, but, you know what? It was almost always easy. This was, without a doubt the easiest book either of us has ever written.

We're friends forever, now. We have had this discussion that publishing a book is not completely unlike birthing a child. This is a thing we've done together. Wow.

Are we writing partners forever? Well … for a while. Is that fair? We both think we have another co-written book in us. And we didn't necessarily think that when we started In Search Of, so who knows what will happen at the end of this one?

Here's a little look-ahead for you – there will be more Cam and Lynsey. We're pretty sure there will be more Hope and Lewis. We're planning to have more Hannah and … well, we have someone in mind for Hannah. And between ourselves, as we work on it, we're calling this one *Noon Whistle* – that could change completely, but for now the noon whistle forms part of the inspiration to get us going. And if you don't know what a noon whistle is, you can Google it ... or read the next book!

Join the Patreon

To read the sequel, head over to **www.patreon.com/InSearchOf**. For just $1 a month you can read all of our chapters and blog posts!

About Us

Tudor Robins

My aim is to write books to make you smile. Someday I may own a horse, but for now my guinea pig, Kiwi, is a better fit for the central-Ottawa neighborhood where I live; commuting by bicycle and following my teenage boys around basketball games and curling rinks. When I'm not writing, I love riding, skiing, running, and spending time on Wolfe Island.

Mara Dabrishus

Aside from my Texas beginning, I spent the first two decades of my life in the Arkansas Ozarks. I primarily write young adult fiction about my first love – horses – although I've also been known to write speculative and paranormal fiction. And now I'm apparently writing romance! When I'm not writing, I'm a librarian at a small college outside of Cleveland, Ohio. I live with a husband, two ridiculous cats, and a bossy toddler.